PRAISE FOR *RECLUCE TALES*

"This collection of tales set in the world of Modesitt's beloved Saga of Recluce series will be most readily and deeply appreciated by fans who are eager to revisit old friends and explore Recluce anew. However, Modesitt's imagination and storytelling power will easily attract newcomers, and the easy exposition and rich descriptions will most likely provide a marvelous gateway into the Saga, as well."

—*RT Book Reviews*

"A nostalgic walk through a well-appreciated series."

—*SFRevu*

"Freed from the length of the novel, the beauty of the world that Modesitt creates becomes even more apparent."

—*Booklist*

PRAISE FOR THE SAGA OF RECLUCE

"An exceptionally vivid secondary world."

—L. Sprague de Camp

"A refreshing use of the traditional fantasy elements."

—Andre Norton

"Modesitt has established himself with his Recluce series as one of the best nineties writers of fantasy. The fantasies are characterized by a highly developed and consistent system of magic."

—*Vector*

"Modesitt presents an interesting study of Chaos versus Order,

Good versus Evil . . . and the attractions each of them has for all of us."

—Robert Jordan, author of the Wheel of Time series

"Unique and refreshing."

—Robin Hobb, author of *Fool's Quest*

"My favorite thing about L. E. Modesitt's books is that they don't go stale. I enjoy rereading them as much as I enjoy them the first time."

—*SFRevu*

L. E. MODESITT, JR.

RECLUCE
TALES

Stories from the World of Recluce

TOR

A TOM DOHERTY ASSOCIATES BOOK
NEW YORK

RECLUCE TALES

Copyright © 2016 by L. E. Modesitt, Jr.

A Tor Book
Published by Tom Doherty Associates
175 Fifth Avenue
New York, NY 10010

www.tor-forge.com

Tor® is a registered trademark of Macmillan Publishing Group, LLC.

The Library of Congress has cataloged the hardcover edition as follows:

Modesitt, L. E., Jr., 1943– author.
    Recluce tales : stories from the world of Recluce / L.E. Modesitt, Jr.—First edition.
    p. cm.
    "A Tom Doherty Associates book."
    ISBN 978-0-7653-8618-2 (hardcover)
    ISBN 978-1-4668-8619-9 (ebook)
1. Recluce (Imaginary place)—Fiction. 2. Magic—Fiction. I. Title.
    PS3563.O264 A6 2017
    813'.54—dc23

2017288133

ISBN 978-0-7653-8620-5 (trade paperback)

Our books may be purchased in bulk for promotional, educational, or business use. Please contact your local bookseller or the Macmillan Corporate and Premium Sales Department at 1-800-221-7945, extension 5442, or by email at MacmillanSpecialMarkets@macmillan.com.

First Edition: January 2017
First Trade Paperback Edition: February 2018

Printed in the United States of America

0 9 8 7 6 5 4 3 2 1

COPYRIGHT
ACKNOWLEDGMENTS

To Tom Doherty and David Hartwell

CONTENTS

The stories and vignettes are arranged in the internal chronological order in which they take place in the world of Recluce so that the earliest events occur in "The Vice Marshal's Trial" and the last events in "Fame."

RECLUCE
TALES

Behind the "Magic" of Recluce

When I initially decided to write *The Magic of Recluce* in the late 1980s, I'd been writing science fiction exclusively. There was scarcely a single word of fantasy in any of my published stories and novels. My educational background included some basic hard science, a stint as a Naval aviator, which, for some reason, also included courses in atomic weapons and power, and both academic preparation and occupational necessity as an industrial economist, followed by a number of years as a political staffer in Washington, D.C. Then, in roughly 1987, as I recall, I attended a large and well-known eastern regional science fiction convention, which shall remain nameless, where I was on a panel dealing with economics and politics in fantasy and science fiction. The comments of both the other authors— all fantasy writers—and the audience were truly a revelation, because it struck me that economics, politics, and hard science were foreign subjects to many of them. As an aside, I will admit that the situation has improved greatly since then. Because it was my first convention, and because I was caught somewhat unaware, I was less than politically and socially astute. In fact, I conveyed a certain dismay about the lack of concern about economic, political, and technological infrastructures in various fantasies then being written and published in the field.

The clear but muted reaction of those others on the panel to my comments was to suggest that I, as a science fiction writer, had a lot to learn about writing fantasy. In fact, some comments even intimated that it would be a rather chill day in the theological nether regions before I ever published a fantasy novel. Being primarily Irish in ethnic heritage, while still retaining the arrogance and impetuousness of youth well past that chronological age, I resolved that I would and could write a fantasy novel. That was the emotional motivation for undertaking the writing of *The Magic of Recluce*.

Still, I faced the very real problem of creating a magic system that was logical, rational, and workable within a practical economic, political, and technological structure that was neither particularly exotic nor borrowed lock, stock, and barrel from western European history . . . or anywhere else. Most fantasy epics have magic systems. Unfortunately, many of them, particularly those designed by beginning authors, aren't well thought out, or they're lifted whole from either traditional folklore or gaming systems and may not exactly apply to what the author has in mind.

While I had a fairly solid grounding in poetry, and actually had had a number of short poems published in small literary magazines, and despite my obvious love of word and rhyme, I had great difficulty in accepting the idea that mere chanted spells would accomplish much of anything in any world, particularly in any world about which I wanted to write. As a result, I began by thinking about some of the features and tropes of traditional fantasy. One aspect of both legend and folklore that stuck out was the use of "cold iron" to break faerie magic, even to burn the creatures of faerie, or to stand against sorcery. Why iron? Why not gold or silver or copper? Not surprisingly, I didn't find any answers in traditional folklore or even contemporary fantasy. Oh, there were more than a few examples, but no real explanations except the traditional ones along the lines of "that's just the way it works."

For some reason, my mind went back to astronomy and astrophysics and the role that nuclear fusion has in creating a nova. In a stellar population I star—one initially composed of hydrogen—the nuclear fusion at the heart of the star begins with the fusion of hydrogen atoms to form helium. Once a sufficient quantity of helium is created, after many millions of years, the fusion process begins to fuse helium into a form of beryllium, then lithium. Each of these fusion reactions creates a heavier element and releases energy, what physicists call an exothermic reaction. While my description is a vast oversimplification, this proton-proton reaction continues in the center of the star until the fusion process begins to create iron in large quantities. According to more recent studies I've read, the reaction process only proceeds to the level of producing iron in the most massive of stars, because of the high temperatures and pressures required.

The proton-proton reaction that produces iron, however, is different, because it is an endothermic reaction, that is, it does not produce excess energy, but requires additional energy to complete the fusion. In the larger and more massive stars where this occurs, the buildup of iron in the stellar core results in a shrinkage and a cooling of the core, until the point when the outer layer collapses upon the relatively cooler core, and then explodes outward, creating a nova, or a supernova, according to some astrophysicists.

At the same time, the fact that metals such as copper or silver conducted heat and electrical energy suggested that they were certainly less than ideal for containing electrical energy. Gold and lead, while far heavier than iron, do not have iron's strength, and other metals are too rare and too hard to work, particularly in a low-tech society.

At this point, I had a starting point for my magic system. I couldn't say exactly what spurred this revelation, but to me it certainly made sense. Iron can absorb a great amount of heat.

If you don't think so, stand on an iron plate barefoot in the blazing sun or in the chill of winter. Heat is a form of energy. In fantasy, magic is a form of energy. Therefore, iron can absorb magic and, by doing so, bind it.

But how would such a magic system actually work?

At that point, I began to think about "order" and "chaos." As I saw it, order is the structure of the universe, and chaos is the "power source." Energy is often created, for example, when a structure is destroyed, as in the case of a fire burning a log. In a simplistic sense, what is left afterwards is heat and less structured matter. Even in the case of nuclear fusion, there is destruction on which a higher-level order is imposed, and that higher-level order incorporates even more energy.

So why wouldn't this also be true of magic?

Then, I thought about string theory, and the idea that the universe is created of tiny infinitesimal "strings" which comprise fermions and bosons, which include quarks, leptons, and hadrons, which in turn form the components of atoms, which in turn make up the ordinary matter of our world. To me, it seems logical that, in a "magical" world, those "strings" would be either order strings or chaos strings.

If there were more order strings in this magical universe, they would eventually choke out the chaos strings, and if there were more chaos strings, they would eventually destroy the order strings and leave formless low-grade energy—exactly what some physicists have predicted will be the eventual fate of our universe. Thus, to have an ongoing working magical universe, there has to be a fundamental overall parity between order and chaos, as well as a means for containing them both so that they do not destroy each other in the way that occurs when matter and antimatter collide. This led to the concept of the Balance, based on the indestructibility of the basic order and chaos strings, a magical version of the law of conservation of energy and matter.

One of the next realizations was something that I'd always understood and even verbalized, but I hadn't applied it to the idea of magic in a fantasy universe. Mankind is a tool-making and tool-using creature. As a species, we improve tools that work and discard those that don't or those that work less well in favor of those that work better. Yet seldom had I seen that concept applied in fantasy at that time. In too many books, there were inept wizards, or wizards who could not tell when or if their magic would work. And then there were powerful evil wizards who often found themselves defeated by those with inferior sorcery or no magic at all, but with a "good heart." I realize that I'm generalizing, but these generalizations do in fact have a basis in fact. After all, logically, there is no way that Frodo should have triumphed, uplifting story that *Lord of the Rings* is. And the economic systems Tolkien used wouldn't have worked, either, but that wasn't the point of the trilogy.

I also couldn't see any rational general or marshal entrusting his army, or even a part of his forces, to a half-baked wizard or warlock whose magic might work—or might not. Real professional soldiers, as opposed to warriors, tend to be more than a little skeptical of untested or erratic weapons and forces. Yet, again, in those days, there were more than a few "wish-fulfillment" fantasy novels where the kingdom was saved by exactly that—the untested mage, the good-hearted youth, etc. I'd already seen, often directly and personally, what had happened in the Vietnam War era, when ill-modified and not fully tested equipment was used, and when equipment and weapons designed for one combat environment were employed in another—and the results were anything but good. Yet, often individual soldiers and units would adapt and modify such equipment until it worked, often at a lower level, reliably. But reliability was the key.

In practice, this would mean that human cultures in a world

based on magic would employ it as a tool and incorporate it into their social structure, most likely in very different ways, based on their requirements of the culture at hand. Those who could more easily master chaos would appear to have the edge in matters of military power, because they could focus destruction upon their enemies. This was the origin of the concept of the white wizards. BUT—pure chaos is unfocused and uncontrolled, and even a chaos wizard must be able to employ some level of order to handle chaos.

By the same token, an ordermage has a greater ability to confine and resist chaos, but without the underlying power of chaos, which is in effect also the life force of all biological beings, he or she can do nothing.

Implicit in this construct is the understanding that neither order nor chaos is "good" or "bad." Also implicit is the fact that people have trouble dealing with this ambiguity. As in our world, in the world of Recluce cultures find different ways to socialize and control such forces. The Council of Recluce effectively bans all use of "free" chaos, and for much of the history of Recluce, chaos use is stigmatized as "bad." This outlook results in a society that is often too hidebound for its own good. Social and technological advancements rest on those who are willing and able to "stretch" the rules, such as Dorrin, and often those who could offer more, such as Lerris or Rahl, are exiled because people are comfortable with what they know and resist change.

On the other side, the chaos mages of Fairhaven view the restrictions of Recluce as unworkable and artificial, and they develop a society which institutionalizes what they believe is the controlled and practical use of chaos, but that structure, as in the case of many societal structures, effectively rests on power. The High Wizard is almost always the most powerful of the white wizards, and might truly makes right, and, in turn, leads to a far more corruptible society.

Cyador, on the other hand, attempts to deal with the order-chaos dichotomy by controlling and directing the power of chaos mechanistically through the "chaos towers" and splitting power between three social groups—the mages, the merchants, and the armed forces. This works for a time, but the reliance on mechanical means for amplifying chaos powers creates not only strength but also a longer-term vulnerability.

The druids of Naclos deal with the potential order-chaos conflict in another fashion, by creating a social structure in which each individual with the ability to handle order and chaos must face an individual trial which tests the individual's ability to balance, practically and ethically, order and chaos. Failure to pass the test usually results in death. Needless to say, the druids have great power individually—but there are far, far fewer of them because the costs of failure are so high.

The matriarchal society of Westwind uses geographical isolation and a brutally effective compulsory military tradition to protect itself and effectively exiles all those who would use either order or chaos as a weapon, but as the world becomes more technological, geography also becomes less effective in protecting Westwind.

All of these cultures, as well as others which develop later, address the order-chaos structure in different ways, but each of these structures seems effective, acceptable, and workable to those who live in each—and that was the goal, because I saw and see that anything as basic and powerful as "magic" has to be a rationalized and structured part of a fantasy culture.

And that is the story of the magic behind *The Magic of Recluce*.

Over the years, readers have pleaded with me to write a book about the beginning of Cyador. My editor has pleaded that I not do so. In the spirit of compromise, here is a story about one aspect of the founding of Cyador.

THE VICE MARSHAL'S TRIAL

The gray-haired man walked slowly into the receiving hall, his eyes glancing toward the malachite throne. He shook his head, then turned and retreated through the inconspicuous side door to the small private study. There he seated himself. After a time, he opened the green-sheened, silver-covered book, one of a pair, turning pages until he reached the lines that fit his mood.

> *Should I recall the Rational Stars?*
> *There I had a tower for the skies,*
> *where the rooms were clear,*
> *and the music filled the walls.*
> *The light clothed the halls,*
> *and the days were long.*
> *The nights were song . . .*

After a time, he closed the book, stood, and walked to the balcony from where he looked out at the city of shimmering white and brilliant green. How did it all come to this, a strange glory he had never imagined? Another set of lines crept into his thoughts.

We stand in a world we did not know
reaping lives and deaths we did not sow . . .

"*Except we did . . . oh, yes, we did,*" *he murmured, as his thoughts went back through the long years, the years that inspired another verse set in the volume few will ever read.*

Worlds change, I'm told,
mirror silver to heavy gold,
and the new becomes the old,
with the way the story's told.

But who else would know the way the story actually happened? His thoughts went back . . . across the years.

I

Vice Marshal Kiedral Daloren walked through the air that felt as though it steamed around him, under a green-blue sky and a white sun that could not coexist under any astrophysics he had ever studied. The crisp color of the sky created a contrast with the rich air that seemed equally improbable, but then everything that had happened since translation had been either impossible or improbable. Even before he stepped fully inside the plast-foam dome that served as the operations center of Colonization Force Five, a comm-tech called out to him.

"Ser! There's still no word from the eastern terraforming team. Marshal Keif wants to know what you're going to do about it."

Of course he does, not that he understands much about this world. Then, none of them did, least of all Keif, whom most of the senior officers called "the emperor" behind his back.

Kiedral didn't hide his frown. He'd been the one who'd insisted on sending the team so far. If they didn't reach out, then they'd just huddle around one small settlement, and history had shown that didn't work on colony worlds. *Were you too ambitious in ordering them to cut back that odd forest for pastures, cropland, and a river port?* He stopped short of the crude wooden table that served as his desk. "How long since we've heard?"

"The regular report at sixteen hundred yesterday, ser. There wasn't a morning report. They don't answer their comm. There's not even an indication of a carrier."

"Half the time, the damned things don't work anyway, especially there." *Not that anything works the way it should—except for the fusactors that this world that shouldn't exist has transformed into what resemble mirror towers.* How simple digital commsets carried more static than meaning while the output of the mirror towers was staggering was beyond him—and beyond the ken of the engineers. The "emperor" didn't even acknowledge any of that, either.

"Do you want us to send the flitter?"

"Not yet. Not until we can figure out how to repower it." Nothing was working the way it should, and most of the powered equipment was failing, except for the dozers, and that was because they were truly low-tech, simple enhanced-ethanol-powered earthmovers, with converters that could turn almost anything organic into fuel. The idea had been to leave them with the colonists. Except that the colony ships in orbit weren't going anywhere, their drives and translators fused to slag in the freak translation that had brought them to this misbegotten world where the summers were near unbearable, instead of in a system guarded by the deep space towers of the Unity. At that thought, Kiedral blotted his forehead.

"What do you want us to do?" asked Subcommander Kharl, young for his rank.

Aren't we all? But that was what happened in a war that lasted generations, especially against the Sybrans and their damned United Faith Alliance, although he had to admire their ability. What he didn't understand was how a culture like that of the Sybrans that was based almost totally on personal combat and weapons skills had a workable economic system. *And they have the nerve to call themselves "angels."*

"I'll take one of the groundscouts out there myself with a half squad of combat techs . . . and the best comm unit we have left." The groundscouts were rechargeable lightly armored personnel carriers, not designed for combat, but certainly well-enough protected against local fauna, especially with a top-turret gunner able to direct osmiridium expanding shells in a complete circle around the vehicle. The other advantage of the groundscout was that, under the apparently freakish laws of physics or nature that applied on the planet, they held their charges a good ten times longer than they should have.

One of the few areas where local conditions are working for us.

"Ser, that's three days close to nonstop. Maybe more if there are problems with the road."

"I know, but I think it's time for an on-site inspection." *Besides which, it will be easier than waiting here without comm while Keif breathes down my neck.* "I haven't been out there, and I need to see what the problems are. Besides, everything here is going as well as it can, and Commander A'Kien is perfectly able to do anything I could do." *And it won't hurt to get away from sewers, water lines, reviewing decisions on what gets built where by whom . . . all of it, especially arguing with Keif.* He almost laughed. A'Kien thought that what Kiedral did was so easy. Let him see for himself, especially with all the useless micromanaging from Keif. "I'll leave a delegation order for him. And a message for the marshal telling him that I'm personally inspecting. How soon can we leave?"

"I'll have the groundscout and combat techs ready in half an hour, ser. Will you need to get your gear?"

"I've got a kit bag here."

"Yes, ser. I'll let you know."

Kiedral nodded and settled behind the table, picking up the tablet that displayed the latest status reports on the various building projects, nodding as he noted that all the initial sewer mains had been laid and that the biotechs were seeding the modified water lilies and adapted biosphere to deal with wastes before releasing them into the river over the stone sluices designed to give the water a last dose of sunlight.

The bay formed a naturally protected harbor, and the land to the north and east of the river was on solid bedrock that sloped gradually uphill in a way that would allow expansion over the years as the city, and the colony, grew. The same bedrock underlay the land on the west side of the river, but a bridge across it could wait.

At present, while a street system had been laid out, all of the colonists remained in the temporary plastfoam barracks, although most of them had opted to build their own quarters on streets that, except for the buried waste collection and water systems, were still little more than packed dirt and clay tracks. They were allowed to sign out equipment on a rotating basis, and some dwellings actually had stone walls that were close to chest-high, although the engineers were using the fusactor-powered lasers most of the time to cut stone in order to shelter the fusactors from the weather, creating what looked like white stone towers.

Kiedral had to admit that the stone, something like a cross between alabaster and limestone, except harder, made not only an excellent building material, but an attractive one as well, and there was certainly plenty of it in the hills to the east of the harbor.

He frowned as he studied the second report on the tablet, the last one from the eastern terraforming team. The team had crossed the hills to the east and was reshaping the land bordering the road into gentler contours, as much as they could with the earthdozers, and cutting back the strange forest. They reported the loss of one laser-tech, who had been killed by a creature that was black like an extinct Terran panther, but larger than either the equally extinct tiger or a lion.

What sort of biosphere supports a predator that large? What does it prey on? He used his light stylus to note the question, but he had to concentrate on doing so, as if the device did not want to work unless he was focused on it. *Something else to go wrong.*

With all the reports and details, as well as the message to the marshal, with whom he avoided talking any more than absolutely necessary, it only seemed a few minutes before Sub-commander Kharl announced, "Ser, the groundscout is here."

"Good." Kiedral flicked his index finger over the tablet, putting it on standby, then stood, pulled the kit bag from under the table, and hurried out of the dome. There was little sense in taking the tablet. The netlink barely covered the area planned for the town that he hoped would one day be a city.

Standing outside the dome, he studied the combat techs as they filed into the rear of the groundscout, six men and a woman. The woman had brilliant red hair, if cut short, a particular shade that had appeared after the strange ship translation among a handful of officers, crew, and even colonists. There was something about her . . .

As if she had sensed his eyes on her, she turned and looked at him, if but for an instant, far too short a period for such a look to be termed either unprofessional or disrespectful, yet Kiedral had the feeling that he'd been assessed and weighed in some fashion.

Ridiculous! She barely passed her eyes over you. But that bothered him slightly, too, he had to admit. After all, he was second in command of the colonization force, and the actual force behind most of what had been accomplished.

"Ser?"

At Kharl's voice, Kiedral turned. "Yes."

Kharl handed him a slip of paper, only a slip, since paper was getting scarce. "Those are the techs and the driver."

"Thank you." Kiedral smiled, glad that the subcommander had covered for him. Kharl knew that Kiedral made a habit of addressing subordinates by name.

He slipped into the seat beside the driver, also a combat tech, and closed the hatch, immediately lowering the glastic window because of the heat built up inside the groundscout. Given the distance they had to cover, using the cooling system was out.

"The techs are loaded, ser," said the driver.

"Take the way along the main east-west avenue." Kiedral wanted to see how work was progressing on the main power complex. He'd feel happier, he knew, once the fusactors were all shielded in stone. No matter what the engineers said about altered anomalous-metal containment, anything that had once been transformed could be altered again—and much already had been a second time by the freak translation.

"Yes, ser." The driver turned the groundscout back toward the center of what would soon be, Kiedral was convinced, a well-planned and thriving town from which the colonists could extend their efforts to convert a wilderness into a thriving nation capable of adding its capabilities to the rest of the Unity.

Kiedral scanned the roster.

> Thaeron, Tech2, squad leader
> Baeltyn, Tech4
> Fhostah, Tech3, driver
> Gorran, Tech3

Jaslak, Tech4
Ryaelth, Tech3
Zhalert, Tech4

Alphabetical, except for the squad leader, and not by rank, but easier to recall that way. Kiedral suspected that Tech Ryaelth was the woman, but he'd find out sooner or later. He eased the slip into his summer uniform coveralls, which, light as they were, still felt far too warm most of the time.

As the groundscout moved onto the avenue—the only thoroughfare paved from one end to the other thus far—Kiedral's eyes moved from the largely completed stone walls of what would be the operations and administrative center to the plaza some hundred meters seaward from the building. The plaza was so far merely a paved circular space, with a smaller raised circular paved area in the center. The groundscout was, of course, the only vehicle on the avenue as it circled the plaza and then continued eastward.

Kiedral had insisted on having the center plaza paved, with the beginning of all the avenues and boulevards started in stone, to give the colonists the immediate idea that the dirt streets were only temporary necessities to lead to the fields beyond the staked boundaries of the township, and that before long the remaining main thoroughfares, at least, would be paved in that tough white stone that held the faintest tinge of green.

A half kay east of the plaza rose the stoneworks surrounding the fusactors, all looking shorter than they were, because Kiedral had insisted that the ground be cleared down to bare rock, and the rock fused solid. He nodded. To the eye the stonework looked finished, although he knew it was still a few weeks from completion. *If nothing else goes wrong . . . which it will.*

When the groundscout reached the edge of the cultivated fields, Kiedral could hear the squad leader's voice from the aft compartment. "Zhalert, you got the turret for the first shift."

That meant Zhalert was likely the least accomplished gunner.

Kiedral looked eastward along the road ahead, if "road" happened to be the right word, since it had been cut, roughed out, and packed down by the dozers sent east to terraform some of the land and begin the layout of what would be a river port town. The trees and vegetation cut along the way had been rendered down into biomass to fuel the dozers.

The other senior officers had been aghast at Kiedral's insistence on creating two highways, each more than six hundred kays long, one to reach another port city location and the other to reach a point in the middle of an endless forest. Although the northern road that the groundscout followed, the one to the middle of the forest, was less than a highway and more than a packed track, it was largely straight and level, and capable of bearing significant weight and resisting even torrential downpours. In time, Kiedral was determined, it would also be stone-paved.

Cultures with good roads survive.

II

Slightly after midday, when the indicators read that the groundscout had covered a hundred kays, Kiedral studied the terrain outside, still a mixture of hilly ground and scattered trees, almost like the hilly savanna of Afrique, although it would not be long before they entered the odd forest that covered most of the area west of the mid-continent mountains and south of the grassy hills that bordered on being desert. He turned to the driver. "Time to pull over and stretch, Fhostah."

The golden-haired and pale driver nodded. "Yes, ser."

Even as the groundcar eased onto the shoulder of the crude road, Kiedral found himself smiling. There was no need to leave the road. They were the only ones on it and would be for the entire trip. *Old habits die hard.*

Before he stepped from the groundscout, Kiedral lifted the portable comm unit from the holder between his seat and the driver's and thumbed it on. "Main base, Star One, comm check."

"Star One. Clear and strong."

"Main base. Good signal this time. Out."

Kiedral slipped the portable comm unit back into the holder, then opened the door and stepped out. His left hand brushed the holstered slug-thrower at his waist, which was turning out to be far more reliable than many of the standard Anglorian energy weapons. *But then, half of them don't work the way they're supposed to . . . and none of the armorers can say why.*

The air wasn't nearly so damp as at the main base, but it wasn't nearly as dry as the hilly grasslands led him to believe. He watched as the techs stepped out of the groundcar, all seven of them wary, their eyes rapidly surveying the terrain as they moved. The last to emerge was Zhalert, the tech4 who had manned the turret.

Six of the techs spread out, moving away from him and the groundscout. Kiedral and Squad Leader Thaeron waited as they swept the area, not that Kiedral thought they'd find anything inimical so close to the colony. *Except you never know.*

The red-haired combat tech—one of the comparatively few women in such a capacity in the Unity forces—was the last to return, slipping back from the area to the north of the groundcar with graceful movements. She turned to Thaeron. "All clear to the north, Squad Leader."

"Nothing moving there, Tech Ryaelth?"

"No, Squad Leader." The hint of a smile quirked her lips, suggesting something.

Her expression intrigued Kiedral, but she said nothing more as the other techs reported, and as Thaeron turned to the vice marshal. "Area appears clear, ser."

"Thank you, Squad Leader." Kiedral nodded, then walked some thirty meters up a small rise to get what he hoped would be a better view of the land to the north and east. Ryaelth and another tech—Gorran, since he was the other tech3—flanked him.

From the top of the grassy rise, Kiedral surveyed the terrain. The area within a kay or so of the road appeared to be mixed grasslands and trees, but farther to the north was forest, the tall and dark forest that the team had reported as "strange." While he'd repeatedly asked for a better description of what they'd meant by that, the best any of the road-building and exploration teams had been able to say was that it felt like they were being watched. Yet they'd seen not the slightest sign of any local inhabitants, unlike in the lands to the east of the midcontinent mountains. Of course, that was why he'd picked the western lands for the colony. The last thing they needed was an immediate conflict with the locals, human as they appeared to be, most likely the descendants of another ship or ships gone astray. With his luck, they were probably Sybran, and that would just make matters worse.

In the distance, just at the edge of the strange forest, he thought he saw a large horned quadruped, almost like an elk, but in moments it was gone . . . if it had ever been there at all.

"Did either of you see that?"

"See what, ser?" asked Gorran.

"The elk?" asked Ryaelth. "It looked like an elk, but it just vanished."

"Yes," replied the vice marshal. "It did look like an elk."

"Ser," ventured the red-haired tech, "is this a terraformed world? Before us, I mean. If that was something like an elk . . ."

"It would appear so . . . or it's the greatest instance of convergent evolution we've ever run across." *But neither would explain why there's higher life on a moonless world.* He shook his head. "We need to keep moving. Back to the groundscout."

"Yes, ser."

III

The following morning, the scout had barely reached a point fifteen kays farther east from where they had bivouacked that first night when Kiedral noted that there were trees sprouting less than five meters beyond the shoulder of the road. Those trees were far more than saplings, and he couldn't believe that the construction team had left them so close to the road.

"Fhostah, pull over here."

"Yes, ser."

When Kiedral left the groundscout, he immediately walked to the nearest of the trees, then the next one. Both were large enough that they had to be five or six years old, if not ten. Somewhat farther away was an even larger tree.

As Kiedral made his way toward it, flanked by Baeltyn and Jaslak, he could see that the "new" trunk, a good twenty-five centimeters across, had grown out of the center of an older stump, one a good meter and a half across, that had been left when the road team had felled the large tree.

In less than three months . . . as much growth as in ten years?

Twwirrip! A yellow-and-black bird with yellow-banded wings offered an annoyingly cheerful series of chirps.

Yet there was something about those chirps . . . Kiedral's hand went to the slug-thrower, and he had it up and aimed at the scaly flying creature that had launched itself directly at him from another tree to the north.

Both shots struck the small monstrosity, and it plummeted

to the ground, writhing for a moment. Kiedral's mouth opened as he watched reddish-white streams of *something* flare from two points in the creature's chest, a good half meter across.

"What the frig is that, ser?" Jaslak's voice held an edge.

"Looks like a flying dinosaur," added Baeltyn.

Kiedral took in the four razor-sharp claws on each leg, and a beak that appeared sharper than any knife, as well as the heavy muscular body and triangular tail. *It looks too heavy to fly.*

"It's burning up," said Jaslak. "What did you hit it with, ser?"

"Regular slugs." Kiedral looked closely at the creature, seeing that the strange reddish-white fire was indeed consuming the dead predator. Then his eyes went to the other trees for a moment.

The yellow-and-black bird was long since gone, as was the sense of danger.

In a few moments, all that was left of the scaly flying beast was a pile of warm gray ash.

"Weird . . . ," muttered Jaslak.

That's an understatement.

Once he was back in the groundscout and they were on their way again, he entered a description of the flying monstrosity in the scout's data bank.

The whole episode had seemed almost unreal, from trees regrowing impossibly quickly to the attack itself. He'd *known*, in a way he couldn't explain, that he was about to be attacked. Had the annoyingly cheerful bird somehow warned him? How had he known it was a warning? If the bird hadn't warned him, how had he known? Yet he'd reacted without knowing why or how, and that bothered him most of all.

He pursed his lips, his eyes on the road ahead, not really seeing it, as he continued to ponder what had happened.

What possessed you to decide to do this in person? What in the name of the Rational Stars gave you the thought that this was a good idea? He shook his head. *Just to get a break from the "emperor"?*

IV

Over the next two days of travel, Kiedral saw more and more trees that had regrown or regenerated impossibly quickly—but not a single ground animal of any sort, and only a few birds, and those at a distance. That bothered him almost more than the attack on the second day had.

The first solid indication he had that the terraforming team had faced more than a communications problem was a mass of blackened vegetation and charcoaled tree trunks that appeared on each side of the road less than two kays west from the last reported position of the exploration team. The last few kays of the road, Kiedral noted, had been far less cleanly graded and cleared.

"The lasers should have been able to do far more than just char the trees and undergrowth," he said quietly.

"Yes, ser," replied Thaeron, from the rear of the groundscout. "I've got Gorran in the turret, and all the others are armed and ready."

"Good." Kiedral watched closely as Fhostah guided the groundscout along the uneven surface of the rough-graded road, the first time that they had encountered such roughness. On each side, the trees had been removed a mere ten yards or so back from the shoulder of the road, with only low-cut stumps remaining—but there were already shoots rising from the stumps, and it appeared to Kiedral that the bark with scars and burns on the trees beyond the cleared area was already beginning to heal over.

Another kay ahead, the road ended in a wall of trees, none

of which showed any sign of burning or cutting. What Kiedral did not expect was to see the pair of dozers parked neatly beside a temporary plastfoam dome. Farther to one side was the biogester with its biofuel tanks. None of the vehicles appeared damaged. Nor did the plastfoam dome show any signs of an attack . . . except that the door flap was open.

Kiedral lifted the portable comm unit. "Main base, Star One, comm check."

There was a crackle of static . . . and then nothing. He frowned and checked the power indicator, but the unit showed full power. He'd been able to reach main base less than a stan before, with a clear signal.

Fhostah glanced at him for a moment. "Must be some sort of dead area, ser."

"Must be." *You hope it's just that.*

After a moment, Kiedral turned. "Squad Leader, we'll hold here in the groundscout for a bit to see if anyone on the team appears."

"Yes, ser."

After a quarter standard hour, during which neither local animals nor team members appeared, Kiedral decided it was time to look around. "Thaeron, leave Gorran at the turret. The rest of us will disembark and check out the situation."

"Yes, ser."

Recalling the encounter with the miniature flying dinomonster, Kiedral had his slug-thrower in hand when he stepped out of the groundscout. All the combat techs also had their weapons at the ready.

"Have them check out the dome," ordered Kiedral.

"Jaslak, Zhalert, you two look into the dome." Thaeron gestured toward the whitish dome that looked like a very out-of-place overgrown mushroom against the trees that were within meters of the curved plastfoam.

Kiedral slowly turned in a full circle, taking in the trees surrounding the clearing that had been created by the team. The trees seemed to be of two general types, large overarching giants that stood close to seventy-five meters, if not taller, and lower undergrowth trees, below which were knee-high to shoulder-high bushes and vines, although Kiedral could see spaces between the bushes that might have been paths. All the leaves, whatever their shapes, were a deep dark green, not surprisingly to Kiedral, given the greenish-blue sky and the too-white sun. The trees were so tall that, even at mid-afternoon, much of the clearing was still in shade.

From every stump rose green shoots, some of them more than a meter in height.

In four days?

"Ser! There's no one in the dome," called Jaslak, backing away from the doorway. "Just gray mounds."

"The whole inside is filled with things like mushrooms," added Zhalert, following the other tech back from the dome.

"Is there any sign of the crew?" asked Kiedral.

"There's no way to tell unless we burn away that gray slimy stuff."

"Go ahead and do it." Kiedral suspected what they'd find, but he had to know. "Just burn through the plastfoam from outside, and keep as much distance as you can."

Zhalert widened the beam focus, leveled the laser at the side of the portable dome, then triggered the weapon. Immediately, the thin foam vanished under the heat, but in moments, a fine spray of *something* spewed into the air from the gray mass that had been inside the dome.

"Jaslak!" snapped Kiedral. "Widen your beam and sweep that dust or spray! Don't let it get close to you or anyone!"

Jaslak barely managed to get the beam wide enough before a tendril of the grayish spores reached him. He kept sweeping the beam across the spores as Zhalert kept his weapon on what had been the interior of the dome.

"The rest of you watch the trees," Kiedral ordered, belatedly following his own advice, if occasionally letting his eyes scan the smoking mass that had been a portable dome—theoretically strong enough to stop any creature ever encountered. But then, he, or the creators of the portable dwelling, hadn't considered carnivorous fungi, or the equivalent.

When the two techs finished, the upper dome was completely vaporized, and all that remained on the smoking plastform floor, so shot through with holes that it resembled a sieve, was bits of metal—from uniforms, boots, and equipment.

"Not even bones . . . ," murmured the squad leader.

In less than five days. Kiedral wanted to shake his head. Instead, he turned, once more scanning the dark and looming forest, before asking, "Can you tell how many were caught in the dome?"

After several moments, Thaeron replied, "Look to be four belt buckles."

"That's only half the team. Check the dozers." Kiedral continued to scan the surrounding forest. For all the stillness, or perhaps because of it, he couldn't help but feel a sense of imminent danger. While the remaining combat techs also kept scanning the trees, in looking them over, Kiedral had the feeling that only the redheaded Ryaelth shared his sense of danger, although he couldn't have said why.

He eased toward the dozers, well back of Thaeron and Baeltyn.

"There's more stuff growing into the dozers. The composites and organics are half-gone," said Thaeron, his voice containing a tone halfway between amazement and horror.

"The plants don't like metal, then," suggested Kiedral.

"Doesn't seem so."

"Are there any small animals there?"

"No, ser."

"Any sign of other team members?"

Before the squad leader could respond, a black shape appeared to fly out of the trees to the east of the dozers, then bounded toward Thaeron and Baeltyn, stopping abruptly short of the shoots that had grown from some of the stumps before it flared into flame as Ryaelth beamed the shoots. The huge catlike creature paused, and in that moment, Ryaelth did not try her weapon on it, but instead turned the beam on one of the charred tree trunks, letting the laser cut through the tough wood. How she managed it, Kiedral wasn't certain, given that the exploration team's lasers hadn't managed the task, but her judgment and aim were accurate enough that the heavy trunk slammed down on the creature's hindquarters, pinning it in place—although the scream it uttered not only shivered his ears, but split through his thoughts.

What sort of creatures are these? Kiedral didn't have time for more speculation. A massive green lizard, far larger than any replica of any ancient dinosaur he'd ever seen, glided out of the deep woods to the west, surging toward the groundscout, despite the blasts from the turret that shimmered off its shining scales.

Kiedral lifted the slug-thrower, firing directly at the beast's left eye.

White flame flared from the lizard, somehow meeting and deflecting the slug.

Kiedral fired again, this time *willing*, if against hope, the slugs into those saucer-sized black orbs.

Both eyes exploded in reddish-white flame, and the giant lizard threshed in pain, its tail whipping back and forth and snapping the trunks of several of the smaller undergrowth trees. After a time, the threshing subsided, and the huge body lay still. By then, Kiedral had reloaded.

"How . . . did you . . . do that, ser?" stammered the squad leader from behind Kiedral.

"It might be that the slugs are metal." Kiedral had the feeling there was more than metal involved, but he wasn't about to try to explain that feeling.

"It could be," Thaeron half-agreed.

"Burn away enough of the vegetation around the dozers so that we can tell if any of the team died there."

"Yes, ser."

The vice marshal walked quickly toward Tech Ryaelth.

Her eyes snapped toward him, and he almost reeled at what lay there . . . yet . . . she was the one who took a half step back. "Ser?"

"How—" Kiedral stopped after that single word, realizing that his honest question would sound like an accusation if he continued in that hard tone "Excuse me, Tech Ryaelth," he began more quietly, "how did you manage to cut through that tree with a laser beamer . . . when the exploration team couldn't manage it with high-powered cutters?"

"I couldn't say, ser."

Kiedral waited, hoping she'd say more, and knowing she wouldn't if he jumped in with more questions. Instead, he smiled knowingly and sympathetically.

"I really couldn't say, ser." She paused. "I did what you did when you shot that small dinosaur out of the air. I just concentrated on making sure the weapon did what I thought it should."

Kiedral almost said something, but didn't. Rather, he thought about what she had said . . . and then realized what lay behind the words. Then he nodded. "Just keep doing that."

He walked closer to the now-dead black cat creature, careful to stay well out of reach of the thing as he studied it. Overall, it was close to twice the size of a tiger, if with similar musculature, and a jet-black coat. The claws, still extended in death, looked razor sharp and extended far more than finger length, and the black fangs were twice the length of the claws. He couldn't help but wonder what it hunted. The giant lizards? Or something else equally fearsome?

He looked toward the forest again.

"Too quiet, ser," said Ryaelth. "Far too quiet."

"I'm afraid you're right." He turned and walked back to where Thaeron stood beside the dozers. Smoke and steam wreathed the damaged equipment.

"There's no sign of anything, ser," said the squad leader. "The laser cutters in the tool bins still seem to work."

"The bins are metal?"

"Yes, ser."

"We'll cover all the cleared area—weapons at the ready," announced Kiedral.

It took more than a stan for him and the combat techs to walk the entire area that the exploration team had cleared. They found no trace of metal or anything else that might have indicated a fallen exploration tech. One thing that did strike Kiedral as strange was that there was a patch of ground—the only patch, besides the areas that had been burned or the road that had been cleared by the exploration techs—where nothing grew. When he looked more closely, he saw that it was an outcropping of the greenish-tinged white stone that the colony was using as a building material.

"We won't bivouac here," Kiedral finally announced. "We'll take the groundscout back to where there's open ground." As the old maxim went, there were times when discretion was the better part of valor, and so far as Kiedral was concerned, this was one of those times.

"Yes, ser," replied Thaeron, nodding his agreement as well.

"We'll check back on this area tomorrow."

"Yes, ser."

Kiedral could sense far less agreement with that, but he was the only one to nod.

V

Needless to say, Kiedral didn't sleep all that well, disturbed by strange dreams filled with inchoate thoughts and emotions, and images of creatures even stranger than the green lizard and the giant black cat . . . or even the smaller flying monster.

By seven hundred, after reporting to main base, which wasn't difficult once they were clear of the forest, they were back at the exploration team site, completely in shade cast by the tall trees to the east. The plastfoam dome floor remained, as did the dozers. There was no sign of the carcasses of either the giant cat or the massive lizard.

"Even the scavengers in this forest must be large," said Kiedral dryly, hoping for at least a smile.

The only one who showed any expression was Ryaelth, whose lips curled upward slightly at the corners.

"Ser . . . what's the plan of action for today?" asked Thaeron.

"To spend some time trying to determine how best to deal with this . . . forest," replied Kiedral. "It's clear that there's something about it that blocks our comm, among other things, as I reported to base last night."

"You got the comm to work, ser. I couldn't," Thaeron pointed out.

That was another thing Kiedral couldn't explain, except that he'd essentially *willed* the comm to operate, and it had.

"We're not a full combat or development team, ser," the squad leader pointed out politely.

"I didn't say we'd deal with it, but we need to know more before we send anyone else out." *Or if we just have to write off this part of the continent.* And Kiedral didn't want to do that. If he had to, that was one thing, but if that happened to be the case, he wanted to know why and what the full range of dangers might be for any colonists near the forest. "First, we'll check the dozers and the biogester to see if the forest has done any more damage. Then we'll probe the forest . . ." He went on to explain.

Less than a half stan passed before the techs reported that there had been little change since they had left the night before. Then they set up both of the heavy laser cutters facing the forest to the north of the cleared area.

As if it had been watching them, another of the massive lizards pushed its wide head from between the lower trees and moved out of the forest and onto the cleared area that already showed regrowth. A bolt of yellow-reddish-white streaked toward the combat techs, slamming into Fhostah, who stiffened, then toppled backwards onto the dirt of the road.

"He's still breathing, ser," said Zhalert, who'd knelt quickly, while keeping his eyes on the advancing lizard.

"Get him to the groundcar." *There's almost an aura of reddish white to everything coming out of the forest, the frigging enchanted— or accursed—forest. What if you think of darkness when you shoot?* The whole idea felt stupid, yet . . . will seemed to play a role in everything around the forest, from shooting the lizard the day before to operating the comm.

Ryaelth had made that point to him as well, if quietly.

"I'll take the laser cutter," Kiedral said in a voice that brooked no argument as he moved forward.

Baeltyn slipped aside, and the vice marshal eased the laser into focus in the center of the lizard's low forehead, then pressed the stud, concentrating as he did on adding a stream of reddish white to the focused energy.

The lizard's head exploded, and grayish ash drifted down over the slumping body.

Kiedral didn't have time for any self-congratulation, because a bear larger than any he'd ever seen charged from the woods to the northeast, directly at Ryaelth, but before he could turn the laser she'd fired her laser beamer, putting a hole right through the beast's skull. Kiedral blinked. He could have sworn that her beam had *bent* in striking the bear.

A movement at the edge of his vision caught his eye, and he swung the heavy laser cutter on its tripod, zeroing in on yet another green lizard, larger than the first, whose heavy legs crushed the bushes and understory trees as it moved toward the team.

Before Kiedral could focus his weapon, another stun-bolt flashed from the lizard, seemingly bending around Kiedral to strike Jaslak. Kiedral pressed the stud again, cold anger behind his cutting beam, a beam that widened enough to sever the lizard's head from its body. The ground shook as the two sections of the beast crashed into the already crushed undergrowth.

After the second lizard, Kiedral felt drained, as if he'd been running for stans, carrying a heavy pack . . . or struggling against a multiple g-load in combat. *But this is combat, another kind of combat.*

A massive triangular head appeared at the edge of the forest, that of a serpent that wound its way swiftly toward Kiedral and the techs still standing.

A surge of anger filled Kiedral—and he swept the laser across the trees of the forest.

An area of the massive trunks and the branches above them a good ten to twenty meters deep and close to a hundred meters wide vanished in an instant blaze—along with the serpent.

"Oh my God . . . ," murmured someone.

Kiedral didn't look to see who, keeping his eyes on the forest.

An uneasy quiet filled the late morning.

A serpent rose above the trees, then vanished. Then the sun vanished, and Kiedral was surrounded by gray.

The gray turned into bulkheads, ship bulkheads, before which was a long table covered with green cloth. Behind the table were seated five marshals of the Anglorian Unity. Kiedral knew none of them.

"Vice Marshal Kiedral, you are charged with dereliction of duty, willful endangerment of the *A.U.S. Nelson* and the colony vessels you escorted . . ."

Kiedral could not move. *Dereliction? Endangerment? Where were they when nothing worked?*

Part of his brain realized that the scene before him and in which he was enmeshed could not be transpiring. *But how? The damned forest is alive . . .* He swallowed. *It's doing this.*

He pushed aside the false images, only to find himself face-to-face with a young woman, one wearing the Institute dress uniform, her short black hair barely long enough to sweep back over her ears. Her eyes were bright.

"You asked for orders to the Far Fleet, didn't you? And you accepted them, didn't you?"

What could he say? He had.

"You couldn't accept Home Fleet duty? That wasn't enough for you. I wasn't enough for you."

"But you are," he protested, knowing that he lied.

She shook her head and vanished, and a flying monster, just like the one he had killed days before—or was it years and years later?—streaked toward him. All he could do was throw up an arm. Claws gouged his forearm, and an explosion of pain shot up his arm, like a current running from his fingertips to the top of his head.

He staggered back, tumbling through dark grayness . . .

. . . and found himself in the clamshell seat of a needle-boat, concentrating on the mental images fed directly to him.

Screen one displayed Wing three—Ambergy—shields amber and collapsing, with a UFA needleboat angling in on him. Screen two showed a UFA corvette sliding past the wreckage of another Anglorian needleboat, heading toward the mirror tower that anchored sector four's defenses. There was no other Anglorian defender between the mirror tower and the corvette.

Wing two, Wing three, shields failing this time . . .

Kiedral winced, but kicked up the thrusters to full, knowing he didn't have the reserves to intercept the corvette and return to the *Kirkendal.* All he could do was target the corvette and close to where he hoped that his remaining torp would be adequate.

Sweat dripped off his brow, and his back was clammy despite the chill in the clamshell, as the overstrained thrusters vibrated the entire needle.

Wing two . . . The transmission cut off as the other needleboat vanished from the screens.

Kiedral continued to focus on the UFA corvette, watching as it shifted power from shields to drives. In turn, he dropped his own shields and fed the power to the rapidly overheating thrusters.

Just before the corvette neared an approach position for its own attack, Kiedral launched his remaining torp, hoping it would suffice.

It did, and mass became a cloud of energy . . . just as Kiedral's own thrusters died.

Abruptly, Ambergy appeared before him, his face anoxia blue, his lips barely moving. "You left me, Kiedral. You left me to suffocate in the cold. You got a commendation. I died."

Kiedral *knew* Ambergy would never have said those words. Yet they still stung. *What was I supposed to do?* Abandon pursuit and let the UFA corvette destroy the mirror tower that held the system defenses? Save his friend and doom hundreds in the tower and open the system to an invasion?

The scene *blinked*. That was the only way Kiedral could have described it, but before the damned forest could dredge up another painful memory, he threw an image at the grayness—one of massive animals, the lizards, the giant bears, the serpents, all fighting, all gorging on each other, year after year, violence and death leading to nothing but more violence and death.

He could sense something like surprise . . . and he followed it up with another image, that of a gigantic forest fire sweeping down from the mountains, incinerating everything in its path, animals fleeing, killing others in a headlong pursuit to escape, leaving the forest behind to burn away into gray ashes . . .

The grayness vanished, and as Kiedral again stood watching the trees behind the empty space he and the laser cutter had created, an image appeared before him, that of a calm pool of deep green-blue water.

Now what? Kiedral waited, ignoring the gashes on his arms, and the blood oozing from his scalp.

The image remained.

Finally, he tried to express the feeling of a question.

The quiet pool vanished, and a second image filled his mind. He stood facing another enormous green lizard. Behind the lizard were crumpled brilliant white plastfoam domes, the kind they had set up all around main base, one after another crushed and crumpled. Beyond the domes, the half-built white stone walls had been flattened.

Kiedral could sense the white fury of the stun lizard, but in turn, he projected back the fury of an Anglorian battle fleet, its lasers and disruptors turning the very ground into ash, kays and endless kays of ash.

A third vision appeared. This time, white stone houses and other buildings radiated from the stone piers rising from the waters of a blue-green harbor, and those buildings followed exactly the plans that Kiedral had laboriously created. Except . . .

the streets were vacant, and grass grew between the paving stones, and the green shutters flanking open windows sagged, and the glass was absent from many of the windows and cracked and crazed in others.

Kiedral walked up and down the streets, but all were vacant. He saw not a soul anywhere.

Abruptly, the scene shifted, and he beheld blackened and smoking trees, and the carcasses of dead lizards, black cats, armored tortoises, and more creatures than he had yet beheld at the edge of the forest.

Is this what you wish . . . ? They are one and the same. The words were not spoken as such, but that was the impression created by the juxtaposition of the two scenes.

Kiedral saw no one, but the question remained.

He finally spoke, although he did not know to whom he addressed his words. "I wish prosperity for all, for both."

The scene of forest desolation vanished, replaced by a searing and brilliant reddish whiteness. From somewhere, he knew not where, he grasped for a darkness to balance that brilliant reddish whiteness . . .

So be it. . . . Again . . . there were no actual words, but a feeling, followed by another image, so clear that Kiedral seemed to be there, standing beside a white stone wall a good five yards in height, if not more. A road ran beside the wall, and on one side were houses and domes. On the other side was the towering forest looming above the stone wall.

From there, the vision shifted to another image, where Kiedral stood in a high-ceilinged chamber.

A man, not young, but not so old as Kiedral, who wore a strange green uniform, one different, yet similar to one of Kiedral's own dress uniforms, walked deliberately down the center of a great hall toward a throne of green stone and silver set upon a low dais. Behind him followed a red-haired woman, also in green, carrying an infant. Her bearing was as regal as his, and each step they took was measured. As the man neared the empty throne, he inclined his head.

Kiedral could see clearly both the man and the woman, and yet there was not only a linkage between the two of them, but between him and the red-haired woman. He could not explain it, only sense it. And there was another linkage . . .

The vision, if that is what it was, vanished, and Kiedral once more stood at the edge of the forest.

"Ser?"

He glanced around, his eyes lighting on Ryaelth. She turned toward him, as if seeing him truly for the first time.

His eyes met hers.

"The giant lizards . . . the serpent . . . the forest. You did that, didn't you?"

"We all did that," he said quietly, without bothering to explain what he meant by "we."

"And the images?"

"What images?" asked Thaeron.

"Call them afterimages of the lasers," said Kiedral, waiting for the squad leader to turn to attend to the fallen Jaslak before he smiled at Ryaelth.

She smiled back, if briefly. Her eyes widened as she belatedly took in the gashes and the blood.

"Collateral damage," he explained, his voice dry.

VI

As the groundscout turned to leave the great forest behind, the vice marshal's eyes lingered on the tall dark-leafed trees for a long moment before he looked at the road, a road that would be paved with greenish-white stone before long.

The spirit of the forest and he had fought to a draw. *An agreement. For now.*

But he would be back, and the second time, he would supervise the boundaries of that agreement, for their draw—of sorts—necessitated that, with the forest and its spirit confined within limits. *But only confined, if within large boundaries . . . and not forever.*

That, too, he knew.

He could only hope that those who follow would understand. He knew Ryaelth did.

The Emperor turns from the balcony and walks back toward his private chambers, where he will rest, for a time, perhaps many times, before the long rest that he dreads . . . and welcomes. Another set of lines echoes through his thoughts.

> *Do I regret the stars that cast me here?*
> *No more than knowing life is fragile, dear,*
> *and fleeting, or that my words die unread,*
> *for words cannot contain what souls have said.*

This story comes from the other end of Candar, in the early history of Lydiar, and I wrote it because a reader asked a question.

MADNESS?

We all know about the Pantarans. By the time she's five, every little girl knows enough to blame the unfortunate, but unobserved, accidents on them, even the ones caused by older brothers that no one ever questions, despite the fact that no one even knows if the Pantarans existed, save for the rare coin that may occasionally appear from somewhere that bears no known language and is ascribed to them. Likewise, in days to come, days so far from us that none will be able to sort fact from fable from fancy, some may recall the day when my brother became mad. Truly mad, they will say. Was he?

I was sulking in the reading room that had been Mother's because my brother had chased me out of Father's library. The sulk wasn't because he'd chased me out, but because he wouldn't tell me why. Heldry was ten years older than I was, and he usually was kind about explaining why I had to do something. That was because he could show his superiority. But he'd refused to say, and that was wrong. After all, I was his only sister, and I wasn't a small child. I was twelve and almost as tall

as any of the women who flocked around both Father and
Heldry.

Father had even said that in another year or so, I could sit at
the formal table as his lady. No one had since Mother died. That
was another reason I was mad and sulking when Heldry refused
to say why I had to leave the library. I was the only woman in
the family, and he was dismissing me. The worst thing was that
I couldn't even try to hide, because Heldry would have known
where I was, at least . . . if he bothered to think about it.

Still . . . after half a glass passed, I slipped out of the reading room and tiptoed oh-so-slowly into Father's sitting room
and then down the hidden stairs—the tiny circular ones—to
the small robing room that adjoined the audience hall where
Father was hearing petitions. The audience chamber was the
largest room in the palace, and the closest to the harbor, positioned so that both the land breezes and the sea breezes off the
waters of the Great North Bay swept through it. Grandsire had
built it that way, or so he had said, because he wanted to be
comfortable when he was handling the uncomfortable tasks of
listening to petitions, dispensing justice, and arguing with his
treasurer and head tariff collector. Like the rest of the palace,
it had white marble walls and columns and floors. That kept it
cool in the summer, but, in winter, even when the great doors
were shut tight, it often felt colder in there than it did outside.

From there, I took the service hall to the rear door of the
library. That was where Father went to read when he wasn't in
the study where he met people. I opened the door ever so quietly, except it wasn't that silent. But it didn't matter because I
heard voices. Heldry was talking to someone. He was talking
to a girl—a woman! I had to know who it was, and if he was
talking to someone he wouldn't be trying to find me. They
were in the alcove behind Father's desk, sitting in the window
seat that overlooked the walled garden. I tiptoed closer, keep-

ing close to the bookshelves on the east wall. I had to stop just
before I got to Father's desk.

I couldn't see her without them seeing me, and they were
talking in such low voices I could barely make out what they
were saying.

"They say it's awful." Her voice was low, with that throaty
sound that men love. I'd heard Father say that to one of the
lords who tried to flatter him at the balls, the balls Father said
I was too young to attend, but he didn't know I'd been to many
of them by watching from the hidden galleries. "Some of them
come up in the ore baskets and their hands are blue for almost
a glass. Then they send them down again. Most of them are
brands . . . just because they can't get other work . . ."

"If they can't get other work . . ."

"It's not right, Heldry. Some have already died, Vyanna
told me."

"I suppose you're right."

"I am right. You know I am. Hard work is one thing. Brands
need to learn that, but learning shouldn't kill them."

"You'd think the factors would care. . . . It does cost when
you break in a new worker."

"Not that much when you're paying the brands half what
they pay a real miner. Less than that, sometimes." There was
a long pause. "Promise me that you'll look into it."

"Since you've asked . . ."

I could hear some movement, but no more words.

"Heldry . . ."

There was a sigh even I could hear. "I'll talk to my father
about it."

"Try to persuade him to summon the factors to an audience.
They won't dare lie to him."

"They might."

"You listen to them. You can tell if they're lying. Please."

Heldry sighed again. "I can't let him or them know I can tell for certain. You know that."

"I have to go. I shouldn't be here at all."

"I'm glad you are."

"I can tell that." The woman laughed softly.

A moment later I heard her boots on the stone tile floor, along with Heldry's heavier steps. That puzzled me. Most women didn't wear boots. All I could do was flatten myself against the bookcase and hope they didn't look my way.

As she and Heldry walked away from me toward the main door of the library, I could see that she wore green trousers and a green tunic. That explained the boots, because the color meant she was a healer. I didn't move because they might have heard me. She had flame-red hair, though, and it was cut too short.

Heldry stayed just inside the door as she stepped out. He didn't want her to be seen with him. After several moments, he turned and saw me. Before I could have fled, he was in front of me looking down. He wasn't pleased. "Shaeldra . . . what were you doing here?"

"Listening. Who were you talking to?" I wasn't about to admit how much I'd heard.

"Someone."

"Who is she?"

"She's a healer," Heldry said in that way that told me she was more than that, not that I didn't already know it.

"Is she pretty?"

"Shaeldra . . ."

"Is she?"

"That wasn't why she was here. Her . . . the woman who's teaching her to be a better healer . . . she was sent to Hrisbarg, to try to heal one of the master miners."

"Is that what Father was mumbling about in the hall last night?"

"In a way," he admitted.

"Again?" I couldn't help but ask because every summer since we'd been old enough to understand, or so it seemed, there was trouble with the miners, if not those in Hrisbarg, then those in Kleth or the tin miners to the northwest near Lavah.

"They're claiming that the shafts have gotten too deep for good ventilation, but the metal factors are insisting that's not so and threatening to turn them out of their homes."

"How can they do that?"

"The factors built the houses for the miners. They own them."

"Then why is Father involved?"

"Because he's the Duke of Lydiar, and he owns all the rights to the metals. He leases . . . rents—"

"I know what leaseholds are," I snapped. I hated it when Heldry got that superior tone in his voice.

"He leases the rights to the factors, and they pay him part of what they make from mining and smelting the iron."

"Can't Father have his mages do anything?" I smiled winningly at my big brother. "Can't you? You're a mage, too, aren't you?"

"They're *iron* mines, Shaeldra. Iron. You know . . . the metal that binds chaos?"

"Even when it's just ore?" I was pleased with that. I'd just learned about how metals had to be smelted or melted out of ore and how all that was left was slag.

"The ore there is so rich it takes little furnace work to turn it into workable metal. That means it can bind chaos to a great degree . . . and any chaos mage who tried to use chaos to widen the vent tunnels might turn himself into ash. Besides, I only have a little talent."

I didn't know about mages turning into ash, and maddening

as Heldry could be, I certainly didn't want him to turn himself
into ash for a bunch of miners and factors. "You didn't tell me
if she's pretty," I reminded him.

"Shaeldra . . ."

"She is, isn't she?"

"I suppose so."

"What's her name?"

Heldry didn't answer.

"If you don't tell me, I'll start asking people in the palace.
I might even have to ask Father."

He glared at me. Finally, he said, "Klyanna. Don't you *dare*
tell anyone else."

"I won't. What are you going to do about the miners in
Hrisbarg?"

"Talk to Father. What else?"

"What will you tell him?"

"What he needs to know."

"Heldry!"

"That's enough, Shaeldra."

"I want to know what happens. I should know."

Heldry started to frown. Then he laughed. "Actually, you
should. If I can persuade Father to summon the factors, you
can watch from one of the hidden galleries."

Heldry did persuade Father to summon the factors. I didn't
know how, and he wouldn't tell me, but he did keep his promise. Three days later, the two of us stood side by side in the
listening gallery above and to the side of the audience platform where Father sat in the gilded chair. Five men in rich
clothing faced him, and all of them had sweaty faces. It wasn't
that hot because it was still spring. They all had thick beards,
too. I never liked beards. They're scratchy even when women
tell men they're soft, but I know why they have to do that.

Father looked at them silently for a time before he spoke.

"I have received reports that you are using unsafe practices in mining the deeper shafts of the iron mines in Hrisbarg."

The two men on the ends looked down. The one in the middle looked squarely at Father. His look said that he knew more about mining than the Duke of Lydiar did. "Your Mightiness, we have taken as much care as possible in mining the deeper shafts, but with the costs of mining and the share that we must pay you, we must do all we can to use the deeper levels. That is where the best ore lies."

Father cleared his throat. "Yet I've heard that one master miner is so crippled that he can no longer work, and that you are using brands. Several of them have died."

"Those miners died because they did not listen," replied the middle factor.

"You are using brands as miners because you can pay them less," declared Father.

The youngest-looking of the factors—maybe that was because his beard was blond and short—was the one who answered. "It is true. That's because many miners have left for the mines in Certis. The Viscount pays exorbitant wages to lure our miners away."

"Exorbitant?" asked Father mildly.

"As much as three coppers a day and lodging. He can do that because he can set the price for his copper for all the factors, and all of Candar pays more for copper because of it."

"All of Candar?"

"All Candar east of the Westhorns . . . and some traders are bringing copper ingots from Lornth because they can make a profit with prices so high."

"Perhaps it would be best if I came to the mines and made an inspection myself," said Father mildly.

"Perhaps . . ." One of the factors started to speak, then abruptly closed his mouth.

"We would welcome you, Your Mightiness," said the center factor. "We will meet you there whenever you wish."

"Let it be so. My seneschal will send word."

With that, the factors bowed and left the audience hall.

"I'm going, too," I told Heldry.

"That's up to Father, Shaeldra."

"I know . . . but you can tell him I should . . ." I smiled as winningly as I could. "Will Klyanna be there?"

"It's possible."

"She should be."

Heldry sighed, but he didn't say she wouldn't be.

More than an eightday passed, and I heard nothing. So I cornered Heldry after breakfast before he could go anywhere. "When are we going to Hrisbarg?"

"I don't know. Father said it will have to wait."

"He doesn't want me to go."

"It's not about you, Shaeldra. I haven't had a chance to tell him you should go."

"Why not? You promised."

"Because . . . You wouldn't understand."

I glared at him. He was the one who didn't understand.

"If you could wield chaos, little sister, I'd be ashes right now." He grinned.

"You . . . Something's gone wrong, hasn't it?"

"I wouldn't say wrong. Something else has come up. The Duke of Hydlen is sending an envoy."

"For what?" I was getting tired of pulling everything out of him.

"His daughter . . . ," admitted Heldry.

"He wants you to consort his daughter?"

"His younger sister. She's about my age."

"And she's not already consorted? She can't be very pretty."

"Her portrait shows her as attractive."

"Portraits lie." They did when someone was trying to get a relative consorted, especially a sister. "Besides, why do you want to consort someone you don't even know?"

"I told Father that. That's why the envoy is escorting Chelynn. Father doesn't know exactly when they'll arrive. That's also why he doesn't want to set when we go to Hrisbarg. The trip takes several days."

I knew that, but I didn't like it.

I was right not to like it because almost an eightday passed before the envoy arrived from Hydolar with the Duke's daughter. Even before Chelynn entered the palace, Aunt Ealdra arrived. She was there to "accompany" me. I knew what that meant. She was there to keep me away from that wench who wanted to consort Heldry except when it was unavoidable.

When I was finally allowed to meet Chelynn, it was just before the official welcoming dinner in the receiving room off the dining hall. She was one of those pale, thin women with breasts too big for her shoulders, a waist better suited to a wasp, and shimmering black hair. The kind all the older men, especially, kept staring at when they thought their consorts weren't looking.

"Shaeldra," said Aunt Ealdra, giving me a warning glance that no one could see but me, "this is Lady Chelynn."

"I'm so pleased to meet you, Shaeldra." Chelynn gave me a smile that was as false as a Pantaran silver. Her voice was just as deceiving. She spoke like a little girl, with that husky sound that scheming women use to sound appealing. I'd heard those voices around Father ever since Mother died.

"I've so wanted to meet you." I could be just as sweetly false as she was.

"Your brother has said so much about you." Another nothing smile followed her words.

"And I've heard nothing but compliments about you." Of

course that was true. No one was going to say anything nasty about the Duke's daughter, at least not where anyone could hear.

"And I've heard only the best about you." She smiled again.

After we traded more sentences saying nothing except—by lack of meaning—that neither of us happened to like the other, I returned to being the naïve little sister and said, "After you leave, we're going to Hrisbarg."

Chelynn smiled that smile that Mother would have called a pleasant nothing. "Oh? That's a mining town, isn't it? Why might you be going there?"

"To see why miners are dying." I wasn't supposed to say anything like that. Well-bred young ladies were to keep their opinions to what could be shown in tone and look. I'd never be able to do that.

"Miners and men who work at hard labor do die at times, Shaeldra," Chelynn replied. "That's not something a ruler can change."

"Even when they shouldn't die?"

"Who can say when they should or shouldn't?"

"A healer."

"Healers should confine themselves to healing."

I hoped that Heldry had heard that. Before I could bait Chelynn into saying more . . . or revealing how insipid she was, the end table nearest to her tottered. The large decorative urn slid off and then fell to the marble floor. The crash was so loud that Chelynn couldn't have heard a word I said. Even if she could have heard, she was too busy moving those long skinny legs to avoid the porcelain fragments skittering toward her feet.

"Oh . . . dear . . ." That was Aunt Ealdra. She looked at me, as if it had been my fault.

It hadn't been, not directly. I did know how it had happened, though. I looked toward where Heldry stood in the archway.

He didn't just glare. I felt the gold choker I wore tighten around my neck. For a moment, I couldn't even swallow. That's what happens when your brother is part-mage. I gave him my most evil look, but the choker just tightened. So I swallowed— or tried to—and turned back to Chelynn, offering a sympathetic smile I didn't feel in the slightest. "Are you all right?"

Before she could say a word, Heldry moved into the room. He offered a winning smile, the one that warmed you, even if you knew it was all too practiced. "It wasn't a totally priceless urn." He managed to convey dismissal while acknowledging that the urn might have had some value. "Perhaps we should join the others before we repair to table."

At table, Chelynn sat at Father's left, across from Heldry. I sat beside him, and the envoy from Certis sat beside Chelynn. He was a round-faced man with a big belly and a square beard. His eyes were small and bright, like a rat's.

Once everyone was seated, and their goblets filled with the deep red wine from the hills, Father stood and lifted his goblet. "To our most honored guest, the Lady Chelynn, and to her father the Duke of Hydlen, for sharing one of his most prized possessions with us for this short period of time."

As Heldry raised his goblet, his left hand reached out under the table and squeezed my knee in a grip like iron. "Do nothing here," he murmured in a voice lower than a whisper.

After that, both Heldry and Aunt Ealdra watched everything I said and did. So I was utterly charming. I could do that. I'd been trained well.

When the dinner was over and Aunt Ealdra escorted Chelynn and Heldry away to the salon, Father beckoned to me. I smiled and joined him in the corner of the dining hall.

He looked down at me, sadly but kindly. "Shaeldra . . . your dislike for Chelynn was all too obvious. Do you think I would allow Heldry to consort with a lady with . . . attributes . . . you

and others might find less than attractive—unless such a consorting were absolutely necessary?"

"Why is it so necessary?"

"There are reasons . . . very good reasons."

"So that you don't have to go to war with Hydlen? Or
because Chelynn will bring thousands of golds."

"It's simpler than that. There are no other suitable young
women in Certis, Vergren, or Hydlen."

"What do you mean by suitable? Heldry doesn't have to
consort a ruler's daughter, does he? There's nothing to stop him
from consorting someone else, is there?"

"No . . ."

That told me Father wouldn't be pleased if Heldry tried to
consort with the healer Klyanna . . . and that meant it wouldn't
happen. I hadn't met the healer, but she was a healer, and that
was something. Chelynn was nothing except a duke's daughter
without a thought in her head except keeping her position or
bettering it. Her heart would go to the fullest strongbox.

"I trust you understand, Daughter."

I smiled as sweetly as I could. "I do understand, Father."
I just didn't like it.

"Good. I'll see you in the morning."

With that, I was dismissed. I couldn't even go to the salon
and think evil thoughts at Chelynn. It was so unfair. It was even
unfair to Heldry.

I didn't see Chelynn again. Father and Aunt Ealdra saw
to that. She and the Hydlenese envoy left two days after the
banquet.

Then, three days after that, on threeday morning, Heldry
had me awakened early and told to make ready for a trip to Hrisbarg. That was another thing I hated about him. He was always
telling me things at the last moment . . . or not telling me at
all, and letting me find out through surprise.

The trip did take two days, a day and a half, really, and the weather was good, not too hot, and there was a cool breeze. I enjoyed riding Shadow. I called him that because his coat was dark gray. Heldry said it fit him because he was a gelding and a shadow of what he could have been. Once we rode outside of Lydiar, though, two healers joined us. One was Klyanna, and the other one was Vaerel. She was older, but I got the feeling she was there more as a chaperone than because she knew that much more about healing. Heldry made sure I didn't get to talk to either one by myself.

So . . . on fiveday afternoon on the last eightday of spring, we arrived at the mines. I thought an iron mine would have tunnels into the side of a mountain with huge wheeled carts rumbling out of those tunnels. Instead, what I saw was a bowl-like depression in the midst of low hills. There were two tunnels that didn't look to have been used in a long time. One of them had a wooden wall, more like a fence, in front of it. There were two tall wooden towers . . . well, they were timber frameworks with heavy ropes going down into holes in the ground. The holes had to be the mine shafts. Beside each tower was a circular pen that held oxen in yokes. The yokes were attached to heavy poles, and the poles ran to a big wheel.

After I dismounted, while I was waiting, I watched for a time. The wheel turned, and that turned gears attached to other wheels, and those had the ropes attached to the big baskets that came up out of the shaft filled with rock. When a basket came up, the oxen stopped, and a team of men swung the basket to the side and tipped it somehow so that the rock, I guess it was the ore, slid down a ramp into a stout wagon.

Over the hill to the west, I could see smoke rising. That had to be where they were using the furnaces to smelt the iron.

"Shaeldra!" hissed Heldry.

I jumped.

He glared. He was good at that. I understood and hurried
to catch up with him and the two healers as he followed Father
toward the nearest of the shaft towers. Three men stood several
yards from the shaft. Because they had guards behind them,
they had to be factors.

I'd almost caught up with Heldry and the healers when
Father stopped. The rest of us halted behind him, and the guards
stopped behind us.

"Where are the factors Nebliat and Yoraln?" Father asked, his
voice hardening as he looked at the three who stood before him.

"I cannot say, Your Mightiness," replied the blond-bearded
factor. "They said they would be here."

"We will see." Father paused. Then he asked, "How deep
are those shafts?"

None of the three replied.

"Do you know, Alurn?" Father looked at the young blond
factor.

"Around two hundred yards, they say."

"You don't know? Have you ever been down those shafts?"

"No, ser. I'm not a miner."

"Pultrun . . . Mocoza . . . have either of you been down those
shafts?"

After a long moment, both of the other factors shook their
heads.

One of the big baskets coming up out of the shaft halted,
and several men, smudged with reddish dirt or grime, slowly
clambered out. One of them staggered. Father gestured, and
Klyanna stepped forward and stopped beside him.

Father glanced at Klyanna, nodded, and spoke again. "I
would talk to those miners there. Oh . . . and I will have the
healer with me."

Even I could see the factors stiffen, tiny as their reactions
were. I'd have wagered most people wouldn't have seen that.

Most people weren't raised in a palace. What I didn't know was why they were worried, unless they worried that the healer could tell which miners had been injured in the past and how.

"Don't worry. I have never met her before now. I have asked the healers to provide one of their number that I had never met," Father added, almost as an afterthought.

That didn't seem to cheer any of the three, but none of them said a word as Father and Klyanna walked toward the shaft and the miners. I could see that one of them had fallen, or maybe he'd fainted. I wanted to go with them, but the look Heldry gave me was more than enough to keep my boots planted where they were.

All Heldry and I could do was watch as Father and Klyanna and all the guards but one walked to the nearer shaft. I looked to the gray-haired healer who remained with us and the guard. Her eyes were fixed on Klyanna. I didn't say anything, but looked back to the shaft. I tried to hear what Father was saying or asking, but he was too far away. Then I looked at the factors. They had turned and were watching Father.

After more than half a glass of talking to the miners, Father turned, gently, and so did Klyanna. He started to walk back toward us. His steps were determined. Heldry avoided looking at me. That told me that he was worried. The three factors also watched silently as Father walked away from the miners and the shafts.

When he neared us, he turned and looked at the factors. "Close the deep shafts. If they are not closed in the next two eightdays, you will all lose your leaseholds."

"But . . . Your Mightiness . . . ," protested one of the factors.

"But what, Factor Mocoza?" asked Father.

"We cannot pay rents if we cannot mine, and we cannot mine without using the shafts."

"You five share the leasehold rights that extend a kay on

a side. You can dig shallower shafts in other places. If you are not interested in doing so, I imagine there are others who will be."

"It takes time to dig such shafts . . . and two eightdays are not enough."

Father did not speak for several moments. Finally, he said, "You have four eightdays."

The three exchanged glances. After a time, the third factor spoke, "We will do what we must."

"Pultrun . . . you will convey those terms to the other factors who did not see fit to join us. I will hear if you do not, and you will lose your share of the leaseholds even if the shafts are closed."

"Yes, Your Mightiness."

"And you will inform me when the shafts are closed."

Pultrun nodded. His forehead was sweaty, and it wasn't that hot.

"Let it be done." Father nodded brusquely, then turned.

We followed him.

I waited just a bit before I said anything to Heldry. "They didn't like Father having a healer when he talked with the miners. Why not?"

"Because some healers can tell when people don't tell the truth. Or when they are telling the truth."

"Can Klyanna?"

He nodded.

"Will you tell me what the miners said? When you find out?"

"I don't know that Father will tell me."

"Klyanna will." I knew that.

"Not if Father asks her not to tell anyone. She won't break her oath as a healer."

"Not even for you?"

He shook his head.

I could tell he meant it. Even if I wouldn't find out, that

made me respect Klyanna more. A lot more than that twit Chelynn.

Father looked tired when we got back to the palace. I didn't see much of him for several days. By the next fourday, though, he was cheerful at breakfast. He even told me that I'd ridden well on the journey to and from Hrisbarg. But he was tired by that evening, and I thought his face was a little gray.

He died three days later. I couldn't believe it. I didn't cry. Not then. Not until I was alone that night. How could it have happened? Father wasn't that old. Some of the palace servants were white haired, and they could do their duties. Father's hair only had a few streaks of gray.

The next morning I went looking for Paetyk. He was Father's healer. It took me two glasses to find him. He was in a tiny room on the lower level, just sitting there and looking at the wall. He looked as sad as I felt, but that didn't stop me from asking, "Why couldn't you save him? You're a healer?"

"Your brother asked me the same question." He sighed. "When a man's heart stops beating, I know of no way to get it to beat again."

"But why? Why did it happen?"

"Sometimes it does. Especially when a person has been very sick in the past, with something like the red flux. You know your father had that, didn't you?"

"I knew he had the flux. But he got well."

"Not as well as he was before, Lady Shaeldra."

I asked more questions, but the answers were the same. It couldn't have been something Paetyk did, I didn't think. Not the way he felt and acted.

After Father's memorial and the dedication to order, Heldry became duke. Well . . . he was already duke, but there was a quiet ceremony. Heldry said he didn't want a big celebration after such a sad happening. He was duke, and that was the way it was.

I didn't hear anything about Chelynn, either. But when I asked Atalar—he was still the seneschal—he just said that the Duke had deferred any decision while he was still in mourning.

That wasn't good.

There wasn't much I could do, and I thought I'd better not say too much. I found out that I'd said too much at breakfast the next morning.

"I hear you asked Atalar about Lady Chelynn yesterday," Heldry said.

There wasn't any point in denying it. "I wanted to know."

"Shaeldra," he began with a tone almost like Father's except he sounded more exasperated, "sometimes, at your age, it's better not to know."

"It is not. I should know."

"Then I'll tell you. Someday, in a few years, you'll be in her position. Maybe then, you'll have some sympathy for her. She didn't ask to be consorted to someone she scarcely knows . . . whether it's me or Khoran of Vergren."

"You're going to do that to me?"

"You have to be consorted to someone. . . ."

I was so mad at him I almost forgot how sad I still was about Father. I didn't even finish my egg toast. I just walked off and ran into the gardens below the veranda. There were places there that no one could find me. But he didn't even try. That made me madder. So I avoided him as much as I could for almost an eightday, and I'd only say what I had to when we were together.

I still wanted to know what was happening, though. So I kept watching to see who Heldry met with. I couldn't believe that he met with the mining factors, and I didn't like the way they looked when they left Father's study, except it was Heldry's, even if I thought of it as Father's. And I didn't like the way Heldry looked after he met with them, either.

Then, near the end of harvest, I saw Klyanna make her way to the library, not to the study. That meant Heldry wasn't supposed to see her, or that he didn't want Atalar and some of the others in the palace to know he was meeting with her. Before he showed up, I sneaked in through the back entrance and hid under Father's desk. Klyanna stood back from the window seat and the open window and kept looking toward the main entrance. She didn't even see me.

Heldry arrived before long, and he closed the door and looked around.

"I shouldn't be here . . . ," murmured Klyanna.

"There's no one else . . . no one else."

I couldn't see what they were doing, but the library was very quiet.

". . . have to do something . . . ," Heldry said. ". . . can tell when a great storm might form . . ."

". . . can usually tell . . ."

"Good!"

What was good I didn't hear because Heldry lowered his voice even more.

He was still whispering when Klyanna protested, "You can't do that."

"What would you have me do? Become an obedient ox for the factors?"

"But that . . . ?"

"I *can* do it . . . if you'll help. You saw what they did to Father. Would you have that happen again?"

Father? He knew that the factors had been why Father had died? And he hadn't told me? I was so upset that, for several moments, I wasn't paying attention. By then, Heldry had guided the healer away from the desk. I peeked out a little, enough to see that they were next to the open window overlooking the bay. I kept watching. I hoped they wouldn't look my way, but

Heldry gestured toward the veranda balcony that overlooked the harbor and the Great North Bay.

Klyanna shook her head several times. Finally, she nodded, but it wasn't a happy nod. When she started to turn, I had to jerk my head back out of sight. I could hear her boots leaving the library. Then, in a bit, Heldry went out. The servants would know, but no one had actually seen them together, and Heldry was the duke. I waited for a time and left by the other door, the one used by the servants. You can do that when everyone thinks you're just a girl.

I kept worrying about what Heldry had said, but I didn't want to bring it up too soon. So I waited. It seemed like forever.

"You never told me how Father died," I finally said to Heldry at breakfast two days later. I'd made myself wait that long before bringing it up.

"The healers said that his heart stopped."

"Klyanna?" I knew what Paetyk had said, but I wanted to know what she had said.

"No. Paetyk."

"How would he know? He's old."

"He was also Father's healer since before Father became duke. No one knew Father's health better." Heldry paused. "Father's heart hasn't been as strong as it should have been ever since he had that nasty bout with the flux three years ago. You *should* remember how sick he was, and how Paetyk worried that he might die then."

I remembered how ill Father had been . . . but no one had said he might die. Paetyk hadn't even told me that when I'd asked.

"You were only ten, Shaeldra. No one wanted to worry you."

But that was all Heldry would really say, and I knew there was more, but no matter what I said, I didn't learn more. Heldry could be so stubborn. I never did find out what else he'd said to Klyanna, either. I couldn't ask any more than I had without revealing that I'd heard his conversation with Klyanna, and I didn't want to do that. He just might have confined me to my chambers. Then I wouldn't have been able to find out anything more at all.

But Father hadn't died of a weak heart. Or not just of that, and Heldry thought the factors had something to do with it. Poison? A chaos mage? I couldn't believe Father had been smothered, not in the palace, but the factors had done something, and Heldry was worried. He was the duke, and that worried me.

Another eightday passed, and suddenly there were workmen removing the stone balustrade at the end of the stone veranda off the audience chamber. Atalar would only tell me that the workmen and artisans were following the plans and instructions Heldry had approved before he left on his trip to Hydolar to return the visit made by Chelynn.

That made me furious. He'd told me he was going hunting. He *knew* I didn't like that cow-eyed vixen, and he went anyway! And he lied about it. Except he didn't. Not totally. He made sure I'd find out . . . after he'd gone and before he returned. That meant he hoped I'd get over being mad.

When he came back in the middle of harvest, more than an eightday later, I was still mad. But I was polite, and the next morning at breakfast, because that was the only meal we shared, mostly alone, except for the serving girls, I asked him, "Why are you having the veranda balcony extended? Does it really need those ugly columns in a semicircle over the lower garden? What *was* the lower garden, I mean? And why are the centers made of copper?"

"You were the one who told me the lower garden was ugly and useless."

"That was because Mother made me weed it."

"That was because you threw a temper tantrum, and she

wanted you to understand that you weren't any better than the gardeners, only more fortunate. Anyway, once the rebuilding is done, I could have them create another set of gardens on each side of the extension to the palace."

"I'll think about it."

"Don't think too long." He gave me that condescending big brother smile I hated.

That made me even madder. Besides, he didn't answer all my questions.

Then he announced that he was having an afternoon reception for the factors who held the mining leaseholds in Hrisbarg and that he was including several others. He told me that I could watch, but not be present. That made sense, but I was still irritated over the destruction of the lower gardens. Maybe that was because Heldry hadn't done anything about replacing them.

When the fourth glass of sixday afternoon arrived, I'd placed myself as close as I could. That was the hidden gallery halfway back in the audience chamber.

The first factor to arrive was Deault. He was younger, younger even than Alurn, I thought, and he was one of the factors who didn't even have a leasehold, and who I didn't think had anything to do with Father's death. After that came Zharyn, and he was the oldest factor I'd ever seen, with snow-white hair. He smiled at Heldry, and it was a real smile. I had to wonder why Heldry had invited him.

The minerals factors all arrived at the same time—Nebliat, Yoraln, Mocoza, Alurn, and Pultrun. They all were most polite, and Heldry was effusive to them all. Father trained us to be pleasant and polite when we needed to be, regardless of those we were with. I still didn't see how Heldry could do it.

Once they were all there, a dark-haired, gray-robed server I did not recognize filled the crystal goblet of each factor. She also filled Heldry's goblet. I could tell Heldry was serving them the best wine—the purple ice wine came from the hills near the border with Sligo.

"To all of you," said Heldry, lifting his goblet.

"And to you, Your Mightiness," replied Pultrun.

The others murmured the same, and everyone waited just slightly, until Heldry took a swallow. It was a swallow, not a sip. Then they all drank.

"I've never tasted a vintage so fine," announced Yoraln after lowering his crystal goblet.

"It's usually reserved for family," said Heldry. "I thought you might enjoy it."

"Is this occasion that special?" asked Nebliat.

"I would think so," said Heldry. "Are we not celebrating the continuation of your leaseholds? Is that not special, after all the work you all have put into them . . . over the years?" He took another sip of the wine.

"We have put much work into them. That is true, Your Mightiness," agreed Nebliat. "But your wisdom in allowing us to continue as in the past contributes to your rents and our prosperity."

"Ah . . . wisdom, but is not power more important than wisdom?" asked Heldry. "The wisest man in the world can do nothing without power."

"But you have power," said Mocoza. "You have one of the richest and most prosperous duchies in all of Candar."

The audience hall seemed to dim, but that wasn't because someone had snuffed the lamps. It was because the sky over the Great North Bay was darkening, most likely because of another harvest storm. Those were the kind that came in with lots of lightning, and not that much rain, except when they reached the very south end of the bay. That was where the best lands for crops were. Father had told me that more than once.

"With the factors behind you," added Pultrun, "nothing can challenge your power and your rule."

"Nothing," murmured Alurn.

Outside, gusts of wind whipped across the expanded veranda.

"Come . . . ," ordered Heldry abruptly. "Let us go out upon the veranda and observe the storm."

The five mining factors glanced from one to the other. "Your Mightiness . . . it is raining."

"Of course it is, but it's only sprinkling, and you were telling me I had nothing to fear because nothing challenged my power and my rule. If nothing challenges my power, and I wish you safe, what harm can there be in watching a storm from the veranda?"

All the factors exchanged glances, but they followed him out through the wide doors onto the veranda. The gray-clad server followed, but only so far as the open doors. She remained just inside the audience hall. I could barely see, but there was nothing I could do except peer in their direction. The greenish shade of the dimming light told me that the clouds continued to gather, turning as they did so often from a dark gray into an evil green that was so dark it was almost black.

Heldry stood in the middle of the newly built addition to the veranda, close to right over the center column. He gestured. "See the dark beauty of the storm! See the lightning!"

I thought he was cackling the way his voice rose and fell. It was hard to hear over the wind. People who haven't been in one of those storms don't understand how fast they come and go.

"Come! Join me! You have nothing to fear! Am I not powerful enough to stand up to any storm?"

"The Duke has gone mad! He's mad!" screamed Nebliat. Somehow, he couldn't move his boots.

"He's mad!" echoed Alurn.

"Look!" cried Heldry in a delighted tone. "See how beautiful the lightning is! Oh . . . do it again!" He raised a hand to the swirling clouds above and beckoned.

Mocoza tried to lift his once shiny boots from the stone where he stood. Somehow, he couldn't, either, and neither could Alurn, Pultrun, and Yoraln. The other two factors eased back toward the audience hall.

Then a lightning bolt struck, and it forked into Nebliat and Yoraln. Before I could say anything, another one struck, and Alurn, Pultrun, and Mocoza flared into charred husks.

After the second lightning bolt struck, one of the two remaining factors yelled, "Someone do something! Anything!" It was Deault—

Klyanna stepped forward. I had no idea where she had been hiding, except she wore gray, and there was a dark wig on the stone tiles inside the audience hall. I hadn't even noticed. But there, even as far away as I was, even in the dark grayish-green light of the storm, I could see that her face was drawn . . . and in pain.

Before I could see much more, a grayish fog rose around them . . .

When it cleared, I could see that she and Heldry had collapsed on the stones. I had to squeeze back through the narrow passage and then run back down the service hall and out through the audience hall to reach them.

Both Deault and Zharyn had moved toward Heldry and Klyanna, but I ran past them and went to my knees, fearing what I would find. But both were breathing. The lightning had not touched them, and there was the faintest smile on Heldry's face.

Once Heldry recovered—and Atalar announced that the Duke had fully recovered after several days—he immediately canceled the minerals leaseholds in Hrisbarg and had the deep shafts sealed. He declared that the storms had showed that order had been violated. Ten years after Heldry went mad and was rescued by the woman who became his duchess, he finally allowed other metal factors to dig new shafts in the same areas as the old ones . . . but not so deep, and he never allowed the deep shafts to be reopened or reworked.

No one ever spoke of the day he'd gone mad, not around him, or anywhere I knew, but somehow everyone in Lydiar knew that when he was defied or provoked unduly, Heldry might go mad and do terrible things.

He never did again, of course, but only Klyanna, Heldry, and I knew why, and Heldry and Klyanna didn't know that I knew. Or, if they did, they never spoke of it, and that was fine with me.

Here is a story about a historical figure . . . before he became
a legend to be feared . . . and respected.

THE FOREST GIRL

Under the Rational Stars, far, far away,
There lie the lands of Cyad, cold without fey
Under the Rational Stars, well within day,
There wait in chill light words no druid should say.

I

"Alyiakal . . . have you finished your studies?" The majer looks
into the small library after supper on a spring evening.

"Yes, ser." The youth straightens in the chair behind the
writing desk.

"What have you learned?"

"That chaos must be directed by the least amount of order
possible. The greater the order, the more likely it is to weaken
the force of chaos."

"What does that mean?"

"Mean, ser?"

"If you're going to aspire to the Magi'i, boy, you can't just parrot the words."

"So what do the words mean, ser?" Alyiakal is careful to keep his tone polite. He doesn't want another beating.

"You tell me." The majer's voice is hard. "Magus Triamon says that you can sense order and chaos. Your mother would have been disappointed by such sophistry."

Alyiakal holds the wince within himself at the reference to his mother. "Chaos has no order. It will go where it will. Order is necessary to direct chaos, but order reduces chaos. The skill is to direct chaos without reducing the power of chaos."

"Alyiakal . . . you understand. From now on, every stupid question will merit a blow with a switch or lash."

"Yes, ser."

"Your supper should have settled. It's time for your blade exercises and lessons."

"Yes, ser." While Alyiakal is almost as tall as his father, he is barely fifteen, and slender, lacking the physical strength of his father. Until the last season, he had dreaded the blade lessons. Although they practiced with wooden wands, he had always ended up with painful bruises. Now, as he walks to the rear terrace of the quarters, he is merely resigned to what may be. He understands all too well that if he fails to satisfy the Magi'i he will follow his father into the Mirror Lancers.

The practice wands—wooden replicas of Mirror Lancer sabres—hang on the rack by the door. As Alyiakal eases his wand from the rack, he considers his lesson. Order must direct chaos, but it also must direct a blade, for an undirected blade cannot be effective. Can he use his slight skills at sensing order to determine where his father's blade must go? He takes a deep breath. It is worth the effort. He cannot be more badly bruised than he has been in the past. He makes his way to the terrace and waits.

He does not wait long, for the majer appears in a moment, his own wand in hand. "Ready?"

"Yes, ser."

Instead of concentrating on his father's eyes, he tries to sense where his father's wand will go before it does. For the first few moments, he is scrambling, dancing back, allowing touches— but not hard strikes. Then . . . slowly, he begins to feel the patterns and to anticipate them.

He slides his father's wand, and then comes over the top to pin it down, but he cannot hold the wand against Kyal's greater strength, and he has to jump back.

"Good technique . . . but you have to finish!" The majer is breathing hard. "Keep at it!"

By the end of half a glass, Alyiakal can slip, parry, or avoid almost every attack his father brings to bear, but he is sweating heavily, and his eyes are blurring when Kyal abruptly says, "That's enough for this evening."

Alyiakal lowers the wand.

"You worked hard, and your defense is much better. Just apply yourself that hard to your studies, and you shouldn't have that much trouble."

"I'm still bruised in places, ser."

"At your age, that's to be expected." His father nods. "You're free to do what you will until dark. Don't go too far. If you're going to walk the wall road, don't forget your sabre."

"Yes, ser. I won't." Alyiakal is sore enough that he isn't certain he wants to go anywhere. At the same time, being free for a glass or so is a privilege not to be wasted. Still . . .

He decides to at least take a walk, if only to show that he appreciates and will use the privilege. He follows his father inside and carefully racks the wand, then goes to wash up and cool down.

Less than a quarter glass later, he walks out the front door, the ancient Mirror Lancer cupridium blade in the scabbard at his waist. He does not breathe easily until the officers' quarters at Jakaafra are more than a hundred yards behind him. Before long he is walking southeast along the white stone road paralleling the white stone wall that contains the northeast side of the Accursed Forest. That wall is five cubits high and extends ninety-nine kays southeast to that corner tower where it joins the southeast wall.

He glances to his right. Between the wall and road, there is neither vegetation nor grass, just bare salted ground. To the left are fields and orchards, and a few cots and barns, fewer with each kay from Jakaafra . . . until the next town, kays away.

He keeps walking along the road flanking the white wall, glancing back, but he sees no one, and no Lancer patrols, not that he expects any. While his eyes remain alert for any movement, especially near the wall, his thoughts consider what had happened during his blade practice . . . and how he had not previously thought of using order to help in using a sabre.

How else might I use order? He doesn't have an answer to that question, but he does not have time to pursue it because, some fifty yards ahead, at the base of the sunstone wall is a black beast, a chaos panther, lowering itself, as if to spring and charge him. He draws the antique Lancer sabre, knowing that its usefulness against such a massive beast is limited at best.

Then . . . the black predator is gone, and a girl—a young woman, he realizes—stands beside the wall. He starts to walk toward her . . . and as suddenly as she was there, she is gone. He looks around, bewildered, but the salted ground between the patrol road and the wall is empty—for as far as he can see.

Carefully, if unwisely, he knows, he moves toward where both the black catlike creature and the young woman had been.

Once there, he studies the ground. There are boot prints, but no paw prints, and the boot prints lead to the wall, not away from it, as if someone had walked from the road to the wall. He can find no boot prints leading away from the wall.

A concealing illusion? It had to be, but he can sense neither the heavy blackness of order nor the whitish red of chaos.

Finally, he turns and begins to walk back home, thinking.

II

Alyiakal blots the dampness from his forehead as he steps into the coolness of the quarters. The walk from the dwelling of Magus Triamon in Jakaafra proper was not short, and the summer day had been warmer than usual . . . and summer around the Accursed Forest was sweltering on the best of days. After standing for a moment in the small entry, he walks into the library, takes down two night candles in their holders, and sets them side by side on the writing desk. Then he uses a striker to light one, an effort that takes more than a few attempts.

Following Triamon's instructions, he concentrates on the lit candle, as much with his senses and thoughts as with his eyes. In time, he begins to get what is almost an image of golden reddish white around the tip of the candle wick . . . as well as a faint blackish mist above the point of the flame. Yet he sees neither the white nor the black with his eyes. Of that, he is certain . . . but they are there.

Next, he concentrates on replicating the pattern of golden whiteness around the tip of the wick of the unlit candle. Sweat beads on his forehead. Nothing happens.

"You must not be doing it right," he murmurs to himself.

He shakes his head, then closes his eyes, and takes a deep breath. Finally, he concentrates once more. The wick of the unlit candle remains dark.

Do you need to look at the candle?

This time, he closes his eyes and tries to visualize the dark wick, and the pattern of golden whiteness around it. He opens his eyes quickly, only to see a tiny point of redness, visible to his eyes, wink out.

"You can do it," he says quietly, redoubling his efforts.

Sweat is running into his eyes a quarter glass later when the candle flickers alight . . . and stays lit. Alyiakal only allows himself a brief smile and a moment of rest before he blows out the candle and repeats the effort. After a deep breath, he once more blows out the candle . . . and relights it—just by focusing order on chaos.

He hears the door open, and the heavy footsteps of his father, steps seemingly far too ponderous for a man as small as the majer.

"What are you doing with the candles?" asks Kyal, not quite brusquely.

"Practicing an exercise that Magus Triamon showed me. He told me to work on it until I could do it instantly."

"Lighting a candle?"

"Lighting it without a striker, ser. He says it's the first step in mastering chaos."

Slowly, Kyal nods, as if he is not certain about the matter.

At that moment, there is a series of knocks on the front door, followed by a loud voice. "Majer! Ser!"

The majer turns and walks swiftly from the archway to the front door, which he opens.

Alyiakal does not follow, but listens intently.

"Majer Kyal . . . ser . . . it's happened again."

"What?" snaps the majer, whose voice is far larger than his stature.

"Another dispatch rider is gone. The morning patrol found his mount and the dispatches. There's no sign of him. The men claim they saw a black chaos cat, one of the big ones. It was prowling outside the wall, just to the southwest of the northern point."

"Send a squad with fully charged firelances. I'd like a report of what they find. Or what they don't."

"Yes, ser."

Kyal closes the door and walks back to the archway into the small library. "We'd best eat early. There's no telling when we'll get another chance." He pauses. "Are you finished with the exercises?"

Alyiakal nods. "I did what the magus wanted."

"You can tell me about it at supper. We need to wash up. I'll tell Areya to get the plates ready."

When the two are finally seated at the table, Areya sets a platter of mutton slices covered with cheese and a yellow-green glaze of ground rosemary. One smaller platter holds lace potatoes, and another thinly sliced pearapples.

Kyal serves himself, then passes each platter to Alyiakal. "What about the exercises?"

"Every flame holds both chaos and order, but there's much more chaos. Magus Triamon taught me how to sense both order and chaos in the flame. He says that's the easiest way to sense them at first. Once I could sense them, and he made sure of that by swirling the patterns, he made me try to move the chaos myself. Then he sent me home with the exercise. That was to light a candle, and then learn to light another one by duplicating the pattern of chaos around the wick. It took a while, but I did it three times in a row. Next, I have to light a candle without using another candle as a pattern."

"Do you think you'll ever be able to match a full magus?" asks the majer.

"Magus Triamon thinks I can . . . if I keep working."

Kyal nods slowly. "I'd advise you to work very hard, Son."

"I will, ser." After a silence, Alyiakal looks at his father. "Is that because I will not match you in might, ser?"

Kyal laughs. "Oh . . . you'll be able to do that in another year or so. It looks like you'll be taller and broader than me. No . . . it's because too many Mirror Lancers are being killed fighting the barbarians who swarm across the grass hills. We need better weapons. Perhaps you'll be able to become a great enough magus to create them. Even if you don't, the Magi'i are the ones who keep our weapons charged."

"You don't want me to be a Lancer officer like you?"

"I'd like it very much. But the son of a Lancer majer from Jakaafra is likely to do no better than his sire, if his talents are limited to the blade and skill at arms alone. Why do you think I insist on your reading about tactics and logistics?"

"But . . . Magus Triamon . . ."

"You may become a great magus. You may not, but a Lancer has three weapons—his sabre, his firelance, and his mind. Fire-lances are powered by chaos. If you do follow in my steps, the more you know and the more you can do with chaos, the better you will be with your weapons. The more you study with the magus, the more you will know what I cannot teach you, and that will sharpen your mind even more." Kyal clears his throat. "There is one more thing. All the senior Mirror Lancer officers come from the great families of Cyad. If you wish to rise farther than I have, you must become more capable than all of them. You must be so clearly so superior that none can contest you." Kyal smiles wryly. "That, you will find, is true in all areas where a man must make his way." His words turn sardonic. "At times, even that is not sufficient."

Alyiakal sits, silent. Never has his father talked so bluntly.

"It's time you began to learn more of how the world works . . . really works. Now . . . eat your supper. I'll have to leave soon to see what that squad has found. You can walk a bit tonight, but go the southeast way."

"Yes, ser."

"And be careful."

"Yes, ser."

Once they finish eating and the majer leaves the quarters, Alyiakal fastens on the old swordbelt and scabbard, checks the sabre, and then slips out into the early evening air, still steaming, but not quite so unbearable as it had been several glasses earlier. Once he is away from the quarters buildings of the Mirror Lancer outpost, he studies the wall even more closely, but he sees no sign of anyone or anything on the road or near it.

Then, in the early twilight, when his eyes move from the small stead on his left to the cleared and salted strip of land on his right, he sees a large black panther cat crouched at the base of the sunstone wall. *Where did that come from?*

He stops and studies the beast. While his hand rests on the top of the hilt of his sabre, he does not attempt to draw the weapon. The black panther cat's eyes remain fixed on him. There is something . . . something he cannot fathom . . . yet he has no doubt that his sabre will likely not suffice against such a creature. What will?

Fire! All wild animals fear—or are wary of—flame. *Can you create a flame large enough to startle it?* He smiles. It cannot hurt to try.

He looks directly at the panther cat, then concentrates on replicating the flame pattern of a candle—a very large candle.

A flare of light flashes up in front of the creature . . . then vanishes.

Alyiakal feels as though his head has been cleft in two, and for several moments he cannot move.

Abruptly . . . the giant cat vanishes. A black-haired young

woman, scarcely more than a girl, he thinks, stands there. She laughs. "Fair enough!"

"Who are you?" he asks, moving forward, if slowly.

"A girl of the forest and the town," she replies. "Nothing more."

He laughs softly. "Nothing more? When you can take on the semblance of a giant black panther and then vanish?"

She frowns.

Now that he is closer, he sees that her eyes are as black as her hair, for all that her skin is a lightly tanned creamy color. "I saw you do that eightdays ago. You didn't really vanish, did you? You just made it seem so."

"Why do you say that?"

"Because I followed your boot prints, and you climbed over the sunstone wall into the Accursed Forest."

"It's not cursed. It's just different."

"You've actually been in the . . . forest . . . and you're alive?"

"You sound so surprised. Why?"

"Lancers die every season from attacks by the black cats or the stun lizards."

"That's because they consider the cats and lizards enemies, and the cats and lizards can feel that."

"I think it's more than that," says Alyiakal, looking directly at her. Up close it is clear she must be at least several years older than he is; it is also obvious that she is striking. Not pretty, but something beyond. What that might be, he is far from certain.

"Can you use that blade?" she asks.

"Yes."

"Then you must be Alyiakal."

"Why do you think that?"

"Magus Triamon said it was a pity you were already so proficient with such a weapon. No one else near Jakaafra uses a blade and can also sense both black and white."

"You're obviously far better at that than am I."

"I'm older."

"Not that much," he protests.

"You're young, and you're kind. Trust me. I am older."

"What do you do in the forest?"

"You don't have to do anything in the forest."

"You didn't answer my question."

She smiles. "No, I didn't."

"Then show me."

"I can't do that."

"Why not?"

"If anything happened to you, your father would seek those responsible. Magus Triamon would have to flee or die, and I could never see my parents again—if they survived your father's wrath."

Alyiakal thinks, then says, "Could you show me some of the forest from the wall?"

A smile that becomes a wide grin crosses her lips. "You'd do that after all the Lancers your father has lost?"

"How do you . . . how much do you know about me . . . and my father?"

"He's in charge of the Mirror Lancers here in Jakaafra, and you live with him in the quarters, and you study with Master Triamon." She shrugs. "Other than that . . . very little, except that you have courage and are willing to look beyond walls."

"Will you show me?" he asks again.

"Since you're asking. But you must promise not to enter the forest."

"You said it wasn't dangerous." He offers an impish grin.

"It isn't . . . if you know what you're doing. You don't."

Alyiakal can accept that. "I won't."

"Then climb up." She turns and scrambles up the sunstone so quickly that she is looking down at him before he even begins.

He discovers that the stone is smoother than it looks. He almost loses his grip twice, but soon he is perched on the flat surface of the wall beside her, looking into the part of the Accursed Forest that cannot be seen from the wall road.

Less than thirty yards from the base of the wall beneath Alyiakal is the rounded end of a pool, whose still waters look to be a clear deep green in the gloom created by the high canopy of the taller trees and the lower canopy formed by the under-growth, trees still taller than any Alyiakal has seen anywhere outside the Accursed Forest. A long greenish log lies half in, half out of the water, except that when the log moves, Alyiakal realizes that it is a stun lizard, not that he has ever seen one, but only drawings of the beasts.

"The stun lizard . . . are they all so big?"

"That's a small one. Some of them are more than ten yards from snout to tail, and they can stun an entire squad of Lancers."

"How do you know that?"

"Shhhh . . . watch."

An enormous black panther pads along the side of the pond opposite the stun lizard, which freezes back into resembling a log. A cream-colored crane with silver-green wings alights at the far end of the pond, standing motionless for the longest time. Then, suddenly, the long beak stabs into the water and comes up with a squirming flash of silver.

"Try to see the order and the chaos in each of them," she suggests.

Alyiakal had not thought of that, and even as he wonders why he should, he attempts what she has suggested. At first, all he can sense is swirling flows of order and chaos . . . but as he keeps watching, he can soon discern that the order and chaos within each of the forest creatures is locked in a tight pattern, and that while the patterns are different, there is something about them that is the same.

"You need to go," the woman who looks like a girl says quietly.

He glances to the west. While he cannot see the sun, the angles of the shadows tell him that it is far later than he realized. Has that much time passed? He looks to her. "Thank you."

After he drops to the salted ground beneath the wall, he looks back up. She is still there, looking at him.

"You didn't tell me your name," he says.

"No, I didn't."

"Why not?"

"It's better that way."

"Why don't you want me to know your name?"

"I don't care if you learn my name . . . just so long as you don't discover it from me."

Then she smiles . . . and vanishes.

For several moments, Alyiakal can sense a web of darkness on the wall, but he sees nothing. Then the darkness drops away, leaving the top of the wall empty of order . . . and her.

He turns and begins the walk back toward Jakaafra, walking quickly and hoping he will not be so late that Areya will tell his father.

III

When Alyiakal arrives at the small square dwelling under the canopy of the overarching oak trees on twoday, as often occurs, he has to wait for Magus Triamon to open the door and admit him. Rather than sit on the bench on the porch, he finds himself pacing back and forth until Triamon opens the door and appears.

"You seem eager this morning," says the gray-haired magus as he ushers Alyiakal into the study.

"I came across another student of yours, Master Triamon."

"Oh? Which one?"

"The black-haired young woman."

The gray-haired magus nods and smiles. "How did you meet her?"

"She gave the image of herself as a great black panther cat. I created an image of a large flame. She dropped the image and laughed."

"You must have amused her. Otherwise, you never would have seen her."

"Who is she?"

"That, my young pupil, you will have to discover for yourself."

"She said the same thing. Are you both so frightened of my father?"

The magus shakes his head. "Your father is but an officer, a strong and honest one. But he is a Mirror Lancer, and one does not anger the Mirror Lancers."

"Why would telling me her name upset anyone?"

"She has the gift of the Magi'i, and the powers of altage and those of the Magi'i would be less than pleased if I facilitated any acquaintance between the two of you."

"But I've already met—" Alyiakal breaks off the remainder of what he had been about to say as the import of what Triamon said sinks in. Then he asks, "Because you are of the Magi'i?"

"Exactly. There are . . . agreements . . ."

"That's absurd. I don't intend to consort her."

"Consorting is not precisely the problem."

"Then why are you teaching me?"

"To determine if you can become a magus. If the Magi'i accept you, then the Mirror Lancers will not want you. If your talent is only minor, such as lighting candles and healing, then you will never become a magus, and you are acceptable to the Mirror Lancers."

"Just acceptable?"

"They prefer Lancers who have no talent with order or chaos, but limited ability, especially healing, is acceptable in junior officers."

"Then why should I study with you?"

"Why indeed?" Triamon smiles.

"Another answer I must find for myself?"

"In the end, we all must find our own answers." Triamon's smile vanishes. "Do you wish to proceed with your lessons?"

"Why would I not?"

"Good. Today, we will begin work on the importance of focus . . ."

After his glass of instruction and practice with Triamon, Alyiakal makes his way to the market square, rather than return immediately to his quarters.

He begins his inquiries with the woman who sells grass and reed baskets.

"Good woman . . . would you know the black-eyed young woman with black hair?"

"The child of forest and night?"

"Yes . . . I believe so."

"No . . . I have seen her. I do not know her."

"Do you know her name?"

"No. It would not be wise to ask."

"Thank you." Alyiakal makes his way to the next stall.

He visits more than a score of carts and stalls before he comes to the one-eyed beggar propped against the wall. He has always avoided the beggar before, but ashamed of himself for his lack of compassion in the past, he places a copper in the near-empty bowl.

"Heard your question of the weaver, boy. They all fear her, you know?"

"You don't, I think," replies Alyiakal with a half smile.

"What's to fear? Her name is Adayal, and her father is a carpenter. Her mother . . . who knows?"

"Thank you." Alyiakal puts another copper in the bowl.

"Just be careful in what you'll be wanting, young fellow. Great wants call to great danger." With that, the old beggar closes his one good eye.

Great wants call to great danger? How could wanting to know Adayal's name be a great want?

With a smile he turns and heads back toward the quarters, hoping to arrive before his father.

IV

Despite all his walks along the wall, and his forays into the town, the summer days pass, and his instruction from Magus Triamon widens, so that he can call up a limited concealment and more illusions than merely flames. Even so, Alyiakal does not see Adayal, or any large panthers, either. Often he climbs the wall of the Accursed Forest and perches or sits there, watching what goes on beyond, trying to hold a concealment as he does, but when he does, he finds he cannot see, and can only sense through his limited use of order. But for all his efforts, he does not encounter the forest girl. He thinks of her as such, even though it is clear that she is truly a woman.

At breakfast on threeday of the seventh eightday of summer, the majer clears his throat. "I received a dispatch late last evening. You were not around."

"You said I could walk so long as I was careful."

Kyal continues without addressing Alyiakal's observation. "I'm going to have to leave this morning and accompany Third Company to Geliendra. Commander Waasol wants to see all the majers posted to duty near the Accursed Forest. Areya will come in to fix your dinner. You're to fix your own breakfasts and keep up with your lessons. I'll likely be gone an eightday. I've sent word to Magus Triamon. You're to see him both morning and afternoon. I've told him to keep you challenged and busy. You're to do exactly what he tells you."

"Yes, ser." Alyiakal does not point out that he has never not followed the instructions of the magus. He also does not mention the times when he has done things that would have been forbidden, had he asked.

After breakfast, Alyiakal bids his father good-bye and then practices perceiving order. Two glasses later, he leaves to walk to his morning lesson with Magus Triamon. On this day, he does not have to wait, and Triamon ushers him into his study almost at once.

"There are many shades to chaos," begins Triamon. "To be even the lowest of healers, you need to know the shades and what each signifies."

"Why do I need to know about healing? Are not the most valuable talents of a magus those that can be used to store and channel chaos?"

"They are . . . but you are more grounded in order, and order suits healing. If the Magi'i accept you for training, the more you know the better, and because many Magi'i deal more with chaos than is healthy, you should know your limits. Without understanding healing, you will not. If you do not become a magus, then you will be a Lancer, and it will help if you can aid healing of your men. That will keep you from losing too many rankers and give them cause to support you when you need it."

Alyiakal frowns.

"Mirror Lancer officers will always need the support of their men at least once, if not more often. The ones who don't get it generally die before they make majer." Triamon's words are delivered in a dry sardonic tone that emphasizes their verity.

Alyiakal starts to protest, then closes his mouth. His father does know field healing, even if he does not have the skill of even a beginning healer magus.

"The lowest and least focused chaos is a dull red, infused with gray. Sometimes, even a bad bruise will show this . . ."

Alyiakal forces himself to concentrate.

V

Even with two lessons a day for close to two eightdays, Alyiakal has more than enough time to continue his walks along the wall, but he sees neither Adayal, nor any large panthers, either. He still studies the creatures of the Accursed Forest from the wall, and he can now distinguish most of them by their patterns of order and chaos, or rather chaos held in patterns by order. But summer gives way to harvest, and Alyiakal has yet to see Adayal, even though he now knows her dwelling . . . yet she is never there . . . or she has created a concealment so perfect that his order senses cannot penetrate it. How is he to know which it might be, or both . . . or neither.

On the second threeday of harvest, early on another evening when his father is away, Alyiakal has removed himself from the quarters to a place on the wall from which he can watch one end of the pool some thirty yards away, the same pool that Adayal had shown him the first time he had looked into the Accursed Forest. He can barely make out the stun lizard half-concealed by a fallen log, although it is small, from what he has seen over the past season, only two and a half yards from nose to tail. That is more than large enough to stun a man and a large horse.

He hears a rustling and the faintest of scrapings on the stone . . . and Adayal sits on the wall beside him.

"You have grown," she says. "There is an order about you."

"Magus Triamon has been teaching me how to use order to manipulate chaos so that the chaos does not break down the order of my body."

"You've learned well."

"I've been looking for you all summer and since."

"I know. Would you like to walk through a little part of the Accursed Forest with me?"

"Have I learned enough to be safe?"

"Enough so that I can keep you safe. Perhaps more."

"I would like that."

"Then let us go . . ." She slips down from the wall onto the mossy ground beside the sunstone.

Alyiakal follows, and when he stands beside her, she reaches out and takes his hand. "This way."

"Should I hold a concealment?"

"There is no need of that." Her voice is throaty yet warm.

She leads him down a path. "Look carefully, beyond that fallen trunk . . ."

He studies where she has pointed, then sees a tortoise, or perhaps it is a turtle, whose shell stretches two full yards with a pattern of light and dark green diamonds that hold the faintest light of their own. Farther on, he sees two gold-and-black birds perched on a limb, the like of which he has never seen.

Adayal stretches a hand out. "Wait."

Alyiakal waits. His mouth opens as a giant serpent slithers across the path some fifteen yards ahead of them, its scales a mixture of greens and browns that blend so well into the forest that he can only make out the part of its body crossing the darker path.

In time, after she has shown him more creatures than he ever would have believed existed in such a small part of the forest, they come to a tree whose trunk contains a small door. Adayal opens the door and gestures for him to enter.

He senses nothing within and follows her gesture. Once inside, after she closes the door, he can still see, because of a faint greenish illumination that somehow surrounds them.

"There is something else you need to learn, Alyiakal," she says gently, turning to him. "I would not have you too innocent or too unlearned about women . . . or learning from rough Lancers." She reaches up and draws his head down, and her lips are warm upon his.

"Slowly . . . ," she murmurs drawing him down onto the soft pallet he had not noticed. "Slowly . . . let me show you."

Alyiakal, surprised beyond belief, does . . . so afraid that the moments that follow will end, but they do not, not for glasses.

Finally, she draws her garments back on and around her. "I shouldn't keep you any longer. Try to keep some of that sweetness."

He dresses slowly, not wanting the night to end.

After a time, they both stand at the base of the wall, outside the forest. Alyiakal looks through the darkness, sensing Adayal as much as seeing her. He remains stunned by both the warmth and the fire Adayal had shown, and touched by the gentleness behind both.

"That is how it should be between a man and a woman," she says softly. "Never forget."

"How could I?" Abruptly, he adds, "You're not leaving Jakaafra and the forest, are you?"

"No. I am part of the forest, and it is part of me. I will always be here."

For all of her words, he can sense a sadness and a regret.

"You must go," she says. "It is late."

Too late, he thinks as they separate and leave the wall in different directions.

It is well past midnight when Alyiakal slips back into the quarters, only to find too many lamps lit. He sighs, if silently, and makes his way into the study.

"Where have you been?" asks the majer.

Alyiakal inclines his head politely, hoping his father will answer the question himself, as he sometimes does.

"Out walking the wall road, no doubt, and peering into the forest." The majer shakes his head. "No matter."

Alyiakal tries not to stiffen at the resigned tone of voice.

"I've been talking to Master Triamon. He says that you have some talent. He also says that you're not suited to the Magi'i. You are too ordered, and your interests lie elsewhere. He feels that you'd never be more than the lowest of the Magi'i, if that."

Alyiakal does not sigh in relief, although relief is indeed what he feels. "Yes, ser."

"That being so . . . young man, next oneday you're leaving for Kynstaar."

"Kynstaar, ser?"

"That's where they take the sons of Lancer officers and see if they can train them to be officers. Some of what they teach, you already know. Much you don't. It's time to see what you can be. There's nothing more you can learn here."

"Yes, ser," replies Alyiakal, although he has his doubts about that, given what he has learned earlier in the evening, but there is little point in protesting. Already, he knows to pick his battles. That much he has learned from his father, from watching the Accursed Forest . . . and from Adayal.

VI

On fourday, Alyiakal searches Jakaafra for Adayal, but can find no trace of her. Nor can he do so on fiveday, or sixday. On sevenday, he leaves the quarters just after dawn, determined to find her.

She is not at her parents' house, nor anywhere along the wall.

Finally, he walks to where she had found him on threeday. She is not there. He looks to the wall, then nods. He quickly climbs the wall and stops on the top. Does he dare to enter the forest without her protection?

Do you dare not to?

He takes some time to create a concealment around himself, not one like he has raised before, but one more like the interlocked patterns of the great forest creatures. Hoping that it will suffice, he eases himself down into the forest and onto the shorter path, the one Adayal had led him back to the wall along at the end of their evening. He cannot see, not with his eyes, but must rely on his senses. He walks as quietly as he can, not wishing to alarm any creature needlessly, but he must see Adayal one more time.

He slips around the last curve in the path before her tree bower . . . and senses that she stands by the door, as if she has expected him.

He hurries to her, dropping the concealment, then stops as he sees the sad smile. "Adayal . . . I have to leave."

"I know. I knew then." She smiles more happily. "You can walk the forest now, whenever you wish."

"I learned it from you." Quickly, he adds, "I have to go to be trained as a Mirror Lancer officer . . . if I can be."

"You will be, if that is what you want."

"Will you be here when I finish training? I want you to be with me."

"Alyiakal, you have seen me. I cannot be far from the forest, and you are meant for one kind of greatness. I cannot share that greatness. Nor would you be happy if I were by your side, because I would be but half there."

He finds he can say nothing.

"I will walk back to the wall with you," she says gently. "I cannot tell you how it moved me that you would enter the forest for me."

Alyiakal's eyes burn, but he nods. He does not trust himself to speak.

She takes his hand in hers, and they begin to walk.

Two large tawny cougars, perhaps half the size of the great black panther cats, appear and walk before them.

"They . . . they do your bidding."

"No . . . they are here to honor you. For your courage and your understanding of the forest."

Alyiakal has his doubts, but he does not voice them.

When they reach the wall, there is a flicker, and Adayal appears as the great black panther and springs to the top of the wall. Alyiakal studies her with his senses, but she is indeed what he sees. He climbs to the top of the wall, where Adayal has returned to being the black-haired, black-eyed, beautiful woman who has loved him.

"Do you see now?" she asks softly.

He nods.

"Do great deeds, honest deeds, and do them with all your heart. You can."

Now. After a long moment, he slips down the wall and then steps back to look at her once more.

The two tawny cougars have joined her on the top of the sunstone wall, flanking her. She looks down at him, then speaks softly, as if to a beloved, yet her words are clear in his ears and thoughts. "You are a part of the Forest, and part of it will always be with you."

"Because of you."

"And you," she replies.

She stands there for a moment, then reappears as the great panther, framed by the two smaller tawny cougars. An instant later, the top of the wall is vacant.

Alyiakal just stares for long moments that seem to last forever, her words reverberating in his thoughts. Finally, he takes a deep breath.

After a last look at the empty wall, Alyiakal turns and begins the walk back to Jakaafra.

North of the Rational Stars, far, far away
There lie the lands of Naclos, warm and so fey
North of the Rational Stars, well beyond day,
There wait in tall trees words no altage dare say.

In Magi'i of Cyador *and* Scion of Cyador, *there are allusions to a history between the Emperor and his consort, but only allusions. Here is a bit of the backstory.*

THE CHOICE

I

The cool misting rain that has briefly enfolded the Palace of Light begins to lift, and the white sun struggles to shine through the mist to bless the greenery of the City of Light, as if to reclaim the first city of Cyador from the gray green of winter. The lightest of breezes whispers into the palace through the half-open window, mixing the scent of old leaves with the faintest hint of trilia and aramyd. As the tall and slender Toziel strides across the polished white stone tiles toward the bedchamber of his mother, the Dowager Empress, he glances toward the tinted panes of that eastern window and out across the green-tinged white stone buildings of the Quarter of the Magi'i.

One of the palace guards opens the door to the antechamber, and Toziel steps inside, making his way through the sitting room that his mother so seldom used and into the bedchamber beyond.

Propped against the pillows of the large bed, a woman surveys him. Her hair is silver, but the silver of the Magi'i, not the often lifeless silver of time and age. Her green eyes remain intent, despite the darkness under and around them, and that intensity almost makes Toziel forget the gauntness of her face.

"Come closer," she commands.

Toziel complies, with a faint smile that contains amusement and sadness, and comes to stand beside the bed.

"My time is short . . . ," she begins, lifting a trembling hand slightly, as if to stop any words he might issue, "and I want a promise from you."

"Of course." Toziel knows well what she will say.

"Do not humor me!" The force behind the words takes much of her energy, and when she is finished, she sinks back into the pillows for a moment, but her eyes remain fierce and focused on her son. Shortly, after several breaths, she continues, "You, my son, carry the elthage lineage, yet your magely talents are so slim as to be nonexistent. That may not be for the worst, for in your reign and life, much of what has sustained Cyad and Cyador may well begin to fail. Your father thought such might occur in our time. We were fortunate . . ." She coughs . . . then swallows laboriously.

Toziel waits.

"You must choose a consort . . . and one who will love and support you."

Toziel forebears to say that he is not exactly unfamiliar with her views on that subject or that he is neither a youth nor exactly ancient at twenty-seven years.

"Promise me . . . once the formalities are all observed when I am gone . . . that you will hold a ball . . ." Her voice fades, and even her eyes dim for a moment. "You know why . . ."

"I believe I understand, Mother."

"You don't understand enough, my son." For an instant, the

firm and cutting tone he has heard all his life fills the room, then fades. "Do you see that book on the table?" Her voice is strong, but even Toziel can tell that the words take all her strength.

He nods, then says, "Yes," as he realizes that her sight is failing as well.

"There was once another . . ." She coughs once more. "They should be a pair . . . united . . . but that . . . about that I can no longer worry." Another silence follows before she gathers her fading strength. "That book will tell you the proper choice of consort, my son. Trust it more than you trust your heart. Your father did . . . as did his . . ." A cough racks her body.

Toziel leans forward.

"You . . . can do . . . nothing for me." She gathers her strength. "Trust the book and read it well." She tries to moisten her lips and fails. "Trust the book. . . ."

He would say more . . . but there is nothing to be said, and he takes her hand and waits for the inevitable that will not be long in arriving.

II

Within the private study of the Emperor, Toziel stands by the wide window overlooking the harbor he can barely see through the mist. He is clad in shimmercloth black, with only the silver and malachite sash to distinguish him from the others at the memorial that he has just conducted in the great audience hall.

Outside the Palace of Light, the mist of winter has gathered once more, though Toziel knows that it will soon fade under the growing intensity of the afternoon sun. Still . . .

"Fitting for the day." He turns, but does not step onto the Analerian wool carpet of subdued green-and-gold geometric designs that has graced the study from the time of the Emperor Alyiakal.

Instead, he lifts from the table the volume with the green-sheened silver cover and opens it to the first page and the title—*Meditations upon the Land of Light*. He quickly turns to the second page that holds a dedication: *To those of the Towers, to those of the Land, and to those who endured.* Below the dedication is a name, one all too familiar to Toziel, if in a far different context—Kiedral Daloren, Vice Marshal, Anglorian Unity.

Then he turns to the page with the green leather marker, and reads the lines there slowly, aloud.

> *Virtues of old hold fast.*
> *Morning's blaze cannot last;*
> *and rose petals soon part.*
> *Not so a steadfast heart.*

"Trust the book," he murmurs.

He walks to the table desk and seats himself, turning to the beginning, seeing yet another set of lines. "Verse . . . to be trusted more?"

Still, he begins to read the opening lines.

> *Although the old lands are in my heart,*
> *in towers that anchored life with certain art,*
> *in eyes that will not again see bold*
> *the hills of Angloria or surf at Winterhold,*
> *I greet the coming evening, and the night,*
> *proud purple from the strange and setting sun . . .*

Toziel lowers the small volume, but does not close it. The words are not archaic, not quite, but they do convey a sense of loss and longing missing from the official records and the histories.

III

The early summer air is perfumed and heavy. The warm, slow breeze seeps from the south, past the fluted bars on the balcony grillworks with barely enough force to create a trilling and humming from the bars pleasant and loud enough to foil eavesdroppers. While cupridium ornamentation or elaborate-appearing flowers might have served the same function, the lines of the Palace of Light are clean, elegant, and without decoration, even carved inscriptions. To the south, and downhill, beyond the trade quarter and the warehouses, are the white stone piers of the harbor of Cyad, where lie moored three white-hulled fireships. North of the piers and below the palace, the sunstone walks and white-granite paved streets half-glow in the twilight of the spring evening.

Toziel surveys the tranquil scene spread out before him. In a few moments, he will leave the sitting room and walk up the steps to the grand ballroom, whose outside verandas overlook all Cyad. There, he will see, among the Magi'i of Cyad and their wives, all too many young women, many of them beautiful, and certainly none of them ugly, not in Cyad, the City of Light. He will dance with a number of them, converse with others, and be pleasant to all. And then . . .

A wry smile crosses his lips. And then, what will be . . . will be.

After a time, there is a single knock on the door. "Everyone has arrived, ser."

"Thank you." Toziel takes a last look at the harbor, then turns and walks to the door, opening it.

Outside are a pair of palace guards, and a round-faced man dressed in formal greens who inclines his head. "Your Mightiness, everything is as you requested."

"Thank you, Dauret."

Dauret leads the way to main staircase, that magnificent edifice that bisects the palace and leads to the uppermost level . . . and the grand ballroom. Toziel follows. When he reaches the top of the white stone steps, he follows Dauret to the left and around the opening for the staircase to the center archway into the ballroom.

When Toziel halts, Dauret gestures. A single trumpet sounds, clear but low and melodic, and all the muted conversations and whispers immediately cease.

"His Mightiness, Toziel'elth'alt'mer," announces Dauret, his mouth twisting as he finishes, as if he wanted to add all the titles that protocol would dictate should follow Toziel's full name, titles that Toziel had insisted would be inappropriate for the occasion.

As Toziel enters the ballroom, the musicians, as instructed, begin to play—music suitable for dancing, again not customary, but he'd explained it simply. "It was her last wish."

No one had brought the matter up again.

He walks at an angle across the ballroom, seemingly almost aimlessly, but he watches all those he passes, without seeming to do so.

A willowy blonde in a blue that matches her eyes lowers her head slightly, just enough to signify that she is interested, but does not wish to seem brazen or forward.

Toziel steps forward and smiles. "Might I have this dance and your name?"

"Halaria'elth."

"That's a beautiful name." Toziel takes her hand in his and places his other on her back, easing her out onto the polished wood of the dance floor.

Several senior Mirror Lancer officers, as also instructed, immediately take their consorts and join him, so that in moments, many couples are dancing.

"Tell me about yourself, Halaria, if you would," asks Toziel gently. "Do you live in Cyad?"

"No, ser. We come from Fyrad. My father . . . he is the magus in charge of the Mirror Towers at the port."

A second level adept, reflects Toziel, *but loyal*. "Have you any brothers or sisters?"

"My brother Abram is a student magus here. They say he has talent in understanding the Mirror Towers."

"Have you thought about being a healer?"

"I do not seem to have that talent, ser, though my mother and little sister do."

"It is indeed strange," Toziel replies warmly, "which talents go to which children and why." In the few moments he has danced with her, he can feel that she is not even a possibility.

His next partner is Istyla, a brunette with an effusively warm manner. Too effusive. And after that, there is the silver-haired Gaylena.

"What is it like, being who you are?" she asks.

"That's a good question," he replies. "Some days, it's quite clear, and, on others, I ask the same question. What of you?"

"I'm a Magi'i daughter. I can heal a little, but not a lot. It's not enough to be a healer . . ."

Toziel can sense that she has more than enough ability to be a healer and after a short dance moves on. He scarcely remembers the next three young women, pretty and warm as they are. Then he spies a slender woman in a clinging black gown that reveals a modestly womanly figure, with gray eyes and clear skin set off by the shimmering brilliant silver hair of a true daughter of the Magi'i. As he nears her, she turns. Her smile is dazzling, yet seemingly honest and open.

"Your Mightiness . . ." Her voice is firm, but warm.

"A dance, if you would."

She glides into his arms, and Toziel, as he guides her out

onto the polished wood dance floor, finds that dancing with her is effortless.

"I never asked your name."

"Cythera. Cythera'elth, of course."

"Of course?" he asks humorously.

"You only invited daughters and families of elthage background, except for your trusted senior officers. Isn't that so?"

"It is indeed."

"So I'm just one of a number of women who are here so that you can see if you like them . . . and they you. Not that such matters to most."

"But it does to you?"

"It does. Shouldn't it? I'd think that a life of power and responsibility would be almost unbearable unless those cares were shared. Sharing doesn't work unless both care."

"Tell me more," he says, not quite teasingly.

"My father brought me here, to the Palace of Light, when I was very little. The only thing that made it warm was the way your father looked at your mother. I remember that."

"When was that?" Toziel couldn't remember an occasion where that might have happened.

"More than fifteen years ago . . ." She pauses. "It was a festival, for the turn of fall. You looked very serious. You were wearing a green uniform, like a Lancer."

Toziel does remember. He'd hated the uniform, because he'd asked for an officer's uniform and his father had said, "Heir or no heir, you don't know enough to be an officer. Not yet." And his father had made Toziel wear the uniform identical to that of a Lancer recruit. At that recollection, Toziel laughs.

Cythera looks surprised, if but for an instant.

"You're kind," Toziel explains. "I was behaving like a spoiled child because my father had reprimanded me—and made it stick."

She cannot quite hide her smile.

He finds her amusement, and her attempt to hide it, attractive.

Before long, the dance is over, and he inclines his head to her. "Please do not leave early this evening."

"Since you ask, I wouldn't think of it." Her smile is less dazzling but warmer than the one with which she greeted him.

Toziel's next partner is another blonde, named Carliana, attractive and a good dancer, and all too polite. As he leaves her, he catches sight of a redhead, a woman he suspects is closer to his own age. She stands well away from the dancers, talking to an older couple and a younger woman in black and silver, with the silver hair of the Magi'i. The younger woman has creamy skin and a perfect profile, yet Toziel finds his eyes lingering on the redhead, who wears a gown of green somewhere between teal and the shade of the Great Eastern Ocean in summer, her fair skin lightly freckled under thick fire-red hair holding a golden luster. She also is a daughter of the Magi'i, if of a less illustrious heritage, he suspects, but a healer as well, for only healers can wear that green in a formal setting.

He finds himself making his way to her, bowing slightly and asking, "Might I have this dance?"

"You might, Your Mightiness," she replies with a warm full voice that is not in the slightest throaty or husky.

Toziel can sense a slight confusion among the three that he and the redhead leave behind as they walk the few yards to the dance floor. He can also sense the redhead's amusement. "I never asked your name."

"Ryenyel'elth."

"And you're a practicing healer?" he asks as they begin to dance. "Where?"

"I work with the Mirror Lancers most of the time."

He cannot help but frown. "Here in Cyad?"

"I seem to be good at helping them recover from injuries that others feel could not be remedied."

"Go on," he prompts.

"There are some whose backs were injured in fighting against the barbarians in the Stone Hills. They could barely walk. One squad leader could not walk at all."

"And you healed them?"

"Not all of them. Some were beyond me, but more than a few."

"How long have you been doing this?"

"Almost ten years."

"Since you came of age?"

She actually grins at him. "Are you asking my age, Your Mightiness? I'm twenty-six, older than most of the young ladies you invited."

Older than almost all of them. "And you've never been consorted?"

"No. I've never been interested in merely being an appendage to someone else, even a highly valued appendage."

Toziel shakes his head. "Are you always this direct?"

Abruptly, she smiles warmly and pleasantly. "I was only seeking to do what you requested, ser." Then the smile drops away, to be replaced by a totally honest grin. "For tonight, direct honesty is best, don't you think?"

For the first time all evening, Toziel's formal boots seem to lose track of the music, yet in instants, somehow, he regains his rhythm. *Or did she do that?* At the moment, he is not about to ask. Instead, he goes on, "Your family?"

"They live in Summerdock. I have been staying with my uncle and aunt and my cousin Elthya."

Toziel smiles. "And since my invitation included all eligible women . . ."

"I thought I would take advantage of that. I have never been to the Palace of Light. I did not expect you to ask me to dance."

"I didn't expect to, either," he admits. "You are . . . different."

"For better or worse, Your Mightiness, I am who I am."

"But you can conceal it rather well, I suspect."

"For healers, that is possible. We are judged by what we can do, and so long as we are polite and pleasant . . ."

"And charming," he adds.

"That is slightly more difficult." A touch of irony colors her words.

In time, barely longer than he has spent with the more interesting of the young women with whom he has danced, Toziel escorts her back to her aunt and uncle, and then asks for a dance from Elthya. That dance is far shorter, charming though the younger woman is.

Over the next glass, Toziel dances with nine other eligible women, before finding himself with another green-eyed healer, Kierstia, whose silver hair is as perfect as possible.

"Where do you practice your healing?" he asks as they begin to dance.

"In the Hall of Healing here in Cyad, Your Mightiness."

"How long have you been there?"

"Just three years, but it is so rewarding, especially when you can help a child or a mother."

Toziel is touched by the intensity of her feelings and asks, "Are there other healers in your family?"

"Not now. My great-grandmother was, I'm told. They say she was a healer here at the palace. I never knew her."

"What would you like to do in life?"

Kierstia's eyes drop for an instant. "Whatever I can do to do good."

Toziel smiles. "Then you will be an outstanding healer. Does your family still live here in Cyad?"

"My father does. He's a Magi'i engineer who repairs the fireships. My mother . . . she died when I was young."

"Is that why you became a healer . . . besides having the ability?"

She nods.

In time, Toziel ends his dance with her and takes yet another partner, and then another.

Somewhat before the glass at which the ball will end, Toziel bows to his last partner, a sweet, if slightly insipid young woman named Tyantha'elth, and steps away, looking around the grand ballroom until he finds Dauret. After a moment, he catches Dauret's eyes, then gestures. The older man slips around several couples and joins Toziel. Those near the two pretend not to look, but Toziel still knows that, while the musicians still play and others dance, the attention of many is indirectly focused on the two of them.

"You have the names of all those with whom I danced?"

"Yes, ser."

"There are two with whom I would like to meet . . . for what you arranged."

Dauret nods, waiting.

"Cythera'elth and Ryenyel'elth."

Although the assistant steward does not show any outward reaction, Toziel can sense his surprise at the second name. "Wasn't that the purpose of the ball?"

"Yes, ser."

"Escort them to the small sitting room, just before the glass strikes. I'll be waiting there. Their parents or escorts can wait in the reception hall." Although Toziel has said this before, he wants no mistakes.

Dauret nods.

Then, Toziel turns and walks from the grand ballroom, out through the right, or north archway, and into the small sitting room, the one to which his mother often retired to refresh herself during the long formal seasonal balls.

Behind him, the musicians play "Land of Light," the traditional ending to every formal ball held in the palace.

IV

Although it seems almost as though a glass has passed before the sitting room door opens, it can only have been a fraction of that when the two women step into the chamber where Toziel stands, waiting.

Cythera enters first, and bows slightly, as does Ryenyel. Both murmur, "Your Mightiness."

Toziel replies with a smile, one he hopes does not convey his own nervousness, and studies the two—the one in a clinging black gown, the other in a shade of healer's green. "If you two would follow me for a moment . . ."

Cythera inclines her head, a movement of grace and resolution, yet without arrogance or submission, and so poised that there is not the slightest movement of the clinging black fabric of her gown.

Ryenyel offers a shy smile and the words, "As you wish, Your Mightiness." Yet the tone of her voice holds the sense of a question, but not enough of that question to determine what it might be.

Toziel leads the way from the sitting room back down the massive staircase to the next lower level of the Palace of Light and onto a corridor on the north side. Their feet barely seem to brush the polished white stones of the corridor as the three glide toward the private study of the Emperor, trailed discreetly by a pair of palace guards, both wearing green uniforms edged in silver trim and carrying small firelances.

The door before which Toziel halts is open, a single portal. "If you would enter," he suggests.

As the two step into the study, Toziel studies each once more as she moves past him.

Cythera is slender, her straight nose perfectly proportioned, even the black stone clips in her silver hair matching the fabric of the slightly scoop-necked gown that hints at, but does not reveal, the exquisite figure beneath. Her lips curl slightly, as if she can sense his evaluation as she passes.

Toziel has no doubt that she can, for most daughters of the Magi'i can do that . . . and far more.

Ryenyel steps past him in turn, and he sees her thick and dark red hair, hair somewhat too coarse by the standards of Cyad to be considered that of a beauty, but the green-faced silver clips accentuate an aliveness in that redness, an aliveness mirrored in green eyes that almost laugh, for she does not conceal that she knows she is being studied, nor that she knows her figure is somewhat too full to be called imperially slim.

Toziel smothers his own amusement, nodding to the palace guards to close the study door before turning. As the door shuts behind him, he walks slowly toward the polished desk that holds but four objects, stepping to the left and then turning to face the two. "My mother was not a woman who cared greatly for things, but she did value most highly several personal possessions," Toziel says, his voice quiet but warm. "I thought you might like to look at each." He gestures toward the desk.

The first of the four objects, the one farthest from Toziel, is an exquisitely simple tiara of a metal that shimmers like silver, but seems to gather and reflect light simultaneously, with three delicate lobes faced with modest white diamonds that seem to have the faintest silver tinge. The second is a small box, seemingly enameled in black, but with a circular oval that depicts a silver-white winged bird with a long, curved neck, unlike any ever seen in Cyador, swimming from left to right across a pond with a background of golden-green rushes. The third is a small volume, a book with a silver-tinged cover that bears the faintest hint of green, while the fourth is an emerald solitaire ring, the stone cut so precisely that even in the muted light of the study lamps the gem seems to dance like a green flame.

For several long moments, neither woman moves or speaks.

Finally, Toziel smiles gently. "Cythera . . . Ryenyel . . . they're only possessions. Tell me what you think, what one evokes the most for you, if you will."

Cythera steps forward first, toward the side of the desk closest to Toziel. Ryenyel waits for a moment, then takes a position even with the silver-haired woman, with perhaps a yard between them.

Toziel notes that neither woman more than surveys either the tiara or the ring, and he can sense that their acts are not artifice. That pleases him.

"Might I ask what the bird is?" asks Cythera, gently lifting and holding the enameled box.

"An Anglorian swan, a cigoerne," replies Toziel. "Not that I've ever seen one."

The silver-haired woman opens the box, her long fingers delicate and careful, as she studies it inside and out before replacing it gently on the desk. "She used this box often. It was her favorite."

Toziel nods.

Cythera frowns slightly. "I have the feeling it might be one of a pair."

That does surprise Toziel, for he has never seen another box like it. "You may be right, but I don't know of another."

Ryenyel turns her eyes on the box. "I think she's right."

"Does that evoke the most for you as well?" asks Toziel.

Instead of replying directly, Ryenyel slips around Cythera and gestures to the silver-tinged book. "Might I open it, Your Mightiness?"

"I'm scarcely mighty, but you may."

He watches as her fingers touch the silver-sheened cover, then lift and open the book. She turns one page, then the second. Her eyes widen as she begins to read the third page.

"It almost seems as though . . . as though . . ." Ryenyel does not complete the sentence.

"As though what?" he inquires.

"Is there another one, just like this?"

Toziel wants to smile, but counterfeits a frown. "Why should there be?"

"I could not say, Your Mightiness. It is only a feeling." Ryenyel turns the page and her lips almost move.

Toziel forces himself not to move, but his eyes keep returning to Ryenyel as she reads yet another page. He can sense the feelings the words bring up in her, and he desperately wants to hold her.

He does not move.

Cythera glances from Ryenyel to Toziel, then back to Ryenyel.

Neither notices as the silver-haired beauty slips from the private study of the Emperor Toziel'elth'alt'mer. Nor does either hear the faintest click of the door, turning as they do to face each other, their eyes meeting . . . and their fingers entwining.

There are love stories, and then there are love stories, and the latter often show what another story about the same person does not.

THE MOST SUCCESSFUL MERCHANT

"If you would send my regrets, Leityr, and your acceptance in my place . . ." The white-haired merchanter coughs, a sound more like retching.

"You're not going to the heir's consorting ceremony?" asks the young man who is barely more than a youth. *"Only the most highly regarded merchanters are invited, and you are among them. I know the Emperor and Empress esteem you above all other merchanters. I have seen the tokens . . ."*

"My son, the Empress will understand."

"The Empress, but not the Emperor? What of him?"

"He will understand more than anyone, and he will appreciate my absence."

"But why? How can that be?"

"You know I have been as kind and honorable, and as loving a consort as I know how to be. You also know that I did not consort young. There was a reason for that. . . ." The old man is silent for a time, and then begins to speak, quietly, but clearly. *"Many years ago, I began my life in trade as a runner, a mere messenger who carried*

dispatches between the trading houses, those both large and small . . .
and even some that were not even properly houses . . ."
   Leityr settles into the chair at the corner of the table desk to listen.

Eileyt was hurrying down the Road of Benevolent Commerce
when he saw Merekel, the only runner with whom he talked
more than infrequently, coming the other way. Merekel waved
and kept going, most likely toward one of the Houses to the
north.

   Eileyt wondered whether he should bother with the Clanless Traders, who seldom needed runners, but the day had been
slow. He shrugged and hurried off the Road and along the front
of the converted warehouse that served a variety of those small
traders. None on the lower level needed his services, and he
reluctantly climbed the wide staircase to the upper level.

   "Runner!" called a voice.

   Eileyt turned. A red-haired woman gestured from a far
doorway on the upper level, a door that fronted on a space little
larger than the smallest of storerooms. He hurried over, only
to discover that the person he had thought was a merchanter
woman appeared barely older than a girl. Although she was definitely shaped like a woman, and her blue eyes were focused and
anything but dreaming, she appeared years younger than Eileyt
himself. *And very beautiful.*

   "Can you take a pouch to Siedyk at Kysan House?" Her
voice was firm, traderlike, but with a hint of huskiness.

   "Two coppers." The fee was set for all runners, two for a
pouch and four for a case, but Eileyt had never seen her before
and wanted her to know . . . just in case.

   "Two coppers, Lady," she said firmly.

   "Yes, Lady."

   "Your pledge plaque, if you would?"

He offered the small bronze oblong.

"Eileyt." She jotted down his name in the dispatch ledger.

He noted the grace and precision of her script, then accepted the copper she proffered, hoping he could get a return run so that he did not have to come back for a single copper.

"I'll hold it for you if you can't get a return run."

The way in which she spoke convinced Eileyt, and he nodded, then headed back down the steps.

He did not get a return run, but early the following morning, just after he'd left his pallet in the almost dilapidated Hall of Runners, little more than a narrow warehouse too small for most merchanters, while passing Yuryan House, he was summoned and given a large pouch for Ryalor Trading, on the upper level of the House of the Clanless Traders. He did not even realize that the pouch was for the red-headed young woman until he saw the entwined *R* and *L* above her doorway.

When he knocked on the open door, she stepped forward and handed him his copper. "Thank you." The way she said those two words made him feel as though she truly did appreciate his services.

"I also have a pouch for you from Yuryan House." Eileyt handed her the receipt for the pouch.

She studied it quickly, made an entry in the ledger before handing him a second copper, one that was not required. "Thank you for that as well."

"Thank you very much, Lady." Eileyt paused, then asked, "Might I ask . . . Lady . . . when did you . . ."

"I've been here for the past eightday. If you want work, come by here more frequently."

"I will, Lady," he promised, and he returned that very same afternoon.

She surprised him by handing him a dispatch pouch and a copper. "For Trader Fuyol at Yuryan House."

Over the next few eightdays, Eileyt made a point of stopping by the House of the Clanless Traders. More often than not, the red-haired young lady merchanter did have runs for him. What surprised him was that she seemed to have business of some sort with most of the larger merchanting clans in Cyad—not only Yuryan House, but Bluet House, Hyshrah House, and even the feared Dyjani House, as well as with an Austran merchantman porting in Cyad.

One afternoon, the fifth threeday of spring, he stopped once more. She was seated behind the table desk, looking at entries in a ledger, while looking at figures she had set down on another sheet of paper, then occasionally adding one to the paper.

"You're taking figures from the ledger, not entering them?"

"I'm calculating the change in the prices of cuprite."

"You trade in cuprite?" Somehow the idea of the merchanter lady trading in cuprite surprised Eileyt. He had supposed that she dealt in small items, such as gems, or lamps, or jewelry.

"You're the curious one, Runner. What is your name?"

"Eileyt, Lady."

She nodded.

"The copper, Lady . . . ?"

"For us, such trades make more sense. Or shares in merchanter cargoes." Her eyes caught his, and Eileyt saw the humor in them and in her face before she continued. "Goods we have to take possession of or hold for more than a short time will come later. It takes more people and a large warehouse to handle small items in quantities large enough to be profitable. The same goes for unique goods."

He pointed to the ledger and the figures on the paper. "How do those help?"

"Men lie. So do women. The coins do not. They only allow men to deceive themselves." The red-haired merchanter woman did not smile. "That is why an accurate ledger is so important. So is knowing who paid how much for what."

"You could write down anything you wanted, and no one would know whether it was right."

"That isn't the point. Accuracy isn't for them. It's for me, for the House."

Eileyt did not laugh. Somehow, she conveyed the impression that her small space was in fact a merchanting house. And he knew that she had more than a score of dispatch pouches all embroidered with the intertwined *R* and *L*, and that often there were almost none in the smooth wooden box beneath the table desk beside the doorway. *But . . . shares in cargoes?* Those cost tens of golds, not coppers or silvers.

"If you would return the pouch . . ."

At her reminder, Eileyt nodded. "Yes, Lady." He turned and set off, still thinking about golds and dispatch pouches.

As a mere runner, Eileyt could not afford to frequent the Honest Stone, the coffeehouse where so many young merchanters gathered to talk and to trade gossip, hoping to tease out hints about what other houses might be doing or to let slip misleading tidbits of information. On slow days, he could pause near the tables outside, hoping for a run. Most times, he did not get a run, but some days he did, as he did in late morning on the following sevenday, usually a very slow time for trade runners.

A dark-haired young trader, attired in the finest white cotton, over which he wore a shimmercloth vest of maroon trimmed in pale green, gestured. "You there! Runner!"

Eileyt hurried over. "Yes, ser?"

The trader finished writing something on a sheet, then folded and sealed the paper before tucking it inside a maroon pouch. "You know Ryalor Trading in the House of the Clanless?"

"Yes, ser."

The trader proffered a copper. "Take the pouch there. You'll get the other when you return the pouch to me or to Nylyth House."

"Yes, ser." Eileyt moved away quickly, then, after several steps, knelt to tighten his sandals, hoping to overhear more of interest.

"You're trading with her?"

"She knows things . . . and she's good to look at . . ."

"Your sire might not see it that way . . ."

The trader laughed. "He'd see it very much that way."

Although it was no business of Eileyt's, except as a merchanter runner, the young trader's words bothered him as he rose and trotted toward the House of the Clanless.

Once he was there, the merchanter lady took the green pouch, frowning as she untied it and took out the folded square. Without a word, she handed the pouch back to Eileyt—empty. Then she gave him a copper. "You can return the pouch to Nylyth House."

"No reply, Lady?"

"Ghulaan's traders want too much for too little."

But . . . denying even the smallest of the major merchanting houses . . . Eileyt did not speak those words, only saying, "Yes, Lady."

His eyes dropped to the sealed envelope on the side of the desk. He could not make out the name, only the words "Undercaptain, Mirror Lancers" and the name Isahl. That must be a town or a Lancer Post, although he had never heard of it. *If she is even remotely related to a Mirror Lancer officer . . .* Eileyt looked into the chamber behind her, but he only saw file chests, and not a single barrel or bale.

"I rent space in the warehouses of others, Eileyt."

The runner barely managed to avoid blushing. "I will return the pouch now." *To Nylyth House.* Eileyt wanted no part of the young trader's anger or frustration.

As the eightdays went by, Eileyt found he was running messages more and more for the young lady merchanter . . . and getting the impression that she was far more than she seemed. He didn't even tell Merekel, but then, Merekel shared little. Most runners didn't.

Then, one sixday evening, he stood in the shadows a block away from Bronze Bowl. The Silver Chalice was better, he'd heard, but he didn't have the coins, and they'd throw him out just because he was a runner and not an enumerator.

From the nearer shadows came two voices. Eileyt eased closer.

". . . got an easy one . . ."

". . . easy?" The other young man laughed. "Nothing's easy."

". . . red-haired merchanter girl, insists on being called 'Lady.' Jiulko wants her dead."

"It's not the first time he's wanted someone gone . . . must have told him no . . ."

". . . hear she's pretty . . . but it's business . . . tomorrow night . . . when she leaves . . . always leaves late . . . no one around . . ."

Eileyt remained unmoving in the shadows as the two silver blades walked on. Although he had never heard the name Jiulko, he concentrated on remembering it. *Should you do anything? Can you?* Eileyt was not a bravo. He might have held off a sneak thief with the truncheon at his waist . . . but to deal with even one of the night's silver blades? He wouldn't even have wanted to encounter one of the ruffians who called themselves, half-mockingly, the bronze blades. He shook his head.

Yet . . . he had made more coins in the past half season than ever before, and she was kind and often gave him extra coppers.

In the end, he made his way to a gray stone building set at the end of a well-swept narrow lane, also of gray stone, to meet a man he had known once, years before.

The graying man wore a gray tunic and trousers so dark that

they were the color of charcoal, yet not black. He frowned as he saw Eileyt. "You're not cut out to be even a bronze blade."

"That's not why I'm here. There are two silver blades. They're going to kill the red-haired merchanter lady, the one who calls herself Ryalor Trading," Eileyt explained. "Tonight . . . when she leaves the House of the Clanless."

The kind-faced—though scarcely kind, Eileyt knew—clerk looked bored. "Eileyt . . . the Guild doesn't do favors."

"I know. I'll pay."

"*You'll* pay? With what?"

Eileyt laid five silvers on the polished wood.

"That's only half."

He showed the other five.

The clerk shook his head. "A runner with that many silvers? You're risking your own neck. Where did you get them?"

"I've been careful." In fact, the ten silvers—a whole gold—comprised most of his life savings, savings he had been amassing in hopes of eventually posting the five-gold bond necessary to become an enumerator.

"And you'd spend them on a pair of silver blades? They'd as soon kill you as spit. To save a merchanter girl who'll get consorted and never look to you?"

"I won't always be a runner. You'll see."

The clerk snorted. "You sure you want to do this?"

"I'm sure."

The older man made an entry in his ledger, then wrote on a parchment plaque, which he handed to Eileyt. Only then did he take the five silvers. "That's only for the one with the blade."

"I know." Eileyt hoped that the assassin's friend wasn't with him, but he didn't have two golds. One was all he could scrape up.

Sevenday evening, Eileyt waited in the shadows of the side

lane across from the steps to the upper level of the House of the Clanless. It was almost full dark, and already in the sky to the southeast the Rational Stars shone bright and pitiless when she came down the steps, moving confidently. She turned north on the stone sidewalk flanking the west side of the Road of Benevolent Commerce. Eileyt wanted to hurry to the red-haired woman. He did not. Instead, he waited until she was almost out of sight before he left the shadows.

Cloaked in the dark gray half-cloaks of silver blades, two figures followed her like shadows, their boots barely whispering across the stone. She never looked back as they silently drew closer. Then, as the first blade passed a narrow alley, he stopped, staggered, and reached back to put out his hand to the stone wall. His hand never touched the wall before he pitched face forward.

From the other side of the road, Eileyt swallowed as he saw two figures, or a figure and a shadow. The shadow was the Guild Assassin, and he was slipping away back down the alley. The remaining figure was the other silver blade. He stooped and cut away his friend's wallet, then straightened and continued following the lady merchanter, as if nothing at all had happened. Eileyt found he was clenching his teeth, but there was nothing left to do, but follow . . . and hope that he could do something.

The lady merchanter suddenly dashed across the road, just in front of a coach headed south, and into a narrow lane. The silver blade let the coach pass, then went after her.

Eileyt kept moving, then stopped as the lady merchanter emerged from the lane, walking swiftly and not looking back. Ever so slowly, Eileyt approached the narrow lane. He heard nothing. He did not want to enter it, or look into it. He finally did. In the dimness past a rubbish barrel, he could make out a pair of boots. The boots had feet and legs in them. Eileyt took

two steps, and then two more, just enough to see the blood—
surprisingly little—and the fact that the blade was dead and
that his wallet had been cut away.

Eileyt stepped back and glanced north along the Road of
Benevolent Commerce. He saw no sign of the merchanter
woman. After a long moment, he smiled, although he could
not have said why, especially after having spent most of what
he had saved over the past two years.

Eileyt did not run on eightdays. Most merchanters were
closed, and those that were not seldom needed runners. He
waited until eighth glass on oneday before he made his way to
the upper level of the House of the Clanless Traders. As he had
hoped, she beckoned to him, and he hurried toward her, then
stopped. "Where to, Lady?"

She ignored the question and looked directly at him. "Eileyt,
someone followed me Sevenday night. You followed them . . .
and then the one who followed me no longer did. What happened? What did you have to do with it?"

Eileyt's face turned to stone. She had known about the
silver blades, but how had she known he had followed them?

She smiled, gently. "I see more than most people know."

He gambled that the truth would suffice. "I overheard two
silver blades talking. One was hired to kill you."

"Do you know who hired the silver blade?"

"The only name I heard, Lady, was Jiulko. I do not know
who that might be."

"I do." Her blue eyes turned as hard and cold as lapis, so hard
that he could have sworn they held the same streaks of gold as
the stone. Then she looked at Eileyt, and her eyes were no longer
stone, but they were not warm, either. "How did you stop him?"

"I'm no blade, Lady."

She nodded. "So . . . you hired someone to protect me."
Her words were not a question.

Not trusting himself to speak, Eileyt nodded.

She reached into the smooth wooden box and handed him a coin—a gold. "I appreciate your concern, and I know you could not afford that."

"Lady . . ."

"No protestations, Eileyt." She smiled again. "How would you like to become an enumerator? You're smart enough. You work hard. You're trustworthy . . . and I can teach you."

"Lady . . . I can't post the bond."

"That is the responsibility of the House, and we need an enumerator."

"We?" Eileyt had never seen anyone but her.

"I have a silent partner. He has . . . certain ties. We've need an enumerator. In time, we will need others, but you will be the first beside the two of us."

A silent partner? The Mirror Lancer officer she wrote? "I would be honored, Lady. Are you sure?"

"If I cannot trust someone who would spend nearly all he has to protect me, I can trust no one. I will pay you half what a junior enumerator makes while I teach you."

Eileyt couldn't conceal his surprise. His mouth opened. He closed it.

"Since today is oneday, you might as well start now . . . or right after any run you have."

"Yours would have been my first."

"You will still run for me while you learn, but after the first eightday, the coppers go in the till."

He almost frowned, but then asked, "You will pay by the eightday?"

"Good."

By that word, he knew he had passed another test of some sort.

Eileyt knew his numbers and his letters, and his hand was

fair. That he'd been told before his parents had died of the white flux, when his chances of becoming an enumerator, or even a trader, had been far more likely to be realized. Fair was not good enough for the lady merchanter, whose name, he finally learned, was Ryalth. Nor did he know the shape of merchant-er's digits, slightly different from common numbers so that they could not be mistaken or easily altered in a ledger or on a contract of bill of sale.

Only after two eightdays did his hands and fingers stop aching at the end of each day, but he had a difficult time not smiling every moment. He did stop smiling when he realized that, once Ryalth listed him as an enumerator, he could no longer sleep in the Hall of Runners. The merchanting houses of Cyad did maintain rooms, little more than spaces big enough for a narrow bunk and a few chests, but those cost three coppers an eightday. He stopped worrying when he received a silver and three coppers for his first eightday's pay, and that was only half the pay of a very junior enumerator. Ryalth kept him running when she needed runs, but otherwise, every free moment for close to half a season more was spent learning one thing or another. He also ended up entrusting most of his wages to her strong-boxes, because having silvers that were increasing every eightday was asking for trouble in the Hall of Runners.

He had pushed the incident with the silver blades almost aside until the fifth oneday of summer when, just after he had washed up at the small fountain at one end of the Hall of Run-ners, Merekel turned to him. "Did you hear?"

"Hear what?"

"You know that nasty Nordlan trader, Juko or Jullko . . . anyway, someone slit his throat in his own little trading house, likely on sevenday evening."

"I hadn't heard that," Eileyt admitted. "I've heard of him. I never did a run for him."

"You're the fortunate one. He was always shorting runners on the return coppers. Can't believe someone didn't crush his skull before now." Merekel shook his head. "We don't see much of you these days."

"Most times, I'm running for Ryalor. They keep me busy."

"She's a handsome lady. Wish she'd keep me busy."

"Not that way. I wouldn't dare. Her partner—he might be wanting to consort her—he's a Mirror Lancer officer. His family might be even Magi'i. She's never said . . . but . . ." Eileyt shrugged. "She pays well for runs."

The other runner nodded. "Smart of you. Don't want to cross altage or elthage."

Eileyt knew that. He wished it were otherwise. But it was not.

When he reached the upper level of the House of the Clanless Traders that morning, he saw a stooped and graying man, wearing the blues of a senior enumerator, standing talking to Ryalth just outside Ryalor Trading.

As Eileyt approached, she turned. "Eileyt, this is Master Enumerator Chaeralt. He will examine your skills to see if you are ready to be a junior enumerator."

Eileyt bowed. "Master Enumerator, ser." He hadn't expected to be examined so soon.

"Let's look into your skills, young fellow." Chaeralt's voice was neither warm nor harsh, just matter-of-fact, a contrast to his severe expression.

"You can use either of the table desks inside," Ryalth said.

Chaeralt nodded and stepped through the doorway.

Eileyt followed.

"Sit down there." Chaeralt pointed to the nearer table desk, the one Ryalth usually used.

Eileyt felt uneasy sitting there, but he did.

The enumerator handed him several sheets of paper. Each

was a ledger sheet. "I'm going to read you figures, and you're to copy them, and then sum them in merchant digits . . ."

Eileyt thought he would be nervous, but that feeling passed as he did what the enumerator requested, especially as it became clear that what Ryalth had taught him was far more exacting than what Chaeralt demanded.

At the end, the stern-faced enumerator actually smiled. "You'll do fine. You could likely pass the enumerator's exam right now, but there's no point in doing that. You need at least a year as a junior." He nodded to Ryalth, who had eased into the chamber. "As soon as we receive the bond . . ."

"I posted it yesterday."

Chaeralt laughed. "I'll send the plaque as soon as it's ready."

"Thank you."

"My pleasure, Lady." Then, with a smile, the senior enumerator turned and left.

Eileyt watched him go, still not quite believing that he might actually become an enumerator after all the years of running.

"Eileyt . . . ?"

He turned. "Yes, Lady?"

"You looked like you wanted to say something when you arrived this morning."

"No, Lady." He smiled pleasantly. "I did hear that Trader Jiulko was found with his throat slit over eightday."

"That shouldn't be a surprise. People who cause others misery often reap what they sow. Those who help others and inspire trust need to be rewarded." She smiled. "Don't you think so?"

"Yes, Lady, I do. Very much so."

"Then we are agreed." Her smile broadened. "I took the liberty of ordering your blues so that you can wear them as soon as Chaeralt sends your plaque." She gestured toward one of the chests, the one placed forward of the others, on which was set something wrapped in cheap muslin.

Eileyt could see a hint of blue at one side where the covering cloth had come loose. "Thank you, Lady. I didn't expect . . ."

"I know. That's one of your best traits."

As she turned and moved back from the table desk, the smooth cloth of her sleeve pressed momentarily against her forearm. For an instant, Eileyt saw the bunching of cloth that could only mean that she wore a forearm sheath, the kind that usually held a black iron dagger, if not something even more deadly.

Eileyt swallowed . . . and yet his eyes burned. *She is still so very beautiful, but so is a fine blade.*

The old merchanter clears his throat. "That's how everything began."

"She never knew how you felt?"

"She may have known. So did he. He also knew I had protected her when he could not. He knows everything."

"You loved her, didn't you?"

"She loves him and always did. He loves her and always did. We would all be poorer if it were not so . . . and we have prospered and been happy. What else can a man ask for?" The old man coughs again . . . a sound even more wrenching than previously. "I have lived a full and prosperous life. If the Rational Stars are gracious, I will live a few more years. If not . . . I have gained all that a man could possibly desire"—almost all—"including the gratitude of an empress. What else could a man reasonably ask for?" Yet his smile is somehow sad. "Go to the consorting ceremony, and offer our felicitations and thanks . . . and mean it, for we would have little without them."

"Yes, ser." *The young man nods deeply and turns, slowly leaving* the study.

But you loved her.

The old man can hear those words as if they had been spoken, as if they still hung in the air.

There are references and allusions to the events in the follow-ing novella in several Recluce novels, but since there is noth-ing about this side of one of the great pivotal events in the history of Candar, I thought it should be told.

HERITAGE

I

"Lady . . . the Emperor is on his way."

"Thank you, Viera." The Empress, Lady Mairena of Light and Healing, immediately closes the green leather folder and slips it into the drawer of her desk, beside another thin volume, one much older, that still shimmers silver green. She stands. "You may go for the evening."

"You will not be wanting me more this evening?"

The Empress smiles, faintly. "No. Not this evening."

The dark-haired maid inclines her head. "Thank you, my lady."

Once Viera has left the study, Mairena walks to the open window. For a time, she stands there, letting the slightest trace of the ocean breeze cool her, not that the early summer has been all that warm, and looks out into the darkness, out over the white stone dwellings, shops, and other buildings, all with green awnings by decree of the Emperor, that stretch to the east and to the north, radiating away from the Palace of Light that has stood as a symbol of the might of Cyad and Cyador for endless generations. *Not endless*, she corrects herself, *but well over six centuries. And now . . .*

At the sound of her door opening, she turns and waits.

The man who enters her chamber does not wear the silver robes of the Emperor, for all that he is physically commanding, but the white uniform of a Mirror Lancer, although his service was years in the past and brief. In a similar fashion, although his heritage is elthage, he would never have even been accepted as a student magus, in spite of his minor abilities in handling chaos, except for the fact that he was the heir to the Malachite Throne. Mairena notes that his short-cut but thick brown hair shows more silver strands than before his visit to Fyrad, quite a few more. She inclines her head slightly. As Emperor of Cyador, and the man to whom she is consorted, he does deserve that.

"Good evening," she offers.

"It's settled," announces Lephi.

She lets an expression of puzzlement cross her face, an expression that is not totally feigned. "What is?"

"The Magi'i have agreed that the *Kerial* will begin sea trials tomorrow." Lephi shakes his head. "The firecannon has not been fully tested, but that can wait. It's past time. With all their concerns . . ."

"The *Kerial*—you mean the fireship?" Mairena knows full well the name of the ship and far more besides, much of which she has learned from the plans in the green leather folder her consort does not know she has created and possesses.

"What else would I mean?"

"You had not decided on the name. You were considering *Lorn, Kerial, Alyiakal*, or *Kiedral*."

"So I hadn't. Well, I've decided. It's the *Kerial*. The last truly great emperor."

She offers a measured nod. "You need a symbol of power to

show the Duke of Lydiar and the others, even the Hamorians. And especially the barbarians of Lornth—"

"Do not ever speak that name! I will not have it."

Mairena reproaches herself silently. She knows better. The very mention of the town named after perhaps the greatest emperor of Cyador upsets Lephi, because the barbarians have held the town for the last several generations as the power of Cyador has slowly waned, a waning that her husband strives to reverse . . . at a cost he—and Cyador—cannot afford, and a cost that he will not, cannot, admit, even to himself.

"And the Duke?"

Lephi snorts. "The Duke is a problem. So are the pirates out of Ruzor. The Hamorians? They're little more than an irritation. Hamor is a land split between three dukes who distrust each other . . . not to mention that the other third of Hamor is divided among warring clans little more than barbarians on horseback. Not one duke is strong enough to overpower the others. I wouldn't be surprised if two companies of Mirror Lancers couldn't take any of their holds . . . except the rewards of such a campaign aren't worth it."

"Nor do you have the Mirror Lancers to spare now that you are dealing with the barbarians to the northeast." *Nor have we had the vessels to transport such a force, not until the fireship.*

"We will beat them back. They are barbarians."

"What of the dark angels of the Westhorns?" asks Mairena.

"What of them? There are few of them, and a handful helping the barbarians will make little difference. The cold of the heights will destroy them in another generation. It could be even sooner."

Mairena nods politely, deciding against pressing the issue, for Lephi has made up his mind. Once his mind is set, she knows from bitter experience, there is no changing it, not without paying a high price, a price she will only pay when her views will change matters, and only when absolutely necessary. This is not one of those times, not when she does not have enough allies among the Magi'i and the Mirror Lancers to make her husband understand the folly of his coming campaign.

"Have you had any of your visions about what will happen?" His voice rumbles, and his tone carries amused condescension, a condescension she has found more and more irritating with each passing year.

"Only that your fireship—"

"Not my fireship. The *Kerial*."

". . . that your fireship will sail the Great Western Ocean."

"And the others as well!"

"And the others as well," repeats Mairena, knowing that she has not seen that.

"You have doubts?"

"I have doubts about your efforts against the Accursed Forest, the barbarians, the traders, and building a fireship and firecannon all at once, with too few Magi'i and fewer young people being born to the Magi'i every year."

"The symbolism of the chains will help," he counters. "Women must understand that home and hearth are the strength of any land."

And allowing them to be chained, even symbolically, will increase the number of children they are willing to bear?

When she does not speak aloud, he goes on, his voice strengthening. "You will see, my Empress and healer. The entire world will see Cyador rise once more, stronger and more powerful than ever."

"May it be so," she replies, understanding that, once more, he will not hear what he does not wish to hear, especially from her . . . and even less from any other woman.

"It will be." He pauses. "I wanted you to know about the sea trials. You'll be able to see the *Kerial* set forth from here."

"I will be watching with great interest." And she will, if not precisely for the reasons Lephi would appreciate, nor does he know that she has studied not only the plans presented to him by the white engineers, but other documents as well, and made her own preparations. But then, there are some things he will never know.

"Excellent! Excellent! How is Emerya coming in her trials as a healer?"

"She has passed all but the last, and that she could do now, but there must be a season between trials."

Lephi nods. "The same as for the Magi'i." Then he frowns. "That will make a match for her difficult."

"You have a son. An immediate match for Emerya is not necessary. Besides, healers should not marry young."

"Unless they intend to marry within the Magi'i," he reminds her.

"That might create even greater . . . complications."

"True." He pauses. "Is there . . . anything else?"

She smiles softly. "Why would there be? I do little except what healing is considered appropriate here in the palace, and you know when I leave the palace and for what purposes. The children are fine, although Kiedron is scarcely that anymore, and you know as much as do I about his activities."

"Triendar says that he has more ability than do I, but he could also be a healer. Of sorts, at least."

"He has enough ability to be elthage, without question, and he has a good mind." *When he chooses to use it.*

"A good mind in a sound body." Lephi smiles, but the smile fades as quickly as it had appeared. "Well . . . good evening."

"When will you be leaving?"

He raises his eyebrows.

"Not this evening. I meant . . . to deal with the barbarians. You said that you were considering it."

"I did?"

"The other night, after dinner."

"Oh . . . that is unlikely. The reinforcements Queras dispatched should be more than adequate to deal with them."

"Even if they are advised by the dark angels?"

His eyes narrow. "The dark angels . . . I told you. There are only a handful of them. Do you really think they can stand against the firewagons, the Mirror Lancers, and the Shining Foot?" His voice increases in volume with every word.

Mairena decides against pressing. She has tried to suggest the danger they pose, a danger she has sensed on more than a few occasions, and her husband has dismissed her concerns time after time. "Their powers are unknown. I worry, but you and the Magi'i know more about them than do I." She doubts that, but saying so will merely enrage Lephi, and she is weary of pressing facts upon him that he will not accept.

"Themphi has used his glass often to see their actions. They build upon the Roof of the World, and that is all. They are no threat. We could call in more of the white wizards among the Magi'i, if necessary. But it is not necessary. Not necessary at all."

"That is good." *Especially since calling them away from the Accursed Forest will allow it to spread across the entire east.*

When Mairena says nothing more, Lephi nods and once more says, "Good evening."

"Good evening."

After Lephi leaves her study, she walks back to the window and takes a long, slow breath, even though there has been little intimate contact between the two of them in years. Lephi finds the order abilities that have grown over the years in Mairena too painful to bear, especially as she has become more and more adept as a healer. In turn, she has found his rage at that pain has resulted in far too many bruises and far too many angry conversations—if listening to tirades qualified as conversation, she reflects.

What can you do . . . with what will come? After a moment, she answers herself, but only in her thoughts, for even in her chambers the walls may have ears. *Prepare as you can and must, for Lephi will not listen.*

As if he ever had.

II

The Empress hurries from her chambers in the dark grayness well before sunrise, all too early, given that it is just past mid-summer in Cyad. She stops before the nearest guard in the Palace of Light and orders, "Send for the Third Magus. Now!"

The green-uniformed man glances around, as if to question the fact that there is no one to take his post.

"That doesn't matter. Find Tyrsalyn! He should be here in the palace."

"Yes, Lady."

The Empress turns and walks swiftly down the wide corridor of polished white stone tiles to the chambers of her daughter. After entering the sitting room, she strides into the bedchamber. "Emerya! Time to get up. This moment."

"What is it?" Emerya blinks and shakes her head, brushing back long strands of brilliant copper-red hair from her face. "Where is Viera?"

"On her way here, I hope, for her sake. We need to leave Cyad as soon as possible. Without dithering and without delay."

"At this glass of the morning? If it isn't still night? Where are we going? Why? What about the ball? Father said he would be back in time for the ball."

"There isn't time for questions, or answers. I doubt there

will be a ball or . . ." Then the Empress thinks better of what she might have said. "You have only a few moments. Don riding clothes. Gather the rest of your riding clothes and boots and put them in a travel bag. One gown. One! If the bag is not packed and you are not dressed quickly, you will wear your nightclothes to the ship. Oh . . . and bring every piece of jewelry you own. Every last one, even those you don't like."

"Even the chains?"

"Even those. Gold is valuable. Wear the gold-and-malachite healer's bracelet. I know you haven't passed your last trial, but wear it anyway."

Emerya's face contorts. "You said 'ship'? We're going on a ship? That means somewhere far, doesn't it?"

"It may be necessary," declares the Empress as she turns.

"Necessary?" asks the redhead as she struggles out from the shimmercloth sheets of the palest green.

Her mother is gone, already striding down the wide and high-ceilinged corridor and into the larger apartments in the corner of the Palace of Light, those opposite her own study.

A set of greens covers the back of the chair set at an angle behind the table desk in the sitting room, and a pair of boots lies on the floor. Mairena knocks peremptorily on the door to the bedchamber, then pushes the door open. "Kiedron. Time to get up."

There is no movement from the dark-haired young man lying only half-covered by the tangled shimmercloth sheets. His eyes do not move.

Mairena walks to the side of the bed and says loudly, "Kiedron, get up!"

Again, there is no motion. She shakes her head and picks up the plain crystal goblet set on the bedside table, concentrates on it for a moment until frost begins to form on the crystal, then throws the icy water on her son's face.

"Oh!" The youth bolts up and to his feet, as if ready to fight. His dark blue eyes look slightly wild and unfocused.

"I told you it was time to get up."

"But I was up late last night."

"That was last night. We have to leave Cyad immediately."

"Why? Are the barbarians attacking? They can't have crossed all of Cyador from the northeast."

"It's something different. Wear your greens and pack as many other sets as you can into that kit bag you were going to take to Kynstaar. A spare pair of boots and any necessities. Also any personal jewelry and any golds or silvers that you have. All of them. We need to leave the palace and board the fireship as soon as we can. Meet me in the upper foyer. Bring your sister. By force, if necessary." Mairena adds just a touch of order to her last words, then turns and leaves her son open-mouthed.

As she makes her way back toward the wide landing at the top of the grand staircase, she cannot keep the frown from her face. *Are you certain what you have seen . . . truly certain?* She pushes that thought away. The strength of the image that woke her only confirms what she had feared . . . and prepared for, not knowing for certain when what she has seen would occur. If she is wrong, she will be embarrassed, certainly disgraced, possibly even executed, for Lephi might well appreciate an excuse for such. If she is right, and does not follow what she has seen and prepared for, she—and her children—will be dead.

She reaches the landing and glances around. No one is there, except for a guard who appears coming up the wide white stone steps.

He is breathing heavily as he comes to a halt several yards from her. "Lady Empress, the Third Magus will be here in a few moments. He was on the lower level."

"Good. Would you tell Captain Altyrn to proceed with the

loading of the duty company? And make certain the Imperial coach is waiting."

"Yes, Lady." The guard's face betrays puzzlement.

"He'll know what you mean." *Lephi would be appalled to see me ordering around his officers.* She does not reveal the wry smile she feels as the guard hurries back down the steps, past the figure of the Third Magus struggling up the staircase.

"You summoned me, Lady?" The Third Magus wears the crossed lightning bolts on the breast of his white tunic, as have all the Magi'i since almost the time of Kiedral, the Second Emperor of Light. Tyrsalyn is not that much older than the Empress, for all the tiredness in his green eyes, and the gray shot through his red hair, but true chaos mages, even the highest of the Magi'i, are fortunate to see a full five decades.

"As I told you might happen one day, we need to get the heirs and all the Magi'i you can find, and their families, on board the fireship and reach the open ocean within the next two glasses. Sooner, if possible. Also, please convey to Captain Altyrn that if he can obtain any more Lancers to join his company, it would be to everyone's benefit."

"The fireship is not finished, Lady Empress," stammers Tyrsalyn.

"The engines work, and the hull is sound, is it not?" asks Mairena. "It can travel under its own power, can it not? And is there not a partial crew on board?" *And did I not arrange for one boiler to be kept ready at all times?*

"Yes . . ."

"Then summon all the remaining mages and their families— all that can be on the *Kerial* in a glass or less."

"You want them all on board? Now?"

"If they wish to live. And I expect to see you on the pier in less than half a glass."

Tyrsalyn pales slightly, but Mairena cannot discern whether

that is because of her words or her assumption of authority that, before this morning, has always been exercised under the guise of written orders of the Emperor, who she fears is meeting his fate in Syadtar . . . and equally fears that he may not be. Yet seldom has what she has foreseen not come to pass, although those foreshadowings have been infrequent.

"I would appreciate it if you would not say that to them, but only that it was the Emperor's wish and that he would look upon their failure to accommodate him most unfavorably."

"Yes, Lady Empress." He pauses. "It is said that you have at times seen what may be."

"At times, that has been so."

"So did the Second Emperor of Light, it is said." Tyrsalyn smiles, faintly. "I will do as you asked. I had best hasten."

"Thank you." Mairena turns and looks along the wide corridor. It is empty.

Moments pass, and then more moments, perhaps as much as a tenth of a glass before Emerya emerges from her chamber, struggling with an overstuffed kit bag—one she likely borrowed from her brother—while Kiedron appears moments later, almost sauntering before catching up with his sister. Then he walks along beside her carrying his own kit bag, not at all bulging. Behind them is Viera, looking totally bewildered.

Mairena raises her voice slightly. "Kiedron, escort your sister downstairs to the coach. Emerya, put the jewelry bag inside the travel bag. I'll meet you at the coach in a few moments. It should be in the portico by now." *The coach I can order, and no one will say anything.* "Don't dawdle. You, too, Viera." She heads down the grand staircase, her children and the maid who has served her and Emerya for years immediately behind her.

When she reaches the entry level of the palace, she sees that Captain Altyrn is waiting before the fountain under the dome in the reception hall of the Palace of Light. His graying hair is ever so slightly disarrayed. His eyes flick to Kiedron and Emerya as they walk past their mother and then past him, then center on the Empress as she stops before him. He pays little attention to Viera.

"Lady Empress, I know there are written orders—"

"There are indeed. The Emperor is wise and has left orders covering all possibilities. He instructed you to assure that we are safe. This is one of those circumstances. Is the duty company on the way to the fireship pier?"

"Yes, Lady. Might I ask why this is necessary?"

"You might. My answer is that events will show that necessity, and that failure to obey will be fatal for both of us."

The hint of a frown crosses the older officer's face.

Mairena knows that he is not that far from leaving the Mirror Lancers on a stipend after long service and asks, gently, "Have I ever asked the unreasonable of you, Captain?" She adds a touch of order to her voice.

"No, Lady."

"Then we should be leaving."

"I will ride ahead of the coach with the duty squad, Lady."

"That would be appreciated. We will make better time, and that is important." *All too important.* She knows she cannot become too insistent, much as she worries, because she has pressed more than would be considered either wise or prudent for any woman of Cyador in these times, and if she is seen as unduly unreasonable, all will fail. She knows she is balancing her position as Empress against the Cyadoran presupposition that women seldom take the initiative.

How did that come to be? Was it because of . . . She has no time to meditate on the immediate past history of Cyador. Instead, she walks swiftly out through the arched entry and toward the gleaming cupridium coach in which Kiedron and Emerya wait. Viera is seated up beside the coachman.

Once Mairena is seated, she calls to the coachman. "Follow the captain and the Mirror Lancer escort to the fireship pier. They will be here shortly."

"Yes, Lady Empress."

Mairena forces herself to wait, and the moments drag as she waits for Altyrn and the four Lancer rankers to arrive . . . and for the coach to move.

"You didn't mention the fireship," says Emerya.

"Please keep your voice down," replies Mairena.

"What is this all about?" asks Kiedron, his voice low.

"Surviving what will come. Do not ask me more. Not yet. Everything will become quite clear in another two glasses."

Kiedron and Emerya exchange worried glances. Emerya looks to her brother, but he shrugs, and she turns to look toward the harbor. Finally, the coach begins to move, easing away from the green-tinged white stone mounting blocks and down the gradual incline to the boulevard leading to the waterfront.

"Your mother is neither mad nor willful," Mairena replies to the unspoken queries. She looks to her daughter. "Do you remember the time I would not let you ride that gray across the bridge in the hunting park?"

"Yes?"

"What happened?"

"The bridge failed and killed the Lancer escort who said it was safe."

Mairena turns to Kiedron.

"I know," he says quickly. "There was the time you dragged me from the ocean just before that big wave came from nowhere and washed all the people away. And there have been more. But what—"

"That is all you need to know for the moment."

"Something awful is going to happen?" ventured Emerya.

"You will see. No more questions, especially where anyone can hear."

The second glances between brother and sister are uneasy . . . and followed by wary looks at their mother. Mairena ignores them, instead surveying the white stone of the boulevard, her eyes taking in the green awnings, most still folded up for the night, the clean white stone sidewalks and alleys. The doors to the well-kept shops are still closed in the early faint light in the half glass before sunrise.

Here and there are wagons at loading docks along the wide alleys, and there will be more in the next glass, Mairena knows.

Should you tell everyone? She shakes her head. The *Kerial* is the only substantial ship at the many white piers, except for the handful of small coastal traders and an Austran bark and a Nordlan ocean schooner. Cyador's navy has dwindled to the point where it is almost nonexistent, and while traders visit Cyador regularly, there have seldom been that many outland vessels at once in recent years, although the merchanters of Cyador remain a force, if far less than once. If people believed her, and she has doubts of that, the few trading ships would be swamped and would save none. Nor would they be able to get under way quickly enough, not under sail with the still air that cloaks the city. And those she has summoned will more than tax the capacity of the *Kerial*. *If you are even right.* Yet how can she disregard what she has seen, seen with a preternatural clarity?

At the boulevard that fronts the harbor, the coach turns eastward. Mairena can see several other coaches ahead of them, also hurrying toward the third pier, the one where the *Kerial* waits. Those coaches are halted by the Lancers stationed at the foot of the pier, who make room for the Imperial coach to pass. Even in passing Mairena can sense, as healers usually do, the worry and concern emanating from the women in the coaches, for there are few full Magi'i left in Cyad, not after Lephi's

demands for Magi'i support in his war against the barbarians—
and the dreadful dark angels, whose powers Lephi has treated
dismissively all too often.

Farther along the pier, more Mirror Lancers stand waiting,
in excess of a full company. That they have not been allowed to
board is a situation Mairena had feared. Still, they are present,
and behind them are a score of Magi'i families. Then there are
the student Magi'i, doubtless puzzled at why they are standing
on a pier before sunrise. The Lancers of the duty company move
aside at the command of Captain Altyrn and allow the driver
to bring the Imperial coach to a halt opposite the gangway
from the white stone pier to the *Kerial*.

Standing short of the gangway is Tyrsalyn, although Mairena is not certain how he has managed to notify as many Magi'i
and families as stand behind the Mirror Lancers and still reach
the pier before her.

Always dependable, reflects Mairena.

"Wait here in the coach until I summon you," she directs
Kiedron and Emerya. "It won't be that long."

When she steps onto the pier, she surveys the *Kerial*, an
impressive vessel with a white metal hull that stretches more
than a hundred yards from end to end, with twin stacks. While
the firecannon has not been tested, its forward turret does not
appear unfinished, and there are four iron-shuttered gun ports
spaced evenly just forward of the middle of the deck below the
main deck. *The gun deck*. There are four ports on the far side as
well, all for weapons not constructed or used in generations,
unsurprisingly, given the effort it has taken to create just the
guns for the *Kerial*.

Unfortunately, she can also see that the gangway is barred
by a pair of armed ship's marines. That is hardly surprising. For
the moment, Mairena ignores the marines and turns to Tyrsalyn. "Third Magus, you've done wonders . . . again."

"Is that not the task of the Magi'i?" His voice is dry.

"Now we must persuade Captain Heisyrt to cooperate."

"He does not know?"

"He has written orders to have the *Kerial* ready to depart on a moment's notice." *That was the best I could manage.*

"I see."

Mairena suspects Tyrsalyn understands too well, but the Empress and the Third Magus step toward the gangway.

As she nears the ship, Mairena can see the perspiration on the brows of the ship's marines who bar the gangway. "You'd best summon the captain."

"The captain is otherwise occupied," states an officer who moves down the gangway and stands behind the marines.

Mairena sees the linked silver bars, suggesting, if the insignia means the same as it does for the Mirror Lancers, that he is a relatively junior officer.

"Lieutenant," offers Tyrsalyn firmly, "if anyone is going to deny the Empress of Light permission to board, it had best be the captain, don't you think?"

The junior officer's eyes widen. He starts to speak, closes his mouth, and finally states, "I'll send word."

Before he can turn, another figure walks down the gangway, a dark-haired officer wearing the silver starburst insignia on his uniform collars. The lieutenant moves back and lets the older officer pass, as do the marines. The senior officer's eyes take in the Third Magus and then Mairena. "Empress . . . I have not expected a visitation from you. Nor did I know that the *Kerial* was open to visitation."

"It is not," replies Mairena politely. "Your task, Captain Heisyrt, is to allow the Mirror Lancers and the others summoned to board, and to then get the *Kerial* and all on board out of the harbor," states the Empress. *And we are running out of time.*

"I have no orders, Lady Empress." The captain's voice is

firm, and she can sense his resolve . . . also the sense that he will not take orders from a woman . . . unless forced.

Still . . . she will try, if briefly. "You had written orders from the Emperor to have the *Kerial* ready to leave port at any time. Why would you have such orders if they were not needful?"

"I report to the Marshal and the Emperor. I have received no orders to leave Cyad, and the firecannon has not been tested."

"You would ignore the written orders of the Emperor?" she asks gently.

"They do not specify . . ."

Seeing and sensing that nothing short of force will suffice, Mairena turns to Tyrsalyn. "If he does not comply in ten counts, turn him to ash. We have no time for niceties or orders that will not come. The life of the heir to the Malachite Throne is at stake."

Tyrsalyn turns to Heisyrt. "Will you obey the Empress . . . or will you die?"

The captain swallows. "I will comply, if under protest."

"That is a good choice," offers Mairena warmly. "I can promise you will not regret it. If you would escort the Third Magus and me to the bridge so that you can make ready for immediate departure."

"As you wish." Heisyrt's voice is polite, but his eyes are hard.

Mairena turns and calls, "Captain Altyrn, begin loading, with the heirs, if you would, then the Mirror Lancers. Do not worry about stowing gear. Just get everyone aboard as quickly as possible."

"Yes, Lady Empress," returns the Lancer officer.

"You are in haste. That is not wise in getting a vessel ready for sea," says Heisyrt.

"Except when one faces a storm that will cast every vessel

in the harbor upon the rocks," replies the Empress. "To the bridge."

Heisyrt glances to the clear skies to the south, out over the Southern Ocean.

"You will see," promises the Empress.

"You said the heir . . . ?"

"Kiedron is in the coach."

The captain turns and addresses the junior officer. "Lieutenant, prepare to cast off once the loading is complete. Send word to fire all remaining idle boilers. Then escort the heir to the Emperor's stateroom."

"Yes, ser."

Heisyrt then leads the way up the gangway, his steps measured.

After climbing metal ladders up three decks, Mairena is more than glad she has worn riding gear and boots. The covered bridge sits forward of the first stack, overlooking the firecannon turret. Before she follows the captain onto the bridge, Mairena looks back down at the pier, then nods as she sees the Mirror Lancers, packs on their backs, filing up the gangway.

She slips through the open hatchway onto the bridge, her eyes on Heisyrt.

The captain reaches for the engine bellpull, then jerks it twice. "I've sent the order for all boilers to be bit lit off and brought up to full power."

"How long before they are?" asks Mairena.

"It will take another quarter glass for them to be at full power. They should be ready by the time all the Mirror Lancers . . . and the others . . . are aboard."

Mairena glances toward the Palace of Light, studies it, trying to compare what she sees to what she has seen. *There is some time. Let us hope it is enough.*

As she waits, every few moments Mairena walks to the pier

side of the bridge. After a tenth of a glass, when it appears that everyone is aboard, or at least there is no one on the pier except for Captain Altyrn, she steps back through the hatchway onto the top of the ladder and calls, as loudly as she can, "Captain Altyrn!"

The captain looks up, finally locating her, and she gestures for him to board. Once he is on the gangway, she re-enters the bridge and looks to Captain Heisyrt. "It's time to leave."

Heisyrt nods to a seaman at the end of the bridge, and a series of whistles fill the air, followed by the clanging of a bell somewhere below the bridge.

Mairena watches and listens.

"Cast off all lines!"

"Gangway up!"

Heisyrt gives the engine bellpull a quick series of pulls, followed by a pause and a single pull.

Although the Empress can feel a muted shuddering in the plates beneath her boots, for several moments nothing seems to happen . . . except she realizes that the *Kerial* is easing forward and away from the long white stone pier.

"To where do you wish us to be bound right now?" asks Heisyrt.

"To the Western Ocean. Head directly to sea along the deepest channel."

"That is not the course best steered . . ."

"The deepest channel," repeats Mairena.

"That will take longer, if haste is necessary."

"I understand. The deepest channel, please."

"Left two points. . . . Then steady as she goes . . ."

The Empress continues to stand back from the helmsman, almost shoulder to shoulder with Captain Heisyrt. Tyrsalyn slips to the back of the covered bridge, his tired eyes moving from the Empress to the captain and back across the bridge.

After a time, perhaps a quarter glass, Kiedron appears in the hatchway through which Mairena had entered the bridge. Behind him is Emerya, and behind them a junior officer, very fresh-faced and with a single collar bar.

Mairena gestures for her children to enter the bridge and stand against the metal bulkhead that forms the rear of the superstructure. She says not a word, but turns to watch the captain and the helmsman, and the progress of the fireship away from the shore—and Cyad.

After another quarter glass, when the ship has begun to pitch slightly as it makes its way through the low waves, Mairena walks to the right side of the bridge and then through the hatchway and out onto the railed lookout's platform. She looks aft. The *Kerial* is well clear of the wide harbor, heading south-southeast, as well as Mairena can tell, perhaps three kays out, so that the structures of Cyad seem like miniatures, with the Palace of Light rising just slightly above them, barely standing out on the gentle slope that rises to the north of the harbor. At that moment, the rays of sunrise creep across the water and bathe Cyad in yellowish light that will soon turn white under the greenish-blue sky.

Soon . . . too soon.

She steps back to the hatchway and beckons to Kiedron and Emerya. "Come here, both of you." Mairena nods to Heisyrt. "You, too, Captain. Just to the lookout platform." She walks back out onto the railed lookout platform, gesturing for the other three to join her.

Tyrsalyn follows, but remains in the hatchway.

"Emerya and Kiedron, watch Cyad," commands the Empress. "Do not take your eyes off the Palace of Light, distant as it is. Especially you, Kiedron."

Kiedron looks to his sister. Emerya nods. Heisyrt frowns.

Behind them, so does Tyrsalyn.

Just as the sun's rays begin to shift from yellow to white, and the Palace of Light brightens to a greenish-white starpoint in the middle of Cyad, an unseen lance of blackness flares, enfolding Mairena in a blackness so deep she cannot see. She can feel herself falling . . .

III

Mairena wakes to find herself being held erect by Kiedron. She glances around. Emerya is white-faced, sitting on the wooden planks of the lookout platform. Tyrsalyn lies sprawled facedown across the raised lower lip of the hatchway to the bridge. Kiedron's face contains lines of strain, and he massages his forehead with his left hand, his right around his mother's waist. When he sees she is alert, he immediately releases her.

Heisyrt stares shoreward, looking back to the north, to the coastline.

Mairena steadies herself on the railing and also looks northward.

Where Cyad and the Palace of Light had stood, there is only a wall of darkness and dust. In every direction, the land is still shaking, and in many places, chunks of cliffs are toppling into the water. Spikes of dust spray into the air. Lower areas of land slump into the water, and yet, well off the shore south of the harbor, a long and low isle of land slowly rises out of the sea.

Even as Mairena watches, the harbor floor appears, as if the harbor and the channel are being drained. Then an enormous wall of water surges toward the ruins of Cyad, pouring over the piers and the seawalls, still shuddering as they vanish under the massive wave that surges up the gentle incline on which the City of Light had stood for centuries. Spray rises into the air, mixing with darkness and dust.

The captain studies the waves, then abruptly turns and commands, "Bring her two points to port! Now! Then steady on that heading." Then he vaults over the prone form of Tyrsalyn and through the hatchway onto the bridge.

"Coming port, ser!"

The *Kerial* has barely straightened on the new heading when the ship pitches abruptly forward into a deep trough in the waves, a trough that races southward away from the fireship as water sprays across the forequarter. For several moments, the entire ship shudders, although Mairena does not know why.

She forces herself to look back at where Cyad had stood.

The water again recedes and bares the harbor floor, but the white stone piers have dropped so that only their upper surface is visible—and only for a time, until a second gigantic wave surges over them and over the debris that had been a great city.

Shortly, the *Kerial* pitches forward once more, if not quite so steeply as previously, and the shuddering lasts only moments before ending.

By now, the entire coastline is shrouded in mist and dust and darkness, and there is no sign of Cyad . . . or the white stone piers of the harbor.

From the decks below come cries of despair, wailing, and loudly voiced questions, some against the Rational Stars . . . and others which Mairena chooses to ignore. *You did what you could.* Even as she believes that to be true, she cannot help but wonder.

After a time, less than a quarter glass, Heisyrt returns to the lookout station, easing past Emerya, who is attempting to use her healing skills to rouse the Third Magus, who has begun to moan and mumble.

Heisyrt looks squarely at the Empress. "Why didn't you tell everyone?"

"You didn't believe me. Why would anyone else? I had

visions. Nothing more. I had another this morning. I was guessing that it would occur this morning. What else could I have done, Captain? Were there any other ships that could have escaped in time? With no wind? As it is, those aboard will likely tariff your stores." She pauses. "Had I been wrong . . . I would have been disgraced . . . possibly executed for commandeering the fireship." Then she looks at the captain. "Would you have risked what I did on a vision, Captain?"

After a long moment, Heisyrt's eyes drop. Finally, he asks, "What happened?"

"I don't know," she answers honestly. "I only know that whatever it was came with a bolt of order, something so powerful I have never sensed its like."

She looks down, sensing that the fallen Third Magus has recovered enough to offer what he may have felt.

With Emerya's help, Tyrsalyn slowly rises to his feet, then puts out a hand to steady himself on the nearest railing. He moistens his lips. Finally, he speaks, slowly and deliberately. "In all my life . . . I have . . . never . . . felt such power. It was like the Accursed Forest, but . . . a hundredfold stronger . . . perhaps even more than that." He swallows as his eyes take in the wall of clouds and dust that have obscured the mass of debris that had, less than a glass before, been the City of Light, Glory of Cyador, and wonder of all Candar.

Mairena follows his gaze, her eyes traveling west, then back east across the northern horizon. Although a large area is blocked by the superstructure of the *Kerial*, everything that she does see is similar—devastation everywhere.

"The destruction is likely worse elsewhere," Tyrsalyn says slowly.

"Why do you say that?" asks Heisyrt.

"Because it had to come from the Accursed Forest, and it is hundreds of kays to the east."

"You said it was stronger than the forest," pointed out Kiedron.

"I did . . . but it could be nothing else . . . although . . ."

"Although what?" demands Kiedron.

"There was some other order as well . . . a different kind of blackness . . ."

"The dark angels?" suggests Mairena.

"They might have involved the Accursed Forest . . . ," muses Tyrsalyn.

"How?" asks Emerya.

"I do not know." The Third Magus glances back northward. "The greatest force was, I think, directed at where chaos was the most powerful."

Emerya looks to her mother. "Father . . ."

"Most of the strong Magi'i were near your father," observes Tyrsalyn.

"You will likely be holder of the Malachite Throne, Kiedron, sooner than any of us thought," says the Empress, "although we shall see." She inclines her head to Heisyrt.

Still ashen-faced, Heisyrt turns to Mairena. "My apologies, Lady Empress. It is just that . . ."

"I understand, Captain. I do." *For you also must have lost those near and dear . . . and then, who would believe the visions of a mere woman, even those of an Empress and a healer?*

After a long moment, Heisyrt asks, "What are your orders, Lady?"

"We should see if there are other Cyadoran vessels near . . . and see the extent of the destruction. If the devastation is as vast as I fear it is, then we should consider setting a course for Swartheld—"

"Swartheld? What about other cities in Cyador?"

"The Accursed Forest has already spread beyond its bounds and is growing by more than a kay a day because all the white wizards who could control it had been sent to fight the barbarians—and the dark angels—in the northeast." She does not say "Lornth," not after Lephi's reactions, although she knows in her heart that he, too, has fallen to the power that has destroyed Cyad and Cyador. Mairena gestures. "I fear all is like that." She pauses. "We should still travel the coast, in case I am mistaken."

"I fear you may not be, Empress," replies Heisyrt, "but it is our duty to do what we can."

Mairena nods. Abruptly, she feels drained, as if all her strength has flowed out of her and into the ocean that surrounds the *Kerial*. She puts out a hand to the railing.

"If you will excuse me, Empress . . ."

"Captain . . . I would not keep you."

Once Heisyrt has left and re-entered the bridge, Kiedron looks to his mother. "If all is like this, why Swartheld? Why not Austra? It is far closer."

"Hamor is the weakest of the other continents. You are the heir, Kiedron. In a few years, if not in months, most of Cyador will be claimed by the Accursed Forest. Where else can you re-establish the Malachite Throne?"

"The Accursed Forest cannot—"

"It already has," interjects Tyrsalyn, his voice raspy and tired. "Earlier last spring, the forest overran the old wards and overgrew the towns close to the walls. Almost all of the strongest white wizards were trying to hold it close to the old bounds. They were failing, even before your father the Emperor called them away to destroy the barbarians . . ."

"Why?" asks Emerya plaintively. "Why . . . why did it happen? Why did it all happen now?"

No one answers her plaint.

Mairena looks toward Cyad, but all that she can see is towering dark clouds that rise from the shore and the waters beyond . . . and cloak everything—except for the flashes of lightning that flare intermittently.

IV

When Mairena wakes in the gray gloom, for a moment she does not know where she is. She lifts her head and glances around. She lies in a wide double bed, in a room with little more than an armoire fastened to the paneled wall. *Bulkhead*, she corrects herself as she sees the portholes and the memories of the disasters of threeday flood over her. She shudders, then forces herself to sit up.

The Emperor's quarters on the *Kerial* are spacious for a vessel, but cramped by any other standard, reflects Mairena. There is a modest sitting room, or cabin, little more than four yards by five, which holds a rectangular center table and chairs. There are two armchairs for reading and a small desk built into a corner. Off the sitting room are three sleeping chambers, one with the large bed from which Mairena rises, and two others barely large enough for beds that might accommodate two if neither man nor woman happened to be particularly large, with an even smaller washroom/jakes off the sitting room. There is also an adjoining cabin—if a space barely large enough for two bunks, one above the other, can be called that—for servants, occupied at the moment just by Viera.

After washing up, Mairena dresses quietly in the same riding clothes and boots she had worn the day before, then eases back into the main cabin. From what she can tell, both Kiedron and Emerya continue to sleep in their quarters. She does not see Viera. She crosses the room, avoiding the heavy table bolted to the deck, opens the door-shaped hatch out onto the open second-level deck on the port side of the *Kerial*, steps out into a cool wind, closes the hatch softly, and walks to the railing. She looks out over the water.

Fourday has barely dawned, if darkly, with endless gray covering the sky. The ocean waters that will look a deep blue green in full sunlight appear leaden gray. The wind whips her copper-red hair, its silver strands concealed with an order-based tint, across her neck and back, and she twists it into a rough knot at the back of her neck. *Viera would scarcely approve.*

The coast, perhaps three kays away, looks as desolate as all that they had passed the day before. It is difficult to tell how much reflects the way it had been or whether the shore had been battered by the same type of waves that had swallowed Cyad, but there are no indications of any habitation. She does not expect otherwise, especially since the part of Cyador they now pass was largely grassland before the devastation. In another day or two, they should reach the coastal towns to the west of Fyrad, and that will likely determine their eventual destination. *A destination you know, but one that Heisyrt will have to come to accept.*

She can but hope that it will not take him too long to accept the inevitable.

She smiles ruefully at the thought of dealing with the captain, then peers once more toward the land she can barely make out. The fireship is proceeding on a southeastward course, as she and Heisyrt had agreed on the previous day, toward Fyrad, at a speed that is not wasteful of the coal in the bunkers while keeping watch for other Cyadoran vessels . . . and signs of un-ruined towns or cities along the coast. None had been sighted when Mairena had gone to sleep the evening before, exhausted.

How long she looks at the featureless gray that still hovers over the land that had been Cyador, Mairena does not know, only that it cannot have been more than half a glass, if that, before a white-clad figure climbs the portside ladder and approaches. She half-turns and waits.

"Lady Empress . . . ?" offers Tyrsalyn.

"Yes, Third Magus?"

"Might I join you for a moment?"

"You may. You don't even have to be that formal," she replies with a smile.

Tyrsalyn moves to the railing, but not too close, his eyes on her. "Did you know . . . Lady? And when?"

"Know? Absolutely?" Mairena shakes her head. "No. What I told the captain was true. I had visions . . . glimpses, if you could call them that. I always have had them. Some of them seemed fanciful, but many have happened . . . as I saw them. The Emperor disregarded those I saw. In some cases, what he was told by his marshals was not anywhere close to what happened, but he chose to believe them. So, over the years, I have said less and less—except where I could do something."

"You were prepared for this?"

"Why do you ask?" she counters.

"I have made a few inquiries and observed. While you were overcome by the power of the dark angels and the Accursed Forest, you recovered more quickly, and you were not surprised. Not as much as you should have been."

"I've always been noted for my reserve, Third Magus," she replies with a touch of archness.

"That reserve has served you well." He clears his throat. "I would also note that the ship is overprovisioned for a vessel not quite fully completed . . . and other matters. Yet the captain was stunned by what he saw, and so was everyone else, including your children. Only you were calm. I ask you again . . ."

"I was as prepared as much as I could be. It was costly . . ." *Both in golds for bribes, and the extra bribes for those offering them to others, and for supplies that Lephi never knew about . . . or the orders so carefully forged and sent amid other orders.*

"It was also dangerous, was it not?" he asks, his voice low.

"Had Lephi or the First Magus discovered . . . yes."

"I salute you, Lady Empress."

"I did what I thought best." Rather than dwell on that, she asks, "Do you have any sense of what may have happened . . . in the northeast?"

"I have tried a glass to see what might be there, but I can see nothing, as if that dark order of the Accursed Forest covers everything. In the past, I have been able to sense the First Magus . . . and others. Now . . . there is nothing. I fear, as do you, that the Magi'i accompanying the Emperor's forces have all perished."

"Can you see anything in the glass?"

Tyrsalyn shakes his head. "I can see what is on the ship. I can see Summerdock and Dellash. They are in ruins, but they were not swallowed by the sea. Biehl was damaged, but the Jeranyi hold it now. I think they fled Jerans . . ."

And that would mean some of Jerans is also in ruins. Mairena finds herself shaking her head. "So . . . little of the cities of Cyad remains standing?"

"If what I have seen in the glass is what has happened . . ." Tyrsalyn's words are cautious.

"What would you suggest?"

"Let the captain see what does not remain of Fyrad before you press him."

"What else?"

"For now, Lady and Empress, I would also suggest a guard or two be posted at the bottom of the ladder I took to reach you. There may be some who will not look upon your actions with complete favor."

"I do not doubt it. They will want to demand why I could not warn everyone or save more. I only knew it would happen before winter. I did not know *when* until the moment I woke early yesterday morning. Preparing for something that *may* be . . .

and may not be . . . in a way that leaves few traces is . . . diffi-cult." *Especially for a woman in Cyador, even an Empress.*

"I imagine it is difficult when every move you make is observed."

"No . . . only every move that is suspect for a woman." *And that will change.*

"It is said that a land survives by its traditions, Lady."

"Until those traditions fail it, Third Magus," Mairena replies with a polite smile. "Some of those traditions might be left in the destruction."

Tyrsalyn inclines his head. "You would know best which those should be."

"Together we should discuss such once we know our course."

"I remain at your service, and at that of the heir."

"Who will likely have to play a different role, and who will need the support of both of us."

"I do stand ready to support him . . . and you, Lady."

Because you can see no other course. "Thank you."

The sky lightens slowly after the Third Magus departs, but the clouds remain thick enough that Mairena cannot make out the position of the sun. She turns to see Viera step out onto the open deck.

"Lady, I have arranged for breakfast for the three of you," offers the petite dark-haired maid who has served Mairena for almost fifteen years.

Mairena smiles. "I take it that you're telling me that it is ready and getting cold."

"That is possible, Lady."

"Do I need to wake anyone?"

"Lady Emerya is awake and dressed."

That Kiedron is not is not exactly unexpected.

"Rap soundly on Kiedron's door and tell him it is time to eat."

"I did, Lady."

"Thank you." Mairena re-enters the sitting room, noting the three platters on the table, then turns to Viera. "Did you take some for yourself, I hope?"

"Some, Lady."

"You are to take what you need."

Viera nods.

Mairena watches until Viera does so. Then she walks to the narrow door to Kiedron's sleeping chamber and opens it. Only the main sleeping chamber has an inside bolt on it, as specifically ordered by Lephi. Mairena offers a bitter smile as she recalls that, then stands in the open door. "Kiedron, get up. Now."

"Why do I have to get up now? It's not as though there's anywhere to go." Kiedron turns toward her and yawns.

"If you want to eat, you'll join us. The ship is likely over-crowded as it is, and the cooks won't have time to fix special meals for you. You won't get a chance to eat again until late this afternoon. The galley can only handle two meals a day for as many as are on board."

"But . . ."

Mairena looks hard at her son, willing him not to say anything about being the heir . . . or possibly even the Lord of Cyador.

Kiedron stiffens, as though he can sense her unspoken command. His mouth opens, then closes. "I'll be there in a moment." His voice is flat, just short of sullen.

"Please arrive in a pleasant mood, a very pleasant mood." Mairena offers a warm smile she does not feel, yet one that is near-effortless, after all the years of practice. "You need to set a good example for others." She steps back and closes the door, with a gentleness she does not feel.

As Mairena settles herself at the head of the table, Emerya murmurs, "He still does not understand."

"Then we must make sure that he does," replies Mairena in an equally low voice, addressing herself to the bowl that contains some sort of warm and bittersweet concoction that is most likely gruel or porridge. The egg toast is too brown, but better, and the tea is barely warm.

Slightly later, while Mairena sips her tea, the door to Kiedron's sleeping quarters opens, and he steps out into the sitting room. "A good morning, Mother . . . Sister," he offers in a falsely cheerful voice. He wears the same uniform greens of a Mirror Lancer officer trainee he had worn on threeday, but without the jacket, and his hair is unkempt. He slumps into the chair across the table from his sister.

"My . . . what a sight," observes Emerya.

"You're not exactly a formal image," replies her brother.

"None of us are likely to be dressed formally for some time," Mairena says. *If ever, should matters go astray.*

"What *is* this?" asks Kiedron, looking down at his platter, then at his sister, and finally at Mairena.

"Breakfast," replies Mairena.

"Thick porridge with a dash of molasses and grilled egg toast," Viera finally says. "I persuaded the cooks to add the molasses."

Kiedron looks down even more dubiously than the first time. "I'm supposed to eat this?"

"If you don't want to go hungry," his mother replies. "It's likely no worse than what you would have been eating at Kynstaar."

"And the company is better," adds Emerya, straight-faced.

"The tea is cold," says Kiedron.

"It would have been warmer had you arisen when others did," says the Empress.

Kiedron looks from his mother to his sister. "Father wouldn't let you two talk to me like that."

"Your father seldom liked to hear anything that was not to his liking, however true it might be. That has been a failing of recent emperors. It's one you cannot afford. Too much has happened that is not to your liking. Even more will happen, if we survive."

"If we survive?" Kiedron's voice is close to incredulous.

"You're saying Father is dead . . . aren't you?" asks Emerya.

"We don't know that for certain, but the Third Magus fears that all the Magi'i near your father and his forces are dead."

"He could still be alive."

"If he is, it will be weeks, if not seasons, before we know. We may never know."

"We could ride to find him."

"On what? It did not appear that any of the great roads out of Cyad survived. The Third Magus can find no traces of any Cyadoran city in his glass. None. You had best eat before it gets colder."

Kiedron scowls, but does begin to eat, if reluctantly.

After they have eaten, although the three still remain at the table, the Empress beckons to Viera.

"Yes, Lady?"

"If you would find Captain Altyrn of the Mirror Lancers. I would see him at his earliest convenience." While Mairena would prefer to seek out Captain Altyrn herself, she knows it is wiser to send Viera.

Once Viera has departed through the main door into the center passageway, Mairena looks at Emerya, then Kiedron. "There will be some necessary changes immediately. More may be required later."

"If something has happened to Father, I'm the Lord of Cyador. Isn't that so?" asks Kiedron.

"If he has indeed perished, you will be his successor," replies the Empress. "Once you are of age."

"I should be now, if he's gone. There's no Regency Council."

"But there is," says Mairena. "Two of the three members of the Regency Council are the First Magus and the Empress. Who is likely First Magus now? That is, if anything has happened to your father?"

"Oh . . . I had not thought of that."

"Kiedron," Mairena says in a low but firm voice, "there is much about which you have not thought. You will need to think through more than you ever have, and you will need more training."

"Training?" Her son's voice is wary.

"You need to learn to handle a blade far better than you do. That was one reason"—*one of many*—"why your father was sending you to Kynstaar. You still need that training, and that is something you can do aboard the *Kerial*."

"I suppose so."

"Kiedron. There are two companies of Mirror Lancers aboard. Just two. They may be the last Mirror Lancers in all Cyador. You need to be worthy to command them. That requires more training. You will need to study many things that you would have learned at Kynstaar, but we will find those aboard who can help you learn."

"What about people in Fyrad or Syadtar or Guarstyad or Summerdock? Or other towns?"

"It is likely the destruction at Fyrad is even worse than at Cyad," replies the Empress. "It is far closer to the Accursed Forest."

"And don't say that you haven't thought of that," adds Emerya tartly before Kiedron can speak. "You can't ever use those words again."

Mairena manages to conceal her surprise at her daughter's comment and adds, "I'm afraid Emerya is correct, Kiedron. A young man who will be a ruler cannot ever afford to appear thoughtless. That is a luxury of youth that you have just had taken from you."

Viera steps into the cabin through the corridor hatchway. "Captain Altyrn will be here shortly, Lady."

"Thank you. How are our inadvertent passengers faring?"

"The Mirror Lancers are well settled. The Magi'i families and students are . . . less settled."

"There should be some spaces for them. The fireship does not have a full crew." *Not close to a battle crew.*

"The Mirror Lancers have taken the spaces for the ship's marines. The others are where the crew settled them. It is cramped."

"We will all feel more cramped before this is over, I fear." Mairena rises from the table, steps away from it, and waits.

Kiedron does not look at either his mother or his sister.

Before long, the Mirror Lancer captain enters the stateroom, inclining his head to Mairena, then to Kiedron.

"If you would join me on the deck, Captain." Mairena leads the way, but says nothing more until the two of them stand alone on the windy deck under the heavy gray clouds, with the hatch to the stateroom closed. "Thank you for coming so quickly. I expect that you have had many demands on your time, and I fear I will make yet another, or at least a task for you to oversee."

"Lady Empress?"

"It may be necessary for Lord Kiedron to lead troopers. He was to be sent to Kynstaar. That is not possible. Even if events do not necessitate such leadership, he needs to learn how to handle a blade far better than he does, if only to understand what is required of Lancers. He has had training. It will not be sufficient. He must be pushed to his limits, until the blade is part of him."

The older captain nods slowly. "I can see the necessity. He is the heir. Will he be willing?"

"He believes he is. He is not. He will be willing. I must talk to him first, but I thought it might take some time for you to consider and work out the best way for him to learn. He also needs to learn about tactics. We are likely to have some eight-days before . . . what may come."

"That is not much time . . ."

"He *will* learn, Captain." Mairena's voice softens. "I am not placing on you the need for him to have that will. That is between him and me." She can sense the captain's doubt, but she merely adds, "It will be so."

Altyrn inclines his head. "I will see to it and inform you."

"Thank you."

"I also have posted a guard at the foot of the ladder. I hope he will not be necessary."

"Again . . . my thanks."

The captain bows, then makes his way down the ladder.

V

After breakfast on fiveday, Mairena looks across the sitting room table at Kiedron. "Your blade tutor will be here shortly."

"I still don't see the hurry in this," he replies.

"Do healers start to learn healing the day of battle?" asks Mairena. "Or after someone sickens?"

"I know that," replies Kiedron in an exasperated tone, "but it's not as though I'm going to be going into battle."

"Haven't you heard a word I've said?" Mairena glares at her son. "I'm not talking about battles. I'm talking about your being able to defend yourself. Your father and your grandsire, and every Emperor after Lorn, who was the last to actually take the throne with both blade and chaos, had armies to protect themselves. Regardless of what happens, you won't. There are exactly two companies of Mirror Lancers here, and they'll be hard-pressed to defend the ship and the Magi'i families on board. Besides, you need to get in the habit of working."

"What about you?"

"You don't think it was work saving you both? You think that the ship being ready, with a boiler fired at all times, just happened?"

"You arranged this? You didn't tell Father? You did it behind his back?"

"I told him." *You told him as much as you could, without him flying into a rage.* "He dismissed what I saw as the dreams of a frightened and weak woman." Mairena smiles coldly. "Do you, my son, want to follow his example?"

"I can't believe—"

"Father has never listened to Mother or me," interjects Emerya. "What's worse is that he didn't even notice that he didn't."

"You could have told the First Magus."

"I tried. He was too frightened of your father. Triendar tried to reason with your father, but he was ignored as well. And don't tell me that the honorable Major-Commander Quaeras, the fearless leader of the Mirror Lancers, would ever listen to a mere woman, who avoided the most high and signal honor of wearing chains only because she was a healer." Mairena does not bother to hide the blazing sarcasm of her words.

"Father never made you wear them," Kiedron points out.

"He did insist that I wear the gold-and-malachite bracelet of a healer." *Which was just a different way of making the same point.*

"That's different."

Emerya raises a single eyebrow, an expression Mairena has never been able to duplicate, a fact that has pleased and amused Emerya more than once. Kiedron is so focused on his mother that he does not notice.

At that moment, there is a single sharp rap on the stateroom door. Viera moves from where she had been seated in the small chair in the corner to the door, where she raises the peephole shutter. "It is Captain Altyrn, Lady."

"Have him enter."

Altyrn steps into the sitting room and inclines his head to the Empress. He is alone and wears the working greens of a Lancer. He also carries two wooden wands shaped like sabres.

"I had not expected . . . ," offers Mairena, moving forward.

"There is little else I can do at the moment, and who else is better qualified to spar with Lord Kiedron to see what will best improve his ability with a sabre? He cannot practice all day, but a glass in the morning and another in the afternoon should afford him a good start. Undercaptain Terazyl will help him with tactics of small units, and he and I will work with Lord Kiedron on logistics and other matters."

"Lord Kiedron and I appreciate your willingness to do this." Mairena refrains from casting a sidelong glance at her son, hoping he will be gracious.

After the barest hesitation Kiedron says, "I do indeed, although I fear I have much to learn."

"We all do," replies the captain. "I had thought the side deck. It is wide enough and long enough . . . and . . . secluded."

"That might be best." Kiedron's tone is suitably wry.

"I would also suggest just wearing an undertunic, ser," added Altyrn. "Sparring practice warms one up."

"Just a moment." Kiedron steps into his sleeping room and removes his green shirt, then returns.

Once the two men leave the sitting room for the side deck, Mairena closes the hatch, then watches through the porthole nearest the hatch, as Altyrn removes his outer shirt as well and folds it over the railing. For several moments, Altyrn asks questions, and Kiedron answers. Although Mairena cannot hear either questions or answers, she continues to watch as both men take their positions. Kiedron, at a prompt from the captain, lifts his wand. In only a few moments, Kiedron's wand is on the deck.

Pick it up. Mairena does not voice the comment, but purses her lips.

Slowly, all too slowly, Kiedron does so. The Mirror Lancer captain says something. Kiedron stiffens for a moment, then nods. As the two resume the sparring exercise, Mairena slowly releases breath she had not realized she was holding.

Again, after several moments, the captain disarms Kiedron. This time, the young man reclaims his wand quickly and immediately takes what Mairena sees as a defensive posture. Altyrn nods. After several engagements, which reveal to Mairena that the captain is indeed accomplished—or at least far more so than her son—Kiedron again loses his weapon.

This time, Altyrn steps up beside Kiedron and positions him, then shows a move in slow motion, directing the younger man to follow his example.

After a time, when she can watch no longer, although Emerya still watches from the adjacent porthole, Mairena crosses the sitting room and leaves by the main entrance. She walks forward along the center passageway to the hatch leading out to the covered but open deck directly beneath and slightly forward of the bridge. The air is warmer, and the sky a lighter gray than it had been on fourday.

She glances forward over the turret that holds the untested firecannon, although none could tell that merely by appearance, a fact that Mairena hopes will prove useful in the seasons and years ahead. Supposedly, behind two gunports are smaller firecannons that work—at least at times. The water has calmed, and the *Kerial* almost seems to glide through the low waves that appear grayish green.

Mairena catches sight of a sail ahead, slightly to port, but the ship, likely a merchanter, does not alter course toward the *Kerial*. In fact, as she watches, the distant ship begins to turn to the west, out into the Southern Ocean, as if to avoid the *Kerial*. She wonders what the master of the fleeing ship thought when he caught sight of the strange vessel, so unlike anything that has sailed the Southern Ocean in generations.

How long she watches the fleeing merchanter, she does not know, not exactly, but it is likely close to a glass because the sails of the other ship are barely visible off the starboard forequarter when someone clears his throat behind her.

"Lady Empress?"

Mairena turns to face the Lancer captain. His green shirt is draped over his forearm, and his undertunic is soaked. "Yes, Captain? How did it go?"

"He is better than I hoped . . . but he has much to learn to meet your expectations."

"It is not a matter of my expectations, Captain. It is a matter of his survival."

Altyrn inclines his head, but does not speak, merely offering a pleasant smile.

"I assume that one of the functions that Kynstaar served was to make that point to sons of the Magi'i and Mirror Lancers who persevered and went on to become officers."

"I would not disagree with your observation."

"Then you will continue to press him?"

"Most assuredly. The task will be to make him angry enough to press himself without demanding more than he thinks he is capable of."

"While you increase the demands bit by bit?"

The captain nods.

"Thank you."

"In turn, I will thank you. Many will not." Altyrn's smile is rueful. "I had no consort to lose, unlike many on board."

"I appreciate that. I fear you are right, and that unhappiness will begin to show itself in the days ahead."

After Altyrn leaves, Mairena again surveys the calm sea, so at odds with the gray clouds that are beginning to lift from the ravaged land that had been Cyador. *And that will never be called such again.*

VI

Early on eightday morning, not long after dawn, Mairena stands at the railing of the deck off the stateroom quarters as the *Kerial* makes its way past a rounded cape. Somehow, it is familiar, although it has been years since she sailed from Cyad to Fyrad with Lephi . . . and that was a time when he was but the heir, a ruler-to-be with great dreams, and very much in love—*or lust*—with her.

How much life changes . . . As she half-watches the coast, not nearly so devastated as the shores nearer to Cyad, she considers those changes, how some, such as her life with Lephi, are gradual and how others, like the devastation that struck Cyador, are brutally swift. *And neither has been favorable.* She also wonders why some emperors, like Lorn and Alyiakal, who faced decline, were able to reverse that trend, while Lephi, for all his efforts, was not. *Is it the times or the man? Were the circumstances more favorable? Or were their consorts more able? More supportive?*

After a brief time, she glances back at the cape. Could it be Cape South? If so . . . what has happened to the tall spire that graced the top of the hill? Or is she mistaken? It has been so long . . . and so much has happened.

A few moments later, hearing the slightest sound of footsteps, and order-sensing the approach of someone, Mairena turns to see Captain Heisyrt approaching. "Good morning, Captain."

"Good morning, Empress. We have passed Cape South," says Heisyrt. "Did you notice?"

"I thought the cape was familiar, but I was not certain. I did not see the spire."

"Nor did I, but it is Cape South nonetheless. Everything else matches the charts . . . and I have sailed this way too many times not to know it. What the Accursed Forest did must have toppled the spire. After hundreds of years . . . it is gone."

Mairena nods. *Gone . . . like everything the Magi'i built over centuries, wiped out in an instant.*

"One can hope that some shred of Fyrad remains . . . or some other city."

"One can hope," agrees Mairena, knowing full well the ambiguity of her words, even as she knows the likely falsity of that hope.

"I must hope until it is proven false." Heisyrt inclines his head to the Empress. "Until later, Lady."

"Until later, Captain."

After Heisyrt has departed, climbing the ladder up to the bridge, Mairena again studies the coast, not that she expects to see much, for there had been no towns and villages immediately east of Cape South even before the devastation. *Is there less destruction on the land here because there were fewer towns?* She has no answer to her own question.

Some short time later, Viera slips out the side hatch and walks quietly to the Empress. "Lady . . ."

"I presume you're telling me that breakfast, such as it is, awaits us. Is Kiedron up?"

"Yes, Lady. Both he and Lady Emerya are awake."

"And your place is also set at the table?" Mairena's voice is firm.

"Yes, Lady."

"Have you heard anything I should know?" Mairena asks.

"Very little, Lady," replies Viera. "Some of the women are asking the Lancer captain and the ship's officers when they will be able to return to Cyad."

"Didn't they see what happened?"

"Some think that you created an illusion."

"I'm not a chaos magus, and healers can't do that." Mairena shook her head. "If Fyrad is also destroyed . . . will that convince them?"

"Some . . . perhaps."

"Hasn't seeing the devastation along the coast, day after day, given them some thought that it cannot be an illusion?" The Empress shakes her head sadly. "I suppose the destruction of everything one thought imperishable is too much to bear."

"And you, Lady?" asks Viera. "How are you bearing up?"

Mairena is struck by the kindness in the voice of the younger woman, although Viera is less than ten years her junior, so struck that it takes her several moments to reply. "Better than most, I think." *The result of fewer illusions, no doubt. Oh, Lephi . . . how did it ever come to this?* After a moment, she asks, "What about you, Viera?"

"The same as you, Lady. I had few who knew me, and I lost none who cared."

Few who knew Viera, thinks Mairena, *and how many really know you, especially as a person, and not as the Empress of Light? Or love you?* Lephi had, once, too many years before. She almost shakes her head. "We'd better join them. Poor breakfasts are even poorer when cold."

When Mairena enters the stateroom, she sees that Viera has set a place for herself, but on the side where Emerya sits, with an empty chair between her and the young healer.

For now . . . that will do. Mairena seats herself at the head of the table, knowing that Lephi would be outraged. *Except you don't have to worry about that.* That thought is accompanied by a feeling of sadness, made sharper by her recollection of the happier times that had been . . . if years ago.

Mairena seats herself at the head of the table, and Viera slips into her place silently. In moments, both her son and daughter appear. Emerya says nothing as she seats herself.

"More peasant porridge," mutters Kiedron, wrinkling his nose.

"It won't hurt you," replies the Empress, "and it might give you a better understanding of what most people eat."

"I understand—"

"Kiedron . . . please think before you speak." Mairena's measured words are iron hard, but hold a hint of exasperation.

"I didn't finish what I was going to say."

"You didn't have to," interjects Emerya.

Kiedron glares at her.

His sister ignores him, taking a mouthful of the grayish porridge.

Mairena thinks about saying more, but decides against doing so. She eats silently.

Not long after they finish eating, Captain Altyrn arrives. The Empress refuses to go to the porthole to watch Captain Altyrn instruct her son, much as she would like to see how he fares. Instead, she forces herself to concentrate on how she might best accomplish her aims in the days ahead. She does look up from the armchair where she has been sitting when Kiedron re-enters the stateroom.

Her son's undertunic is soaked, and he drops, rather than sits, into one of the chairs by the stateroom table.

"How did your session with Captain Altyrn go?" asks Mairena.

"I'm getting better. I can tell that, but I still can't lay a blade on him."

"He has a lifetime of practice."

"But he's getting *old*," replies Kiedron. "He's got gray hair."

"Aren't older Magi'i still powerful? Aren't older healers better healers? Why shouldn't an older Mirror Lancer still be good?"

"But I'm soaked, and he's just damp."

"That's technique, dear. He knows the blade so well that he doesn't have to work as hard as you do. In time, if you keep working, it won't take as much effort for you, either."

"How much time?" asks her son sardonically.

"As much time as it takes. That is the way with everything, you'll discover. It's one thing your father never understood."

"Nothing comes to those who wait," is his rejoinder.

"That is not what I said. Nor what I meant. Some things take longer. Some take less. A ruler must have the skill to determine which. The captain has practiced with a blade for years, but most likely not that much at one time, except perhaps when he was your age. If you work hard and long now you should come close to his skill in a much shorter time."

"I don't see why—"

"Kiedron, if you wish to be a ruler of anything, you must show that you are a leader. With Cyad gone, you cannot lead just because your father was Emperor. The more skills you can show, the more likely people will follow you. You need the Mirror Lancers to make sure they do and to protect the people whom you wish to lead. The Lancers respect skill with weapons. Do you understand?" Mairena's voice hardens with the last words.

"That's also why you can't say stupid things," adds Emerya. "You haven't learned a thing from what's happened."

Mairena offers an icy look at her daughter.

"But . . ." Emerya's voice dies off.

"You two need each other. Who will protect you, Emerya, when I am gone? And who can you trust to heal you then, Kiedron? You can honestly disagree, but I will not have cruel statements between you two."

Emerya lowers her eyes for a moment, then says, "I'm sorry." She looks to her brother. "But I was right about what you can't say."

"Yes, you were." Mairena turns to her son. "You need to listen better. You also need to ask why someone agrees with you or why they disagree. A man or woman who wants something is likely to agree with the most foolish notion you express. A man who is a schemer may disagree to tempt you into rushing into a rash act because he angers you. You need to consider not only what people say, but why they say what they do."

Kiedron actually nods in response to her words.

Mairena can but hope that he has actually taken in the meaning of her words. *And hope can be such a frail reed.*

VII

Early in the afternoon on oneday, Captain Heisyrt sends the same junior officer who had escorted Emerya and Kiedron on board to request that the Empress join him on the bridge. She follows the fresh-faced undercaptain, or whatever his equivalent rank must be, up the ladder to the bridge. As soon as they enter the bridge, Heisyrt steps away from the helmsman and toward the hatchway to the port lookout's platform. Mairena follows him out onto the platform. The lookout stations himself as far from the two of them as possible.

"We are approaching Fyrad, Lady . . . or where Fyrad once

was." While Heisyrt's words are even, he looks intently at the Empress.

"You sound doubtful, Captain."

"I can see a plume of water that must be from the river, but I see no signs of the city, where it should have been, only an enormous bay surrounded by mud flats filled with fallen trees and other debris."

"Then that is what is left of Fyrad."

"You are not surprised, Empress?"

"No. Saddened to see what I have felt, but not surprised."

"What would you suggest, now?"

"We make our way to Hamor."

"Why Hamor, Lady? Why do we not land at one of the less damaged ports in Candar . . . perhaps Lydiar?" asks Heisyrt.

"And then what, Captain?" replies the Empress. "Who in all Candar would be willing to allow the heir to the Throne of Light and two companies of Mirror Lancers to set foot on their soil? And if we did fight our way to shore, how long before we are overwhelmed?"

"The same will happen in Hamor."

"It will not. We will purchase land on the Swarth River, upstream of Swartheld, and agree to defend it for the Duke of Afrit against the Heldyans and Meroweyans. He can use the golds, and we will quietly re-establish the Malachite Throne there. Unlike those in Candar, who have always chafed at the power of Cyador, the Hamorians will see little danger in a single ship, especially when that ship can hold the upper river and, by doing so, protect the lower river from river raiders coming from the south."

Heisyrt's face screws up in disbelief. "My lady . . ."

"Did I not save you and this ship . . . and all aboard?"

"I do not know that we have enough coal . . ."

"Your bunkers are full, are they not? Who do you think made sure you were provisioned and ready for sea?"

Heisyrt inclines his head in acceptance of her statement. "Still . . . there is the matter of coal . . . Hamor is not exactly near."

"Two boilers can be converted to burn wood, also," the Empress points out.

"You know much about the *Kerial*, Lady."

"I have seen all that the Emperor saw." *And likely studied it longer and with greater care.* Not that she is ever likely to say that. "And he had great foresight in having the *Kerial* built."

"Should we not see what other Cyadoran vessels may be near?"

"For a few days, perhaps," Mairena replies. While she doubts that many, if any, vessels, even Cyadoran ones, will near the *Kerial*, she knows that she will need to make some concessions to keep from turning the captain even more against her.

"That would be good. We should head back toward Cyad. We're more likely to encounter Cyadoran merchanters there."

"Then we will see," concludes the Empress.

Heisyrt nods.

Once she has left the bridge and returned to her quarters, Mairena sends Viera—who else can she dispatch?—to request that Captain Altyrn join her on the side deck, then slips from the stateroom that is a sitting room of sorts out onto the deck to wait for the Lancer officer. Her eyes drift to the large bay and the mixed swirls of muddy water, darker river water that holds the remnants of who knows what, and the blue-green waters of the Western Ocean.

In less than a quarter glass, Altyrn climbs the outside ladder and presents himself. "What do you require of me, Empress?"

"I need to address all the Magi'i and those of the Mirror

Lancers you think appropriate and tell them what has happened."

"What will that be?"

"That Cyad and Cyador are no more."

"I have feared such with each kay of devastation we have passed."

While Altyrn works with the Lancers and the crew to clear a space on the main deck, Mairena once more summons Tyrsalyn. When he arrives, she gestures toward the mixed muddied waters and the mud flats that appear to compose nearly all the land around the bay, although Mairena notices shoots of green in many places and wonders, *Trees, saplings . . . so soon.* She only asks, "Do you recognize where we are, First Magus?"

"Near or above what remains of Fyrad, if what I have seen in my glass is correct."

"What have you seen of other cities?"

"No cities remain in Cyador itself, only scattered small towns . . . and the ruins of Summerdock and Dellash."

The Empress cannot refrain from frowning. "Small towns, but nothing else?"

"I fear that the Accursed Forest and the dark angels lashed out at wherever there was chaos. Small towns often have no Magi'i."

"But Dellash . . . Summerdock . . . and the *Kerial*?"

"Water and distance diminish the effect. Dellash is on the isle. Summerdock is mostly surrounded by water and is close to the farthest point west from the Accursed Forest—"

"And the *Kerial* was in deep water?" *If barely.*

"Exactly, Lady."

"I have summoned everyone to a meeting. They also must know and come to accept what is. You will be beside me."

Tyrsalyn nods.

Almost a glass later, Mairena stands on a small platform

created from several planks laid over the top of a capstan. She faces aft and to starboard, where most of the adults from the Magi'i on board, and a handful of junior Mirror Lancer officers, have gathered. Most of the practicing Magi'i are ironmages or healers, largely women. The others are gray-bearded men, a handful of older but not elderly Magi'i, most likely instructors from the academy where young mages are taught and tested.

The Empress waits until those gathered are silent. Then she begins. "For those of you who do not already know it, the large bay with the waters of mixed colors is all that remains of Fyrad. You have also seen the destruction along the coast of what once was Cyador. This destruction has enfolded all of Cyador."

After another silence, she turns and gestures to Tyrsalyn. "First Magus, what has your glass shown of Cyad, Fyrad, or any of the great cities of Cyador?"

"All of them have vanished, as if they never existed, save for Summerdock. It lies in ruins, and few survive there."

"No!" comes a cry from one of the women in the group. "It cannot be. . . . It cannot be. . . ."

"Who would doubt the vision of the First Magus," declares the Empress, "especially since we have just seen what remains of Fyrad? Whatever there once was has sunk deep beneath the water."

To the side, Tyrsalyn nods slowly.

"In the next few days," declares Mairena, firmly and clearly, "we will decide where we should go."

"Back to Cyad!" exclaims a man.

"Cyad," echo several voices, and heads nod in agreement.

"That is where we are headed. But . . . if there is nothing there, we will have to go elsewhere." Before anyone can say anything else, she steps down off the makeshift platform. She had hoped for greater understanding, but had doubted it would be forthcoming.

VIII

A glass later, Mairena stands in her small sleeping quarters, looking at her daughter. "You have asked me, if not in words, why I have done what I have done."

"I've never said a word."

Mairena smiles, if faintly. "You didn't have to." She extends a deep-green enameled box.

Emerya takes it, looking down. "What is it?"

"The answer, in part, to your unspoken question. Go ahead. Open it."

Her daughter does so. Inside is a lambent cupridium-and-lacquer pin displaying three miniature items: a lance and a jagged lightning bolt crossed over a sheaf of grain.

"Where did you get this?"

"Look on the back," replies Mairena. "That should tell you."

Emerya does so, squinting to make out the tiny letters cut into the untarnished and ancient, but still shining, cupridium. "Lorn'elth'alt'mer," she murmurs, before she looks up. "It belonged to the Emperor Lorn? It really did?"

"Yes, it did."

"You got this from Father?"

"No. I got it from my mother. It has been handed down from Ryalth through daughters and an occasional niece, always woman to woman. It will be yours one day."

"Then . . . you're . . ."

Mairena nods.

"But . . ."

"Your father chose me, not just because I was moderately attractive and a healer, but for other reasons as well, represented by that pin." *From just where do you think you and your brother get your elthage abilities, do you think?*

"You . . . but there has never been an Empress who ruled, has there?"

"No. And now is not the time for that. The best I can do is act as part of the Council for your brother." *And make certain he does what he must to maintain and preserve his heritage . . . and that of all the women who made it possible.*

"You could—"

"Not now. Not when too many traditions and beliefs have already been overthrown. Not when people need to believe in the Emperor to come." *And not when Kiedron is yet unprepared to do what must be done . . . now. Nor should those deeds rest on his shoulders. He will have to bear enough.*

Emerya replaces the pin and closes the box. "When it is time for me to care for it, I will do so." She hands the box back to her mother.

Mairena accepts the small box and nods. "I know."

Whatever there is in or behind the words of the Empress is more than enough that Emerya shivers.

IX

For the next glass Mairena remains alone and out of sight, but after the third glass of the afternoon, she knows what she must do. Rather . . . she has always known, but had hoped it would not be necessary. Seeing the faces that had watched her has convinced her that her instincts were correct, those instincts that Lephi had mistrusted and ignored. She heads for the hatch to the outside deck.

Kiedron, recovering from his afternoon session with the captain, looks up. "Where are you going?"

"To talk to people. Too many of them do not understand."

"They don't need to understand. You are the Empress of Light."

"If they understand . . . matters will be easier." *Much easier.*

Before long, Mairena finds a familiar face, a woman who stands at the railing on the starboard side, looking toward the empty coast.

"Aedina?"

The graying woman turns. "Empress."

Mairena wants to tell her to use her given name. She does not. Instead, she says, "There's not much left."

"I know, but I just want to go home."

"We have no home left. There is nothing there, Aedina."

"Triendar will be there. He always . . ." The graying woman whom the Empress has known since both were girls stops as her eyes rest fully on Mairena, and her words trail off. "He's dead, isn't he?"

"The dark angels and the Accursed Forest destroyed him— and Lephi . . . and all the Magi'i who sought to defeat the barbarians."

"How could that happen? How?"

Mairena gestures toward the shore, now more distant, and the mists that still shroud much of the land. "You saw what that power did."

"Why? Cyador gave the barbarians so much. What did Triendar do to them?"

Besides trying to destroy them for rejecting Cyador? "We cannot change the past, dear Aedina. We can only move forward."

"Where? Where is there to go? They're all barbarians everywhere."

"We go where we can change them. To Hamor."

"That's . . ."

"Across the Great Western Ocean? It is, but I've brought

golds and we have the last great fireship and Mirror Lancers. We are the Magi'i of Cyador . . . are we not?"

"Why so far?"

"Because those golds will go farther and will buy what we cannot build . . ."

In the end, Mairena spends almost a glass with Aedina . . . and that conversation is only the first of many she will need to undertake.

X

On threeday morning, while Kiedron is undergoing another sparring session, Mairena gathers Tyrsalyn and the three Magi'i she judges to be the most powerful and influential of those aboard the *Kerial*, also likely to be three of the most powerful remaining after what has befallen Cyador.

"I've heard rumors, Lady Empress," announces Chamsym, a still-burly magus with iron-gray hair, the most noticeable sign of his age being the bloodshot nature of his eyes and the dark pouches beneath them. "I don't like rumors. Why are we here?"

"To discuss the future of Cyador and the Malachite Throne, of course."

"The Emperor is dead. So are the First and Second Magus, and Cyador has been leveled. What is there to discuss?" Chamsym's laugh is sardonic.

"The heir is alive, and so are we," replies Vaernt. Dark-haired with no sign of gray, he is slender, more than wiry, less than massively muscular.

"That is true," admits Mueryt. "Still . . ." He shrugs with the temporizing gesture that Mairena recalls all too well from the times he has visited the Palace of Light.

"The Accursed Forest is spreading into most of the lands where we once held sway," begins Tyrsalyn.

"Is that what your glass tells you?" asks Chamsym.

"Among other things. My eyes also tell me that what the glass reveals is true."

"Earthquakes and floods happen. Men rebuild and put things right. Men," Chamsym announces. "They don't go run off because things get difficult."

"I see," says the Empress. "The destruction of every city in Cyador and the death of most of their people is just one of those things? A massive wave of destruction that almost every magus and healer sensed, most of whom were prostrated—or killed—that was just one of those little things?"

"I didn't feel a thing," declared Chamsym. "I see no reason to skulk off to Hamor."

"Even if staying here means misery and death for most?"

"It won't. Things will get better."

The Empress restrains a sigh. "I take it that you will oppose my plan to go to Hamor and re-establish the Malachite Throne, then?"

"Far better to land at Summerdock and set it right. You'll go to Hamor over my dead body," declares Chamsym.

"There's nothing left to set right," Tyrsalyn points out.

"Then we'll build it . . ."

"With what?" asks Vaernt.

"Our hands."

"Your hands?" asks Mueryt. "When did you ever dirty your hands, except with chaos?"

"That won't help," says the Empress. She looks directly at Chamsym. "What do you have against rebuilding in Hamor, far from the dark angels and the Accursed Forest?"

"That's giving up, surrendering to an enemy we defeated before."

"Except we were losing that battle even when the Emperor dispatched every magus he could spare to keep the forest within its boundaries."

Chamsym flushes. "We'll retreat to Hamor over my dead body."

"I think you've made your point." Mairena smiles sadly . . . and concentrates.

Chamsym stiffens, as if jolted, and his arms twitch before he slumps in his chair, his eyes wide and lifeless. Almost immediately, the chaos within him, unrestrained by order, begins to transform his remains into ash.

Vaernt looks to Tyrsalyn, then to Mueryt, before his eyes return to the Empress. "You're a healer . . . not . . ."

"The power to use order can be used for more than healing. I'd prefer to have acted otherwise, but what once was Cyador is no longer suited to the Magi'i." She turns to Tyrsalyn. "Is that not so?"

"I fear it is." His eyes take in the other two Magi'i. "If either of you can use a glass, you will see just how much the land has changed, and how it is still changing."

"I've seen," admits Vaernt.

"I'll take your word for it," declares Mueryt. "Using a glass splits my skull . . . and if I'm looking at order . . ." He shakes his head. "What about Chamsym?"

"He got so angry that no one would listen to him that his heart stopped," declares the Empress. *In a way, that is what happened.*

After the other two Magi'i have left, and Viera has swept up the ashes and gathered the few metal articles that are all that remain of Chamsym, Tyrsalyn stands by the table and looks at the Empress. "Captain Heisyrt thinks you are mad to go to Hamor."

"That surprises me not at all. Will the remaining Magi'i support me in this?"

"With Mueryt and Vaernt convinced . . . and all the women you have persuaded, who is likely to object?" He pauses. "What you plan is . . . bold."

"Most would say fanciful . . . or unrealistic. But it is the only way. To struggle against the barbarians, the Accursed Forest, and . . . the dark angels . . . amidst total ruin, where not a single structure remains, except for tiny towns we have no way to reach . . . that would be folly."

"Some would say going to Hamor is folly."

"We have golds. I arranged for that. I sent two small chests to the Emperor's stateroom once it was completed." *Those golds do not include all the jewels I've hoarded and brought.* "There are cupridium blades and even some ancient firelances . . . I assume you and the other true Magi'i could infuse them with chaos, could you not?"

"I can, if given some time, and if the firelances hold up."

"I intend to save them for show . . . or rather, the heir to the Malachite Throne intends to do so. We also have almost two companies of Mirror Lancers, and none of the Hamorians are trained as well as the Lancers are." *Or as Kiedron will be.*

"Or as determined as you are, Lady." Tyrsalyn inclines his head in respect, then turns and walks from the stateroom.

XI

By fourday, the *Kerial* reaches the site of Cyad, where a single lonely merchanter has anchored. Mairena makes her way to the bridge, where Captain Heisyrt steps forward to meet her at the open hatch.

"The merchanter?" asks the Empress.

"I recognize her—*The Pride of Cyador.* She's one of the great ships of Ryalor House."

Mairena manages a nod. *Ryalor House . . . and the name of the ship.* The irony is almost overpowering. "I'd like to talk to the captain."

"You could take the pinnace once we're closer."

"I'd appreciate that."

The Empress watches as the captain raises the large Imperial ensign and as the *Kerial* eases closer to the merchanter, then comes to a halt several hundred yards away. The two vessels exchange flag signals, none of which mean anything to Mairena, before Captain Heisyrt returns to the lookout platform from which the Empress has observed the impressive clipper, a vessel likely to be faster, at least in a favorable wind, than the *Kerial.*

"They are ready to receive you, Lady. They have questions."

Who would not? "Thank you. I will do my best to answer them." *One way or another.*

Two Mirror Lancers accompany Mairena on the short sail of less than half a kay to the clipper trader. *The Pride of Cyador* has lowered a ladder, much like a rope and wood staircase, that makes it comparatively easy for Mairena, and the two Mirror Lancers, to reach the main deck of the merchanter, although climbing even a rope ladder would not have been that difficult in the low swells off the mud flats that are all that remain of the City of Light. When she reaches the deck, the captain steps forward.

"Lady Empress, Captain Elthoryn'mer, at your service."

She smiles, trying to order-project both assurance and warmth. "I'm pleased to meet you. Perhaps we could talk, and I could tell you what has occurred here . . . or, rather, the causes of the devastation."

"I would greatly appreciate that, and so would my officers and men. If you would not mind the privacy of my rather cramped stateroom?"

Mairena nods acquiescence.

The two walk across the main deck to the sterncastle and up the ladder to the second deck. The captain's stateroom is indeed modest, not more than four yards by three, with a small circular table at one end, anchored to the deck.

Elthoryn gestures to the table, and Mairena takes a seat. He seats himself across from her, then asks, "What happened?"

"The dark angels and the Accursed Forest destroyed every city and town in Cyador," Mairena replies simply.

"How could that be?"

Mairena gestures in the direction of vanished Cyad. "You see what has befallen the City of Light. We have just returned from where Fyrad once stood. There is no sign of the city, but only an enormous great bay. There are no towns left standing anywhere along the coast from here to there. The tower that marked Cape South has been toppled and vanished . . ." She goes on to explain what Tyrsalyn and Vaernt have also discovered.

When she finishes, Elthoryn says, "We came from Biehl, and from the south of there, to Summerdock and beyond, all we saw was the same."

"The glass of the First Magus showed that also, even well away from the coast."

Elthoryn then asks, "What about the Emperor?"

Mairena shakes her head. "All the Magi'i who were trying to bring the barbarians under control have all also been destroyed. From what we can tell, only those aboard the fireship have survived . . . and, of course, any aboard your vessel or any other Cyadoran ships that were at sea. The heir to the Malachite Throne is aboard the *Kerial.* So is the former Third Magus, now First Magus, and two companies of Mirror Lancers."

"Might I ask . . . was that a fortuitous happening?"

"No. It was not . . ." The Empress explains in much the same fashion as she already did to Tyrsalyn and Heisyrt, if by adding slight touches of order to certain words and phrases . . . and smiling more than she would otherwise.

When she stops speaking, Elthoryn nods slowly, then smiles ruefully. "I suspect you did not come here merely to recount events and to wish us well."

"No . . . I did not. I wish to see Cyador's heritage renewed and carried out. You could be of assistance, and I believe we can assist you as well . . . since a Cyadoran vessel with no home port and no resources behind it might find it difficult to continue merchanting."

"In what respect might this mutual accommodation take place?"

The Empress tells him, if in terms more suited to trade, again trying to use order as emphasis and persuasion, if subtly.

There are several moments of silence when she has finished.

"I don't know that's the best offer I've ever had, Lady Empress, but it's likely to be the only one available after what's happened. As you've pointed out, Cyadoran merchanters and vessels haven't ever been the most welcomed . . . and without the power of Cyad and many Magi'i behind us . . ."

"I had thought as much. Would you like me to address your crew and officers . . . or would you rather handle that yourself?"

"I think your presence and that of your fireship will suffice." Elthoryn's smile is wry. "Tell me more about the heir and your plans."

More than a glass passes before he escorts her from his stateroom.

After boarding the pinnace to take her back from the merchanter to the *Kerial*, the Empress reflects on her meeting with Elthoryn. In the end, he has proved far more reasonable, at least initially, than Captain Heisyrt about the options open to those who remain the survivors of Cyad and Cyador. But then, those who have had to rely on more than just power to accomplish their ends are often more adaptable . . . and reasonable.

XII

Even so, Mairena allows two more days to pass, each day spent quietly talking in turn with those aboard the *Kerial*, until she has spent time with all but a few of the adults on board. At the end of that time, another merchanter, the *Toziel*, arrives and anchors. Mairena once more employs the pinnace, first to pick up Captain Elthoryn, and then to sail to the *Toziel*.

Her conversation with the captain of the *Toziel* follows much the same pattern as did her initial discussion with Elthoryn, if in less time, given Elthoryn's support and persuasion. Then she has the pinnace convey both captains back to the *Kerial*, where the three of them meet with Captain Heisyrt.

There, the Empress allows both merchanter captains to share their views and feelings with Heisyrt, if neither tersely nor with great verbosity. When she has seen them off to their ships, she returns to the bridge.

Heisyrt looks to the Empress, then inclines his head. "Whenever you give the word, Lady Empress."

"Not quite yet, Captain . . . but soon."

When the Empress returns to her quarters, Emerya is waiting in the stateroom.

"What have you been doing?" asks her daughter.

"Gaining support," replies Mairena.

"Gaining support? Wearing what you were wearing?"

"I'm wearing riding clothes."

"The way you're wearing them . . ."

"Do not question how I do what I do, Emerya," replies the Empress, her voice like liquid ice. "I will do anything I must to assure that the heritage of Cyador continues and that you and your brother carry on that heritage. *Anything* to assure that you can. After all that your father did to destroy it . . . and all the other things he did . . . do not reproach me. Do not even dare to try. Do you understand?"

Emerya steps back, from both the determination in the words and the raw power of order behind them. She drops her eyes. "I'm sorry."

"So am I," replies Mairena, adding, "I have not had to stoop so low as you intimate." *Even if I would were it necessary.* "But I have used some abilities in ways I would not prefer. The time may come for you as well. I hope it is not soon." She settles into the armchair. "Not soon at all."

"What will not be soon at all?" asks Kiedron, walking into the stateroom from the outside port deck.

"The time when you'll have to make the kind of choices I've been making. The time when the entire fate of your heritage rests on your shoulders."

Kiedron starts to reply, then looks to Emerya, and nods. After a moment, he says, "I hope I make them as well as you are."

That does surprise Mairena, but she replies, "I can only do my best, and I can only hope the same for you." She offers a smile that hides the sadness within and adds, "It has been a long day, and I would rest for a time."

Kiedron and Emerya exchange glances, but neither speaks.

Then the Empress walks into her sleeping quarters, closing the door behind her. She does not sleep . . . or rest.

XIII

After another day spent talking to the remainder of the adults on board the *Kerial*, Mairena speaks to Heisyrt. Flag signals are exchanged with *The Pride of Cyador* and the *Toziel*. All three vessels lift anchor, and the *Kerial's* mighty engines throb as she turns to the southeast.

Mairena once more assembles not only the Magi'i, but all of those aboard the fireship, again on the main deck, except a handful of the crew and those on the bridge. When all are gathered out under the mid-morning sun, the Empress begins to speak, slowly and clearly, not just because she wishes to come across as deliberate, but because she infuses each word with the tiniest fragment of order.

"In hopes that we might find some part of Cyador that remains intact, we have traveled for days and days and found nothing. Then we returned to find that nothing of that which was Cyad has remained. The captains of *The Pride of Cyador* and the *Toziel* have found only destruction to the west and north. You have seen Cyad destroyed in instants, and you can still behold that not a trace remains of what once was Cyad, save mounds of mud. Is there a single white stone left upon another? Any trace of the mighty white piers of the harbor or of the Palace of Light? You have seen the great bay that swallowed Fyrad. You have witnessed the entire coast of Cyador from west of Cyad to east of Fyrad. Not a trace of any habitation or house remains. All the Magi'i of Cyador could not prevail against the Accursed Forest, and now but a handful remain—those aboard this fireship. While we cannot prevail against the Accursed Forest, we can indeed prevail against mere men . . ."

As she speaks, Mairena continues to weave a sense of order, of rightness, into the words she utters.

"I cannot promise safety here, nor can anyone. I cannot promise the opportunity to rebuild Cyad where it stood, or anywhere in what once was Cyador, for the Accursed Forest would soon topple anything that we could build . . . so we must find a new land to carry on our heritage, that heritage from the

Rational Stars. . . . The land that offers the most opportunity is that of Hamor, for it is the farthest from Candar, and it is yet divided and weak. Our ancestors crossed the endless gulf from the Rational Stars and built Cyador. Compared to that, can it be so hard to cross a single ocean? We have a great ship. We have Magi'i and healers. They had neither. We have Mirror Lancers and firelances, and we have golds to use to buy what we need and to trade.

"And we have the heir to the Malachite Throne, and he will build another great city . . . one that will endure even longer than did Cyad. That I have seen, just as I foresaw what befell Cyad and Cyador. . . .

"We will prevail. . . . We will triumph."

For long moments, the Empress stands in silence, shimmering in order. Then, she turns and walks to the bow of the *Kerial*, looking to the south and east. She does not look back, either at those she has addressed or at the two merchanters that sail in the wake of the *Kerial*.

Her eyes remain on the eastern horizon—and the unseen and distant land where the heritage of Cyador will be renewed.

Must be . . . and will be.

This story came about as a request by Patrick St-Denis for his short anthology, Speculative Horizons, *and sheds light on a character who walked into the sunset before the ending of* Fall of Angels.

THE STRANGER

The late light oozed over the hills at the foot of the Easthorns that harvest afternoon, a light that gave the early snows on the higher peaks to the east the faintest tinge of orange. I heard the hoofbeats on the lane before I saw the man ride out of the sunset toward the cot and the sheep shed. I had just closed the door behind the flock. In those days, the mountain cats were far more numerous and far bolder, and any shepherd who left a flock outside was tempting fate. The fiercest of mastiffs was no match for a pair of cats. A young herder wasn't, either, and I was barely old enough to sprout a few hairs on my face. I also had no real weapons, just an iron-tipped staff and a belt dagger. Ma had sold the big old sword that had been Da's after he'd died when the Prefect had conscripted all the locals for an attack on Axalt. No one's ever breached the walls of the trading city, and the Prefect's forces didn't then, either. Ma got a death-gold, and that didn't even pay for the three lambs and the ewe that the armsmen took after they gave her the coin.

I glanced back at the shed for a moment. I was worried about the old ewe. She'd gone into season in early winter for the first time in a year, and the ram had covered her before we'd known, and she was showing signs her time was near.

Anyway, the hoofbeats got louder, and it was just before supper when the man rode up to the shed. He wore a black tunic, and black trousers, and even a black leather cloak. He wasn't young, and he wasn't old, but his face had the look of a man who'd traveled some. His hair was mahogany red, but it didn't look that way then. In the sunset, it was more like the color of blood. He was also clean-shaven . . . or mostly so, like he'd shaved a day or two before.

"Young fellow, might a man find a hearth and a meal here?"

I didn't understand his words at first.

He asked again, and he spoke slowly. I still had to struggle to understand him because he spoke the way the traders from Suthya did, not quite the same, but close enough. What they called the old way of talking, sort of the way they did in Cyador, Caetyr told me later.

"We're not an inn, ser."

He smiled, sort of shyly. "I wasn't looking for an inn. I was looking for honest folk who wouldn't mind a few coppers for sharing their meal and letting a stranger sleep. I'd even sleep in the loft of the shed."

By then, Ma had come out into the yard. She just looked at him.

He turned in the saddle and bowed his head to her for a moment. "Mistress, I was asking the young fellow about whether I might pay you for a meal and a place to sleep."

"One way or other, I'm no mistress." She paused. "There's an inn in town."

"A stranger traveling alone is often safer with honest herders." He smiled, and it was sort of a sad smile.

"That'd be so in places."

"And you're closer to Axalt. That's where I'm headed."

"You said you'd pay?" asked Ma.

"I did. Three coppers? Would that suffice?"

"We've only got a thick soup and fresh bread. No ale, nothing like that. Water's good, though. We got a clean spring back side of the hill."

"A thick soup would be wonderful." When he dismounted, I saw that he had two swords at his belt, both on the right side, and both sheathed in something like a double scabbard, and a long dagger on his left side. The two swords were short blades, like nothing I'd ever seen. It was more than warm, but he wore a dark gray leather glove over his right hand, the kind that extended partway up his forearm under the sleeve of his tunic.

He slipped his wallet from his belt and deftly slid out three coppers one-handed, extending them to Ma.

"I guess you're our guest," Ma said with a smile.

"I thank you." He glanced toward the shed. "Might there be a place to put my mare? She's carried me more kays than I'd want to count."

"There's a large stall at the end of the shed," Ma said. "She'll have to share."

"She's done that before."

His horse was a black mare, and she did fine in with the old gelding. The man groomed her with a worn brush that had leather straps that fitted over his gloved hand, and before long the three of us were sitting at the old table by the hearth.

Ma dished out the soup. She even used the better bowls and set the bread in a basket in the middle of the table.

"Would you like to say a blessing?" she asked.

"If you wouldn't mind . . . mine's a little different."

"A blessing's a blessing," Ma said warmly.

He cleared his throat gently before he spoke. "May we all live in order and peace, and may that order keep chaos and evil at bay. May we always understand the goodness of order and the perils of chaos, and live so that others do also, and may we always strive for the goodness that order brings, both for ourselves and others."

"That's a good blessing," Ma said. "Different, but good."

"You talk like you're from the West," I said.

"I'm from a place called Carpa. It's in Lornth." He broke his bread one-handed, with his left hand. I watched him for a moment. He didn't use his right hand at all.

He looked at me. "You're very observant. My right hand was hurt years ago. I can do some things with it, but eating's not one of them."

Ma gave me a look. So I asked, "Where have you been lately?"

"I was in Passera a while ago."

"That's two eightdays' ride," Ma said.

"I didn't ride it. I came downriver to Elparta on a flatboat. It took four days." He shook his head. "It might have been better to ride."

"It take you a long time to get here from Carthan?" I asked.

"Carpa." He laughed, soft-like. "Ten years or so."

"Lornth is beyond the Westhorns. Did you see the ones they call 'angels' when you came east?"

"I have seen them," the man said.

"Are they six cubits high with silver hair and eyes, the way they say?"

He laughed, again. "Some have silver hair. I saw one who had silver eyes. None was taller than four and a half cubits, perhaps not that."

"There must be a lot of them."

"There were only thirty or so who came from the Rational Stars. That's what they told me, and they don't lie."

"All folks lie at times," Ma said.

"They don't bother with it. At least, the ones I knew didn't."

"They're all women, aren't they?" That was what I'd heard.

"Most of them. Not all. One was a black mage, and a smith. His name was Nylan. He could bend the fires of heaven and draw something even hotter from a simple charcoal forge. He hammered out blades there on the Roof of the World that could cleave through the best iron in Candar. He forged other things, too." The stranger's eyes got a faraway look in them for a moment.

"What about the women?" I asked.

"Frankyr . . ." Ma said that in her quiet voice, the one that told me I was being rude.

"I watched the one they called 'the Marshal,' Ryba of the Swift Ships of Heaven. She was tall for a woman, almost as tall as I am. With nothing but a pair of short blades she killed three Lornian armsmen and sliced off the sword hand of a fourth in less time than it takes to tell it." He shook his head. "Folks don't believe me when I say that, but it's true."

"Those short blades the kind you have?"

He looked at me. "They are. They were forged by Nylan."

"They don't seem very big, not like the sword Da had."

"They're very good, especially for close fighting on horse-back. They can also be thrown. Saryn of the black blades could throw one hard enough that it would pierce a breastplate and the point would come out through a man's back."

"You saw that?"

"Once." The stranger nodded, then stood. "I thank you for the supper, and I'll be headed out to the loft."

I watched him from the side of the cot, but he did pretty much what he said he'd do. Then I walked back inside and barred the door.

Ma looked at me. She was still sitting on the bench. "He's a strange man. I think he's a good one, though."

"Someone must be chasing him," I said. "Why would he

want to stay here? What he gave you would almost pay for a meal and bed at the inn."

"He's not a common armsman," Ma said.

"With all that black, you think he's an assassin or a bravo?"

"He might have been . . . before he hurt his hand." She shook her head. "He doesn't swagger."

"Maybe he was a captain or an undercaptain."

"He doesn't want to say . . . but he's not common."

Neither one of us said what we were thinking—that with his weapons and his skills, he could have taken anything he wanted. In the time before I dropped off to sleep, I wondered why he'd avoided the town.

The next morning, once we opened the door, it wasn't long before the stranger appeared. He'd brushed his clothes clean. He must have found the spring, because he was washed up, and he'd shaved. Cleaned-up, he looked a little younger, but I'd have guessed he was still more than ten years older than me, but not so old as Ma.

She offered him maybe a quarter of a loaf, and he gave her a copper, then stood on the stoop and ate the bread with water from the mug Ma offered.

"You led armsmen, didn't you?" Ma asked.

He finished eating before he answered. "I did. I have to admit I wasn't too successful. I haven't done that in years."

"What are you doing here in Spidlar?"

"Like I told you last night, I'm passing through on my way to Axalt. There's no way to get there from Passera without crossing the Easthorns and then crossing them back—except through Spidlar."

Ma looked at me. "You'd best take the flock before it gets too hot."

I wanted to hear what the stranger might say, but Ma was right, and I took the iron-tipped staff that had been Da's and headed out to the shed. I didn't worry about the stranger. Maybe I should have, but there was something about him. Besides, if he'd meant harm, he'd already have done it, and with those blades of his, I couldn't have stopped him. I did look back a couple of times, but by the time I'd reached the hilltop with the flock, he was walking back to where his mare was stalled.

We hadn't grazed the hills to the southwest in a time, and that was where I headed, with the old ram and me leading the way. The grass there wasn't bad, but it was browning earlier than it usually did, and that meant we'd likely have a dry summer, an early winter, and a long one.

When I brought the flock back in late afternoon, Ma and the stranger were out by the shed, and there was a pile of coal there piled against the west wall, tall as he was and four times that far across. I don't know as I'd ever seen that much coal in one place before that.

"Where did all this coal come from?" With all that coal we wouldn't be hoarding wood and scraps and freezing, the way we had the winter before. That was if we were careful, but it looked like it would last a while.

"I was walking up in the hills, and I saw a few little pieces in the dry wash, and I started following them." The stranger shrugged. "I showed your mother where the seam comes out. I wouldn't tell anyone. Someone would just come and take the land and the coal."

"It's our land."

"That may be, but unless you've got golds to hire armsmen or you're armsman trained, you'll lose it to those who have coin or weapons. Coal that good's worth a shiny silver."

"That's not right."

"Was it right that your father got conscripted to attack Axalt?"

I didn't answer for a moment. Ma had been talking. I hadn't

said anything about Da. I looked at her and then at him and wondered what else might have been happening.

"Nothing," he answered, as if he'd been able to hear my thoughts. "The mare needs another day of rest. I rode her too hard getting here. That was because I thought I could reach Axalt yesterday."

"He spent all day walking up to where he found the coal, chipping it out, and putting it in bags for the gelding to carry back. It took all day," Ma said. "Then he washed up."

I didn't say anything.

"It's going to be a long, cold winter," he said.

"You didn't have to do that," I told him.

"The world would be a pretty sorry place if we only did what we had to, don't you think?" he replied.

I'd heard words like that before. Seeing him standing there, with the one hand still gloved in gray, and looking at a pile of coal it would have taken me days to lug anywhere, what he said sounded different. He hadn't just said the words. He'd said them after he'd done something to show that he meant them.

I just stared at him, because I didn't know what to say and because Ma was looking at me with a disgusted expression on her face.

"Someone's coming." He turned toward the lane from town, quicker than a mountain cat. "Get in the cot."

Ma looked at him.

"Inside." His words were so powerful that I grabbed Ma by the arm and dragged her back to the stoop. But we didn't go in. We stood half in and half out of the doorway watching.

Four men on horses trotted up the lane, fast enough that the dust billowed almost to the girths of their saddles. The stranger stood there, halfway between the cot and the sheep shed, waiting, like he knew them.

Two of the riders were big men, maybe not quite so tall as

the stranger in black, but broader across the shoulders. The third rider was smaller, and even from where we were, he looked mean, with a slash scar across one cheek, and a lash in his right hand. The last rider waited behind the other. He wasn't big, and he wasn't small, and he wore a shoulder harness with two blades in it.

The stranger didn't say anything. The first three riders reined up some fifteen yards away from where he stood.

"You won't be getting away this time!" called the big rider in the middle. He had a big blade out, laid across his thighs for the moment.

The one on the right also had a big blade. He just smirked.

"You don't want to do this," the stranger replied. "I'm leaving Gallos. You could turn around and leave."

"After chasing you for hundreds of kays?" The one with the whip laughed. "We're here to get our golds." He paused. "Unless you'd like to pay more than the Prefect will."

He lifted the whip hand, and I could see that the butt of the weapon was fastened around his wrist with leathers. I guessed that was so he didn't lose it.

The stranger was the one to laugh. "You're not that honest. If I gave you golds you'd cheerfully take them and then still try to take me."

"Hear that," said the one in the middle. "The teacher fellow doesn't think we're honest. Teach us something, teacher fellow."

All four of them laughed.

When the laughs died away, the stranger spoke, and his voice filled the yard. He wasn't shouting. His words just carried. "No one can teach you. No one can teach another anything unless the listener wants to learn. I can speak, but you cannot learn if you will not find the order within yourselves."

The three front riders all laughed again.

While they were laughing, the stranger did nothing . . . except somehow, he seemed *blacker*, darker, more solid. And he had a blade in his left hand. It looked real small compared to the ones that the two big men on horseback held.

"I guess we'll be doing the teaching, then," said the middle rider, looking to the rider with the lash. The four rode forward a way and then stopped.

The man with the whip flicked it in the direction of the stranger, and it cracked just short of him.

The stranger didn't move.

"The teacher fellow wants us to think he's brave," said the big man in the middle. "Roart, see how brave he really is."

The whip lashed out at the stranger, but it didn't strike him, but wound around his short blade. Then he jerked and turned or something, and the rider with the whip was pulled right out of the saddle, and one boot caught in the stirrup for a moment, and then he arched into the air and came down on his head. Hard. He didn't move, and it didn't look like he would. Ever.

The other three froze for a moment.

Then the lead rider lifted his blade and spurred his horse forward. The horse barely had taken three strides when I saw a black blade sticking out of the man's chest.

The remaining rider of the front three charged the stranger. My mouth was open as the second black blade buried itself in that bravo's chest. At that moment the stranger started to move toward the big blade that had dropped from the hands of the man who'd done most of the talking.

I ran from the door because I could see that the stranger wouldn't get to the blade before the last rider did. The rider looked to be a Kyphran nomad. The staff wasn't much against a big blade, but it was the only thing I had. Ma tried to grab me, but she was too slow.

The Kyphran was already swinging one of those hand-and-a-half swords when he rode toward the stranger, who was still crouching, because he'd had to dig the fallen blade out of a rut in the yard. The rider was already by me, but I took the staff and lunged, and I swung it at the back of his sword arm and hit him as hard as I could. The blade flew clear, and he turned the horse and pulled out another blade almost as big as the first.

"You're going to be sorry for that, boy." The bravo cut down at me.

I got the old staff up in time to keep that blade from going through me, and it stopped the blade and held. My legs didn't, and I sprawled on the ground, and when I hit, I lost hold of the staff. Then I tried to scramble out of the way.

The bravo came back and was bringing his sword down when he got this funny look on his face, and then slumped forward in the saddle. His head lolled a funny way, and then the horse stopped, and he fell face-first out of the saddle and into the dirt.

The stranger was standing on the other side of the horse, and he already had the reins in his left hand, and the big blade of the other bravo—that was the one he must have used—was lying in the dirt.

It took me a moment to climb to my feet. When I did, the stranger handed me the reins. "Can you tie this horse up in the pen by the shed?"

"Yes, ser." I don't know why I called him "ser," but it seemed right.

I started to walk the big courser toward the pen, but I looked back to see where the other three horses were. The one that was the farthest away—he was almost a hundred yards south—had this wild look that I saw even from where I was.

The stranger turned toward the wild-eyed horse. Then he called, "Here, fellow." Demon-flame if the big horse didn't stop and sort of snort and snuffle before he began to walk toward the stranger. He did that with all three of the other mounts, and before long, we had them all four tied up in the pen beside the sheep shed.

Ma had been out in the yard for a time, looking at the four dead men, then at the horses tied in the pen, then at the stranger, and finally at me. "You shouldn't have done it with the staff, Frankyr. You could have been killed."

"No, if you'd done the careful thing, you shouldn't have," said the stranger as he fastened the gate to the pen, "but careful isn't always right. I'm glad you did the right thing. Otherwise, things might have turned out differently, for all of us." He turned to Ma. "I'm sorry about all this. I didn't think they'd be able to track me here."

"That why you took the flatboat downriver?" asked Ma.

"I hoped they'd leave me alone." He shrugged. "I should have known better, but I tried not to have things turn out this way."

"This way?" Ma's voice wasn't cutting, but it had a touch of the edge she put on the words when she didn't believe me.

"The killing. I don't like killing, for all that I once tried to gain a holding by it. It didn't work out. That taught me something, and I've tried to avoid it ever since." He took a deep breath. "The problem is that, sometimes, when you try to avoid something too much, it's like you draw it to you."

"So how did not wanting to kill draw these fellows after you?" Ma gestured at the bodies, but she didn't look at them.

"I've been in Gallos for a while, telling people about order and how it works." He stopped and looked hard at me. "Most young people don't understand. I didn't, not until I ran into the angels. But that's another story. Anyway . . . it's like this. Rulers all tell a story, and it's usually a story that makes them look good. If they know people won't believe that story, then they talk about how evil someone else is and how everything they do causes the problems folks have. Once I was one of those who believed the stories. That was before the angels came, and I

watched and listened to the great mage Nylan. He showed me
how the world really is. So I've been traveling and telling people
what little I've learned from the angels. The new prefect of Gallos didn't care for my teaching, because he's been trying to tell
the story that all the problems in Gallos, maybe everywhere in
Candar, have been caused by the angels. The angels live in a
tower—one tower on the Roof of the World. It's high and cold,
where no one ever lived before. They never left the Westhorns
until they were attacked, both by Lornth and Gallos. So how
can they have caused all these problems? A handful of people
on top of the Westhorns?" The stranger laughed, sort of ruefully. "The new prefect didn't like my telling people that. His
armsmen came and burned the temple I'd built in Passera. It
wasn't very big, but it was where I was telling people about order. I wasn't there at the time. That made him so mad that he
put a price on my head."

"For telling folks what was really happening?"

"Well . . ." The stranger smiled sheepishly. "I did fight off
a couple of armsmen who tried to capture me and take me to
Fenard so that I could be drawn and quartered. One of them
died, I think, but I didn't stay to find out. I thought that, if
I left Passera, there wouldn't be any need for them to kill me or
me to kill them in order to stay alive. The Prefect didn't like
that. I was charged with treason for pointing out that the way
of the angels brought down great Cyador and defeated the
forces of both Gallos and Lornth. So I thought I'd best leave
Gallos. But they sent a whole squad of armsmen to block
the road east of Passera. It seemed like a better idea to take the
river north and head for Axalt this way. Otherwise I'd have to
go through Certis, and the ruler there is friendly to the Prefect,
while Axalt has no love of him."

Ma and I knew that.

Suddenly, he cocked his head, then stood and hurried

toward the sheep shed. There, he unbarred the door and slipped inside. I hurried after him, and so did Ma, after she ran inside the cot and came back out with the lantern.

The old ewe was against the wall of the shed, and the others had given her space.

"She's not going to make it," Ma said. "I can tell."

The stranger knelt down on the soiled straw, close to the ewe, and she let him. I don't know what he did, but one moment, the old ewe was bleating in distress, and the next, he was putting his left hand on her head, and it stopped. Then he began to talk to her like she was a sick child, and this black mist . . . or something like it . . . blacker than the darkness in the places where the light from the lantern couldn't reach . . . it sort of ran down his good arm and into the ewe.

Ma and I just watched.

He didn't seem to do anything, and yet he did.

It must have been a good glass that passed while she delivered the two lambs . . . and the afterbirth. He touched both of the newborns somehow with that blackness, and before long, both lambs were nursing, and the old ewe was acting years younger, like nothing at all had been wrong.

When the stranger stood and turned, so that the light from the lantern fell on his face, he looked older, worn-out, a lot more tired than after he'd fought the men who'd been chasing him, and his face was all sweaty. "They should be all right now."

"What did you do? You some kind of mage?" asked Ma, so soft that I could tell she was half scared and half plain shocked.

"I'm no mage, not the way the angels are. I've just learned a few things along the way." He looked at me. "Anyone can learn some things about order." He shook his head. "We still need to get rid of the bodies. If they're found around here, you'll be the ones blamed."

"They tried to kill you . . . ," I began.

"That doesn't matter. Anyone who helps a traitor is guilty, and I don't think you want to be hung or leave everything and head for Axalt." He looked at Ma.

She shook her head. "I'll get the spade."

We walked outside, and Ma hurried to the cot and then back with the spade and sort of thrust it at the stranger's right hand.

He wasn't looking and the shaft struck his glove. It sort of *clunked*, dull-like, and he grabbed the shaft with his left hand. "I'm sorry. My right hand isn't that limber."

It didn't sound limber at all. It sounded like there was metal under the glove. I wondered if he had some sort of wrist guard or brace there, but before I could ask, he said, "We'll need to use the gelding to carry the bodies, one at a time. Can you do that, Frankyr, while your mother shows me somewhere over the hill where we can bury them?"

"Yes, ser."

We finished burying the four of them on the far side of the hill sometime before midnight. The stranger insisted that we dig deep, and he and I did the digging while Ma held the lantern.

He gave us all the coins that the riders had, and there were fifteen coppers and five silvers, and one plain gold ring. "You could have gotten that anywhere. I'd not sell it for a season or so, though, just to be safe."

Then, after we stalled the gelding, he saw us to the cot and walked back to the shed. I heard him climb up to the loft.

When I woke just after first light and went out to offer him breakfast, he was gone. So were the four horses. There was a cloth pouch tied to the bar on the inside of the sheep shed, with six golds inside, and a scrap of parchment with words written on it.

I'd never been to school, and I couldn't read what he wrote. Ma couldn't, either, but the golds spoke for themselves, and who could we have asked to read it right then? Years later, when no one was asking about the riders who disappeared, when I went to Axalt to sell some sheep, I had a merchant there read it to me, and he said that it read:

You and your mother deserve half.
    Remember—believe in order, and live in order, and all will be right.

Under the words was just a letter. I could tell that. It was an *R*.

I guess we follow order. Anyway, I tried. A good herder might bring in a gold a year, and we had six. So we spent a few silvers here and a few there for a good ram or ewe, and before long Ma could buy a loom, and one thing led to another.

The one thing that bothered me, and it still does, is that we never even knew his name. I suppose we didn't need to. The lambs grew into strong ewes, and they lived twice as long as any we ever had. They also stayed black, and so did all their lambs, and the lambs that came from them, and we get twice as much for their wool. That's how we could build a real house here and buy more of the land. We've kept the coal to ourselves, though.

You might say that all that came from the blackness of a good-hearted stranger.

There are always those who think that the arts, especially those involving words and music, are somehow "soft." But when songs can change the present and the future, how soft are they, and how much of the ensuing suffering falls on the singer?

SONGS PAST, SONGS FOR THOSE TO COME

I

The silver-haired druid lies on his narrow bed in the chamber whose naturally polished wooden walls seem to curve without doing so. His eyes are wide, both unseeing and seeing too much as the images only he can apprehend swirl before him . . . one after the other . . .

. . . a room walled in white stone, sitting in which is a man all in white with bronze starbursts on the collars of his tunic . . .

. . . a dark-haired woman looking intently at him, as if listening . . .

. . . a silver-haired youth, blank-eyed, carrying heavy white paving stones, blood seeping from his feet and oozing from the holes in his boots . . .

. . . the same dark-haired woman as before in a black uniform walking into a large hall, when crossbow quarrels transfix her . . .

. . . a younger, silver-haired woman, also in a black uniform, standing above the model of a walled and towered structure, just as the model explodes, shredding her form with metal splinters and engulfing her in flames . . .

. . . a blinding light pouring from the sky like a second sun, melting the buildings beneath it as if they were wax . . .

. . . a city of black buildings surrounding a harbor from which strange ships come and go . . . amid a sense of order and peace . . .

And there are others, many others, but those are the images that matter, and which pierce him to his very quick.

He shudders as his eyes unglaze, and murmurs, "Not again . . . you ask too much." Except he knows that he addresses no one. After eightdays of the same dreams, there is no one to address.

Except himself.

II

The druid's niece stops behind the low stone wall and studies the narrow forest pool that holds a small stun lizard, sunning itself on a rock barely protruding from the water, a rock that catches one of the few shafts of sunlight passing through the high canopy of the Great Forest. She smiles briefly before turning and continuing along the path. In time, she reaches her destination, a small dwelling set back from the main path, but linked to it by a second path, this one covered with a fine gray gravel that would sparkle in the light, if any direct sunlight could penetrate the high canopy of branches that protect the structure beneath that appears to be set unduly tightly between the massive trunks of two trees—except that the walls of the dwelling flow into those trunks.

She opens the door. "Uncle!"

There is no response to her call. So she steps into the tiny foyer of the ancient dwelling and glances around, her eyes taking in but not truly seeing the woven grain of the wood so carefully grown into the shape of the chamber long years before she had been born. There is no one there, nor in the small sitting room beyond the archway.

"He must be in back."

After closing the door, she takes the gray path around the southernmost of the massive tree trunks and makes her way through the middle of a garden of mixed flowers, whose scent changes daily. The path ends at a circle of green moss.

At the western end of the moss is a bench that appears, only appears, to have been carved out of an enormous tree root. The man seated there wears a simple brown shirt and trousers, with boots of the same color. His hair and beard are silver.

"Greetings, Lynahra."

"Didn't you hear me, Uncle?" She crosses the moss and seats herself on the end of the bench, turning slightly so that she can look directly at him.

"I knew you'd find me if you thought it important." His deep green eyes hold a smile.

"Why have you grown that beard? You look old."

"That is the idea. No one pays much attention to an old bard."

"You're leaving the forest again? Why?"

"There are songs of summer yet to be sung," he says gently, "even by one lost in endless autumn."

"When you speak that way . . ." The silver-haired younger woman shakes her head. "You don't have to go."

"But I do." *Better that than chaos left unbalanced . . . and unending dreams that will only worsen.* That he knows from bitter experience. "There are matters that must come to be."

"And you will make them happen with song?" Her voice is sad, rather than skeptical.

"I cannot forge black iron, nor can I bend the forest to my will. Order must have a focus to balance the white city."

"You're not going *there*?"

"Only for a little while. What order needs is much closer."

"Then why are you—"

"Going that far?" He lets the silence draw out for a time before he goes on. "Because even great and violent acts require fertile ground and cultivation, and what is most effective often requires time and a wandering journey." *And others to believe it is their idea.*

"And songs to sing?"

"Is that not what I do?" *For all must seem the doing and will of others.*

III

The mare he had bought in a small town south of Clynya eight-days earlier lifts her head ever so slightly. The bard can sense that she smells something on the light breeze that comes out of the northwest.

Almost four eightdays have passed since he first entered the lands of the Tyrant, then left them. Spring has given way to early summer. The Westhorns are behind him—*for now*—and, if he recalls correctly, for it has been all too many years since he passed this way, the small town of Vryna lies ahead, if too far to reach before the sun drops below the rolling hills of Gallos stretching westward behind him. Beyond Vryna lie the Easthorns, far less daunting than the Westhorns that shelter Westwind within their stern and chill heights, and beyond the Easthorns lie Certis and Montgren . . . and the white city that rules both in fact, but not in name.

He can smell the hint of wood-smoke, suggesting a camp just ahead, and one likely with guards, since lone travelers would be more circumspect. He continues to ride, and in some fraction of a glass, he sees the encampment, with two wagons flanking a fire. He nods and rides slowly, but directly, toward the fire, fingering the leather grip of the time-and-use-polished wooden truncheon at his belt. He does not slip his hand through the wide leather strap.

"Stranger . . . best you stop there."

The silver-haired and bearded bard reins up. "As you wish."

"What are you doing out so late and alone?" The shadowed speaker is a woman, who holds a small crossbow aimed at him.

"I've been riding far later, and I always travel alone. Why are you camped so close to the town? Vryna was once friendly to traders, not that I've been through here in years."

"What's in the pack, old man?"

"A guitar." That is absolutely true, but not the whole truth.

"Minstrel or not, you're old to be traveling alone," says the hard-eyed woman with the twin blades at her wide belt.

"And you are far from Sarronnyn, lady-blade. There must be a story behind that."

"That's for me to know. What's your name?"

"Bard."

"Is that a name or a title?"

"Both."

"Fair enough, Bard. You can tie your mare with the others. She's not in season, is she?"

"No." *And she won't be.*

"There's a tie-line beyond the wagons."

"Thank you."

"You were once a blade?" asks the armswoman.

"Of sorts," he admits. "Why do you ask?" He knows full well why, but wishes an answer from her.

"Old as you are, riding into a strange camp is a danger."

"Not when the guard once served with the Tyrant's forces and still keeps the blades."

She laughs, if with the slightest trace of bitterness. "Go tie up your horse. There's not much left from supper, but no one would grudge you that in return for a song or two."

"It has been a long day," he replies with a smile, then dismounts and begins to walk the mare toward the wagons, the fire, and the tie-line beyond.

"There's a minstrel headed to the tie-line!" calls out the guard.

As he walks the gray mare into the haze of smoke and the flickering light cast by the fire, his eyes take in those standing near the end of one wagon—a heavyset and black-bearded man, an older graying man who would scarce cast a shadow even in full sunlight in early morning or late afternoon, a second armswoman with graying blonde hair, and a younger man barely beyond youth who sports a scraggly and uneven beard that only emphasizes his lack of experience. The bard nods to the four. "Good evening. I appreciate the welcome."

"There's a mite of trail soup in the black pot," offers the black-bearded man.

"That would be much appreciated."

"You're not from around here."

Bard shakes his head. "From the West, beyond the Westhorns, not far from Clynya."

The older armswoman stiffens, but says nothing.

As Bard approaches the tie-line, the gray gelding at the end sidles away, most likely because he sees and smells the mare and the stranger.

"Easy there, fellow," he offers, placing a hand high on the gelding's withers.

The gelding whuffs, then almost seems to nod.

Bard takes a lead from the saddlebags and secures the mare to the tie-line. He sets the saddlebags and his pack well back from the horses before uncinching the saddle and removing it and the thick blanket. He glances around, knowing even before he does that the older armswoman is moving toward him along the shadowed side of the wagon.

"Clynya," she says flatly. "That's awfully close to the Great Forest. You're silver-haired, too." She keeps her hands well away from the hilt of either blade at her belt.

"I am, and it is." His words are soft.

"I'll be interested to hear what you have to sing. After you eat."

"I'll do my best."

"I'm certain you will." She turns and walks back toward the fire, without so much as a glance back at him.

He finishes and sets his saddle and gear on the wagon tailboard, although he will have to move them later. Before he leaves the mare to follow the armswoman, he studies the shadowed side of the nearest wagon, then lifts the pack that holds the guitar and two other items with him as he moves to join the others around the fire.

The trail soup is acceptable, and definitely edible, most likely because of the contributions of the two experienced armswomen, and he needs no encouragement to scrape the heavy iron cookpot clean.

He has barely finished when the heavyset trader with the square-cut short beard asks, "What news do you have from the West? Oh . . . I'm Hardyn. Leydon is the thin one, and the young fellow is Gerhard."

"All from Certis, I'd wager." At Hardyn's momentary start, the bard goes on, "The wagon's built of Montgren pine, but I've never heard of traders from Vergren. Most folks there are herders or the like. Jellico's the best bet, since most traders out of Rytel stick to the river." He turns to the graying blonde. "And you're?"

"Eltara. Delana is my partner."

Bard understands both messages, unnecessary as it was for Eltara to voice them, at least to him. Before the others can speak again, he continues, "There's a new prefect in Fenard. He's hiring armsmen. Some say that's to garrison the forts on the passes through the Westhorns. Others . . ." He shrugs and looks to the armswoman. "What might you think?"

"Why ask me?"

"Because you once served the Tyrant."

"Not willingly and not for long."

She lies, but he lets the lie pass and says, "Still . . . you would know whether the Tyrant would stand behind the Marshal."

"I could care less about either, old minstrel. What do you think?"

"Even if the Tyrant despised the Marshal, she'd likely support Westwind, just to keep the Westwind Guards between Sarronnyn and Gallos."

"Any smart ruler would," observes Leydon, the thin man. "Best to let another do your fighting."

Gerhard does not look at the bard.

"What other news might you have?" asks Hardyn.

"The women who took over the broken-down port that used to be the great city of Cyad have pushed all the Delapran troopers out of the whole area. They killed hundreds of the troopers. The Duke sent reinforcements, and they slaughtered or routed all of them, too. They're calling their land Southwind."

"Cyad? Never heard of it," says Hardyn.

"It's only a small port, these days," although he has dreams of when it was not, long before his birth. "It's the first one with a harbor west of the druids' port at Diehl. I think the Duke of Delapra called it Eastport. Most of the women came from either Sarronnyn or Westwind. They started coming years ago."

"How did a bunch of women manage that?"

"There were quite a few of them. I gather they'd trained like the Westwind Guards and the Tyrant's Finest." *And they had some other assistance.* Bard was not about to mention that assistance or its nature.

"Why'd they do a chaos-fired thing like that?" asks Leydon.

"Word is that they didn't like the way women ruled in Sarronnyn and in Westwind, or the way men ruled anywhere."

". . . can't imagine why . . . ," murmurs Eltara in a voice so low that the bard is the only one to hear her words.

"Don't care much for news about women," says Hardyn dismissively.

"The Sarronnese have found and re-opened the lost Cyadoran copper mines," replies Bard.

"Those were played out years ago, I thought."

"Centuries back," adds Leydon.

"The mages in the white city are paying more for copper. They need it to make their white bronze. That made the lower-grade ore remaining worth the search and mining. The price of tin will likely go up as well, if it hasn't already. . . ."

A look passes between Hardyn and Leydon, suggesting that that particular piece of information might be useful in some fashion.

". . . and one of the Jeranyi clans crossed the Stone Hills and raided Biehl. They fired part of it before the Duke's troopers could muster and drive them off . . ." Perhaps half a glass later, he clears his throat. "If you'd like some songs . . ." His tone suggests that his voice will not last for the entertainment if he keeps talking.

Hardyn nods. "That'd be good."

Bard loosens the ties on the pack and eases out the guitar—wrapped in a neatly trimmed section of an old blanket—then checks the strings and tunes it. He frowns. Does he sense the white mist of chaos to the north of the camp? He seats himself on one end of the log that has been set on the west side of the fire, forces a smile and runs his fingers over the strings, then begins.

> When I set out for Lydiar
> A thousand kays away . . .
> That spring, it scarcely seemed that far,
> A season and a day . . .

By the second stanza the four were smiling . . . and laughing as he finished.

> When I reached my end in Lydiar
> A thousand kays away,
> A journey not so very far,
> My hair, I found, was gray.

His fingers stray soundlessly across the strings for a few moments as he again feels the growing chaos that approaches, the chaos of men bent on violence, still not that close, and thinks about the next song he will sing.

> Once I knew a maid so fair
> When spring had turned the evenings gold
> She was a vision bright and rare,
> But, alas, a druid, truth be told . . .

After the fifth song, he is certain about the approaching chaos on the road from Vryna. While those who create it are yet a kay or more away, he decides he has finished paying for his supper. "It's been a long day, and my fingers are numb." He smiles and stands, for more than one reason. "You're going to have company before long, I think," he says to Eltara.

She frowns.

So does Hardyn.

"I've learned to trust my feel for these things," says Bard quietly. "If you don't mind. I think I'll get my bow ready."

Hardyn looks as though he will complain.

Eltara looks at the trader. "You'd better get ready for trouble. I'm getting my crossbow." She stands and walks toward the farther wagon.

Bard eases the remaining two items from his pack and sets them beside the log, then wraps the section of blanket around the guitar and places it back in the pack.

Eltara returns, carrying a small crossbow similar, if not identical, to the one carried by her partner. Her head tilts as Bard takes what appears to be a circular shape and, using both legs, and both hands and arms, strings the composite bow, turning the near circle into a double curved bow.

"It's a Westwind bow."

Her mouth opens, then closes.

"We all have our secrets," he says dryly as he straps the quiver in place, counting the shafts—twenty—the same number as that with which he began, if about a third the number that a true warrior archer would carry. Then he extracts the thumb ring from his belt pouch and places it on his left thumb. "Shall we join your partner?"

"We should. She shouldn't have all the entertainment to herself."

When they are well away from the three men, Bard looks at the armswoman, the older of the two, if far younger than he is. "It will be better if I act first. Much better. You two are younger." All of that is true, but, again, not the real reason for his suggestion. He knows that he must be accurate and swift, for he will have but a short time before he will be unable to act, at least if there are as many riders headed their way as he fears. Before she can question, he asks, "What did Hardyn do to upset the locals? People usually don't just decide to attack after dark for an evening's entertainment."

"He's got bolts of black wool. He's also got saffron, cardamom, and vanilla, and healer-quality brinn."

"Expensive goods."

"He told the locals he had nothing for sale. He wants to sell it all in Sarronnyn, where he can get much more. The local innkeeper begged him for brinn . . . for his wife. He could tell that Hardyn was lying when he said he didn't have any."

"She's dying or mortally ill from a flux?"

Bard can both hear and sense the movement of the other armswoman.

"Something like that." After a pause, Eltara says in a stronger voice, "Delana . . . we're going to have company."

The other armswoman moves toward them, stopping as she sees Bard and the bow he carries. "That's a—"

"Yes, it is," he agrees. "The nearest rider is less than half a kay away. We should let them get within a few yards without letting them see us."

The fact that both women agree confirms their experience.

Another quarter glass passes before he hears what he has sensed for far longer. The dark-clad riders, a party of ten, move slowly, quietly, as they ease toward the traders' camp.

"Wearing dark clothes and skulking around . . . that's the mark of a brigand," calls out Bard when the lead rider is less than thirty yards away.

The lead rider says nothing, but raises a blade of some sort and rides directly toward Bard, who immediately looses the first shaft, then a second, third, and fourth. His movements are practiced and fluid, almost unthinking, which is even more necessary than his speed and accuracy. He manages seven shafts before the white-tinged miasma sweeps over him. He does manage to extend the bow and cushion his fall with his left hand before everything goes totally black.

Water on his face wakes him, enough that he can feel his skull being pounded by an invisible hammer. Bright points of white pain flare before his eyes, making what he can see intermittent at best. With the help of one of the armswomen—he cannot tell which at that moment—he struggles into a sitting position.

"They didn't wound you, did they? I can't see anything. The light's not the best, though."

"No. They didn't." *You might say that the weight of the past did.* He does not utter those words, however, but merely attempts to concentrate on where he is. After several moments, he asks, "Did you get the last three?"

"We did. How did you know?"

"I see well in the dark." That is also true, but not all the truth. "My bow?"

"It's fine. You didn't fall on it."

Bard can finally determine that Eltara is the one who helped him. "Thank you."

"We'll be the ones thanking you."

"It took the three of us," he replies.

Delana approaches through the darkness. One hand holds shafts. "There are seven. One's broken."

"I'll take it, too." He accepts the shafts and eases them into the quiver.

She says to her partner, "Every one through the eye." She looks back to Bard. "Your entire shaft and the head—they're wood."

"Of course," says Eltara quickly and firmly. "Later. We need to get the bard on his way, and us on ours. We'll only have a few glasses before the locals decide that their raiding expedition was unsuccessful, if that. We'll need to be well west of here."

"Leave the bodies where they fell and take the horses, all but one. Tie the one to a tree near the bodies. I assume you took everything of value."

Eltara fumbles in her wallet then extends her hand. "Of course. A third's yours. That's the rule for traders' guards."

Bard smiles. It is, if he happened to be a paid guard, but to refuse would be an insult. "Thank you. It will make the rest of my journey easier." He lets her drop the eleven coppers into his extended palm.

"Not that much easier," replies Eltara. "They only had a bit more than three silvers in coppers among them."

"Every copper helps when you're traveling." He stands, carefully. The worst is past . . . he thinks. This time. Until he sleeps and dreams.

"You got most of them . . . ," begins Delana.

"I have . . . difficulty finishing a fight," he admits. That is the statement with the fewest omissions he has made the entire evening.

"The way you start," says Eltara, "there's not much finishing needed. Will you need help saddling up?"

He shakes his head.

"Then we'd all better get moving."

IV

The late afternoon sun beats down on Bard's back as he rides from the west city gate into the heart of Jellico. Heat oozes from the cracked paving stones that date back a century or more, and possibly even to the time just after when Kastral held off Fenardre the Great. Before too long, he reins up outside the inn's stable. He glances back at the signboard—the faded image of a bronze bowl. There is no lettering.

A boy hurries out from the shadows beyond the double doors. "You be staying here, ser?"

For a moment, Bard has to struggle to understand the words. *Has the speech changed that much?* Then the accent tells him that the youngster must have come from Montgren or even Sligo, likely indentured by his family after a bad year.

"If there's room."

"I couldn't say, ser."

"A copper to keep the horse while I eat and find out."

"Yes, ser."

Bard dismounts and removes the guitar from his pack before leaving the stable and walking into the inn.

The angular man who has to be the innkeeper stops him in the hall that serves both the inn and the tavern. "We don't give rooms to minstrels. You can sleep by the fire if folks like your songs."

"What's the tariff for a garret with a pallet?" Before the innkeeper can reply, Bard goes on, "A pair of coppers?"

"Three."

"The stable?"

"Copper a night. Another copper for grain."

"And some ale without charge if the public room likes my songs."

"One mug every half glass you sing. If they like you. No food."

Bard studies the innkeeper. Hard as the man's voice is, there is but the faintest trace of white about him, and far more of the blackness Bard wishes to see. He hands over three coppers, holding the fourth back. "For the grain? Now or later?"

The innkeeper pauses, then says, "One for today. We'll see about later."

Bard nods and hands over the fourth copper.

"Garret room for you has a horn painted on the door. Be another glass before anyone wants a song. Maybe longer."

"Then I can eat first. I'm paying. What's good today?"

"Pearapple pork ragout."

"I need to get my gear." With a nod, Bard heads back to the stable to finish the arrangements with the ostler's boy.

Once the mare is settled in a stall to herself, and fed a grain mixture that is mostly oats, Bard uses the stable pump to wash his hands and face, then takes his gear up to the third floor and the corner garret. After securing his belongings in a suitable fashion, he makes his way down to the public room, less than half-full, where he takes a small table with two chairs and places the guitar on the other chair.

Before that long, a serving woman appears. She is neither young nor old, but her hair is bound up in a bun, although a few brown wisps have escaped. Her face is thin and worn beyond her years, and there are circles under her eyes. "Ser?"

"Is the pearapple pork as good as the innkeeper claims?"

"It's not bad, ser."

"Is there anything better?"

"I'd take the pork, ser."

"How much?"

"Three, ser, if you take ale with it."

He eases out three coppers and leaves them on the table.

She nods and moves toward the archway into the kitchen. He smiles as she moves adroitly to avoid the questing hand of an older merchanter at the circular table. The merchanter looks vaguely surprised, then turns back toward the graybeard across the table from him.

Bard listens.

". . . avoid Lydiar . . . Duke's armsmen shaking down small traders . . . cut down a minstrel . . . didn't like what he sang about the Duke . . ."

". . . Sligan black pine up a copper a hundred cubit-length . . ."

". . . might try Spidlaran yellow pine . . ."

The lecherous merchant snorts. "Not with the whites adding a half-copper surcharge for the use of the stone roads into their city . . ."

Bard isn't surprised, although he wonders when the white mages had started the practice. *You should have traveled more.* At that thought, he smiles to himself. Traveling long ago lost its appeal, as dreaming has.

". . . Viscount and Prefect can't do anything . . ."

"Do you blame them?"

Bard continues to listen until he sees the server returning.

She sets the mug of ale on the table, followed by the brown crockery platter with a chip on one edge. A battered tin spoon is stuck into the ragout, and a small loaf of bread, more the size of a bun, perches on the other side of the platter.

He immediately studies the food and the ale, but can sense no chaos of any sort. He hands her the coppers. "Thank you."

The coppers vanish into the wallet at her waist. Another pair of coppers appears in his fingers. "For you and the little one."

Her eyes widen.

"Not a word." He doesn't wish to explain how he knows.

"Thank you, ser." Her voice is barely audible, and she turns quickly.

He breaks off a chunk of bread and uses it to push part of the not-quite-soupy mass onto the spoon. He lifts the spoon and samples the yellowish concoction. To his surprise, its taste belies its appearance, and he has another spoonful. He takes his time finishing, watching as the public room slowly fills.

Finally, he begins to tune the guitar. Then he plays a melody without song, after which he pauses and takes several sips from the mug that is almost empty, before he plays a second tune, and then a third. The notes are faint silver, but silver indeed.

"A song! Let's have a song," someone calls.

He smiles and stands beside the table, his back to the wall. After adjusting the strings again, he begins.

> *Once I knew a maid so fair*
> *When spring had turned the evenings gold . . .*

He offers a comical and wry expression and continues with the next stanzas of the song before reaching the last one.

> *That is why I do but sing*
> *In winter of my wandering ways.*
> *A woman is truly a deadly fling*
> *And I'd like to keep my lingering days.*

There are enough smiles around the room when he finishes that he bows slightly before the next song.

> *When I set out for Lydiar*
> *A thousand kays away . . .*

The song after that is more for the merchants.

> *Sing a song of coppers, pocket full of sky,*
> *Four and twenty traitorbirds, baked into a pie.*

Three others follow before Bard announces cheerfully, "This one's for the fellows in the corner."

> *When the bones roll sole, or sevens thrice,*
> *There's weight out of hand, and the snow is ice . . .*
> *Make your sum with grief, and you'll sleep with ease,*
> *Make it with no effort, and you'll sleep where others*
>   *please . . .*

Several of the older men chuckle. One of the hard-eyed younger men around the corner table stiffens, ever so slightly, and only for an instant.

Bard keeps his headshake to himself and finishes the song, even as he notes that the sad-eyed server has refilled his mug. He is about to set the guitar in the empty chair when a black-haired woman slips into it. Despite the warmth in the room, she wears a long-sleeved and form-fitting blouse that, while showing nothing, reveals everything.

"You looking for company, minstrel?"

"Only to share words over an ale, fair lady. I'll pay, but just for an ale for you."

She raises one eyebrow.

Definitely a practiced expression. "There's another fair lady." And that is also true in its way, truer than his other truths.

"A faithful bard?"

"I know," he replies. "Rarer than an honest ruler or a Rational Star."

"Then I won't take your coin, even for ale." She smiles. "You're from the West, beyond the Westhorns."

"How do you know that?" He takes a swallow from the mug, wondering about her, but there is no free chaos around her.

"When I was very small, I heard a singer. I don't think he was a bard or a minstrel. He had silver hair like you. He didn't have a beard and he would still be younger than you. He sang like you. Do you know him?"

"I couldn't say. Not without knowing more." That is strictly true, but he doubts his guess would be wrong.

"I can remember parts of one of the songs." Her voice drops as she sings, barely above a whisper.

> *Down by the seashore, where the waters foam white,*
> *Hang your head over; hear the wind's flight . . .*

She looks at him inquiringly.

He realizes she is much older than he had thought, enough older . . . "That's an old song. It's a song of mourning for unrequited or lost love. Most wouldn't sing it except in private."

"It was sung in private."

"Since you were small, I'd guess it was sung to your mother . . . or an aunt." He knows it was sung to her mother, who had also been black-haired with intense blue eyes. *How have you come to be here, Rhianna?* A thought strikes him and he glances across the public room to the wall, where stand two men, both wearing nondescript cloaks—private guards. He almost nods. "You've been looking for him for years. You paid to be told if a silver-haired singer ever appears."

She does not appear to be in the least surprised. "Of course. Call it one of my . . . foibles."

He waits.

"Do you know him?"

"I can get word to him."

She purses her lips ever so slightly, then nods. "That might be best." A faint smile appears. "It might, indeed." After a moment, she goes on. "It was my mother. She died almost ten years ago, but the years after she . . . heard that singer . . . she always said they were the best of her life"

"I can tell him that. What about you?"

"I cannot complain. In fact, I have little to complain about . . . except perhaps envying her a bit."

"It's best not to envy." His words are quiet. "What you envy may not be what you think."

"I think I see that. Thank you . . . for her." Her smile is brief before she stands and slips away toward the guards. She does not look back as the guards follow her from the public room.

Bard can feel more than a few eyes turn in his direction.

Once Rhianna has left the room he stands and fingers the strings of the guitar.

> *Catch a pretty girl, and keep her in your heart,*
> *Never let her go, for love may keep you two apart . . .*

A half glass later, he sets down the guitar and takes a last swallow of ale. Then he lifts the guitar and steps away from the table. He fixes his eyes on the hard-eyed young man still waiting to join the bones game. When the man looks up, Bard shakes his head.

The would-be gambler looks away immediately.

Bard hides his sigh. *Those who cannot recognize a quiet warning won't accept a stronger one.* He turns and makes his way up the narrow stairs to the tiny garret room with the single pallet.

He will not dream . . . he hopes.

V

Bard reins up and shudders as he looks at the white tower that dominates the white city and stands across the square from him on sixday afternoon. "Such beautifully ordered chaos . . ." His words are low and spoken only to himself.

He turns the mare and has her proceed at a walk toward the artisans' quarter, where he will stay at the hostel before making his way to the tavern new to him that he has yet to visit, although enough years have passed that revisiting any of those he once frequented would raise no memories. *None at all.*

Three glasses later, as the sun hangs low over the hill to the west of the city, he walks past the inn, which has no name, to the adjoining tavern. The oval signboard over the whitened oak door to the tavern itself reads LAVENDER ROSE, and a carved rose, painted lavender, is positioned under the curved letters.

The server just inside the door glances at him . . . and at the guitar he holds.

"You can't sing for your meal."

"I had not planned on that." He smiles almost shyly. "Is there any objection to my singing after I've eaten and drunk . . . and paid for both?"

"You get one song. If no one complains you get another. It's like that these days. No magery in the music. The white guards will flame you faster than grease on hot coals."

"The only magery I know lies in my voice and the strings of my guitar." That is not quite true, but those will be the only magery he would ever show or use within the white city—in public or anywhere he can be overheard . . . and that is almost anywhere, given the mirrors that the white mages use.

"Keep it that way, minstrel."

There are two small tables that are empty. One has but a single chair, because there are five men at the adjoining table. Recalling what happened in Jellico, he chooses that table and places the guitar on its side under it, leaning against the wall.

"What'll you have?" The server is like so many, worn beyond her years, but she offers a smile that has a tiny trace of warmth.

"What is there? Besides stew?" In the white city, there is always stew, and often burhka, because the spices mask the tinge of chaos that is everywhere.

"Burhka, and papparoiles."

"Papparoiles." The large, flat noodles with brown sauce are peppered just enough to mute the ever-present chaos, a chaos unnoticed even by the few healers and blacks tolerated by the white mages.

Close to a glass later, he rises and strums the guitar. Those at the nearer tables look in his direction. A man and a round-faced woman dressed to look younger than she is exchange glances of resignation.

> *I'll go no more a riding, not under the staring stars*
> *Or by the silent seas.*
> *I'll not be the one to sing, not outside your window*
> * bars,*
> *Or by the tulip trees . . .*

When he bows at the end of the song, there is a scattering of applause. He looks to the tall woman by the archway to the back. She nods.

Given that modest encouragement, his fingers find the strings once more, this time to sing the almost, but not quite, nonsensical contrary song.

> *When masons strive to break their bricks*
> *And joiners craft their best with sticks . . .*
> *When rich men find their golds a curse,*
> *And Westwind's marshal fills your purse,*
> *Then sea-hags will dance upon their hands*
> *And dolphins swim through silver sands.*
> *Hollicum-hoarem, billicum-borem . . .*

The bard can see a few smiles as he finishes the second song, and the tall woman nods again. Even the round-faced woman inclines her head, if but slightly.

He offers two more songs before seating himself, even though he has continued to see approval. *Four songs should be enough . . . more than enough.* Especially since he might have to perform for days before what he seeks might occur.

VI

Bard eats at the Lavender Rose again on sevenday, eightday, and oneday. Each night he sings four songs, and only four. On twoday night, when he enters the tavern, the tall woman murmurs, "Be careful. Fellow in the corner looks like a white guard."

Bard nods. "I'll be very careful."

After eating, he begins with the setting out for Lydiar song, and follows it with the contrary song. After that comes "Maid So Fair."

As the silvered notes die away, he can see that the white guard has left. Perhaps his waiting is over. *Perhaps.*

He shifts the guitar slightly and begins the last song.

> *The minstrel knows what's brewing*
> *For the pair hearing his tunes*
> *He knows well they'll be ruing.*
> *The love he's sparked with his runes . . .*
> *And tell me it's love, sweet love,*
> *Not just a hand in a glove . . .*

When he finishes, he takes a last bow, then walks to the table, where he replaces the guitar in his otherwise empty pack, knowing from the miasma that few in the white city even sense that white guards wait for him outside the Lavender Rose. Then he nods to the tall woman and makes his way to the door.

Outside, standing on the white stone sidewalk that borders the street paved in even larger white stones, wait two white guards and a white wizard.

"You're to come with us, minstrel," declares the wizard.

Bard doubts the wizard has reached twenty-five, if that. But then, most die young. "Of course."

After walking several blocks, the wizard turns toward a white stone building. For the first time since entering the city Bard is surprised. He is less surprised when he is led to the chamber whose walls are made of precise white stones. He has seen that inside wall on too many nights. The pleasant-faced man seated behind the white wooden table is clad entirely in white, except for certain items of white bronze, and the true bronze starbursts on the collar of his tunic. His eyes are sun gold.

Bard nods, both in politeness and in affirmation of the image he has already seen too many times.

"You were very careful, minstrel. With your words. No one—not in years—has managed four songs a night for more than half an eightday. You could have continued for eightdays, could you not?"

"At four a night, I know enough songs for a time."

"What is your name?"

"'Bard' will do as well as any."

The white mage laughs harshly. "I could force you."

"You could. Would it please you if I recited all the names I've gone by?"

"A few of them might be useful." The mage's tone was cold but wry.

"Nylson, Naharl, Hylchant, Lied, Vatyr, Tynor . . ."

"You seem to be telling the truth." The mage smiles.

"I am. It's much easier that way."

"So it is, but what is true is not necessarily all the truth. There is another name that comes to mind."

"I've been called more than a few."

"Since you do not wish to be named, I will not. You sing well, Bard. Were it not so clear who and what you are, you could almost pass for a renegade black, at home nowhere in Candar or anywhere else."

"Home is foreign to a bard."

"Oh?"

"If I do not sing in a way true to myself, then what I sing will turn on me. If I do, sooner or later some listeners will. That's another reason to limit what I sing." Bard shrugs. His laugh is of quiet amusement. "You are among the highest. Why do you trouble yourself with a poor singer?"

"You're scarcely a poor singer. I doubt there's one better in all Candar. We both know you're far older than you look. You sought me out. It does not appear that way, but you did so in a fashion that made sense for me to take an interest. Why?"

"There is too much order in the Westhorns," Bard says bluntly. "It might be best if that changed."

"I cannot believe that you would even intimate that the white city invade the Westhorns . . . or Westwind."

"I cannot believe you don't understand that Westwind poses problems for you."

"We can deal with Westwind."

"I'm certain you can. That's the last thing I would want. Or that any beyond the Westhorns would wish. Wouldn't another kind of change be preferable." *Since as Candar has begun to change, Westwind's end must come.*

"Oh?"

"Think about it."

"I already have. There are . . . possibilities . . ."

"They will take resources you could better use closer to the white city."

"You could do whatever you have in mind without even coming here."

Bard shakes his head. "No. If I do what I must without your knowledge . . . and then you were to do what you feel necessary . . . instead of too much order in the Westhorns, there would be far too much chaos . . ." He goes on for several sentences.

"How do we know—"

Bard's laugh is harsh, at least for him. "You know that we do not lie, and we do not break our promises. You will also know in less than a year."

"You may not lie, but seldom do you tell the whole truth unless it suits you."

"If you agree, I will do exactly what I have proposed."

"But what that will cause, you say . . ." The white mage's lips purse. "That is a long time to wait."

"You would spend half that time just readying a force . . . and you would lose thousands of men. Far better for you to let events take their course. Just think . . . a beloved first-born son . . . there. Is that not chaotic enough for you?"

A faint but hard smile crosses the mage's lips.

VII

The skies are cold and clear, and harvest has faded into autumn when Bard finally reaches the stone guard post that marks what had once been the border between Westwind and Gallos. While the lower lands to the north also belong to Westwind, the Westwind Guards patrol them less frequently. On the rocky peaks to the south beyond the guard post there is already a dusting of snow on the open ground, but none on the needles of the evergreens or on the stone-paved narrow road that leads to the heart of Westwind.

He reins up as two guards step out of the small stone building into the chill wind.

The two guards, each with twin blades in shoulder scabbards, study him.

"What is your business here?" asks the older.

"I'm on my way to Clynya. I thought that some might like to hear a minstrel. I know that this is not a place where many men linger, but news and song might find a welcome for a day or so."

"Lute or guitar?"

"Guitar." He gestures to the pack fastened over the saddle-bags behind his saddle.

"Weapons?"

"There's an old horn bow and a quiver in the pack. No blades except a belt knife."

"Bronze or iron?"

"Black iron."

The older guard studies his hair, then says, "The duty guard captain can decide. You'll have to wait for our relief. Then we'll escort you to our post. That will be a glass or so. You can sleep there tonight. If the captain passes you, tomorrow you can ride with a courier to the keep. That's a dawn-to-dark ride and then some."

"Thank you." Bard does not mention that he has made that ride before, if many, many years ago.

"You can tie your mare in the shelter behind the post and wait there."

Bard accepts the dismissal and rides slowly to the rear of the post.

VIII

Two days later, Bard enters the great hall at Westwind, carrying only his guitar, and accompanied by a junior guard captain named Heldra. It is late afternoon, but well before the evening meal, and the hall is mainly empty, except for the four women seated at the table on the dais at the far end, three in the center of the table and a silver-haired woman at the end.

As he approaches, he studies the three. The black-haired

and tall woman in the center wearing black leathers must be the Marshal, for all that she appears too young, in her late twenties at best. Looks can be deceiving, however, as Bard well knows. The grayed and weathered woman to Bard's left and the Marshal's right is likely the arms-master. The other woman? Someone of import, but of what import, he has no idea.

"This is the minstrel, Marshal," announces Heldra after she and Bard halt before the dais.

"What is your name?" The Marshal's voice is strong, but not unpleasant.

Bard bows, then straightens. "I've had many names. That's because not all have liked what I've sung. Those you may have heard are Naharl, Nylson, Lied, Hylchant, Vatyr, Tynor . . ."

The Marshal glances to the silver-haired woman seated at the end of the table, clearly a healer with order skills.

"He's speaking the truth. He's mostly druid from what I can tell. Possibly all druid."

"How did you come here?"

"Most recently, I traveled through Gallos. I did not stay long in Fenard. The Prefect has forbidden public song. He says it creates chaos."

The Marshal looks to the older woman. "Blynna?"

"Where else have you traveled in the last year?"

"From Clynya I made my way through the southern pass. I tried to stay in the Analerian lands of Gallos. I stopped in many small towns. I sang in Arrat, Desanyt, and Meltosia. I ran into brigands when I camped with traders outside of Vryna. I also sang in Jellico and Vergren, and spent a few days in the white city before leaving and heading west again."

"Not Lydiar?"

Bard shakes his head. "I heard that Lydiar wasn't all that safe, and that the Duke's armsmen have gotten into the habit of killing bards whose songs they didn't like."

A quizzical look appears on the face of the woman who has not spoken.

"You have a question, Aemris? Go ahead."

"Thank you." Aemris turns to Bard. "Why did you spend time in the white city? Isn't singing there dangerous, especially for someone like you?"

"Singing anywhere can be dangerous, but people pay for news as much as song, and the larger cities are where the news is. In the white city, I never sang more than four songs a night." He offers a wry smile. "I did learn a few things, and I managed to leave without more than a few questions from the white guards."

Aemris looks to the healer. The healer nods.

"What did you learn? Especially matters that might affect Westwind?"

"It can't be a surprise to you that the white mages are working to control all of Candar. They feel that Westwind will keep them from ruling the lands beyond the Westhorns. I got the impression that they're thinking about doing something—"

"Got the impression?" asks the Marshal coolly. "How?"

"I heard a white mage talking. He said that the white city could deal with Westwind and there were several possibilities. He didn't mention what those were. I wasn't in a position to ask him."

"Where exactly did you hear this?"

"In a white city patrol building. I was waiting to be questioned."

"And they let you go?"

"Provided I left the city immediately."

"You were fortunate," observes Blynna. "What else did you learn there or elsewhere in your travels?"

"That Sarronnyn has re-opened the old copper mines, and that copper and timber are getting dearer . . ."

The questioning lasts for more than a glass when the Marshal gestures. "You may stay here for a time. There is more that we would know. We would appreciate a few songs after dinner."

Bard nods. "Thank you, Marshal."

He is waiting in an alcove off the main hall when he hears a sound from an adjoining chamber, then a cry. The guard beside him shifts her weight as the cries grow louder.

"Let me sing . . ."

"You're supposed to wait here."

"I can stand in the doorway."

"I don't . . ."

Bard eases to the door, slightly ajar, and peers in. A young girl is rocking a cradle, cooing to the infant, but the cries continue.

He opens the door slightly and, lifting the guitar, begins to sing.

> *Oh, my dear, my dear little child,*
> *What can we do in a place so wild,*
> *Where the sky is so green and so deep*
> *And who will rock you to sleep . . .*

By the end of the second stanza there is a soft "coo," and when he finishes the lullaby, the small chamber is again quiet.

The girl tending the infant looks up with an expression of gratitude.

Bard smiles and retreats, saying to the guard, "I've had a little experience." *More than a little.*

Before all that long the guards begin to file into the great hall. The guard with Bard guides him to a table at the rear.

"The travelers' table."

No one joins him, which is hardly surprising, given how late in the year it is, late for the heights of the Westhorns, anyway. The dinner consists of a cross between a casserole and a stew with a game meat, most likely red deer, accompanied by a healthy slice of maize bread.

In time, he is summoned to the front of the hall where he seats himself on the dais and begins to sing.

> *All day I dragged a boat of stone*
> *And came home when you weren't alone,*
> *So I took all those blasted rocks*
> *And buried all your boyish fancy locks . . .*
> *And took you for a ride in my boat of stone . . .*

The song is archaic, but the melody is lively, and the guards seem to like it, as he'd thought they might.

"Another," suggests the Marshal.

He fingers the strings for a moment, thinking, then plays a series of chords leading into the next song.

> *The way is always too far,*
> *As the west mountains are*
> *As solid as sky towers,*
> *As empty as showers . . .*

In the end, he has sung for close to a glass.

The Marshal merely nods to him before she leaves the dais. Neither Aemris nor Blynna even look in his direction.

IX

Bard sings after dinner every evening for over an eightday. He always sings the first song to the Marshal, and all the others to the guards.

He still dreams the dreams of what he must bring to pass, and he often wakes in the travelers' quarters drenched in sweat and shivering. The smell of that sweat nauseates him, and he must wash up completely and frequently, despite the bone-numbing chill of the water.

On sixday evening, the Marshal stops him after half a glass and motions him to the dais and to a chair placed beside her.

"You sing far too well for a traveling minstrel."

"I will admit I do not travel often. This past half year has been the first in a very long time. I have stayed here longer than anywhere else."

"Do you wish to leave?"

"No."

"Why not?"

"Because I am here to sing for you."

The Marshal looks to the healer, who nods, almost sadly. The Marshal looks back to him. "Then . . . perhaps I should let you. You may accompany me." She stands.

He immediately does as well, then walks beside her, if a half pace back, as she climbs the stone steps to the upper level and a sitting room behind a heavy oak door.

The two guards position themselves just inside the door.

She seats herself in a leather upholstered straight armchair.

He takes a lower stool from the wall and places it several yards from her.

"You're not as old as you look," says the Marshal, a faint smile tingeing her lips.

"Far older in some ways, younger in others." *Otherwise you would not find me here.*

"You've circled much of Candar to gain my attention. Why?"

"The simplest and most honest answer is because I must." His reply is also totally true.

"From one like you, that is indeed a compliment."

"To a woman who will determine the entire future of the world, it is a fact."

"Do you ever lie?"

"No . . . except . . . I do not always tell all I know."

"Truth is the most deceiving of lies."

"It is."

"How are you deceiving me?"

"I've tried not to deceive you about why I am here."

"Why is that?"

"To sing to you, so that what can be, will be."

"Then . . . you should sing."

Without another word, he eases the guitar into position and begins.

> *Catch a falling fire; hold it to the skies,*
> *Never let it die away,*
> *For love may come and fill your lonely eyes*
> *With the light of more than day . . .*

With the words and the silvered notes from the strings, he weaves truth into the song, as much as he can.

Her eyes are bright when he finishes.

"Perhaps a song more appropriate to . . . ," he suggests.

"The season? Of course. Since it is almost harvest . . ."

> *When the plains grass whispers gold*
> *When the red blooms flower bold—*

The Marshal holds up her hand and looks to the two guards. "You can leave now."

The younger immediately rises. The older offers an inquiring glance.

The Marshal merely nods. She does not speak until the door to the chamber is closed and the echo of boots on the stone steps has faded. "Where did you learn that song?"

"From my grandmother . . . quite some time ago." He pauses. "There are others I could have sung."

"Such as?" Her voice is cool, and anything but coy.

He fingers the guitar and begins again.

When I was single, I looked at the skies.
Now I've a consort, I listen to lies,
Lies about horses that speak in the darks,
Lies about cats and theories of quarks . . .

"Enough." The single word is cold. "You never said from where you came?"

"As I told you when I came, I traveled from Clynya to Certis and the white city, then through Gallos. Carefully, of course."

"That's not an answer."

He does not answer, not in spoken words, but his fingers caress the strings.

Oh, Nylan was a mage, and a mighty smith was he.
With rock from the heights and a lightning blade built
he . . .

She frowns. "That's not an answer."

"But it is. You don't know that song. It was banned by Ryba, but it was first sung by the singer who composed your anthem, the one you don't sing when outsiders are around."

From the skies of long-lost Heaven
To the heights of Westwind keep . . .

"You're one of *them* . . . one of the Ancients."

"I've been called that . . . for lack of a better word."

"Why are you here?"

"To sing you songs, at your pleasure. Only at your pleasure."

"The druids have never meant harm to Westwind . . ." The first hint of tentativeness enters her voice, then vanishes. "I would hear your songs, but your songs, not ours."

"I can sing those . . . and others."

"My name is Dylyss." She says no other word, just waits. His fingers once more find the strings.

> *When lightning spares the peaks and splits from one to*
> *   three,*
> *And the stars shine bright enough that the blindest man*
> *   can see,*
> *Then that's when we'll be home, back to the forest free,*
> *That's when we'll face no trials and live within our*
> *   tree . . .*

He can see the puzzlement on her face, but he finishes the song and begins another, one not quite so sardonic.

> *The daring old smith with the hammer of light,*
> *He struck down the Lancers of Cyad so bright . . .*

He sings quietly, warmly, with all his skill and honesty, for well over a glass until he knows the time is right. The last lines of the last song will be absolutely true, but necessary for all that must and will come.

> *When the soareagle takes flight,*
> *You are the fire of the night,*
> *And the light of this day,*
> *The balm for an endless wand'ring way.*
> *You are . . . you are . . . you are . . .*
> *The sun in the shining sky . . .*

When he finishes, he stands and places the guitar on the side table before taking her hand.

She leads him, and that, also, is as it must be, and should be.

X

The bard looks from the small window in the Black Tower toward the ice needle that is Freyja, a spire of ice-sheathed rock that dominates the heights of the Westhorns . . . and Westwind. The white light of the sun catches only the tip of that ice needle, creating the impression of an upthrust dark blade with a shining white point.

The winter has been long, and he has sung almost all the songs he knows, and composed a few more. Some of those he has not sung. Some he may not sing for years. Some . . . perhaps never.

His dreams have largely faded . . . and he only wakes transfixed occasionally. That saddens him, and always will.

Before long the deep snows will melt enough that roads to the west—those beyond Westwind, for the guards keep the major ways within the heights open no matter what—will open. Then he will leave . . . for a time.

He senses a familiar presence on the ancient steps, and hears the bootsteps on the stone, but he does not turn.

"I thought I would find you here. When will you be leaving?"

"I've said nothing."

"You haven't needed to. You need to return to . . . your home . . ." The tall woman in the black leathers does not mention the Great Forest. She never has. Neither has he.

"I will come back."

"When I am dead and gone? Like the others?"

"Late next fall." *Once and no more.*

"You are one who promises little."

"I have never broken a promise. Ever." And, that, too, is true.

She takes his hand. "The roads will not be clear below Westwind for another eightday."

They descend the ancient stone steps together.

In time, he may sleep without dreaming.

In time.

I had written thirteen novels about Recluce, but never a story—until Eric Flint asked me to do so.

SISTERS OF SARRONNYN, SISTERS OF WESTWIND

I

The Roof of the World was still frozen in winter gray, and the sun had not yet cleared the peaks to the east or shone on Freyja when I caught sight of Fiera coming up the old stone steps from the entrance to Tower Black.

I moved to intercept her. "What were you doing, Guard Fiera?"

"I was coming to the main hall, Guard Captain." Fiera did not look directly at me, but past me, a trick many Westwind guards had tried over the years. Even my own sister, especially my own sister, could not fool me.

"Using the east passage?"

Fiera flushed. "Yes, Guard Captain."

"Assignations before breakfast, yet? When did you sneak out of the barracks?"

She straightened, as she always did when she decided to flaunt something or when she knew she'd been caught. "He kissed me, Guard Captain. Creslin did."

Oh, Fiera, do not lie to me. I did not voice the words. "I seriously doubt that the esteemed son of the Marshall would have even known you were in the east passage. It is seldom traveled before dawn in winter. If anyone kissed anyone, you kissed him. What was he doing? Why were you following him?"

Fiera's eyes dropped. "He was just there. By himself. He was walking the passage."

"You're a fool! If the Marshall ever finds out, you'll be posted to High Ice for the rest of the winter this year, and for all of next year with no relief. That would be after you were given to the most needy of the consorts until you were with child. You'd never see the child after you bore her, and you'd spend your shortened life on remote duty, perhaps even on the winter road crews."

This time, my words reached her. She swallowed. "I meant no harm. He's always looked at me. I just . . . wanted him to know before he leaves for Sarronnyn."

"He knows now. If I see you anywhere near him, if I hear a whisper . . ."

"Yes, Guard Captain . . . please . . . Shierra."

"What was he doing near Tower Black?" I asked again.

"I do not know, Guard Captain. He was wearing field dress, without a winter parka. He looked like any other guard." Fiera's eyes met mine fully for the first time.

We both knew that young Creslin, for all his abilities with a blade, was anything but another guard. He was the only male ever trained with the Guards, and yet his masculine skills had not been neglected. He could play the guitar better than any minstrel, and I'd heard his voice when he sang. It seemed that he could call a soft breeze in the heat of summer, and more than a few of those who had guarded his door had come away with tears in their eyes. Fiera had been one of them, unhappily. He'd even called an ice storm once. Only once, after he had discovered he'd been promised to the Sub-Tyrant of Sarronnyn.

Shortly, after more words with Fiera, I walked down the steps to the door of the ancient tower to check on what might have happened.

I always thought that tales of love were romantic nothings meant for men, not for the guards—or guard captains of Westwind—although I worried about my younger sister, and her actions in the east passage showed that I was right to worry. Fiera was close to ten years younger than I. We had not been close as children. I've always felt that sisters were either inseparable or distant. We were distant. Much as I tried to bridge that distance, much as I tried to offer kindness and advice, Fiera rejected both. When I attempted kindness, she said, "I know you're trying to be nice, but I'm not you. I have to do things my own way." She said much the same thing when I first offered advice. After a time, I only offered simple courtesy, as one would to any other Westwind guard, and no advice at all.

To my relief, the Tower Black door was locked, as it always was and should have been. There *might* have been boot prints in the frost, but even as a guard captain, I was not about to report what I could not prove, not when it might lead to revealing Fiera's indiscretion. Besides, what difference could it have made? Fiera had not made a fatal error, and young Creslin would be leaving Westwind forever, within days, to become the consort of the Sub-Tyrant of Sarronnyn.

II

Four mornings later, Guard Commander Aemris summoned the ten Westwind Guard Captains to the duty room below the great hall. She said nothing at all for a time. Her eyes traveled from one face to another.

"Some of you may have heard the news," Aemris finally said. "Lord Creslin skied off the side of the mountain into a snowstorm. The detachment was unable to find him. The Marshall has declared mourning."

"How? . . ."

"The weather . . ."

"He wasn't supplied . . ."

"There are some skis and supplies missing from Tower Black. He must have taken them. Do any of you know anything about that?"

I almost froze in place when Aemris dropped those words, but I quickly asked, "How could he?"

The Guard Commander turned to me. "He does have some magely abilities. He coated the walls of the South Tower with ice the night after his consorting was announced. The ice is still there. None of the duty guards saw him near Tower Black recently, but he could have taken the gear weeks ago. Or he could have used some sort of magely concealment and made his way there."

Not a single guard captain spoke.

Aemris shook her head. "Men. They expect to be pampered. Even when they're not, and you do everything for them, what does it get you? He's probably frozen solid in the highlands, and we'll find his body in the spring or summer."

I tried not to move my face, but just nod.

"You don't think so, Guard Captain?"

Everyone was looking at me.

"I've seen him with a blade and on skis and in the field trials, ser. He's very good, but he doesn't know it. That will make him cautious."

"For the sake of the Marshall and the Marshalle, I hope so. For the sake of the rest of us . . ." Aemris said no more.

I understood her concerns, but for Fiera's sake, I could only hope Creslin would survive and find some sort of happiness. Despite all the fancies of men and all the tales of the minstrels, most stories of lost or unrequited love end when lovers or would-be lovers are parted. In the real world, they never find each other again, and that was probably for the best, because time changes us all.

III

For weeks after Creslin vanished, Fiera was silent. She threw herself into arms practice, so much so that, one morning, as ice flakes drifted across the courtyard under a gray sky, I had to caution her, if quietly.

"Getting yourself impaled on a practice blade won't bring him back."

"They're blunted," she snapped back.

"That just means the entry wound is jagged and worse."

"You should talk, sister dearest. I've seen you watch him as well."

"I have. I admit it. But only because I admired him, young as he was. I had no illusions."

"You don't understand. You never will. Don't talk to me."

"Very well." I didn't mention Creslin again, even indirectly.

IV

Slightly more than a year passed. The sun began to climb higher in the sky that spring, foreshadowing the short and glorious summer on the Roof of the World. The ice began to melt, if but slightly at midday, and the healer in black appeared at the gates of Westwind. Since she was a woman, she was admitted.

Word spread through the Guard like a forest fire in early fall. *Creslin was alive.* He had somehow found the Sub-Tyrant of Sarronnyn, or she had found him, and the Duke of Montgren had married them and named them as co-regents of Recluce. I'd never heard anything much about Recluce, save that it was a large and mostly deserted isle across the Gulf of Candar to the east of Lydiar.

Fiera avoided me, and that was as well, for what could I have said to her? Creslin was alive, but wed to another, as had been fated from his birth. No male heir to the Marshall could ever remain in Westwind, and none ever had.

That night after inspecting the duty guards, I settled onto my pallet in the private corner alcove I merited as a guard captain without a consort.

I awoke in a tower. It was Tower Black, and the walls rose up around me. I looked up, but the stones extended farther than I could make out. The stone steps led upward, and I began to climb them. Yet they never ended, and at each landing, the doorway to the outside had been blocked by a stone statue of an unsmiling Creslin in the garb of a Westwind Guard. Behind the statue, the archway had been filled in with small black stones and deep gray mortar. I kept climbing, past landing after landing with the same statue of Creslin. The walls rose into a gray mist above me. Blood began to seep from my boots. I refused to say anything. I kept climbing. Surely, there had to be a way out of the tower. There had to be . . .

"Shierra, wake up." Dalyra shook me. "Wake up," she hissed. "You'll rouse everyone with that moaning and muttering. They'll ask what you were dreaming. Guard captains don't need that."

"I'm awake." I could tell I was still sleepy. My words came out mumbled.

"Good," whispered Dalyra. "Now go back to sleep." She padded back to her pallet in the adjoining alcove.

I lay there in the darkness under the thick woolen blankets of a single guard captain. I'd never wanted a consort. Not in Westwind, and it wasn't likely I'd ever be anywhere else. Even if I left Westwind, where would I ever find one strong enough to stand up to me? The only man I'd seen with that strength was Creslin, and he'd been little more than a youth when he'd escaped Westwind, and far too young and far too above me. Unlike Fiera, I knew what was possible.

Yet what had the dream meant? The Tower Black of my dream hadn't been the tower I knew. Tower Black was the oldest part of Westwind. Its smooth stones had been cut and fitted precisely by the ancient smith-mage Nylan under the geas of Ryba the Great before he had spellsung the traitor Arylyn to free him and fled with Arylyn to the world below the Roof of the World. The great hall, the Guard quarters, the stables, the craft buildings, all of them were far larger than Tower Black. Yet none of them conveyed the *solidity* of the far smaller Tower Black that they dwarfed.

I finally drifted back into sleep, but it was an uneasy slumber at best.

The next morning, Aemris mustered all the guards, and even the handfuls of consorts and the guard captains, in the main courtyard of Westwind. She stood in the gusty spring wind and snowfall, the large fat flakes swirling lazily from the sky. Beside her stood the healer.

"The Marshall of Westwind has learned that Lord Creslin made his own way to the Sub-Tyrant of Sarronnyn," the Guard Commander began. "They were wed in Montgren, and, as a token of his esteem, the Duke named them co-regents of Recluce.

They are expanding the town of Land's End there on Recluce, and the Marshall will permit some from Westwind to join them in Recluce. The healer will explain."

Aemris delivered her speech without great enthusiasm. Even so, everyone was listening as the healer stepped forward.

"My name is Lydya. I am a healer, and I bring news of Creslin. He crossed much of Candar by himself and unaided. For a time he was imprisoned by the white wizards of Fairhaven, but he escaped and made his way to Montgren. He and Megaera are co-regents of Recluce. They are building a new land, and there is opportunity for all. The land is much warmer and much drier than Westwind, but there are mountains and the sea." She smiled crookedly. "The mountains are rugged, but much lower and not nearly so cold. For better or worse, neither men nor women rule, but both can prosper, or suffer, according to ability . . ."

Somehow that did not surprise me, not from a youth who had crossed much of Candar alone. What puzzled me was that he had married the woman he had left the Westhorns to avoid being consorted to. That suggested that Megaera was far more than he or anyone had expected.

After the healer finished speaking, Aemris added a few words. "Any of you who are interested in accompanying the healer to Recluce remain here. That includes consorts."

Perhaps forty guards out of three hundred remained in the courtyard. I was the only guard captain.

Aemris motioned for me to come forward first.

"You, Shierra?" asked the Guard Commander. "You have the makings of an arms-master or even Guard Commander in years to come."

How could I explain the dream? That, somehow, an image of Creslin kept me walled within Westwind? I could only trust the dream. "Someone must bring his heritage to him," I finally said.

Aemris looked to Lydya. The healer nodded.

"She's the most senior guard who wishes to go," Aemris said. "She should be guard captain of the detachment."

"That she will be." The healer smiled, but I felt the sadness behind the expression.

In the end, Aemris and Lydya settled on twenty-five guards and ten consorts with five children—all boys under five.

For the two days until we rode out, Fiera avoided me even more pointedly than before, walking away when she could, giving only formal responses when she could not. She could have volunteered, but she had not. Instead, she had asked to accompany a trade delegation to Sarronnyn. She hadn't told me. I'd discovered that from others—as I had so many things.

V

The ride to Armat took almost four eightdays. We rode through the Westhorns to Middle Vale and then down into Suthya by the road to the north of the River Arma. Until we reached Suthya, in most places, the snow beside the roads was at least waist-deep, and twice we had to help the road crews clear away new-fallen snow. In Armat, we had to wait another eightday for the ship Lydya had engaged with the letter of credit from the Marshall.

While we waited, she continued to purchase goods in one fashion or another. When the *Pride of Armat* ported, I was surprised to discover it was one of the largest vessels in the harbor, with three tall masts. The ship was heavy-laden indeed by the time its master lifted sail and we departed from Armat three days later. Lydya and I talked frequently, but it was mostly about the cargo, about the guards and their consorts, and about how we would need to use all the wood-working and stone-working tools to build our own shelter on Recluce. That bothered me little. All Guards knew something about building and maintaining structures. Westwind could not have endured over the centuries without those skills. I tended to be better with stone. Perhaps I lacked the delicate touch needed for woodwork.

After more than an eightday of hugging the northern coasts of Candar, the ship had finally left the eastern-most part of Lydiar behind, swallowed by the sea. For the first two days, we'd been followed by another vessel, until Lydya had suggested to the captain that he fly the banner of Westwind I had brought. About halfway across the Gulf of Candar, the war schooner eased away on a different course.

Lydya and I stood just aft of the bowsprit, at the port railing.

"Do you know what to expect in Recluce, Shierra?"

"No, except that it will likely be hot and dry and strange. We'll have to build almost everything from nothing, and there's a garrison of savage men we'll have to deal with."

Lydya laughed. "They'll have to deal with you. None of them are a match for your least trained guards. That's one of the reasons why Creslin needs you, and why the Marshall permitted some of you to come."

"But she drove him out, didn't she?"

"Did she?"

The question made me uneasy, especially asked by a healer. "Why did you come to Westwind?"

"To ask the Marshall for what might be called Creslin's dowry. For obvious reasons, he cannot ask, and he would not even if he were physically where he could."

For that, I also admired him. "How did you come to know him?"

"I was a healer in the White road camp where they imprisoned him. After he escaped, Klerris and I followed him, not to

Montgren, but to Tyrhavven. That is where he and Megaera took the Duke's schooner that brought them to Recluce. Klerris accompanied them, and I traveled to Westwind."

"Is he really a mage?"

"Yes. He may become one of the greatest ever. That is if he and Megaera survive each other."

"Healer . . . what is the Sub-Tyrant like?" I did not wish to ask the question, but I had to know, especially after Lydya's last words.

"She has hair like red mahogany, eyes as green and deep as the summer seas south of Naclos, fair skin, and freckles. She is also a white witch, with a kind heart, and a temper to match the most violent thunderstorms of summer."

"Is she . . ."

"She is as beautiful and as deadly as a fine dagger, Shierra. That is what makes her a match for Creslin, or him for her."

What could I say to that, except more pleasantries about the sea, the weather, and the cargo we carried?

VI

Another day passed. On the morning of the following day, a rocky headland appeared. I could see no buildings at all. There was no smoke from fires. As the ship neared land, and some of the sails were furled, I could finally make a breakwater on the east side of the inlet between the rocky cliffs. At first, I wasn't certain, because it wasn't much more than a long pile of stones. There was a single short pier, with a black stone building behind it, and a scattering of other buildings, one of them clearly half-built. A dusty road wound up a low rise to a keep built out of grayish-black stones. On one end was a section that looked to have been added recently.

The captain had a boat lowered, with a heavy rope—a hawser, I thought—attached to the sternpost. The men in the boat rowed to the pier and fastened it to one of the posts, and then the crew used the capstan to winch the ship in toward the pier. As we got nearer to the shore, I could see that very little grew anywhere, just bushes.

"Lydya . . . it doesn't look like we'll have much use for that wood-working equipment. All I see are a few bushes."

The healer laughed. "Those are trees, or what passes for them."

Trees? They were barely taller than I. I swallowed and turned back to look at the handful of people waiting on the pier. One of them was Creslin. I could tell that from his silver hair, lit by the sunlight. Beside him on one side was a black mage. On the other was a tall red-haired woman. That had to be Megaera.

Once the ship was tied fast, the captain scrambled onto the pier, bowing to Creslin and Megaera. I just watched for a moment.

"Shierra . . . you're the guard captain," said Lydya quietly. "Report to the Regents."

I was senior, and I would have stepped forward sooner, except . . .

There was no excuse. I vaulted over the railing and stood waiting behind the captain. Once he stepped back, I moved forward.

"Guard Captain Shierra, Regent Creslin, Regent Megaera," I began, inclining my head in respect to them.

"Did you have any trouble with the wizards?" Creslin asked.

"No, ser. But then, we insisted that the captain fly our banner. One war schooner did follow us. It left halfway across the Gulf." I couldn't help smiling, but felt nervous all the same as I gestured to the middle mast where the Westwind banner drooped limply.

"You seem to have a full group." Creslin smiled, but he didn't seem to recognize me. Then, why should he have? Fiera had been the one who had kissed him.

"Two and a half squads, actually."

Creslin pointed westward toward the keep. "There are your quarters, rough as they are. We'll discuss other needs once you look things over. We might as well get whatever you brought off-loaded."

"Some carts would help, ser. The healer"—I didn't wish to use her first name, and what else could I call her to a regent?— "was apparently quite persuasive . . ." I went on to explain everything in the cargo holds.

"Now, *that* is true wizardry." Creslin laughed.

The sound was so infectious, almost joyful, that I ended up laughing with him. Then, I was so embarrassed that I turned immediately to the guards. "Let's offload!"

I forced myself to concentrate so much on the details of getting the guards and consorts and the children off the ship and then making sure with the ship's boatswain that the holds would be unloaded in the order on the bill of lading that I did not even sense Megaera's approach.

"Guard Captain?" Her voice carried, despite its softness.

I tried not to jump and turned. "Regent Megaera."

"Once you're ready, I'll escort you up to the keep." She smiled, almost humorously. "They'll have to walk. We're a bit short on mounts. It's not that far, though."

"We have enough mounts for the guards, and some spares." I paused. "But they'll have to be walked themselves after all the time on ship."

It took until early afternoon before we had even begun to transfer cargo and to walk the horses up to the crude stables behind the keep. Once I had duties assigned to the guards, I stayed at the keep, trying to keep track of goods and especially weapons. The wallstones of the outbuildings being used as stables were so loosely set that the stalls would have filled with ice on a single winter day at Westwind. The storerooms on the lower levels of the keep were better, but musty.

I blotted my forehead with my sleeve as I stood outside the stable in the sun, checking the contents of each cart, and directing the guards.

After the cart I had checked was unloaded and Eliera began to lead the old mare back down to the pier, Megaera appeared and walked toward me.

"Guard Captain . . . I have a question for you."

"Yes, Regent?" What could a white witch want of me?

"Recluce is a hard place, and it is likely to get harder before it gets easier. Could you instruct me in the use of blades?"

"Regent . . ." What could I say? Westwind Guards began training almost as soon as they could walk, and Megaera was nearly as old as I was, I suspected. Beautiful as she was, she was certainly older than Creslin.

She lifted her arms and let the tunic sleeves fall back, revealing heavy white scars around both wrists. "I can deal with pain and discomfort, Guard Captain. What I cannot abide is my own inability to defend myself with a blade."

But . . . she was a white mage.

"Magery has its limits." She looked directly at me. "Please . . . will you help me?"

How could I say no when she had begged me? Or as close to begging as a Sub-Tyrant could come.

VII

I was studying the practice yard early the next morning. The sun had barely cleared the low cliffs to the east, and the air was cool for Recluce, but dusty. I wondered if I'd ever escape the dust. Already, I missed the smell of the firs and the pines, and the clean crispness of the air of Westwind. The barracks were stone-walled, sturdy, and rough. From what I could tell, so were the Montgren troopers.

I heard boots and turned.

"You're Guard Captain Shierra. Hyel, at your service." As eastern men sometimes were, he was tall, almost half a head taller than I was, but lanky with brown hair. His hands were broad, with long fingers. Megaera had pointed him out the day before and told me that he was in charge of the Montgren troopers, such as they were, but with all the fuss and bother of unloading and squeezing everyone in, we had not met.

"I'm pleased to meet you." I wasn't certain that I was, but his approach had been polite enough.

"Are you as good as Regent Creslin with the blade?"

How could I answer that question? There was no good answer. I forced a smile. "Why don't we spar, and you can make up your own mind?"

Hyel stiffened. I didn't see why. "I only made a friendly suggestion, Hyel. That was because I don't have an answer to your question. I never sparred against Creslin." That was shading things, because Heldra had, and at the end, just before Creslin had ridden off, even she had been hard-pressed. I certainly would have been.

"With wands?"

"That might be best." Best for both of us. If he was a master blade, I didn't want to find out with cold steel, and if he wasn't, I didn't want to have to slice him up to prove a point.

"I'll be back in a moment."

Why had Hyel immediately sought me out, and before most others were around?

In moments, he re-appeared with two white oak wands that

seemed scarcely used. He offered me my choice. I took the one that felt more balanced. Neither was that good.

"Shall we begin?" Hyel turned and walked into the courtyard. He turned and waited. Once I neared, he lifted the white oak wand, slightly too high. I was less comfortable with the single blade, but the shorter twin wooden practice blades were still buried in the storeroom where they'd been quickly unloaded.

His feet were about right, but he was leaning forward too far.

It took just three passes before I disarmed him.

He just shrugged and stood there, laughing.

I lowered the wand, uncertain of what to say. "Are you . . ."

"I'm fine, Shierra. Might I call you that?"

"You may."

He shook his head. "I always thought that what they said about Westwind was just . . . well, that folks believed what they wanted. Then, when Creslin slaughtered Zarlen in about two quick moves, well . . . I just thought that was him."

"No. He could have been as good as a Westwind armsmaster . . . he might even have been when he left, but there are many guards as good as I am." That was true enough. There were at least ten others. But Creslin . . . slaughtering someone? I'd known he was determined, but somehow, I'd never imagined him that way.

"It wasn't like that," Hyel said quickly. "Creslin and Megaera came here almost by themselves. On the Duke's small schooner with no guards and no troopers. Zarlen thought he could kill Creslin and have his way with her. Creslin saw what he had in mind and asked him to spar. Creslin disarmed him real quick, and Zarlen went crazy. He attacked Creslin with his own steel. Creslin had to kill him." Hyel laughed ruefully. "Made his point."

That made more sense . . . but to see that a man wanted his wife . . . and to kill him like that? The Marshall would have acted that quickly, and Creslin was her son. I'd never thought of it that way. I lowered the wooden wand until the blunted point touched the stones.

"Can you teach me?" Hyel asked.

I could. Should I? "If you're willing to work," I answered, still distracted by what Hyel had told me.

"Early in the morning?" A sheepish look crossed his face.

"Early in the morning. Every morning."

I'd been in Recluce only two days, and I'd already committed to teaching Megaera the basics of the blade and to improving the skills of the Montgren garrison commander.

VIII

With the Regent Megaera, I had to start farther back, with an exercise program of sorts. I gave her stones of the proper weight to lift and hold, and exercises to loosen and limber her shoulders. After an eightday, she found me re-mortaring the stones in what would be the armory.

"Regent." I laid aside the trowel that I'd recovered from the recesses of the keep and stood.

"When can we start with blades?"

I didn't answer her, but turned and walked to the wall where I'd laid aside my harness. I unsheathed one of the blades and extended it, hilt first. "Take it, if you would, Regent."

After a moment of hesitation, she did.

"Hold it out, extended. Keep holding it." That wasn't totally fair, because no blademaster works with her weapon fully extended or with the arm straight, except for a thrust. But it's a good indication of arm strength.

Her arm and wrist began to tremble before long. She fought the weakness, but finally had to lower the blade.

"When your arms are strong enough to hold that position longer," I answered.

Her lips tightened.

"If we start before you're ready, you'll learn bad technique because you won't have the strength you'll have later, and strength and technique won't match."

Abruptly, she laughed. "Strength and technique won't match. That's almost what Klerris said about black magery."

I nodded slightly. I knew nothing about magery, but it seemed that strength and technique should match in any application.

"Did you ever see Creslin work magery?"

How was I to answer that?

"Did you?" Megaera's voice was hard.

I thought I saw whitish flames at the tips of her fingers.

"Only once. I wasn't certain it was magery. He called a storm and flung the winds against the south tower until it was coated with ice."

"Why did he do that?"

"I could not say, Regent."

Megaera smiled. I didn't like that kind of calculating smile. "*When* did he perform this . . . weather magery?"

I could have lied, but she would have known. "After his betrothal to you was announced. He left the great hall as soon as he could."

"Oh . . . best-betrothed . . . if only . . ."

While her words were less than murmured, I might as well not have been there.

Abruptly, she looked at me. "I would appreciate it if you would say nothing of this."

"I will not, Regent Megaera."

"Next eightday, we *will* begin with blades."

Then she was gone.

IX

Several days later, I took one of the mounts and rode up the winding road to the Black Holding. Several of the guards had been detailed to help Creslin build the quarters for him and Megaera. I knew he'd never shirked work, but it was still strange to think of the Marshall's son and the Regent of Recluce working stone. I'd overheard remarks about his skill as a mason, and I wanted to see that, as well as check on the guards working there.

When I reached the structure, still incomplete under its slate roof, I reined up and dismounted, and tied the horse to the single post. The stones of the front wall and the archway were of various sizes, but all edges were smoothed and dressed, and fitted into an almost seamless pattern that required little or no mortar. Had Creslin done that? I couldn't have dressed the stones that smoothly, especially not with the tools we had, and I was the best of the guard stoneworkers on Recluce.

Hulyan appeared immediately. She was carrying a bucket. "Guard Captain, ser, we didn't expect you."

"What are you doing?"

"It's my round to carry water to the Regent. He's cutting and dressing stone down in back, ser."

"Where are the others?"

"They're finding and carrying rough stones to the Regent. That's so he doesn't have to spend time looking."

"You can lead me there, but don't announce me."

"Yes, Guard Captain."

We walked quietly around the north side of the building and to the edge of the terrace. There I stopped and watched.

Below the partly built terrace, Creslin stood amid piles of black stones. His silver hair was plastered against his skull with sweat, yet it still shimmered in the sun. He adjusted the irregular black stone on the larger chunk of rock, then positioned the chisel and struck with the hammer. Precise and powerful as the blow was, the stone shouldn't have split, but it did. One side was as smooth as if it had been dressed. I watched as he readjusted the stone and repeated the process.

Before long he had a precisely dressed black stone block. He only took a single deep breath, wiped his forehead with the back of his forearm, and then started on the next irregular chunk of heavy stone. In some fashion, he was mixing magery and stonecraft, and the results were superb. At that moment, I did not want to look at another piece of stone. Ever.

After a moment, I realized that Creslin must have known that as well. Was that why he worked alone?

I watched as he cut and then dressed one stone after another. I could not have lifted the hammer so strongly and precisely. Not for stone after stone. No stonecutter I had ever seen or known could have.

Slowly, I moved forward, just watching, trying to sense what he was doing.

Despite the brilliant sunlight, there was a darkness around him, but it wasn't any kind of darkness or shadow that I had ever seen. It was more like something felt, the sense of how a blade should be held, or a saddle adjusted to a skittish mount. I kept watching, trying to feel what he did, rather than see.

For a moment, I could *feel* the stone before Creslin, knowing where the faults lay, and where the chisel should be placed . . .

"Guard Captain Shierra!" he finally called, as if he had just seen me.

"Yes, ser. I was just checking on the guards."

"They've been most helpful. We couldn't have done half what's here without them." He paused. "But if you need them at the keep . . ."

"No, ser. Not yet anyway. Thank you, ser." My voice sounded steady to me. It didn't feel steady. I turned and hurried back to my mount, before Creslin could ask me anything more.

I untied the gelding and mounted, turning him back toward the keep in the harbor valley.

Thoughts swirled through my head as I rode down the dusty road.

Was that order-magery? The understanding of the forces beneath and within everything?

What I had seen wasn't what anyone would have called mage-craft. There were no winds or storms created. No one had been healed, and no keep had been suddenly created. Yet those stones could not have been cut and dressed so precisely in any other fashion. What I had also seen was a man who was driving himself far harder than anyone I had known. His body was muscle, and only muscle, and he was almost as slender as a girl guard before she became a woman.

I had thought I'd known something about Creslin. Now I was far from certain that I knew anything at all.

Back at the keep, I couldn't help but think about the way in which Creslin had turned irregular chunks of rock into cut-and-dressed black building stones. Could I do that? How could I not try?

I settled myself in the stoneyard on the hillside above the keep, with hammer and chisel and the pile of large chunks of broken dark gray stone. I set an irregular hunk on the granite-like boulder that served as a cutting table and looked at it. It remained a gray stone.

I closed my eyes and tried to recapture the feeling I'd sensed around Creslin. It had been deliberate, calm, a feeling of everything in its place.

Nothing happened.

Knowing that nothing was that simple, I hadn't expected instant understanding or mastery. While still trying to hold that feeling of simplicity and order, I picked up the chisel and the hammer. After placing the chisel where it *felt* best— close to where it needed to be to dress the edge of the stone, I took a long and deliberate stroke.

A fragment of the stone chipped away. It was larger than most that I had been chiseling away. That could have been chance. Without hurrying, I placed the chisel again, concentrating without forcing the feeling. Another large fragment split away.

Slowly, deliberately, I worked on the stone.

After a few more blows, I had a clean face to the stone, cleaner and smoother than I'd ever managed before, but the face was angled slightly, compared to the other, rougher faces.

I kept at it. At times, I had a hard time recapturing that deliberate, calm feeling, but I could tell the difference in the results.

Learning how to harness that feeling and to use it effectively in cutting and dressing stone was going to take some time. I just hoped it didn't take too long. We needed dressed stones for far too many structures that had yet to be built. Creslin had also asked that some of the stone be used to finish the inn near the pier, especially the public room. That was to give the guards and troopers some place where they could gather and get a drink. I had my doubts about how that would work, for all of Hyel's efforts, and those of Creslin.

X

Exactly one eightday after she had last asked me, Megaera appeared in the keep courtyard, early in the morning, right after I had finished my daily session with Hyel.

"We're running out of time, Guard Captain," she said firmly. "Whether I'm strong enough or not, we need to begin."

"You've made a good start with the physical conditioning. But whether you can master a lifetime of training in a season or two is another question." That wasn't even a question. I doubted that she could, but she could learn to use a shortsword to defend herself against what passed for eastern bladework. In case of raiders or invaders, or even assassins, that could save her life just by allowing her to hold someone at bay long enough for help to reach her.

"There's no other choice."

The way she said the words, it seemed as though she was not even thinking of raiders.

"Creslin's not that hard, is he?" I couldn't believe I'd said that to the Regent, and I quickly added, "My sister felt he was a good man at heart."

Megaera laughed, half-humorously, half-bitterly. "It's not that at all. Against him, I need no defenses. Besides, from what I've seen, I'm not sure that I'd ever prevail by force of arms."

Her words lifted a burden from me. But why was she so insistent that she needed to learn the blade? She was a white witch who could throw chaos-fire. I'd even seen it flaring around her once or twice.

Megaera lifted the white oak wand. "Where do we begin?"

"At the beginning, with the way you hold the blade." I stepped forward and repositioned her fingers. "You must have firm control, and yet not grip it so tightly that it wearies your muscles." I positioned her feet in the basic stance. "And the way in which you stand will affect those muscles as well."

"Like this?"

I nodded and picked up my own wand. "You may regret this, Lady."

"The time for regrets has come and gone, Shierra. There is only time to do what must be done."

"Higher on the blade tip . . . ," I cautioned.

For the first few passes, breaking through her guard was almost laughably easy. But unlike many of the junior guards when they first began, once she had a wand in her hand, Megaera had no interest in anything but learning how to best use it.

Her eyes never left me, and I could almost feel that she was trying to absorb everything I said. Her concentration, like Creslin's, was frightening.

What was between the two regents, so much that they each drove themselves beyond reason, beyond exhaustion?

XI

The following morning, Hyel was waiting for me.

"You're early," I said.

"I wanted to make sure I got my time with you before the Regent Megaera appeared." He laughed easily.

"You don't need that much more work." He really didn't. He learned quickly. His basic technique had never been that poor, but no one had ever drilled him in the need for perfection. I wondered if the Westwind Guards had developed that insistence on absolute mastery of weapons and tactics because the women were both the warriors and the childbearers and every woman lost meant children who would not be born.

"I'll need to keep sparring with you to improve and hold what you've taught me."

True as his words might be, I had the feeling that Hyel was not telling me everything. "And?"

He gave me the sheepish grin. "Who else can I talk to?

You're the only one who commands fighting forces. The Regents are above me, and . . ."

I could understand that. I did enjoy talking to him. Still . . . "If we're going to spar before the Regent gets here . . ."

"You're right." With a nod, he picked up his wand.

We worked hard, and I had to admit that he'd gotten enough better that I had to be on guard all the time. He even got a touch on me, not enough to give me more than a slight bruise, but he hadn't been able to do that before.

When we set down the wands, I inclined my head. "You're pressing me now." I even had to blot my forehead.

"Good!" Hyel was soaked, but he was smiling broadly—for a moment.

"What's the matter?"

"Is everyone from the West like you and the Regents?"

"What do you mean?"

"You never stop. From dawn to dusk, you, Creslin, and the Regent Megaera push yourselves. Anyone else would drop. Some of my men have, just trying to keep up with Creslin on his tours of the fields and the springs. He cuts stone, looks for and finds springs, runs up and down mountains—"

"Compared to Westwind," I interjected, "they're just hills."

"They're mountains to the rest of us." He grinned before continuing. "You and the Regent Megaera are just as bad. You give me and her blade lessons, drill your own guards, cut and dress stones, check supplies and weapons . . . I've even seen you at the grindstone sharpening blades."

"A guard captain has to be able to do all that. That's what the position requires."

"Stonecutting, too?"

"Not always stonecutting or masonry, but all guards have to have at least apprentice level skills in a craft."

"No wonder Westwind has lasted so many ages." He shook

his head. "That explains you and Creslin. What about the Regent Megaera?"

I shrugged. "She's more driven than Creslin, and I don't know why."

Hyel cleared his throat abruptly. "Ah . . ."

I turned. Megaera had entered the courtyard carrying a practice wand.

"Until later, Guard Captain." Hyel inclined his head, and then stepped away, offering a deeper nod of respect to Megaera.

"Can we begin, Shierra?" Megaera asked.

"Yes, Regent."

I turned and lifted my wand.

Megaera had practiced . . . or she had absorbed totally what I had taught her the day before. Once more, she concentrated totally on every aspect of what I showed her. At the end of the practice session, she inclined her head and thanked me, then left hurriedly. I couldn't help but think about what Hyel had said.

Her intensity made Creslin look calm, and I knew he was scarcely that.

After washing up a bit, I was back working on cutting stones. I couldn't match the pace that I'd seen in Creslin, but with each day I felt that I was getting more skilled. That was strange, because I'd felt no such improvement over the years before. I couldn't exactly explain what was different, except that the work went more quickly when I could hold on to the sense of calm and order.

I'd cut and dressed several larger stones when I sensed more than saw Lydya approach. She radiated a calmness that didn't interfere with my concentration. Her presence should have, but it didn't. She said nothing, and I kept working.

Finally, she stepped forward, almost to my elbow. "You're good at cutting and shaping the rough stone."

"I've been working at it."

"You're using some basic order skills, you know?"

"I watched Creslin for a time. I just thought I'd try to do what he was doing. It looked . . . more effective."

"Just like that?" Lydya raised her eyebrows.

"No, not exactly. I already knew something about masonry and stonecutting. But there was a certain feel to what he was doing . . ." How else could I explain it?

The healer laughed, softly, but humorously. "There is indeed a feel to the use of order. If you continue to work on developing that feel to your stonework, you may become a master mason." The humorous tone was replaced with one more somber. "In time, it will impair your ability to use a blade."

"But . . . Creslin . . ."

Lydya just nodded. "Order has its price, and there are no exceptions."

XII

Megaera made solid improvements. By the end of the second eightday of practice, she was sparring at the same level as the most junior guards. At times, she made terrible mistakes. That was because she had so little experience. Each of those mistakes resulted in severe bruises, and she was fortunate not to have broken her wrist once. Even so, she continued to improve. After our sessions, I began to match her against the guards. That was as much to show her that she had improved as for the practice itself.

After one session, she forced herself not to limp, despite a slash-blow to her calf that would have tried the will of most of the guards. She did sit down on the stone bench beside me.

"That was quite a blow you took."

"I should have sensed it coming." She shook her head.

I couldn't help noticing that the circles under her eyes were darker. "You can't learn everything all at once."

"You sound like . . ." She stopped, then went on. "Do you have a sister, Shierra?"

"A younger sister. She's probably a squad leader now."

"How do you get along?"

Should I have answered? How could I not, when she could tell my very thoughts? "I love her, but she has kept her distance from me."

Megaera laughed. It wasn't a pleasant sound.

"Do you have a sister?"

"You know I have a sister. She's the Tyrant."

She was right, but I hadn't known quite what to say. "Is she a mage, too?"

"No. Not many Tyrants have been mages, not since Saryn anyway. She is just the Tyrant. Were you ever close to your sister?"

"I tried to be. But she never wanted to hear what I had to say. She said she had to make her own decisions and mistakes."

Megaera looked away After a moment, she rose. "Thank you. I'll see you tomorrow." Then she turned and left.

Had my comment offended her, by suggesting her sister had only meant the best for her? Did she react that way to everything, taking even harmless statements as criticisms or as slights?

Megaera said little to me for the next three mornings, only what was necessary to respond to my instructions. She avoided me totally in matters involving the upgrading of the quarters and the keep, or even the duty rosters for the guards. Creslin and Hyel discussed the duty rosters for the Montgren troopers, and Hyel and I worked out the rotations between us.

On the fourth morning, before we began, Megaera looked at me, then lowered the practice wand. "Shierra . . . you meant the best."

"I did not realize that matters were so between you and

your sister." I wasn't about to apologize when I had done nothing wrong, but I could say that I meant no harm.

"You could not have known. No one here could have. Even
Creslin did not know until I told him. Sisters can be so cruel."

Could they? Had I been that cruel?

Even as we sparred, Megaera's words crept through my
thoughts.

XIII

Late one afternoon, Hyel found me in the stoneyard. "We need
to get down to the public room."

"Now? We need more stones . . ."

"You know how the troopers and guards don't talk to each
other?"

"We talk to each other."

"Our guards don't talk to each other. Even when they're
drinking they sit on opposite sides of the room."

I'd seen that. "It will change."

Hyel shook his head. "I told Regent Creslin about it. He's
going to do something. This evening. He didn't say what. I think
you should be there."

"Frig! I don't need this." But I picked up my tools and my
harness. "I'll meet you there. I need to wash up." At least, I
needed to get stone dust out of my eyes and nose and hair.

I did hurry, but by the time I got to the half-finished inn
and public room, the sun was low over the western hills that
everyone else called mountains. The windows were without
glass or shutters, and someone had propped wooden slats over
several of the openings to cut the draft.

Hyel was right. The Westwind guards had taken the tables
on the south side, and the Montgren troopers those on the north

side. I should have paid more attention, but between keeping things going and the stonework and the training sessions, I'd had little time and less inclination for going to the public room.

I eased onto one end of the bench on the leftmost table. "What is there to drink?"

"Some fermented green stuff," replied Fylena, "and something they call beer."

"Doesn't anyone ever talk to the Montgren guards?"

"Why? All they want is to get in our trousers."

"Without even bathing," added someone else.

"There's the Regent."

I looked up. Megaera had taken a place at the adjoining table, and beside her was the healer. Across the room, Klerris the mage was sitting beside Hyel.

Creslin walked into the public room and glanced around. He carried his guitar as he made his way to Hyel and spoke. Hyel hurried off and returned with a stool. After a moment, Creslin dragged the stool into the open space and then recovered his guitar.

He settled onto the stool and fingered the strings of the guitar. He smiled, but it was clear he was uneasy. After another strumming chord, he spoke. "I don't know too many songs that don't favor one group or another. So enjoy the ones you like and ignore the ones you don't." Then he began to sing.

> *Up on the mountain*
> *where the men dare not go*
> *the angels set guards there*
> *in the ice and the snow . . .*

I'd forgotten how beautifully he sang. It was as though every note hung like liquid silver in the air. When he finished the first song, no one spoke, but Megaera slipped away from the other table and sat beside me.

Creslin then sang "White Was the Color of My Love."

"Has he always sung this well?" murmured Megaera.

"His father was supposed to have been a minstrel, but no one knows for sure."

Creslin launched into two humorous songs, and both the guards and the troopers laughed. When he halted, he stretched his fingers, then coughed, looking around as if for something to drink. Megaera left me for a moment, carrying her cup to him.

Instead of thanking her, he asked, "Are you all right?"

"Fine, thank you. I thought you might need this." After he drank she took the cup and rejoined me. For the first time, I saw that she was deathly white, and she held her hands to keep them from trembling.

Creslin sang several more songs, and then coaxed one of Hyel's troopers into singing one of their songs.

Finally, he brought the guitar to Darcyl. I hadn't even known that she played. Creslin turned, looking for a place to sit. Megaera rose, taking my arm and guiding me with her. We ended up at the one vacant table. I did manage to gesture for Hyel to join us, and Megaera beckoned as well.

"I didn't know you could sing." Megaera's words were almost an accusation.

"I never had a chance until now, and you never seemed to be interested," Creslin replied, his voice either distant or tired, perhaps both. His eyes were on Darcyl and the guitar.

No one spoke. Finally, I had to. "Fiera said that the hall guards used to sneak up to his door when he practiced."

For the first time I'd ever seen, Creslin looked surprised. "Fiera? Is she your—"

"My youngest sister." I don't know why I said it that way,

since she was also my only sister. "She talked a lot about you, probably too much." I wished I hadn't said that, either, almost as soon as the words were out of my mouth, but I hadn't expected to find myself sitting at a table with just the two regents and Hyel.

"How is she?"

I sensed Megaera bristling, but all I could do was answer. "She went with the detachment to Sarronnyn. She'll be rotated back later in the year sometime. It could be that she's already back at Westwind."

"Where did the guitar come from?" Hyel was doing his best to keep the conversation light.

"It was mine," Creslin replied. "I left it behind. Lydya—the healer—brought it. My sister Llyse thought I might like to have it."

"You've never played in public?" I was trying to do . . . something . . . to disarm Megaera's hostility.

"No. I was scared to do it, but sometimes music helps. The second song, the white-as-a-dove one, probably saved me from the white wizards."

"You didn't exactly sound scared." Megaera's voice was like winter ice in Westwind.

"That wouldn't have helped much," Creslin said slowly. "Besides, no one born in Westwind shows fear. Not if they can help it."

Megaera looked at me, as if she wanted me to refute what he'd said.

"Feeling afraid is acceptable, but letting it affect your actions is not. That's one of the reasons the guards are often more effective than men. Men too often conceal their fear in brashness or in unwise attacks. The guards are trained to recognize their fears and set them aside. Regent Creslin was trained as a guard until he left Westwind."

Hyel raised his eyebrows, then took a long pull from his mug.

For several songs by Darcyl, we just sat there and listened.

Then Creslin rose. He offered an awkward smile. "I'm going to get some sleep."

At the adjoining table, both Klerris and Lydya stiffened.

"I do hope you'll play again for us," Hyel said. "That really was a treat, and just about everyone liked it."

Everyone but Megaera, I felt, and I was afraid I understood why. I was also afraid I'd just made matters worse without meaning to.

Creslin recovered his guitar and looked at Megaera.

"I do hope you'll play again," I said quickly.

Megaera's eyes fixed on Creslin. "I need to talk to you."

"Now?"

"When you get to the holding will be fine. I won't be long."

Her words told me that matters were anything but fine.

Concern flooded Creslin's face.

"Stop it. Please . . . ," Megaera said softly, but firmly.

Before Creslin could move, Klerris stepped up to Megaera. "A moment, Lady?"

"Can it wait until tomorrow?"

"I think not."

As if they had planned it, the two mages separated Creslin and Megaera, Klerris leading her in one direction and Lydya guiding him in another.

"What was that all about?" asked Hyel. "I thought things were going better between the troopers and the guards."

"Between my guards and your troopers, yes."

Hyel's eyes went to Megaera's back as she and Klerris left the public room. "He was singing to her, and she didn't hear it. Was that it?" asked Hyel.

I shook my head. "He was singing to us, all of us, and she needs him to sing for her."

"She's not that selfish."

He didn't understand. "I didn't say she was. It's different." I tried not to snap at him.

"How's he supposed to know that?"

I didn't have an answer, but I knew it was so, and even Fiera would have understood that.

XIV

After the night that Creslin sang to all the guards and troopers at the public room, two things happened. The first was that Creslin and Megaera began to call Klerris and Lydya, and Hyel and me, together to meet almost daily about matters affecting Recluce. Creslin laughed about it, calling us the unofficial high council of Recluce. Usually, I didn't say too much. Neither did Hyel.

Mostly, I watched, especially Creslin and Megaera. Sometimes, I couldn't help but overhear what they said afterwards as they left the hall.

". . . don't . . ."

"I'm sorry," Creslin apologized. "I still can't believe your cousin wants to tax us . . ."

"He doesn't. It has to be Helisse . . . not any better than sister dear . . ."

Creslin said nothing.

"Sisters of Sarronnyn . . . except she never thought of us . . . just of her, of what she thought was best for Sarronnyn . . ."

"Don't we have to think of what's best for Recluce?"

"It's not the same!" After a moment, Megaera continued, her voice softer. "I'm sorry, best-betrothed. You try to ask people. You don't always listen, but you care enough to ask . . ."

Their voices faded away, and I stood there, thinking about

how they had spoken to each other and what they had said—and not said.

The second thing was that, not every night, but more and more frequently, Megaera began to sleep in the keep. Then it was every night.

I didn't even pretend to understand all the reasons why she preferred to share my small room at the keep rather than stay in the Black Holding where she had a fine large room to herself. I also understood why she'd married Creslin. What real choice had she had? I could have understood why she'd never slept with him, except for one thing. It was clear to every person on the isle that he loved her, that he would have taken a blade or a storm for her. Yet she ignored that, and she also ignored the fact that she cared for him. That was what I found so hard to understand. But a guard captain doesn't ask such things of a regent, even one who shares her chamber.

Finally, one night, in the darkness, she just sat on the edge of her pallet and looked at the wall.

"It's not my affair," I began, although it was because anything that the regents did affected all of us on Recluce, "but could you . . ." I didn't quite know what to say.

Megaera did not speak for a time, and I waited.

"It isn't your affair, Shierra. It's between Creslin and me." She paused, then went on. "We're tied together by magery. It's an evil thing. I know everything he feels. Everything. When he looks at me . . . or when he feels I've done something I shouldn't . . . or when . . ." She shook her head.

"Does he know what you feel?"

"He's beginning to know that. The . . . mage-ties were done at different times. I had no choice . . . mine to him was done even before we were betrothed. He didn't even know. That . . . it was my sister's doing. My own sister, and she said that it was for my own good. My own good. Creslin . . . he chose to tie himself to me. He didn't even ask. He just had it done." She turned. "How would you feel, to have every feeling you experienced felt by a man you never knew before you were married?"

I was confused. "Didn't you say that you know everything he feels?"

"Every last feeling! Every time he looks at me and wants me! Every time he feels hurt, like a whipped puppy, because I don't think what he did was wonderful . . . Do you know what that's like? How would you feel if you knew every feeling Hyel had for you, and he knew how you felt?" She snorted. "You've at least worked with Hyel. When I started feeling what Creslin felt, we'd met once at a dinner, and we'd exchanged less than a handful of words. Sister dear and his mighty mother the Marshall decided we should be wed, and that was that."

The idea of having every feeling known? I shuddered. I liked Hyel, and we had gotten to know each other somewhat. The idea that a complete stranger might know all my feelings . . . no wonder Megaera looked exhausted. No wonder she was edgy. Yet . . . I had to wonder about Creslin.

"What about Regent Creslin?" I asked softly.

She shook her head.

Once more, I waited.

"He does what he feels is right, but . . . he doesn't always think about how it affects others. At times, he tries to listen, but then . . . it's as though something happened, and he's back doing the same things." Megaera's voice died away. Abruptly, she stretched out on the pallet. "Good night, Shierra."

Everything Megaera had said rang true, and yet I felt that there was more there. Was that because I had watched Creslin grow up? Because I wanted to believe he was doing the best he knew how? I had watched him both in Westwind and since I had come to Recluce, and I could see how he tried to balance matters, and how he drove himself. But was I seeing what I wanted to see? Was what Megaera saw more accurate?

How could I know?

I lay on my pallet, thinking about Fiera. I'd only wanted the best for her. I'd never even thought of doing anything like the Tyrant had. I wished I could have told her that. But when I left, she hadn't let me. She'd gone off to Sarronnyn, as if to say that she could go where she wanted without telling me.

XV

The warning trumpet sounded while I was just about to begin finishing the stonework reinforcing around the second supply storehouse. I was halfway across the courtyard when Gylara called to me.

"Guard Captain! Ships! At least two warships entering the harbor. They're flying the standard of Hamor . . ."

Hamor? Why were the Hamorians attacking?

". . . Regent Megaera has ordered all squads to the pier! She's left with first squad!"

I should have been the one to issue that order. But then, I shouldn't have properly been doing stonework, except no one else in the detachment had been trained in it, except Doryana, and two stonemasons weren't nearly enough with all that needed to be repaired and built. I was already buckling on my harness and sprinting for the courtyard.

"Second squad! Form up! Pass the word."

Hyel rushed into the courtyard just as we were heading out. I'd hoped we could catch up with first squad. I didn't like the thought of Megaera leading them into battle.

"Get your men! We've got invaders!" I didn't wait to see

what he did, because second squad was already moving. The harbor was close enough that advancing on foot was faster than saddling up. Besides, there wouldn't be enough room to maneuver in the confined area, and we'd lose mounts we had too few of anyway.

Second squad followed me in good order. I didn't bother to count the ships filling the harbor or the boats that were heading shoreward. Counting didn't solve anything when you were attacked and had no place to retreat. The first boat reached the pier before first squad did.

First squad tore into the attackers, but another set of boats was headed toward the foot of the pier. If they landed there, they could trap first squad between two Hamorian forces.

"Second squad! To the boats!"

We managed to reach the rocky shore just as the first Hamorians scrambled from the water. The leading warrior charged me with his oversized iron bar. I just stepped inside and cut his calf all the way to the bone and his neck with the other blade.

After that, it was slash and protect.

Then fire—white-wizard fire—flared from somewhere.

I took advantage of that to cut another Hamorian throat and disable two more. So did my guards.

More wizard fire flared across the sky.

Then the winds began to howl, and the skies blackened. Instantly, or so it seemed. Lightnings flashed out of the clouds. I hoped they were hitting the Hamorian ships, but we weren't looking that way, and the Hamorians who were died under our blades.

"Waterspouts! Frigging waterspouts!"

I didn't look for those, either. "Second squad, toward the water!"

The Hamorians began to panic.

Before long we held the shore to the east of the pier, and the only Hamorians nearby were wounded or stumbling eastward.

"Second squad! Re-form on me!"

Only then did I study the harbor. The water was filled with high and choppy waves, and debris was everywhere. Three ships were enshrouded in flames. A fourth was beached hard on the shingle to the east. I didn't see anyone alive on it, but there were bodies tangled in twisted and torn rigging and ropes.

Then, I turned to the pier. The guards of first squad had been split by the ferocity of the initial attack and by the numbers, but they had re-formed into smaller groups. They were standing. I didn't see any Hamorians. I also didn't see Creslin or Megaera.

"Second squad! Hold! Dispatch anyone who doesn't surrender!"

I scrambled over and around bodies to get to the pier. Half the way toward the seaward end, I found them. Megaera lay on the blood-smeared stones of the pier, gashes in her leathers. Creslin lay beside her, an arrow through his right shoulder. One hand still held a blade. The other was thrown out, as if to protect Megaera. Both were breathing.

Creslin was more slightly built than I recalled, so wiry that he was almost gaunt. He looked like a youth, almost childlike, helpless. Despite the blood on her leathers and face, Megaera looked young, too, without the anger that sometimes seemed to fuel every movement she made. For the briefest moment, I looked from the two, looking young and bloody, and somehow innocent, to the carnage around them. There were scores of mangled bodies, and burning and sunken ships. Ashes rained across the pier, along with the smoke from the burning schooner that had begun to sink.

Hyel hurried toward me, followed by four litter bearers, two of his men and two guards.

"They're alive, but . . . they'll need the healers," I told him. "We'll need to round up the survivors. Some of them are swimming ashore." I glanced around. "Most of your men are on the west side of the pier. You take that area. The guards will take the east."

Hyel nodded. "We'll do it. The lookouts say that there aren't any more ships near."

That was some help.

Once we finally captured all the surviving Hamorians and had them under guard, I headed back to the keep.

I trudged up the steps, only to have one of the Montgren troopers approach and bow.

"Guard Captain, the mage and Captain Hyel are waiting for you in the hall."

"Thank you." I wiped the second shortsword clean and sheathed it.

Even before I stepped into the hall, Klerris moved forward. Hyel followed.

"How are they?"

"Lydya is working with them. They'll live." Klerris glanced at me and then Hyel. "You two are in charge for now."

I looked back at the mage. "Us?"

"Who else? Lydya and I will be busy trying to patch up bodies and spirits. You two get to take care of everything else."

It was pitch dark before I felt like I could stop, and I'd made a last trip down to the pier and back because I'd posted guards on the grounded Hamorian vessel. I didn't want the ship looted. There was potentially too much on her that we could use.

"It's hard to believe, isn't it." Hyel was sitting on the topmost step leading into the keep. "Sit down. You could use a moment to catch your breath."

"Just for a bit." I did sit down, but on the other side of the wide step, where I could lean back against the stone of the walls. "What's hard to believe?"

"People. You get two young leaders, and they start trying to make a better place for people who don't have much hope or anywhere to go, and everyone wants to stop them."

I didn't find that hard to believe. I'd already seen enough of that as a Westwind guard.

"You don't agree?" He raised his eyebrows.

I laughed. The sound came out bitter. "I do agree, but I don't find it hard to believe. People are like that."

He gestured to the north, his arm taking in the small harbor and the last embers of the grounded and burning sloop. "And all this? That's not hard to believe?"

"It's real, Hyel."

"How could two people—even if they are wizards—create such . . ."

"Chaos?" I laughed again. "Creslin's a mage, and she's a white witch. They both have to prove their worth. To the world and to each other." Proving it to each other might be the hardest part, I thought. "We all have to prove things." I stood. "I need to check on the wounded and see what changes we'll need in the duty rosters."

Hyel grinned crookedly, uneasily, as he rose from the step. "What do you have to prove, Shierra?"

"Tell me what you have to prove, Hyel, and then I'll tell you." I started to turn.

His long-fingered hand touched my shoulder. Gently.

"Yes?"

His eyes met mine. "I have to prove . . . that I was sent here wrongfully. I have to prove that I'm not a coward or a bully."

"What if you were sent here rightfully, but you're not the same man that you once were?"

His lips quirked. "You ask questions no one else does."

"I did not mean to say—"

"You didn't, Shierra. I always learn something when I'm with you." He smiled. "You'd better check those rosters."

I could have avoided Hyel's question. He wouldn't have pressed me again. He'd answered my question and not demanded my answer. After a moment, I managed a smile. "I have to prove that I didn't make a mistake in choosing to come here. I have to prove that I've escaped an image."

"The image of a Westwind Guard?"

"Partly."

He nodded, but didn't press. This time, I wasn't ready to say more. "Until tomorrow, Hyel."

"Good night, Shierra."

XVI

Over the next three eightdays, something changed between Creslin and Megaera. I didn't know what, or how, but after they recovered, they both slept at the Black Holding, and occasionally they held hands. They still bickered, but most of the bitterness had vanished.

Our meetings didn't have the edginess that they had once had. Not that there weren't problems and more problems.

A second tax notice came from the Duke of Montgren, and there was no pay chest, either, although the Duke had promised them for a year.

"What about the cargo?" I asked, looking around the table in the keep hall.

"It's paid for," snapped Creslin.

"Did you have to pay, since the ship is the Duke's?" I didn't understand why that was necessary, since Creslin and Megaera were his regents.

"The captain's acting as a consignment agent. If he doesn't get paid now, when would we get another shipment of goods? Would anyone else trade with us?" He went on, pointing out how few wanted to trade with such an out-of-the-way place.

"So they're gouging the darkness out of us?" asked Hyel.

"That's why we need to refit the Hamorian ships for our own trading."

"We can't afford to refit one ship, let alone others," observed Megaera.

"We can't afford not to," snapped Creslin.

Then after a few more words, he stood and strode out. Megaera rose. "He's worried."

After the others left, Hyel looked to me. "He's acting like we're idiots."

"Sometimes we are," I pointed out. "He's paid for most everything we have personally, and he doesn't have much left."

"What about Megaera's sister, the Tyrant? At least, the Marshall sent you and equipment and supplies. The Tyrant hasn't sent anything. Neither has the Duke."

Why hadn't the Tyrant sent anything? Sarronnyn was rich enough to spare a shipload of supplies now and again. Did Megaera's sister hate her that much? Or did she regard her as a threat? How could Recluce ever threaten Sarronnyn?

XVII

Whether it was the result of Creslin calling the storms against the Hamorians or something else, I didn't know, and no one said, but the weather changed. Day after day, the clouds rolled in from the northwest, and the rains lashed Recluce. Fields began to wash out, and we kept having to repair our few roads. No one had ever thought about so much rain on a desert isle, and most of the roofs leaked. After nearly three eightdays, the worst passed, but we still got more rain than the isle had gotten before.

Megaera, once she had fully recovered from her injuries, and once we did not have to deal with rain falling in sheets, continued her sparring and working with me on improving her blade skills. One morning she did not bring her practice blade. Instead, she sat on one of the benches in the courtyard and motioned for me to sit beside her. Her face was somber.

"Shierra . . . something has happened . . ."

What? It couldn't have been Creslin, or Megaera would have been far more distraught. It couldn't have been Hyel, because I'd seen him a few moments before, and enjoyed his smile.

"Creslin . . . he sensed something last night. Something has happened at Westwind. He doesn't know what it is, but . . . it's likely that the Marshall and Marshalle are dead."

"Dead? What about . . . all the others?"

Her fingers rested on my wrist, lightly. "We don't know. We don't have any way of knowing, but we thought you should know what we know. You're the senior Westwind guard here. Creslin and I . . . we thought that perhaps you could tell the guards that you've had word of hard times at Westwind, and that the Marshall and Marshalle have been hurt, but that you don't know more than that."

I found myself nodding, even as I wondered about Fiera. Had she been hurt? Or killed? Would I ever know, with Westwind thousands of kays away?

"I'm sorry, Shierra." Megaera's voice was soft. "I know you have a sister. . . ."

For some reason, hearing that, I had to swallow, and I found myself thinking of Megaera as much as Fiera. How could her sister have been so cruel to her?

After Megaera departed, I did gather the squads, and I told them something similar to what she had suggested.

But the eightdays passed, and we heard nothing.

I kept wondering about Fiera. Was she all right? Would I ever hear? Would I ever know?

Then, one morning at the keep, as Hyel and I waited for the regents, Creslin burst through the door. "There's a coaster porting." He hurried past us and down the steps to the hill road that led to the pier.

Hyel looked at me. Then we both followed.

"That's a Westwind banner below the ensign," I told Hyel. "That's why he's upset."

"Upset?"

I didn't try to explain, not while trying to catch up with Creslin. "We're going to have more guards." Would Fiera be there? If she wasn't, could someone tell me about her?

"More—?" Hyel groaned as he hurried beside me.

"Don't groan so loudly."

We finally caught up with Creslin as the coaster eased up to the pier and cast out lines.

"Do you want to explain?" asked Hyel.

Creslin pointed to the Westwind guards ranked on the deck.

"I still—" Hyel didn't understand.

"I hope they aren't all that's left," I said. *Please let Fiera be there . . . or alive and well somewhere.*

"The Marshall's dead. Llyse is dead, and Ryessa has been moving troops eastward into the Westhorns," Creslin said.

I hadn't heard about the Sarronnese troops. I wondered how he knew, but perhaps the mages or the trading captains had told him.

"If Westwind still existed, there wouldn't be three squads coming to Recluce." His words were hard.

Once the coaster was secured to the pier, the gangway came down, and a blonde guard—a squad leader—stepped down and onto the pier.

My heart almost stopped. Fiera! But I had to take her report as she stepped past Hyel and Creslin and stopped before me.

"Squad Leader Fiera reporting."

"Report."

"Three full squads. Also ten walking wounded, five permanently disabled, and twenty consorts and children. Three deaths since embarkation in Rulyarth. We also bring some supplies, weapons, and tools . . . and what is left of the Westwind treasury."

Hard as it was, I replied. "Report accepted, Squad Leader." I turned. "May I present you to Regent Creslin? Squad Leader Fiera."

Creslin did not speak for a moment. He and Fiera locked eyes. The last time they had met, she had kissed him, and now everything was different.

Then he nodded solemnly. "Honor bright, Squad Leader. You have paid a great price, and great is the honor you bestow upon us through your presence. Few have paid a higher price than you . . ." When he finished, his eyes were bright, although his voice was firm.

So were Fiera's, but her voice was hard. "Will you accept the presentation of your heritage, Your Grace? For you are all that remains of the glory and power of Westwind."

"I can do no less, and I will accept it in the spirit in which it is offered." Creslin looked directly into her eyes and lowered his voice. "But never would I have wished this. Even long ago, I wished otherwise." He tightened his lips.

Even I felt the agony within him.

"We know that, Your Grace." Fiera swallowed, and the tears oozed from the corners of her eyes. "By your leave, Regent?"

"The keep is yours, Squad Leader, as is all that we have. We are in your debt, as am I, in the angels', and in the Legend's."

"And we in yours, Regent." Fiera's voice was hard as granite or black stone, but the tears still flowed.

"Form up!" I ordered, as much to spare Fiera as for anything. "On the pier."

"What was all that about?" Hyel asked Creslin.

Whatever Creslin said, it would not explain half of what had happened, nor should it.

Carts had already begun to arrive. They had to have been sent by Megaera, and at that moment my heart went out to both my sister and to Megaera, for both suffered, and would suffer, and neither was at fault. Nor was Creslin.

With all the need to accommodate the unexpected additional guards, consorts, and children, I could not find a time when Fiera was alone until well past sunset.

I watched as she slipped out the front entrance of the keep and began to walk down the road. I did not know what she had in mind, but I had to reach her.

Following her, I did not speak until we were well away.

"Fiera . . . ?"

She did not respond.

I caught up with her. "I wanted to talk to you, but not . . . not with everyone around."

She stopped in the middle of the rutted road, under a cloudy and starless sky.

"Why?" she asked. "Why did it have to happen this way?"

"You gave him his future. You gave him what will save us all," I told her, and I knew it was true. I also knew that, at that moment, it didn't matter to her.

She said nothing.

"Fiera . . . ?"

"What?" The single word was almost snapped. "I suppose

you have some great suggestion. Or some reason why everything will be wonderful."

"No. I don't. I don't have any answers. For you or for me. Or for us." I rushed on. "I know I didn't do everything right, and I know what I did must have hurt you. I didn't mean it that way. I only wanted to help . . ." I swallowed. "I love you, and you are my sister, and you always will be."

We both cried, and held each other.

There were other words, but they were ours and for us alone.

XVIII

Late that night, I sat on the front steps of the keep. Fiera was sleeping, if fitfully, and Megaera and Creslin doubtless had their problems, and I . . . I had my sister . . . if I could keep her, if I could avoid interfering too much.

"Are you all right?" Hyel stood in the doorway of the keep.

"I'm fine."

He just looked at me with those deep gray eyes, then sat down beside me. For a long time, he said nothing. Finally, he reached out and took my hand. Gently.

Love is as much about wisdom as lust and longing. Fiera had loved Creslin, not wisely, but well, and out of that love, she had brought him the tools to build a kingdom. He would never forget, for he was not the kind who could or would, but he loved Megaera. So he would offer all the honors and respect he could to Fiera, but they would not be love.

Megaera had loved her sister, also not wisely, but well, while I had loved my sister wisely, carefully, I had not shown that love, nor had the Tyrant, I thought. Unlike the Tyrant, who would never show any love to her sister, I'd been given the chance to let Fiera know what I felt, and I, for once, had been brave enough to take it.

As for the future, I could only hope that, in time, Fiera would find someone who matched her, as Creslin and Megaera had found each other, as Hyel and I might.

At times, the ripples of what one life accomplishes affect another, and this is one of those stories, although the end result is less obviously wrenching here than in some cases.

ARTISAN—
FOUR PORTRAITS AND
A MINIATURE

I

The Merchant Princess

The brown-haired girl watched from the balcony as the matching grays drew the open carriage up under the covered portico, ducking back into the bedchamber as the shapely blonde woman turned her head toward the upper levels and called out, "Jyll, dear, we're home!"

Without a word, Jyll walked from the shaded balcony through her bedchamber and into her bath and dressing chamber. There she briefly stopped to behold herself in the mirror, seeing again the pale freckled skin and the fine brown and unmanageable hair she hated so much. Then she made her way back through her bedchamber and sitting room to the upstairs hall. She left the sitting room door wide open behind her as she crossed the hall to the grand staircase, which she descended with grace and without rushing. Finally, she walked through the grand hall to the receiving hall where her thin dark-haired father and her stepmother stood.

"You took your time," said the blonde. "Your father and I worried that you weren't well." She frowned. "You're wearing trousers again."

"I like them. Besides, I went riding this morning."

"Not alone, I hope?" The blonde's eyebrows rose.

"I always ride alone. I have my sabre, and Fieron is faster than any mount in Land's End."

"She's quite safe on Fieron," said Jyll's father.

"You don't know what could happen, Jerohm."

"Artesia . . . this is Recluce, not Sligo or Lydiar."

"I came as soon as you called," Jyll said quickly, looking to her father, standing beside the woman less than ten years older than she was. "I'm so glad to see you, Father. How was the voyage back from Diehl?"

"Well enough. Well enough."

"I thought you might be home earlier." Jyll did not mention that she had drawn out her ride, hoping that she would not return until they were in the throes of unpacking.

"Your father brought you something special, Jyll."

Jerohm extended an oblong enameled box to his daughter. "Artesia helped me pick it out."

Jyll took it, trying not to wince when she saw the garish red-and-black enamel and the yellow crest on the top. "It's . . . very pretty," she said cautiously.

Artesia looked at her stepdaughter. "It's lovely, Jerohm. Perhaps you should set it aside until Jyll is older."

Because Jyll knew exactly what her stepmother was thinking, she smiled sweetly. "Perhaps you should. Perhaps Artesia would be willing to keep it safe for me."

Jerohm's face fell.

"No . . . I'll keep it. I know just where I'll put it in my sitting room." She smiled warmly at her father. "Thank you so much, Father. I'm so glad you're home safely." She didn't have to put the emphasis on "you."

"Well . . . we need to get unpacked . . . and I'll need to get to the warehouse to make sure everything coming off the *Diamond Pride* is properly stored."

"Thank you again, Father. I need to put this where it belongs." She managed another smile before turning and walking swiftly toward the main hall and the grand staircase. Behind her, she could hear Artesia's voice, which, low as it was, carried with a penetrating edge.

"Behind all that sweetness, Jerohm, Jyll is a chaos-wielder."

"She's only a child."

"She's old enough to be consorted."

Only in that backwater you come from, thought Jyll.

"She was wearing that awful orange blouse with lavender trousers," Artesia went on.

You would have called them purple before you married Father. Jyll hurried up the stairs and then into her sitting room, closing the door softly, not because she felt like it, but because she didn't want to give Artesia the satisfaction of knowing she was upset.

She glanced around the room, then decided to place the enameled box on the left side of the fireplace mantel, in turn moving the small Spidlaran knot basket to the side table flanking her reading chair. She forced herself to take several slow and even breaths before she went to the writing desk that doubled as her drawing board. Once there, she took out the smooth paper and the pastels and began to draw, her fingers sure.

By the next afternoon, she was satisfied with the drawing, but the question was whether she could do what she wanted to with the image of Artesia. She'd managed subtler effects before, but this time . . . this time . . .

Rather than ruin the portrait, because it had taken a great deal of effort, she took out another sheet of drawing paper. Once more she drew, or rather sketched, a quick caricature of her stepmother. A good half glass later, when she laid aside the last pastel crayon, she nodded.

Then, she concentrated on ordering her thoughts, on putting aside her anger, and upon creating a compulsion to tell the truth, the truth about love.

He'll see. I'll make her tell the truth.

Somehow, she had to move that compulsion onto or into the crude quickly drawn image, not in a destructive way, but in a fashion so that it would become part of the pastels and paper. With the first attempt, the paper disintegrated and powdered pastels spread across the polished wood of the desk.

A second caricature, cruder than the first, took another half glass to finish. Once more, she concentrated, but even in trying to be gently firm, her attempts to hold anger away from order were still unsuccessful, although the paper merely fragmented into strips, rather than disintegrating totally.

On and off, over the next eightday, Jyll worked on her project. Frustrating as it was, it kept her away from Artesia except at meals, and her father was home for most of those. Finally, by the following threeday, she dared to imbue the pastel of her stepmother with the feelings she felt were only appropriate. It took her almost three glasses before she finished. Her back and neck ached, and her eyes were blurring so much that she had to close them for a time.

When she studied the almost finished portrait, she smiled. While she wasn't totally satisfied with the results, they should be sufficient for Artesia. *Besides, you've spent more than enough time on the bitch.*

Next came the frame, and that took another two days, and another two for the dark oil to dry. But she waited, if impatiently, galloping out on Fieron for glasses at a time, because she wanted both frame and portrait to show the care she had lavished on them . . . and she wanted her father to see that care.

At last, just before the midday meal on eightday, Jyll walked down the grand staircase and into the side parlor off the family dining room. Her father and stepmother were standing by the window overlooking the side garden.

"You're actually early," offered Artesia. "How charming."

Jyll offered an apologetic smile. "I'm sorry if I upset you. I drew something for you." She started to extend the drawing in the simple frame she had made.

"Where did you get the frame?" asked Jerohm.

"I made it. You said I could use the wood-shop when Varren wasn't using it. There was some scrap pine from crates. I didn't think you'd mind." Jyll made her words soft and lowered her eyes.

Artesia stepped forward and took the offering, studying the frame first, running her fingers along the edges. "The frame is quite good. You might do better to become a cabinetmaker."

"Jyll can do better than that. She has the spirit of an artisan," said Jerohm proudly.

Then . . . Artesia looked at the portrait. Her face paled. Her mouth opened. Then her knees gave way, and she crumpled.

Jyll leaped forward and snatched the framed portrait in midair.

Jerohm tried to cushion his consort's fall, but was too late as Artesia collapsed onto the thick Analerian carpet. He knelt beside her, turning her onto her back.

Jyll said nothing as Artesia's eyes fluttered. Then Artesia moaned. Slowly, her eyes opened, and she looked almost in terror at her consort. "Jerohm . . ."

He helped Artesia to her feet, then settled her into one of the side chairs before striding back to face his daughter. Jyll had not moved, nor had she smiled.

"What did you do?" demanded Jerohm.

"I gave her the portrait."

"Let me see it."

Wordlessly, she extended the frame and watched as he studied the pastel drawing.

Finally, he looked up, his face puzzled. "I don't understand." His eyes went to Artesia. "It's a quite lovely drawing of you. You look beautiful."

"It's a demon gift," snapped Artesia. "Burn it."

"But . . . it's lovely," protested Jerohm.

"Burn it!" demanded Artesia.

Jyll managed not to smile, her eyes moving from her father to her stepmother.   •

II

The Student

As she sits on the black stone wall, from where she can see and hear the ocean—she has no idea why the waters north of Land's End are called the Gulf of Muir—Jyll looks to the wiry red-headed young man to her left, intently whittling or carving on a chunk of wood, as he often does. "Why does Lortren always call you 'toymaker'?"

"Because I want to make machines that will make the world better. She knows I make models of them. She calls them toys because she thinks that I'll never be able to make them real." He offers an embarrassed smile. "I think you already knew that."

"I thought it was something like that."

"Why are you here?" He eases the small knife into its sheath. "At the Academy of Useless and Violent Knowledge, I mean?"

"That's not really its name."

"No, but for me, it's appropriate. I'll never be that good with weapons, not like Kadara and Brede . . . or you. You're almost as good as they are."

"My father let me train with a retired Guard so that I could ride alone."

"You never said why you were here," he says gently.

"You don't let up on questions, do you?" Jyll smiles, trying to defuse the edge her words had held.

"If I don't ask questions, I can't find answers."

Should you answer? Finally, she speaks. "I've never told anyone here. I suppose Lortren knows, but . . . please don't tell anyone, not even your . . . friend Kadara."

He does not reply for a moment, then nods.

"I drew a portrait of my stepmother . . ." When he does not speak, Jyll goes on. "It was more than a portrait . . . I did something to it. She looked at it and fainted. She insisted that my father burn it. It was a good portrait. He just pretended to burn it and hid it away. She kept saying that I was filled with chaos and evil. Finally . . . well . . . here I am."

"So you used order to focus hatred on your stepmother? I didn't know that was possible." He frowns.

"No," she replies firmly. "It's not like that. I . . . it's sort of like . . . I knew she didn't really love him . . . so I made the portrait . . . I guess . . . it was sort of an order compulsion to face who she was."

"You . . . put . . . an order compulsion into a drawing?"

"The drawing was really good."

"I know."

"How do you know?"

"I've seen what you've drawn. Loric showed me the one you did of Lisabet."

"Drawing! What use is that?"

"The image of Lisabet wearing a pendant looked almost real. I mean, the pendant did."

"So?"

"What if you made jewelry? People pay for that."

"Make things?"

"They're going to exile us. We'll have to do something."

"You won't be able to make your toys and survive," she points out.

"I can heal a bit, and I am an apprentice smith."

She bit off the reply she almost made.

"Men can get by if they're street artists," he says. "It's harder for women."

"Isn't everything? Except spreading our legs?"

Even in the early twilight, she can see him flush.

"I could teach you about forges . . . ," he finally says. "If . . . if you want to make jewelry . . ."

"You're sweet, but . . . you don't understand. It's not as though I slashed her with a knife. Besides, she seduced Father because he's a wealthy merchant, not because she really loved him. Now, she's convinced herself and everyone else that she does."

"Then . . . does it matter, if that's what she feels? Maybe your order compulsion forced her to truly love him. That is possible."

Jyll feels the blood draining from her head. *Could you . . . could you really . . . ?* A wave of nausea washes over her.

He reaches out and touches her wrist. "Are you all right?"

She does not answer, her thoughts whirling, her stomach churning.

"What's the matter?"

"You don't understand!" Abruptly, she slides off the black stone wall and begins to walk downhill toward the ocean.

Maybe the sound of the waves will drown out everything for a time.

III

The Missing Apprentice

Flaghiern sat at the corner table, staring at the battered pewter mug, half-full, and his third already, for all that it was still light outside, not that the spring air managed to ooze past the smoke and staleness that filled The Overflowing Bowl.

An angular white-haired man slid onto the chair across the small table from him. "Thought you'd still be at the shop."

"No reason to be there now."

"Oh . . . the girl holding it down?" Dowlon laughed. "Your apprentice."

"She's gone, her and the babe. Child now, I guess."

"Gone? Where'd she go? You throw her out?"

"Suppose I did. Didn't mean to." Flaghiern lifted the mug and took a deep swallow, then set it on the table with exaggerated care. "Just wanted her to be more than . . . she was . . . we were."

"That doesn't sound like you threw her out."

"Worked out the same. She left."

"Where did she go?"

"How'd I know? She left a note, not that I can read it." Flaghiern looked into the mug.

"So . . . you'll get another apprentice."

"Not like her." The goldsmith shook his head. "Never like her."

"I'd not want to be prying, but . . ."

"The more fool I was . . . told her she could consort me . . . or leave. She left in the middle of the night." Flaghiern shook his head. "Neath those leathers, pretty little thing she was."

"But . . . you took her in."

"That'd be three years back, now. She worked the first three eightdays for naught. Slept in the stable. She said her da had been a silversmith, but she didn't know other metals, especially not gold. Begged for a chance to show me what she could do."

"What could she do?" Dowlon leered.

"It weren't like that. Don't know that she came from Southwind, but she might have. She wore those paired blades. Last year, some of Baldo's boys came in, found her alone. Thought they'd have some fun. One dead, one without his manhood, and the third lost his arm."

"I heard about that. I thought you were the one."

"I never told anyone otherwise. Better that way." The goldsmith took another swallow from the mug. "Thought so anyway."

"Oh . . . why'd she come here?"

"She never said. Never said how she ended up with a bairn, either. She worked hard. Never saw anyone learn so fast. Don't think she really knew the fine metals, though. Seemed to know about smithing and iron more. Doesn't matter now."

"There's rules for runaway apprentices . . ."

The goldsmith shook his head. "Not ifn it's not in writing. Was a bad year afore she came. You know that. Dimon . . . he was the real goldsmith. When he died of the flux . . ."

"The Guild would still back you."

"Didn't go through the Guild. Everyone thought she was just a shopgirl, tend the counter. Demon rats . . . was me ending up on the counter."

"Why'd you let her . . ."

"Because she was good . . ."

"She the one did those bracelets for the portmaster's wife? The delicate ones?"

Flaghiern nodded.

"She take anything? So's you could send the patrollers after her?"

"No. Nothing except what I owed her. Maybe less . . . Even

left me some fine rings and a bracelet I never saw before. Better than anything Dimon ever did. You know . . . she was even polishing rough stones afore she left . . . had the touch." The goldsmith looked down at the battered wood of the small square table. "Just wish she hadn't been so fine looking . . . maybe woulda worked out . . ."

After a time, he raised the empty mug for the server girl to refill.

IV

The Exiles

The tall man with the white-blond hair, wearing the dark blue jacket of a ship's officer, stopped outside the shop on the narrow side street of Southport. The shop itself was no more than four yards across the front. The door was not centered but at the right side, and there was a single narrow display window, a yard wide, centered between the door and the south end of the shop. The officer looked at the items displayed in the window, taking in a pendant. The brilliant blue stone was oval and set in silver, with a silver chain.

He stepped back, studying the shop, solidly made, everything in place, ordered in all particulars. Then he moved forward again, drawn by the pendant. He frowned. Somehow, the pendant looked familiar. He'd never seen one like it in any of the silversmiths or goldsmiths he'd visited.

Could this be the place? After all these years?

Finally, he walked back over to the door and opened it, stepping inside, and then closing it.

"I'll be there in a moment." The voice came from the back room of the shop.

Was the voice familiar? He wasn't sure.

He looked around. The front room was neat, and largely empty, except for two portraits, one on the wall above the left end of the counter and the other above the empty space between the counter at the right end and the wall. In the middle of the counter was a display area under glass. In it were two rings, another pendant, and an amulet of a design he'd never seen.

The craftswoman—or goldsmith or silversmith—stepped through the narrow archway and up to the counter.

He looked at the fine dark brown hair, still cut to chin length, if now shot with silver, and the dark blue eyes. "Hello, Jyll."

Her mouth opened, then closed. "Loric! What are you doing in Southport?"

"So you did recognize me after all these years." He smiled broadly. "Looking for you, at the moment." *I've looked for years.* "You haven't changed a bit."

"I fear I have."

"Not in the ways that count."

"In more ways than I would like to think."

"You look to be quite successful."

"Thanks to others."

"No. You always had the skill and the talent. When I saw that pendant in the window . . . Didn't you draw one like that, for the portrait you did of Lisabet?"

"I might have. That was a long time ago."

He glanced at the wall to her right. Hanging there in a simple wooden frame was a portrait of a beautiful young woman with blonde hair.

"You did that as well, didn't you?"

She nodded, her mouth offering a wry and rueful smile.

"Is that a relative . . . a . . . daughter, perhaps?"

Her laugh was more rueful than her smile had been. "No . . . the other portrait is her. She doesn't have her father's hair. His generosity, perhaps . . ."

"Jyll . . . you know why I'm here. . . . You must know."

"I've made too many mistakes, Loric. You, of all people . . ."

"Why do you think I've spent the last seventeen years look-ing for you? Why do you think I worked my way up from ordinary seaman? How else could I visit every port in Candar?"

She smiled sadly.

"I have, you know, and every town I could get to, but South-port isn't where . . . I've been able to port in the last few years."

"You've been able to port?" She looked again at his jacket. "You're a captain with your own ship now?"

"A captain, but for a group of merchants. I don't own the ship. That's made it harder to get to certain ports." He took a deep breath. "How did you end up here?"

"It made sense. The Academy sent me to Summerdock."

"How could Lortren . . . ?"

"She didn't know, or she pretended not to know when I wouldn't tell her. The first year was hard. I worked as a scullery maid in an inn . . . then persuaded a goldsmith to take me on as a shopgirl and an apprentice. He was desperate. He wasn't much of a goldsmith. He said . . . he wanted . . . Let's leave it at that. When I left, I had enough silvers for passage to Southport, and I got a real apprenticeship with a woman here."

"You have your own shop, though, don't you? Isn't this yours?"

"It is." Jyll glanced to the portrait of the blonde woman.

He looked at the portrait.

"My stepmother. After my father died, she sought me out. I don't know how she found me, but she did. She insisted she was in my debt. My debt . . . after all . . ." Jyll shook her head. "She said that what I'd done had given her the happiest years of her life. She wanted me to come back. I told her Recluce wouldn't allow that . . ."

Loric smiled broadly, but said nothing and continued to listen.

"She insisted on giving me enough to set up my own shop. I didn't do it all on my own, you see. She also insisted on returning the portrait to me. After . . . what I'd done . . . I couldn't refuse." Her lips quirked. "It's a useful reminder."

"Of what?"

"Of the dangers of hatred."

"I can't believe you . . ."

"That was then, Loric. Leave it at that."

After a moment, he gestured to the portrait of the blonde woman. "Is she still . . ."

"She lives in Land's End. She and Father never had any children. We write occasionally."

"What about your daughter?"

"She tutors some of the daughters of the wealthier women."

"She's well, then."

"She's very well, Loric, and she's been the joy of my life."

He glanced down at the display case. "That . . . and your work."

"Of course."

"You can come back to Recluce, you know. Not to Land's End, but to Nylan."

"The new city?" She raised her eyebrows.

"The black city, where they allow those who have made peace with who and what they are and who follow order in a . . . less restrictive way." He glanced around the shop. "Which you do."

"Who would allow me in?"

"Dorrin, for one. He's the one who's building the city."

"Dorrin? Was he the one? Was it his ship that destroyed the white fleet?"

"Not the whole fleet, but enough. He built and commanded *The Black Hammer*. He's done wonders."

"The toymaker . . ." Jyll laughed. "I wonder what Lortren would have said."

"I don't think she'd have been all that surprised. I once heard her say to Eshierra that he'd either die young or change the world, and she wasn't fool enough to wager on his death."

"He was determined."

"So were you. You still are." He squared his shoulders and looked straight at her. "You could move your entire shop to Nylan. If you won't do it for yourself, think about it for your daughter. I can get you and your cargo free passage. If you worry about . . . me . . . us, there are other captains who owe me favors. . . ."

"Loric, we can't change the past. It's gone."

"No, but you can change the present and the future."

"I . . . I can't do that."

After a long silence, he said, "Please think about it. Grant me that."

Her eyes met his. Then she nodded. "You deserve that. But don't ask me again. I'll decide in my own time."

And on your own terms. You always did. He forced a smile. "I won't ask again. But don't ask me not to stop by again if I port here."

"I won't." Her smile was warm, if still sad.

"I will take the pendant, though, if it's for sale."

"I thought . . ."

"I'm not. I want it for myself." *And because you created it.*

"Oh . . . Loric . . ." She shook her head. "That's as bad as . . ."

"Asking? Then, after I buy it, I won't buy another thing." He laughed gently. "Or ask again. Ever." He paused. "It doesn't mean I won't stop by."

"I'll get the pendant. The price is two golds."

"That's all?"

"That's all, and I'm not giving you a bargain. I never was a bargain, either, and I never will be."

"No, you shouldn't be." He laid the two golds on the counter. Then he laid ten more on the counter. "Those are for her. You're not to tell her, and you're to save them for her times of need."

"Loric . . . there's no need."

There's every need. "She shouldn't be a bargain. Ever." He turned and took in the portrait of the dark-haired girl, looking for a long time before finally looking back to her mother.

She nodded. "Only for her."

"Only for her," he agreed.

When he finally left the shop, he did not look back, knowing he dared not, knowing that the choices would be, as they always had been, hers.

V

The Proprietor

"The shop is new, Dorrin," says the broad-shouldered woman with the short silky brown hair that has begun to show traces of silver. "Kadara said that everything was amazing."

"If she said so," replies the wiry man, "it must be. She's never been fulsome with praise." The breeze off the harbor below ruffles his curly red hair, hair that is half-silver. "Except of Lers, and even there, she's careful."

"It's good that he's enough like his father that he doesn't take her praise too seriously," she says.

"Is that what Leyona says?"

"They're just friends, the way you and Kadara should have been from the beginning."

"They're both smarter than we were," he replies dryly. "Leyona takes after you in that, thank order."

The two walk down the narrow stone walkway flanking the

stone road that leads to the harbor and stretches uphill behind him to the gates in the wide stone wall . . . and far to the north beyond. Before long, they pass several shops still under construction before they reach their destination. The shop-front trim glistens with recently applied green paint, and the stone walk fronting the modest display window has been recently swept and washed. The sign features a curved carved letter *J*, surrounded by a carved oval, both silver gray against the black board. He holds the door and nods for his consort to enter. She does, and he follows.

A dark-haired young woman, a good five years or so older than their daughter, stands behind the counter, smiling pleasantly and waiting. "Are you looking for anything special, Lady, ser?"

"Definitely raised in Southwind," he says with a laugh. "Is your mother here?"

"Might I tell her who is calling, ser?"

"Just tell her that it is an old acquaintance who made toys, if you would." Dorrin conceals a smile.

"Yes, ser." Her polite response does not hide the puzzlement in her face and voice.

As the young woman steps through the archway, the woman who is also a trader looks at her consort. "You didn't have to be so cryptic."

"It won't be cryptic to her, I'd wager," he replies with a grin.

The woman who emerges from the rear of the shop has the same fine dark hair as her daughter, but that hair is shot with silver, and her eyes are deep blue, rather than pale green. Her eyes fix on the man. "Dorrin . . . it had to be you. And you didn't even come to see if I were black enough to stay in Nylan." The last words are offered almost teasingly before her voice turns welcoming. "And you must be Liedral."

Liedral nods, an amused smile playing across her lips.

"I know my limits," Dorrin says into the silence. "As harbormaster, Reisa is a far better judge of people than I am. I'm better as a toymaker, as someone once said."

"An engineer," Liedral corrects him.

"I've looked at your ships," says Jyll. "You're also an artist. There's not a thing about them that's not both beautiful and necessary."

"You see?" exclaims Liedral. "I've told you that."

"You've told me many things, dear, and most of them were right." Dorrin smiles affectionately, but ruefully.

Jyll turns. "Lorica . . . would you bring me the small black box. You know the one."

The young woman immediately slips back through the archway, but returns almost immediately with a black enameled box small enough to rest on the palms of her long-fingered hands.

"Thank you, dear." Jyll lifts the box and then extends it to Dorrin. "Go ahead. Open it."

Slowly, he does, his eyes widening as he sees what lies within. Liedral leans forward as well. On the deep red velvet is a golden ring, a man's ring, neither massive nor delicate, and the smooth curves of gold frame an oblong black stone with simple beveled edges. Cut into the black crystal is an image of *The Black Hammer*. The thin lines that depict the ship seem an almost luminescent gold, yet the miniature image is absolutely precise.

"Ionstone," murmurs Liedral. "Where . . . ?"

"I have my sources."

"I can't . . . ," protests Dorrin.

"You can," replies Jyll firmly. "I know you've said that you don't want anything said publicly. I've heard that you've even threatened people who wanted to do so. That doesn't mean you can't have a personal reminder of what you did."

"But . . . I only did what had to be done."

"You didn't have to do it, Dorrin," replies Jyll. "What is important in life are those who do what has to be done, and those who give all that they have. I would not be here, nor would I have found happiness, if you had not done what you did for all of us . . . the ones who did not fit."

"I can't," he says again.

"Dorrin . . . you cannot always be the giver. That deprives others of the opportunity to give as well. Just accept it gracefully. There are times to put aside everything and accept." She turns to look at the tall man with white-blond hair who has moved silently through the archway following his daughter and whose eyes enfold the artisan who is his wife. "I learned that late . . . but not too late."

Sometimes actions have repercussions years later, and writers are always turning those repercussions into pivots for "great" acts, but those actions also affect others in ways that no one would ever suspect. This is a story that reveals more about an incident that led to the rise of a ruler . . . and how that event not only changed history, but also the life of an "average" man simply because he witnessed that incident.

ARMSMAN'S ODDS

"One and one," grumbled Asoryk, looking down at the dice lying on the battered wooden table, "black demon's eyes." He shifted his weight on the narrow chair, careful not to brush the grimy bricks of the wall with his cyan uniform. That was one of the drawbacks of being an armsman of Lydiar. The captain got upset if armsmen appeared in public in dirty uniforms, especially if the armsmen were squad leaders. That was because the Mirror Lancer officers got angry, not because Captain Gersach cared about a smudge or two.

"They make two, double demons, and that's the basis of order," said Daasn. "Make your point." His eyes did not leave the corner table in the small tavern on the narrow unnamed lane off the south market square.

"Don't you ever think about how two chaos numbers always add up to an order number? The white wizards never say anything about that."

"What I'm thinking is you're going to have the demon's own time making your point." The angular junior squad leader grinned at Asoryk.

"What's your hurry? We've got time. You just want me to pick up the next round."

"I am getting thirsty." Daasn lifted the heavy mug and finished what little ale was left in it.

"You're always thirsty. Especially when you can get someone else to pay." The older squad leader scooped up the dice, cupped them in his hands, shook them, and let them roll out onto the wood. A five and a six. "Eleven. Friggin' left hand eyes. Just my luck."

"Ale's not that costly." Daasn's grin grew wider.

"Easy enough to say when you're not buying." Asoryk scooped up the dice and slipped them into the leather pouch attached to his wide belt, then raised his arm to summon the server. "Why is it that the odds are always against an armsman?"

"I'm an armsman, and they're not against me."

"You know what I mean," replied the older man.

Daasn laughed. "You mean that you're the oldest senior squad leader in the Duke's forces, and that you should have been an undercaptain years ago?"

"Or a captain by now."

"It might be because you're too honest. The Duke doesn't want fair. He wants what he wants. Captains are supposed to get it for him." Daasn raised his dark bushy eyebrows.

Asoryk offered a sour smile at the reference to the skirmish with the Sligan highlanders. His recollections were cut short by the arrival of the server.

Dhuris—the heavyset brunette server—stopped at the table and looked at Asoryk. "Your pleasure?" Her rough voice suggested that serving the two armsmen was anything but a pleasure, even though she'd been serving them on and off for over a year. Klyana, the other server, had always been far more friendly.

"Two ales."

"Be six. Now."

Asoryk laid the coppers on the table. They vanished into a hand far more delicate than the server's voice. As he looked at her hand, he couldn't help but think of Anallya, and, for the briefest of moments he was back in the bushes on the side of the road to Fairhaven, watching as he had struggled out of the undergrowth that Anallya had pushed him into, his eyes wide as she'd hurried toward the mage she'd insisted had been following her.

Before he could even reach the shoulder of the road, a single bolt of fire had fallen, and the white mage had nodded briskly and ridden away from the ashes on the wizard's road, the ashes that had moments before been a young woman. If Asoryk had only been quicker, had understood more . . . but she'd refused to stop and he'd followed her, trying to change her mind about leaving Howlett. She'd been the most beautiful woman he'd ever seen. He might have been young then, but he'd been old enough to know that, and over the years since then . . .

"Asoryk . . . are you going to drink that mug, or just stare at it?"

The squad leader looked at the full mug before him. He hadn't even seen the server put it there. "Sorry . . ." He shook himself. It had been a while since he'd had one of those memory spells that seemed so real that he had felt he had been transported back years. Not that he'd really known Anallya that well. He'd been little more than a beardless youth working as a stable boy when she'd appeared in Howlett, where she'd been a server for less than a season at the inn.

"You want to talk about it?" Daasn's voice held the skepticism of a comrade who felt obligated to ask the question to which he already knew the answer.

Asoryk shook his head. "No good'll come of it. The past is past." He lifted the mug and took a long swallow.

"Once they're cast, you can't change the way the dice came up," agreed Daasn.

"Demon-spawn. No matter how many times you throw, you never can even the odds."

"That's life, too."

Asoryk took another swallow. The ale tasted bitter. "How's your brew?"

"Fine. Just like the last one."

Asoryk lifted the mug and sniffed. Then he took a taste. Was the bitterness just in his head? As he set down the mug, he scanned the public room of the tavern. Abruptly, his eyes stopped as he took in two young men seated at a table against the far wall. Both were clean-shaven, and both wore stained tunics slightly too big for them. "Frig," he muttered.

"What?"

"Over against the wall. Don't stare." Asoryk watched as Daasn took in the pair.

"Mirror Lancers . . . out of uniform . . . what are they doing here?"

"Whatever it is . . . they shouldn't be. They know it, too, wearing workingmen's tunics."

"Maybe they're supposed to be here. Heard the white mages are looking for a renegade black healer."

"Who told you that?"

"Cheira. Seamstresses hear everything."

"Couldn't be more obvious than those two." Asoryk stopped. He almost shook his head. Of course. That was the point. Just as it had been with Anallya when the Mirror Lancers and the mage had showed up at the inn.

As he looked around the public room, he didn't see anyone who might be a white mage. But would he even be able to see a white wizard? Still . . . he had to do something. He rose from the table and walked over to the table against the other wall. "Haven't seen you boys here before." He let his voice fill the room. "Isn't it a bit far from the Mirror Lancers' barracks down here? You looking for someone? Or just seeing how the other half lives?"

A good half of the men in the public room looked up—and then lowered their heads when they saw the grizzled squad leader standing next to two well-muscled younger men.

The younger man at the table—red-haired—started to get up.

The older one put a hand on his arm and smiled at Asoryk. "Squad leader . . . we just heard that the lager here was better, especially if we weren't in uniform."

"Was it?"

The older Mirror Lancer grinned. "No . . . but you can't blame a fellow for trying."

Asoryk let his eyes sweep the room, barely catching sight of a figure in gray ducking back away from the rear archway, the one that led to the alley. He glanced back to the table. The younger man had been watching the archway as well.

"Enjoy your lager." Asoryk nodded to the pair, then walked back to where Daasn still sat, a puzzled expression on his face.

"Why'd you do that?" asked Daasn. "Those Lancers are mean bastards. They won't forget. They'd have cut you down right here if they could."

"They're mean," replied Asoryk, seating himself. "That doesn't mean good." His hand—hidden by the table—briefly brushed the hilt of the iron shortsword.

He turned his chair slightly so that he could watch the archway to the kitchen, as he had the feeling that the two Lancers were. Even from the momentary glimpse Asoryk got of the woman in gray, he had the feeling she didn't belong at the Blue Ram, just as Anallya hadn't belonged in Howlett.

As he sipped the ale, no longer in any hurry to finish it, he also kept studying the room, but all the others were regulars, or with regulars, or seemed to be familiar to the two servers, but then Klyana had always made that easy. Some women did.

Anallya had been the one who'd taught him that, with warmth and kindness, even when she had turned him away.

"You're sweet, Asoryk." That was what she had said, but her smile had been sad.

"There's someone else . . . isn't there?"

"There was . . . and there's my son."

For a moment, Asoryk had been shocked, not by her words, or by the fact that she had a son, something that he never would have guessed, but by the sadness in her wide gray eyes.

"I've never seen your son."

"He lives with my parents."

"What happened?" he had finally stammered.

"Nothing you can change. Nothing anyone can change. You don't want to be close to me." With that she had retreated into the inn's kitchen.

Before he could follow her, the innkeeper's wife had appeared, shooing him back to the stable.

Asoryk shook his head. He'd never even been able to find out anything about her son, either.

When he glanced over at the table where the Lancers had been, it was empty.

"Time for us to go."

"You were just saying that we had plenty of time."

"That was a while ago." Asoryk rose, leaving a pair of coppers on the table, not that Dhuris would appreciate them, and strode toward the door.

Daasn moved after him with the quiet grace that showed why he'd made squad leader so quickly.

When the two stepped into the starlit dimness outside the tavern, it didn't take long for Asoryk to make out the figures of the two Mirror Lancers. It wasn't hard because they'd removed the workingmen's tunics and stood in the pleasant early summer air in their shimmering whites.

"They want to be seen."

"Proud bastards," murmured the junior squad leader.

Asoryk looked back at the tavern, past the weathered signboard showing a ram rampant, barely illuminated by a lantern with a glass fogged with smoke. From what he could tell, there were no entrances on the sides, just the front entrance and, presumably, a rear entrance to the kitchen. "We'll go this way." He walked southward, moving past the alley behind the tavern.

"The post's the other way," Daasn pointed out.

"I know. I want to see something up this street." Asoryk kept walking until they passed another side street and were well out of sight of the two Lancers. Then he took the next narrow street to the left.

"Asoryk, where the frig are we going?"

"Back to the Blue Ram."

"You think the Lancer boys are there to scare someone out the back, and that there's someone waiting—"

"Don't you?"

"Looks that way. Why do you want to mess with the Mirror Lancers?"

"I don't. They're not worth a boar's teats."

"Then . . . why—"

"Because I want to see who they're after." That was easier than explaining why what he was about to do was necessary.

"Best be careful."

"Aren't I always?"

Daasn chuckled.

At the next corner, Asoryk headed back north. When he reached the alley that led to the Blue Ram, slightly uphill of the tavern, he eased into the shadows on the left side, moving as quietly as he could.

Crack. Asoryk's boot came down on a curved shard of broken crockery, and a cat, little more than a flash of gray and white, took three bounds in front of them before vanishing behind a pile of trash behind a shop that Asoryk recalled as a cooperage.

"Scared it, you did," murmured Daasn.

"Quiet now." Asoryk moved into the deeper shadows on the south side of the alley, the side away from the rear of the cooperage. After easing his way along the backs of shops whose function he'd never paid much attention to, he stopped beside a slops barrel, ignoring the stench.

"Why are we waiting here?" muttered Daasn.

To do what I couldn't years before. Except Asoryk did not speak the words. "To even the odds."

"What odds?"

"The ones armsmen seldom have the chance to even. If you don't understand, I'll explain later."

"You'd better."

The senior squad leader did not reply.

After a time, exactly how long Asoryk could not have said, but patience was one thing he had learned as an armsman, the rear door to the Blue Ram opened, and a scullery wench emerged carrying a pail with both hands and clearly struggling with the weight. The faintest of reddish-white light appeared in the dark shadows some ten yards ahead of Asoryk, outlining but briefly a tall figure in white. A white wizard.

His eyes went to the still-open rear door of the tavern, where he saw clearly, if but for a moment, a slender figure in gray—

except that gray had a solidity of a luminous black—and then the woman in gray darted back out of sight.

Asoryk nodded, if only to himself. A black mage, possibly even a healer. The white mages were known for their intolerance—Asoryk would have called it jealousy more than intolerance—of either whites who did not go to Fairhaven to be trained or of most blacks. Why, he didn't know, except it went back in time and was somehow connected to Recluce. But none of that mattered to him. Not tonight. Not once he'd seen the woman trapped in the Blue Ram. Not after years of memories.

The scullery wench finally finished emptying the bucket into the slops barrel behind the tavern and returned to her chores inside, closing the rear door . . . but not quite all the way, Asoryk realized. After he watched for a time longer, he also realized that the white mage was watching the door, and that the black mage—or healer—was watching the white wizard.

Asoryk edged around the slops barrel, keeping close to the rear walls of the shops. He froze as he heard the baying of a hound, but realized it was too far away to be one of those used by the Lancers to track fugitives from Fairhaven.

He flattened himself against the wall as the faint reddish whiteness increased slightly, as if the mage was about to do something. Across the alley, the tavern's back door widened from a crack to a slit.

Asoryk looked to the junior squad leader. "Give me your blade." His voice was low and hard.

Wordlessly, Daasn passed him the iron shortsword.

No sooner had Asoryk grasped the hilt than the white-clad mage turned, lifting his arm, about to point at Asoryk and Daasn.

Asoryk hurled the borrowed blade, hoping his aim was true enough to distract the white wizard. As soon as the heavy blade left his fingers, he sprinted forward, drawing his own shortsword.

Whhsst! Ugly reddish-white fire flared against the dark iron of the flung blade, slowing, then melting it as it dropped to the uneven stones of the alley.

Before the mage could turn his chaos-fire on Asoryk, the squad leader thrust the tip of the shortsword into the only part of the tall, thin mage's body he could reach, the right side of his chest, almost at the shoulder—far from a killing blow.

Yet reddish whiteness flared around the blade. The mage's mouth opened, but no sound came from it. The white wizard seemed to shrivel under the steel, and the white flames died away, leaving Asoryk holding a blade that appeared untouched. In moments, nothing lay on the uneven patchwork of stone and clay that paved the alley except a few bronze buckles and oddments, and a few coins.

Asoryk glanced toward the inn, but the door was half-open. He barely turned in time to see a gray-clad figure running past them on the far side of the alley, almost immediately swallowed by the shadows farther to the east . . . perhaps aided by a certain darkness of another kind.

Daasn stepped up beside the senior squad leader and looked down. He shook his head.

"Must have been hit by lightning . . . or something," Asoryk said.

"Must have been." Daasn nodded slowly.

"Should start back to the barracks." Asoryk leaned and picked up the melted blade, then handed his own to Daasn. "This is yours. We'll take the long way back." He started up the alley, following the unseen steps of the woman who had fled, not that he would follow beyond the street ahead.

Daasn joined him.

This time, at least, he'd been able to even the odds.

He wondered if the black mage, or healer, had a son, not that it mattered. She'd at least have that chance. He also wondered, not for the first time, what had ever happened to Anallya's boy. He shook his head. He'd done what he could, even if he'd have to dispose of the melted blade and pay for a replacement. That was cheap for what he'd gained.

Not all magic, either in Recluce or elsewhere, comes from those who wield order or chaos . . . or even both.

BRASS AND LACQUER

I

The air was crisp, but not chill, that afternoon on the last eightday of harvest when Shaunyce and Talysen walked up the black stone walk to the wall north of Nylan. She glanced at him, stocky and barely taller than she was, not to mention his already thinning blond hair. But he was a black mage, of sorts, as a student engineer, and he *was* sweet.

Talysen gestured to the wall. "It was built over three hundred years ago."

"I know that, silly mage. Everyone does."

"Did you know that a student mage destroyed a good part of the wall right there?" He pointed. "That happened in my grandmother Aleasya's time."

"It doesn't look any worse for it."

"She said it took three masters to fix it."

Shaunyce nodded politely. "What happened to him? The student mage, I mean?"

"It could have been a woman, you know."

"A woman wouldn't destroy a wall. That's stupid."

"Don't you understand how much power that took?"

"It was still stupid. You never said what happened to him."

"She said the masters sent him to Hamor. There was a healer who followed him."

"What happened to her?"

"She didn't say."

"You mean you didn't ask."

Talysen flushed. "Why are you so difficult?"

"I'm not. Any woman would want to know." She did not shake her head. Instead, she turned and walked away from him and to the chest-high black stone wall. There she looked south toward the entrance to the harbor. A black vessel, somehow indistinct, headed outbound into the gray-green-blue waters of the Gulf of Candar. She knew it had to be one of the black ships. She said nothing until Talysen joined her. "That's a black ship, isn't it?"

"Most likely."

"Most likely? You're an engineer. You're studying so you can build them, and all you can say is, 'Most likely'?"

"It is. I'd guess that it's the *Shierra*."

Shaunyce thought he could have said that first. She only smiled. "Have you been on one of them?"

"Not at sea."

"But you've been on one when they're tied up behind the walls at the west end of the harbor. Right below the engineering buildings?"

"Just a few times."

"What does it feel like standing on the front of one?"

"The bow?" Talysen shrugged. "I wouldn't know. I was mostly down in the engine room."

"You could get me to where I could see one up close, couldn't you? Even on board one?"

Talysen shook his head. "No one gets on a black ship except engineers, shipfitters, and the crew. Not even the council members, unless they're a black master."

"I don't believe that."

"That's what the senior engineer said."

"I'd really like to see one of the ships. Just look at it."

"So would every engineer or naval officer from Hamor and every other land."

"I'm just a shopgirl. I couldn't tell anyone anything if I wanted to. It's such a little thing. Why can't you let me see one of the ships? What harm will it do?"

"Probably none at all," Talysen replied, "but I'm just an apprentice junior engineer. Junior engineers follow the rules. That's if they want to become senior engineers."

"Fine." Shaunyce offered the single word coolly. "I'm ready to walk back."

Talysen looked puzzled, but only said, "If that's what you want."

II

She was still angry when she reached the shop on oneday morning, but she managed a smile as Master Brauk said, "Good morning, Shaunyce."

"Good morning, ser."

"Did you have a pleasant endday?"

"I did," she lied, not wanting to admit that she was still angry with Talysen. It wasn't as though she wanted to do anything to hurt Recluce, and how could looking at an iron ship reveal anything at all?

"That's good." He turned away and opened the shutters protecting the front display window. The morning sun glinted off the polished finish of the kettle that adorned the signboard of the adjoining coppersmith's shop. "How is your mother?"

She responded, as she always did, "She's doing well, ser." Brauk never asked more about Nynca, or her pottery, although he must have known that she produced fine pieces, but since he never asked more, Shaunyce didn't feel she should say more, either.

"That's good. Don't forget to dust the display shelves."

"Yes, ser." She headed toward the counter to get the dust cloth.

Two glasses later, Shaunyce was getting hungry and impatient. Brauk hadn't said another word before retreating to his study adjoining the storeroom. She'd heard the side door, the one to Brauk's study that opened on to the alley, open and close several times as traders came and went, but the door to the study muffled their voices.

Then the front door opened, and a balding man walked in. He looked to be a merchanter, and not a poor one, from the black velvet of his jacket.

"Good day, ser," she offered cheerfully.

He nodded brusquely in reply, but did not speak, walking to the open display cabinet set against the north wall, surveying one shelf, then the next. He kept looking at the pair of polished brass creatures standing side by side on the third shelf of the open cabinet. She didn't like the brass figures, each in the shape of a winged beast the like of which she had never seen, with four-clawed feet and a winding barbed tail. The figures were almost identical, except that their long-snouted heads were turned in opposite directions, so that, on the shelf, they looked either toward each other or away, depending on how they were positioned. They were also absolutely flat on the back, and each was hinged, but not exactly in the middle, with the sides bent forward slightly so the figure would balance, giving the impression that each of the creatures was poised to take flight.

"What sort of creatures are these, girl? Why are they hinged? They're too fancy just to be hinges. How much is Brauk asking?"

"They're dracones, ser. Seven silvers."

"Seven silvers? For something no one has ever heard of?" The merchanter shook his head. "Creatures that never were as hinges . . ." His words dying away, he shifted his gaze to a box, the smallest on display, set on the higher shelf. The top of the seemingly plain box, lacquered or enameled in black, or perhaps coated with something similar, had an inlaid circular oval depicting a silver-white winged bird with a long curved neck unlike any ever seen in Recluce or even in Candor, gliding across a pond against a background of golden-green rushes, seemingly moving from right to left.

"I've never seen a bird like that." The merchanter turned toward Shaunyce. "Do you know what kind it is?"

"A cigoerne, ser," replied Shaunyce.

"I didn't ask where it came from, girl."

"Yes, ser. I was told the city of Cigoerne was named after the bird. The cigoerne was a bird from the Rational Stars."

The merchanter snorted. "A mythical bird from a mythical place, and that's what the Hamorians named their capital?" He paused. "Doesn't look that old, though."

Shaunyce just hoped he'd buy something, either the pair of winged brasses or the box, and leave. She didn't like either the bird box or the brass creatures, but each for a different reason.

"How much is it?"

"Fifteen golds."

"Fifteen golds?" The merchanter shook his head. "Your master doesn't want to part with it, that's certain."

"That's just the way it is, ser." Shaunyce had wondered about that, since Brauk had only displayed the box for two eightdays in the three seasons she'd worked for him.

With the sound of the study door opening, Shaunyce knew Master Brauk was headed to the front of the shop. She did not look back, but kept her eyes on the merchanter. She hoped Brauk hadn't heard her words.

The angular merchanter took a last look at the black enameled box, shook his head, and walked toward the display window. Shaunyce slipped from behind the counter, following the merchanter, not intruding, but staying close and trying to convey helpfulness.

Brauk eased forward and gestured for Shaunyce to return to the counter. Then he said something in a low voice to the merchanter. The other man laughed.

". . . might look at the lower shelf on the display case," suggested Brauk, stepping back, but in a fashion that left the way to the display open.

The merchanter nodded, then returned and studied the lower shelf before speaking. "What about this?" He held up a woman's jewelry box, with a hinged top of fine black lorken. The top was simple, with just an inlaid border of twin lines of white birch, and the box was easily five times the size of the more expensive enameled box.

"Six silvers, ser," replied Brauk.

"That's more like it, not like that tiny black box." The merchanter shook his head again. "It's not much good for holding anything."

"Boxes should serve the needs of their owners," replied Brauk.

"This one will do fine," said the merchanter. "Elegant and simple. Priced right, too."

"Is there anything else . . . ?" Brauk's voice was warm, helpful, but neither wheedling, nor intrusive.

"Not a thing." Even so, as the merchanter turned, his eyes went back to the pair of dracones, then lingered on the small black box, the one with the cigoerne on it, for just a few instants.

Once the merchanter had paid for the simple jewelry box, Brauk wrapped it in gray felt and watched as the man left the shop. Only then did he walk back over to the end of the counter where Shaunyce stood.

"Did you see how he immediately looked to the unique pieces? That was the sign of a man who was going to buy. He needed something to placate his consort, or his mistress. More likely his consort. He'd have picked jewelry if it was going to a mistress."

"I'd hoped he'd buy the black box." Because Shaunyce wanted to take Brauk's mind off the merchanter who she felt might have bought more, she pointed. "Where did you get those brass figures? The dracones?"

"You don't remember?"

"You said Thyel, the coppersmith, made them from a drawing. That's all. You never said who did the drawing."

Brauk smiled. "I suppose I didn't. He was an old fellow. He came to Nylan every so often. He wasn't a seaman, but he didn't seem to be a merchanter, and he didn't wear black. Thyel wouldn't make them without silvers up front. The old man paid them and said I could pay him back if they sold. I thought they might. The old man thanked me." He frowned. "He said he'd be back, but it might be years . . . or longer. He couldn't tell. That was more than five years ago."

"He just left them with you?" Shaunyce couldn't believe that. Who would pay to have something made and then leave it for someone he wouldn't see for years to sell? Yet Brauk wouldn't make up something like that. He didn't have the imagination, or the interest in telling stories.

"He said that they could look out for themselves, and when the time came, they'd find the right owner." Brauk paused. "He said one other thing . . . that they always found a good home."

They always found a good home? That suggested . . . Shaunyce shook her head. "What about the black box with the bird on it? You never told me about that one, except that it was rare and to watch it carefully."

"My father always thought it was a copy of something older. I didn't think so. I still don't. That's why it's priced the way it is."

"Did it come from Cigoerne?"

"I'd judge so. Where else?" Brauk walked to the display case and picked up the small box. He carried it back and extended it. "You see? The finish looks like lacquer, but as old as it is, there's not a single crack. Look at the cigoerne itself. Look closely."

Reluctantly, Shaunyce did. After a moment, she blinked. The bird seemed to stand out, against faint ripples, ripples that seemed to move as she looked. She swallowed and looked up. "Order magic? It has to be."

Brauk shook his head. "I've had one of the black masters look at it, several over the years. So did my father, right after . . . They all said it didn't have excess order or chaos."

"You don't really want to sell it, do you? Is that why the price is so high?" Shaunyce frowned. "If you don't want to sell it, why do you have it out?"

"It isn't all the time. I set it out for an eightday or two every year. It's good for getting attention, and it makes the other pieces seem reasonable."

Shaunyce had the feeling there was more to be said and waited.

"Also, I hope that someday, someone might come along and tell me more. Like that old woman did about the ring with the carving of the first of great ships—*The Black Hammer.*"

"The ring you saw was a copy of the original, she said."

"That means there is an original, and it's likely priceless. I can always keep my eyes out for it." He smiled.

Shaunyce wasn't certain his expression was friendly.

"Here." He extended the box. "Hold it. Hold it for a long time. Very carefully, though. You'll see."

The way he said that, she didn't want to, but she took the box in her long and slender fingers, the reason why she worked for Brauk, because those fingers were far too delicate to work the heavy clay the way her mother did, not without getting wrinkled. Besides, Shaunyce hated the way the clay worked up under her nails, and she liked having her nails longer. They showed off her hands better, and her hands were one of her best features.

For several moments, she looked at the image of the cigoerne, but she didn't like the way she seemed to stand out, as if she were alive or trapped in the oval that depicted her gliding across the rush-framed pond.

She? Shaunyce wanted to drop the box, but she dared not, especially with Brauk standing there. An intense feeling of loss and longing swept over her, a feeling that all she held dear had vanished. She shivered.

As she did, Brauk gently lifted the box from her fingers. "You felt something, didn't you?"

Wordlessly, she nodded.

"You felt more than most. I can see that. Everyone feels something different. What did you feel?"

Shaunyce didn't want to say. She shook her head, then asked, "What did you feel?"

Brauk looked sheepish, an expression Shaunyce had never seen from him, then said, "It feels peaceful to me. Now, at least."

"Not to me," admitted Shaunyce.

"I think it brings out what we feel or might feel." Brauk looked down at the box. "I'll leave it on display just for a while longer. Do keep an eye on it."

"Yes, ser. I will."

"You might want to hold it again later. Not soon, though."

At her expression, he added, "The feelings it evokes can change. Mine did." Then he replaced the box in the display case before he walked back to the small study.

Shaunyce stood there beside the counter. She was confused. He had suggested that she hold it again, but not anytime soon. Yet he was only going to leave the cigoerne box out for a short time? Did he think she was going to work in his shop forever?

The rest of the day was better, especially after she ate the cheese and pearapple her mother had sent with her. No one either asked about the dracones or even looked at the small box, and Shaunyce even sold an antique silver-and-sapphire necklace to the young consort of an older merchanter. The age of the merchanter was a guess, since the comparatively young woman came with a guard, a hard-faced man at least a decade older than she was.

A quarter glass before closing, Shaunyce was about to begin carrying the items in the display case—the really valuable ones, like the brass dracones and the cigoerne box, and, of course, the jet-black pearl necklace that also came from Hamor—when Talysen walked into the shop.

"What are you doing here?" She tried to keep the irritation out of her voice, but she did have to put all the valuables into the locked chest in the iron-walled strong room in back before she could leave for the evening. If she spent time with Talysen, then it would take just that much longer.

"I came to apologize. I obviously did something to displease you yesterday. I still don't know what it was, but I'd like to apologize."

"If you—" She managed not to sigh, even as she wondered how a black, even a student who wasn't that close to being a master, could be that dense. She could see the desire to please in every line of his face, and she couldn't help but smile, just a bit. At least, she kept from laughing. "It's a woman thing." That covered a lot, and she hoped he wouldn't ask for more of an explanation she didn't want to give.

"That doesn't tell me much." A rueful smile accompanied his words.

"If I have to tell you something that you should understand, then . . ." She shook her head.

"You're saying that I should be able to know what you're thinking so that you don't have to ask for it or tell me something that's painful for me to hear."

"I didn't say that."

"Whether you said it or not, that is what you meant." Talysen added, his voice warm and slightly amused, "Would you really want me knowing what you're thinking . . . or do you just want me to know it when it's convenient?"

"You're impossible."

"Why is it that people always say that when someone points out an unpleasant fact?"

"That's not true."

"Then tell me why you were so upset at me yesterday."

Shaunyce wanted to scream. She tightened her lips. Finally, she said, "I really wanted to see a black ship. You didn't listen."

Talysen sighed. "I did listen. I told you why the masters don't allow anyone on board who isn't an engineer or a master."

"But I'm not anyone who would do anything to hurt Recluce."

"Anyone who wanted to learn about the ships to use the knowledge against Recluce would say the same thing. And if a lot of people saw the ships, then those who wanted to learn about them could find out from them."

"Not from me," declared Shaunyce. "I wouldn't even know what I was looking at."

"The engineers don't have the people or the time to question everyone who might want to look at a black ship." Talysen glanced toward the hinged bronzes. "Those are the dracones you mentioned?"

"Yes." Shaunyce's reply was just short of curt.

"They couldn't fly, not really. Their wings are too small for their bodies."

"Spoken like an engineer!" Brauk's voice was hearty as he walked toward the pair.

"Ser," said Shaunyce quickly, "this is Talysen. He's a student engineer."

"Apprentice engineer," corrected Talysen. "I'm pretty junior, though."

"You'd better go," said Shaunyce, looking to Talysen. "I need to finish up here."

"Oh . . . I can take care of that," interjected Brauk. "You've worked hard today." He turned to Talysen. "Before you two leave, though, could I ask a favor of you? It will only take a few moments."

"If I can, ser," replied the apprentice engineer cautiously.

"I'm certain you can." The shop owner walked to the display case and lifted the black box off the top shelf, returning and extending it to Talysen. "I'd appreciate your thoughts and feelings on the box, especially your sense of whether the box has an excess of order or chaos."

"I'm not a master, ser."

"I understand that, but I would appreciate your thoughts."

"As you wish, ser." Talysen accepted the box, holding it in his square-fingered hands.

Shaunyce watched as, first, he looked at the box, then half-closed his eyes. After several moments, he opened them.

"What can you tell me about the box?" asked Brauk.

"It's . . . different. There's no excess of order and no excess of chaos. It feels perfectly balanced. Nothing is perfectly balanced.

I don't know that I've ever felt anything quite like it." Talysen shook his head.

"What if you both touched it?" asked Brauk. "Do you think that would change anything? Go ahead." He looked hard at Shaunyce. "Try it. Both of you touch it at the same time."

Shaunyce hesitated.

"Go on," Brauk urged.

While his words were not exactly a command, Shaunyce knew he'd be displeased if she didn't follow his suggestion. Gingerly, she reached out and touched the box that Talysen still held. For a moment, she felt nothing, not even the sense of loss that had swept over her that morning.

Then came an image of a woman wearing a shimmering gray tunic and trousers, her brown hair perfectly in place, with vivid green eyes. Shaunyce swallowed, realizing she was seeing herself—except she wasn't like that at all. She had mouse-brown hair, and a nose that was too strong, with eyes set too close together. And her gray shop tunic and trousers certainly didn't shimmer.

She looked helplessly at Talysen, taking in his too-thin blond hair and high forehead, the slightly stooped shoulders, and the intensity in his eyes . . . and the goodness behind those eyes. A feeling of shame washed over her, and she immediately lifted her fingers from the box.

For another moment, she and Talysen continued to stare at each other.

Then he looked away and toward Brauk. "I'll leave now." He bowed to Brauk. "Thank you, ser. The box was most illuminating." He turned without looking at Shaunyce, then walked out of the shop.

Shaunyce remained motionless, frozen. She finally faced Brauk. "You did that on purpose."

"Did what?" asked Brauk innocently.

"You *knew* he'd learn what I was feeling."

"You don't think he should know? Isn't deceiving him inviting chaos into your life?"

Letting Talysen know that way had just created more chaos. Shaunyce couldn't afford to say that.

"Deception always outs, Shaunyce. Always. And it hurts you, because it wounds the deceiver as much as the deceived, if not more."

Even in her anger and confusion, she could hear a hint of sadness in his voice. She couldn't help but wonder why he'd mentioned her specifically. She was only his shopgirl. Why did it even matter to him?

III

When Shaunyce came to work on twoday, Brauk had already removed the cigoerne box from the array of the more expensive items being displayed. The pair of hinged dracones remained. He did not mention the box, and she did not ask, much as she wanted to know why he had changed his mind.

He did ask, as he did occasionally, "How is your mother?"

"Fine, ser." Shaunyce didn't feel like saying more.

Very few people stopped in the shop that day.

Threeday was different. A Lydian merchanter had ported, and so had vessels from Austra and Southport. The common seamen didn't even pause outside the shop windows, Shaunyce noticed, but that type never did. The better-dressed ship's officers—or mates, if that was what they were called on merchanters—usually did. Sometimes, one would even come in.

The first one who did spoke only old Candaran, the language of Fairhaven, similar to the Temple of Recluce, but difficult to follow. Even so, she sold him a small jewelry casket of worked lorken, inlaid with a border of ivory shaped to look like a chain.

The second man, who eased through the shop doors with the grace of a mountain cat less than a glass later, wore the striped patch of some sort of mate, but he carried himself more like the ship's marines who defended the Brotherhood's section of the harbor where the black ships ported. He was tall and lean, with golden-green eyes and a warm smile as he approached her. "What's a pretty girl like you doing in a place like this?" His Temple was precise.

"It's a very nice shop." Shaunyce managed a pleasant smile. "Are you looking for something special? For someone special?"

"From what I've seen, you're the most special treasure here."

"Treasure? I think not." She gestured toward the dracones. "Those are special. They're the only ones in all of Recluce."

The man's eyes moved from appraising her to the dracones, but did not linger there long, returning to her in far too familiar a manner. "They might be, but . . . they're not what I'm seeking."

"Could I show you some of our fine jewelry?"

He smiled again. "You could . . . but, to be fair, I wouldn't buy any."

"I see." Shaunyce was afraid that she did indeed see, but she didn't dare be rude. She gestured again, this time toward the bookcase against the wall. "Perhaps some rare books?"

"I think not. I'm interested in . . . company."

"You're a very good-looking man, ser," she replied with a smile, "but that's something we don't sell here."

"I didn't think you did. Perhaps you'd be free later."

She managed a gentle laugh. "Not even for a handsome fellow like you." After a pause, she added, "Is there anything we do sell that you'd be interested in?"

"No . . . but you can't blame a man for trying." He smiled a last time before leaving the shop.

After the handsome ship's officer had left the shop, Shaunyce retreated to the counter. He'd been handsome enough, and polite in his approach, direct as he had been, but . . . She shook her head. Even Talysen had been far more respectful.

Then a trader came into the shop—older, bearded, and wearing a shapeless brownish-gray woolen jacket. "Merchanter Brauk, girl."

Shaunyce didn't argue with his rough voice and peremptory and dismissive demand. She'd learned that in the first days of working in the shop. She inclined her head, then turned and walked to the back, where she announced, "A trader for you, ser. He's likely from Hydlen. He's not been here before." Those that had always knocked on the side door.

Brauk raised his eyebrows.

"The way he speaks, ser. He demanded you."

Brauk nodded and rose from the table desk, carefully closing the ledger he had been perusing. Shaunyce followed him as far as the counter, where he stopped and gestured to the trader. The two retreated to Brauk's study, but Brauk left the door open, something he did not do if he knew a trader well. Shaunyce moved back to a position near the counter. She'd have to assist anyone else who entered the shop while Brauk haggled over whatever the trader had brought.

Thinking over what she just said to Brauk, Shaunyce reflected on the handsome ship's officer, realizing that, while he certainly hadn't been from Recluce, his precise Temple had offered no hint of an accent at all. He seemed more like a marine, but the Brotherhood didn't allow warships of other lands into the harbor at all. Or maybe they didn't let the crews come ashore. She wasn't sure which.

Why was she thinking about that?

She was almost relieved when a wiry gray-haired woman strode into the shop and immediately looked for Brauk, peered to the rear of the shop and saw he was busy, then stepped over and stopped in front of Shaunyce. "Brauk's still trying to sell those bronze monstrosities, is he, girl?"

"Yes, Lady."

"Mistress Caryon will do, thank you. I'm no lady. No airs for me. Is that jet-black pearl necklace still available?"

"It is, Mistress Caryon."

"Leastwise, you listen. Still the same ridiculous price?"

"Merchanter Brauk has kept the price as it was."

"He's as bad as any Hamorian." She offered a sound somewhere between a snort and a sniff. "You're too good-looking to be a shopgirl. If you don't have talent, you'd be better working for me. If you do, you're wasted here. Brauk'll use you until you lose your looks, and what will you have?"

Shaunyce didn't know what to say. After a moment, she asked, "Would you like the necklace, Mistress Caryon?'

"Of course. I just don't want to pay what he wants."

"What would you pay?" Shaunyce hated the haggling, but Brauk was still tied up with the Hydlenese trader.

"Two golds, five."

"He won't take that." Shaunyce knew that because Brauk had turned down an offer of two golds eight the previous fiveday.

"Ask him."

Shaunyce nodded and walked back toward the study, standing outside the door and trying to catch Brauk's eye.

After several moments, the shop owner murmured something to the trader and hurried to Shaunyce. "What is it?" Annoyance colored his voice.

"Mistress Caryon offered two golds five for the jet-black pearls. I said you wouldn't take it. She insisted I ask you."

"She can have it for two and seven, not a copper less." Brauk turned and walked back to the trader.

In turn, Shaunyce made her way back to the gray-haired woman.

"Well?"

"Two and seven and not a copper less."

Caryon sniff-snorted. "Better than two eightdays ago . . ." She paused. "Two and seven it is. The box comes with it."

"Yes, Mistress Caryon." Shaunyce didn't know if it did, but it was a simple oak box, without any decoration, and Brauk did occasionally let the boxes go with their display contents.

"If you would get it for me and take it to the counter."

Shaunyce did so. By the time she had retrieved the necklace and the box that held it, Caryon was at the counter and had laid out two golds and seven silvers.

Shaunyce hadn't handled a sale that big, not without Brauk at her shoulder, but she did know what to do. She lifted out the two cards in the bottom of the box, one for the purchaser and one for the store, each listing the item and leaving a space for the purchase price and a signature for both Brauk and Caryon. She filled in the price and handed the cards to Caryon, who signed both and returned them. Shaunyce signed for Brauk, then placed the card in the box, replaced the top, and handed the box to the gray-haired woman. "Thank you, Mistress Caryon."

"You're most welcome." Caryon paused. "You never told me your name."

"Shaunyce."

"That's an attractive name, and one with substance. Don't waste it, dear." She smiled and walked from the store.

Shaunyce waited for almost half a glass before Brauk finished with the trader, showed him out, and then returned to the counter.

"Did she accept?"

"She did. She paid in golds and silvers. Here they are," she said.

"She can spare them," replied Brauk. "I saw that you let her have the box. That was good."

"I know you sometimes do."

"She doesn't come often, and she won't haggle much."

"I was surprised . . . at the amount."

"Because I'd rejected two and eight last fiveday? That was then. This is now. I could use the golds and silvers to pay for what the trader had. Besides, Haellyn had a buyer in mind, someone in Austra, likely. For a silver less, I'd rather sell to Caryon."

"I've never seen her before."

"You'd like to know who she is?"

Shaunyce nodded.

"Have you heard of The Lady's Place? She's the Lady."

"She's the one? She doesn't . . ."

"Sometimes looks reveal, sometimes conceal. That's a line from the past." He looked toward the shop door. "Here comes the dowager. I'm not available. Don't part with anything for less than one part in ten of the original price."

By the time the widow of Merchanter Moraris had reached the display case, Brauk was nowhere to be seen. Shaunyce smiled helpfully and stepped forward.

IV

Threeday passed, and so did fourday . . . and the rest of that eightday. When Shaunyce arrived at the shop on oneday morning she had not seen or heard from Talysen since the previous twoday. Nor did she see him or even receive a note from him over the following eightday, as the middle of harvest arrived, and the weather began to cool, and the clouds began to form in the northern skies, suggesting that the fall rains might descend even before harvest season was over.

More than a few outland merchant officers passed by the shop, and one or two even bought small things from her, but none were that much different from the tall blond man who had been the first to proposition her. She still remembered him, because he reminded her of what Talysen had said about outlanders trying to find out about the black ships. She thought about trying to see Talysen, but the gates to the student and apprentice quarters were closed to outsiders. Even family members had to be vouched for before they could enter. She thought about writing a note, but what would she say—except that she hadn't been fair to him . . . which he already knew? That had been obvious the moment he had left the shop.

She was still mulling over what had happened, or what she had let happen, or what Brauk had caused to happen—or perhaps it had been all three—when a younger man, only a few years older than she was, stepped through the door. He wore the rich brown coat of a successful merchanter over a white ruffled shirt and a light brown cravat. While he looked to be headed for Brauk's study in the back, he glanced in Shaunyce's direction and then headed toward where she stood beside the counter.

"I haven't seen you here before."

"You must have missed me, then. I've been working here since last spring."

"That was my loss. I'm Shefan. I was looking for Merchanter Brauk. Might he be here?"

"He is. Would you like me to tell him you're here?"

"If you would."

"He's in his study."

Although Shaunyce did not gesture for him to accompany her to the back of the shop, he followed, if several steps behind. Since the study door was ajar, Shaunyce knocked quietly, then said, "There's a Merchanter Shefan here to see you, ser."

"Have him come in," replied Brauk.

Although Brauk's words were hearty and certainly loud enough that Shefan must have heard, he remained standing several paces away, looking expectantly at Shaunyce.

"You can go in, ser."

"Thank you." With a smile, a very long look at her, and then a nod, he stepped toward the study.

Shaunyce stepped back and watched as he passed, entered the study, and closed the door. She did not return to the counter, but eased toward the study door, listening.

". . . did you get her? . . . makes the trip from Land's End almost worth it . . ."

". . . more than decoration, Shefan . . . dab hand at selling things . . ."

". . . and you didn't bring her on for her looks?"

". . . must admit . . . the rest was more than I'd anticipated . . ."

At the sound of the shop door opening, Shaunyce immediately turned and hurried back into the shop proper. She reached a position in front of the counter just as the tall gray-haired man stopped in front of the display case that held the dracones. He continued to study them for a time before he turned to her. His brown leather jacket was well-made, if worn, and his boots were scuffed, yet his light tan shirt was of fine cotton, and his brown trousers were of good wool.

"Might I help you, ser?"

"You know, those bronzes don't belong here?"

"They were made by Thyel."

"I'm certain that they were. What are they supposed to be?"

"Dracones, ser."

"How much?"

"Seven silvers."

"How about six?"

Shaunyce thought about countering, but the very *solidity* of the man stopped her. "Six it is, but I countered with six and five and you insisted on six."

He smiled. "Done."

After Shaunyce took his silvers, made out the cards, and then took back one he had signed, she looked at the signature—Sardittar—then at the gray-haired man. "You're not from here, are you?"

"No. I'm from Mattra. I come here occasionally for supplies. Tools, mostly."

"You're a crafter?"

"Woodcrafter." He produced a woolen cloth from somewhere and walked to the dracones, where he carefully wrapped them up. "Thank you. Tell your merchanter that they'll have a good home."

"I will."

Wondering about his last words, she watched as he strode out. Seemingly in moments, the door to Brauk's study opened, and Shefan walked from the rear of the shop to the counter.

"You're still here?"

"Where else would I be?"

"Have you ever thought about leaving Nylan?"

"No. Why would I?"

"Adventure, change, even love, perhaps. I wouldn't think you'd want to be a shopgirl all your life." Shefan smiled.

The smile bothered her, as if he was suggesting . . . all manner of possibilities, none of which appealed to her, perhaps because all of them were linked to Shefan. "I appreciate your interest in my well-being, Merchanter Shefan. You're very kind, and thoughtful, but I think I'd prefer to remain in Nylan."

"You can't blame a man for suggesting possibilities."

The fact that it was the second time a man had used that sort of phrase bothered her, but she managed to reply, "You can't blame a woman for wanting different possibilities."

For an instant, he looked shocked. Then he smiled, faintly, coolly. "I see. In that case, I wish you well . . . here in Nylan." With a nod, he turned and left.

Before long, Brauk walked to the counter. "Shefan didn't stay long. I thought he might."

"He suggested some possibilities. I wasn't interested."

"That's probably for the best. Shefan tends to be interested in anything only for a short time." Brauk glanced at the display case. "What happened to the dracones?"

"I sold them."

"You sold them? To whom?"

Shaunyce handed him the card.

"Sardittar? Never heard of him."

"He said he was a woodcrafter in Mattra."

"And you got six for them? From a woodcrafter?"

"You said I could take six if someone was interested."

"He must be a very good woodcrafter, indeed." Brauk shook his head.

"He said to tell you that the dracones would have a good home."

"He said those exact words?"

"Yes, ser . . . maybe not exactly, but he did say they'd have a good home."

"Very strange. Oh well, life has its turns." Brauk smiled happily and headed back to the study, but not before scooping up the silvers.

V

On the sixth fourday of harvest, late in the afternoon, the blond merchant officer walked into the shop again. He didn't head straight for her, but for the more expensive display case, where the dracones had been, which now featured a pair of black iron daggers, one of which Brauk had obtained from the rough-voiced trader. She was sure it was him, except he wore different garb and a different rank patch on the sleeve of his dark blue jacket. She hadn't known what the first patch had signified, nor did she recognize the second.

"Have you changed ships?" she asked.

He gave her a quizzical glance. "Have we met before?" His words were in Temple, but with a Hamorian accent, unlike the voice of the man she had thought he might be. A warm smile followed. "It would be strange if we had. I've never ported here before."

Was he someone different? Or just pretending? "I don't think so. For a moment, you reminded me of someone. Do you have a brother?"

The man laughed. "You've met Coenyr?" He frowned. "I don't think . . . that's possible, not here in Nylan."

"I didn't say it was here," Shaunyce said. "Is he an officer in the Hamorian navy?"

"He is. That's why . . ."

"He couldn't have come here," she finished his words. "And you're a merchant officer, aren't you?"

He nodded, a puzzled expression still on his face.

"Let's just say it was a long time ago that I saw him for just a few moments. He was rather insistent. Nice, but insistent. I wasn't interested." She smiled politely. "Are you looking for something special?"

"Oh . . . I'm looking for something for my consort. Not too expensive, but something that she can look at and tell that it's from Recluce." He looked at the display case that had held the dracones.

"What's in that case likely wouldn't fit what you have in mind." She eased toward the wall shelves to her left. "There are a few bracelets and pendants here . . ." She stepped back and let him look.

His eyes caught the bracelet, the one Shaunyce had thought might appeal. He picked it up and studied it, his eyes going over the simple designs carved in the polished black lorken and the regularly placed pin pearls.

"This is probably too dear for me . . ."

"Five silvers," she said.

He looked askance. "That's all?"

"It's not metal. It's lorken, and pin pearls aren't that hard to come by here on the beaches below the cliffs. You're paying for the artistry."

"I'll take it." He paused. "Or am I supposed to bargain?"

"We bargained," she said. "You paid full price, but I'm adding in the box. It's a good box, and you'll need it to keep the bracelet safe."

"I can see why Coenyr was interested in you. I would be, too, if I were him."

She could tell that he felt obligated to say something nice. "You're kind, but you're still in love with your consort, and that is something I appreciate."

An embarrassed grin crossed his lips. "She is special."

"I hope she'll like the bracelet. It was made by Loricana. She comes from a long line of artisans."

"Do you know them all? All the artisans in Nylan?"

Shaunyce shook her head. "I have a pendant she made. That's how I know about her."

"From an admirer, no doubt?"

"From my father, before he was lost at sea."

"I'm sorry. I didn't mean . . ."

Shaunyce smiled, if sadly. "That was when I was eight. Will you be away from her for much longer?"

"We're bound back to Swartheld from here. I hope it's not too long a crossing."

The smile on his face confirmed to Shaunyce how he felt about his consort.

He eased out his battered leather wallet and laid five silvers on the counter. She took the cards from the box and filled them out, then had him sign both.

Once he left, Shaunyce couldn't help but think about what he'd said—and what Talysen had said, so much earlier. The brother of the first blond officer had been clear. The first one was a Hamorian officer, but he'd been in Nylan as a merchant officer—or mate, or whatever they were called.

She'd thought Talysen had been inventing things. Now . . . she wasn't so sure.

Even when she had walked the kay to the small house with the shed in the rear that held her mother's studio and kiln, she was still mulling all that had happened during the day . . . and what had happened with the woodcrafter and the dracones and with Merchanter Shefan eightdays earlier. There was . . . something . . . connecting them all, except she couldn't quite figure it out.

She had barely entered the house and crossed the small front room to the kitchen where her mother stood beside the old ceramic stove before Nynca spoke.

"You're still thinking about Talysen, aren't you?"

"Mother." Shaunyce only expressed mild exasperation. "I just got home. Why would you think that?"

"That was a guess, but you're thinking about something. You

always call out a greeting when you first come in, unless you're thinking deep thoughts."

"I haven't seen Talysen in almost a season."

"You were still thinking about him," observed Nynca.

"I was, but not in that way."

"What do you mean?"

"He was interested in me. I liked him, but . . ."

"You weren't in love with him. Not then. It might be better that way."

"Mother . . . how could I consort someone who is just a friend?"

"That's not what I meant."

"What did you mean?"

"I've said enough. You know, you don't have to work for Merchanter Brauk."

"What else can I do? I won't live here and do nothing." Shaunyce didn't add what she'd always felt about working with the clay that wedged itself under her fingernails and dried out the skin of her hands and fingers until she felt that they would split and crack.

"That's a start," said Nynca dryly. When Shaunyce did not say anything, she added, "Still wanting to carry your own weight."

"I've always tried to do that. I never wanted to be a burden on you. Never!"

"That's true enough," replied her mother.

After a long silence, Shaunyce finally asked, "What else could I do?"

"You won't admit it, but you do have a talent with the clay. It wouldn't get under your nails if you'd cut them."

"My skin cracks."

"You never tried using sheep oil."

Shaunyce almost said what she'd always said—"it smells." For some reason, she didn't. "I didn't."

"You are thinking deep thoughts."

"Why don't you let Brauk sell your pieces?"

"Because everyone would say that you were sleeping with him."

"You didn't let him sell them before. Why not then?"

Nynca frowned. "You never asked."

"I didn't think about it. Now that I've worked there, I can see that what you do is better than most of what he sells." The thought struck her again that Brauk sold all manner of goods, except fine pottery and earthenware. "Even if he took a fifth part of what you could sell your best vases and platters for, you'd make more."

"I likely could."

"Then . . . why didn't you?"

"You know . . . I've always told you that telling the truth is best."

"You have." Shaunyce wondered what lay behind her mother's words.

"And that lying can come back to haunt you?"

Shaunyce nodded.

Nynca did not speak.

Shaunyce waited.

"You can lie without saying a word, by letting others think what they will."

"I know." Shaunyce paused. "That's what . . . happened with Talysen. I let him think I felt more than I did. When he found out . . ."

"I wondered about that. But I didn't ask."

"I appreciated that." And Shaunyce did, although she'd never said so.

"I lied to you, too, without saying a word. And that lie has come back to haunt me."

Shaunyce had no idea what lie her mother had told her through omission.

"I didn't know that you had asked Brauk for a job. I wished that you hadn't, but if I'd told you why, then that would have revealed that I'd lied, after a fashion. Several years after your father died, I got so lonely . . . and he was having a hard time, too. We . . . kept company . . . for a time. No one knew. But if suddenly, he started selling my pottery . . . his consort and others might well ask questions. It didn't last long. We knew it was wrong. I also didn't tell you . . . because I didn't want you to think less of me."

Shaunyce just stood there for several moments. Then her eyes burned, and she could not see. "Oh . . . Mother."

For the first time in seasons, she wrapped her arms around her mother.

VI

On fiveday morning, Shaunyce made certain that she was at the shop earlier than her usual eighth glass, early enough that Brauk had to unbolt the door to let her in.

"You're here early," he said as he re-bolted the front door behind her.

Shaunyce didn't want to say what she knew she had to. So she said the words immediately, keeping her voice firm. "I appreciate all your letting me work here, and I appreciate all you've done for me, but I don't think it's a good idea for me to keep working here, ser."

"You didn't think that yesterday," he said mildly.

"When I asked you for a job, I hadn't even told my mother

that I was going to ask you. She never said anything. I noticed that you never carried any pottery or earthenware, but you carry everything else. I never asked about that, but all the pieces came together last night, and I asked my mother why you hadn't carried anything of hers. She told me."

"Do you mind telling me why that made a difference?" A faint smile crossed Brauk's lips. It could have meant anything.

"You showed me—with the box—about unspoken deception. You were right. That's why I can't work here any longer. And I'm very sorry if you thought I was taking advantage of . . . what happened between you and my mother. I didn't know. Now that I do . . . I just can't stay. If you think I was . . . I'll pay back my wages as I can."

"You would, wouldn't you?"

"Yes, ser."

"You don't owe me anything. First, you've been the best shop-girl I've had in years. You more than earned what I paid you. Second, I could tell that you didn't know. I could also tell you hadn't told your mother before you asked me for the position. In that, I deceived you by not saying anything, but I did think it might be better for you to work here . . . at least for a while."

"You got upset by my deceiving Talysen, didn't you?"

"I did." Brauk paused. "What happened between your mother and me . . . it wasn't right . . . but we both needed something. In that, we didn't deceive each other, but we deceived others."

Shaunyce realized something else at that moment. "You've both paid for it, haven't you?"

"What makes you say that?" Again, Brauk's voice was mild, as if he knew what she meant, but wanted her to go on.

"Because you both like each other still, and you don't dare to see each other, and you can't sell her pottery and she can't ask, and she doesn't make as much . . . nor do you."

"You've learned a great deal this season, Shaunyce."

"You knew what the box would do, didn't you?"

He nodded. "I knew it would be painful for you."

"You didn't . . . with my mother . . . the box?"

"No . . . not with her."

Shaunyce tried not to swallow.

"It's not really my box. It's my consort's. It's been in her family for years. She let me borrow it. That's why it was priced as it was. What I told you about it was true, though." He smiled softly. "You can recover from deception . . . if you're honest about it." After a moment, he added, "You could still work here, if you wanted."

"Thank you, ser. I wouldn't feel right about it."

"I still owe you your pay for the last two eightdays . . . and you earned every copper."

She thought for several moments, then nodded. "But nothing more."

VII

Late in the afternoon on sixday, with mist descending on Nylan, Shaunyce stood waiting outside the black stone gateposts that marked the entrance to the engineering buildings on the slope just above that walled section of the harbor of Nylan that held the black ships. Several student engineers—*apprentice engineers*, she corrected herself—walked past without even looking in her direction. The air was cool, but not cold, as the mist and fog thickened and more apprentices, and then some masters in black, made their way out of the gates and toward their quarters or their homes.

Shaunyce looked down at her fingers, and their short-cut nails. The skin on her hands wasn't cracked, at least, and her mother had been right. After a bit, the sheep oil smell went away. Almost another full glass passed before she saw the stocky blond figure she recognized from his slightly forward posture.

She moved away from the gateposts and waited.

As he approached he did not seem to notice her, perhaps because of the fog, although she had her doubts, not until she said, "Talysen."

He turned slightly and took several more steps, stopping perhaps a yard from her. He just looked at her, not speaking.

"Talysen . . ." She concentrated on trying not to sound pleading. "Could I . . . might I . . . have a word? I know you don't think much of me . . ."

"How long have you been waiting here?" His voice was even.

"I . . . don't know. A glass . . ."

"It's well past suppertime. I was working late."

"I . . . I had . . ." She shook her head. "I need to be honest . . . and fair."

"You weren't before."

"I wasn't. I liked you. I still like you. I think you're a good person. I think you're one of the best people I know. You thought more of me than I am. That made me feel special. I wanted to keep that." She swallowed. "I pushed you about wanting to see the black ships . . . because . . . not because I wanted you to do what I wanted . . . but because that would show just how much you thought I was special. After you touched the box . . . and saw . . ." She paused. "I still want to be friends. And, even if you don't, if you can't, I'd like to say that I'm sorry. I wish I hadn't deceived you. I wish I hadn't hurt you."

"You think things could be like they were?"

"No. I wouldn't ever want that. I'd want to be able to tell you what I felt, honestly felt. I'd want you to tell me the same. Even if we're only friends." She looked down, then back at him. "Gently, maybe."

"How am I supposed to believe you?"

"We . . . we could touch the box together . . . again . . ."

"It's not on display, and you don't work there anymore."

"You know?"

"I know more than you think."

"You need to know how I feel. I asked Merchanter Brauk if he'd let us . . . if you . . . if you . . ."

"Stop." His voice was firm, but not harsh.

"I can't. Ever since I saw how you saw me . . . except it wasn't ever since. It took a few days for me to realize . . . ever since then . . . No, that's not quite true, either. It took me almost a season to work things out. I'm sorry about that, too. You deserve better."

Talysen smiled. "Don't I get a say about what I deserve?"

"I can't ask for more than friendship. . . ." She paused. "What did you say?"

"I said that I get a say in what I deserve."

For a moment, Shaunyce didn't know what to say. "Yes, you do. If you don't want even to be friends . . ."

"Stop," he said again. "We're friends. On the terms you suggested." He smiled.

So did she, knowing that, whatever happened, it wouldn't be deceptive.

He reached out and took her hand, and they walked away from the black gateposts, and the black ships that lay well behind them.

ICE AND FIRE

The first snowflakes of winter, except that it was still fall, even in the far north of Austra, drifted lazily out of the gray sky. Faryl shivered and hurried up the wide path from the narrow road. His arms ached with the weight of the old basket. He glanced up as he saw the stocky gray-haired man on the front porch of the cottage, a modest stone-walled structure with a gray slate roof, the only slate roof in all of Cresylet, except for one other, not that there were more than a few score dwellings clustered on the north side of the river. "Grandda . . . what are you doing here?"

"Your da's taken the mule to Vizyn. Your ma's helping her sister . . ." He looked down at Faryl. "Where's your coat?"

"Inside."

"Inside won't do you much good when it's cold outside. In with you." The older man gestured. "There's a fire in the hearth." He paused as he saw the basket. "What do you have there?"

"Acorns . . . for the old sow. Father asked me to gather some on the way back from my lessons."

"Why didn't you wear your jacket when you left?"

"The sun was out, and it wasn't that cold."

The older man waited until Faryl was through the door, then closed it.

"How did your lessons go?"

"Fine." The words were flat.

"What happened?" The older man walked to the hearth, where he bent and added another log to the fire.

"Nothing."

"Then perhaps you'd better spread the acorns on the hearth to dry before you put them in the feed barrel."

"It wasn't raining."

"Faryl."

"Yes, ser." Faryl set the basket by the hearth and began to scoop out the acorns with his hands. Finally, he said, "Grandda . . . Sammel was saying that he'd never be my friend. He said I was like a black and he was a white." Faryl didn't want to say more. He especially didn't want to tell his grandfather about what had happened at the pond. Not when he wasn't even certain it had. But it had. He knew it had.

"What happened?"

"Nothing. I told you what he said."

"You want to know what he meant?"

Faryl nodded.

"They're like ice and fire, boy. Ice and Fire." He looked at his grandson and the puzzled look there, and added, "The whites are like chaos, like the fire there. See how the flames dance. No matter how long you look at them, they're never quite the same, and they're hot. Chaos is like that. Black is order, firm and solid, like deep winter ice. What happens when fire and ice meet, boy?"

Faryl shrugged.

"The same thing as when a drop of water hits a small flame. *Psssst!* The water's gone, and so is the flame. That's why it's best not to have much to do with either pure order or chaos. Little bits of each are fine, because we need ice or water and we need fire."

"But too much fire can burn down a house?"

"And too much ice and winter can freeze you solid," added his grandfather. "Just stay away from both, boy. Mages, white or black, order or chaos, just lead to trouble."

"Why?" asked Faryl.

"The black ones want everything just so. Why . . . you can't have the slightest thing out of place if you live in Recluce. They say that's a sign of chaos. And the white ones . . . they're just plain dangerous, burn you up soon as look at you if you cross them."

"Sammel's not like that."

"Thought you didn't like him."

"I don't. Not now, but he's not a white mage."

"That's good. I brought a bit of meat pie for your supper . . ."

Even cool, the meat pie was good. After eating and sitting a time by the fire, Faryl climbed under the old stiff blanket on his pallet not that far from the hearth. He remembered what he had done at the pond, when he'd somehow kept the water Sammel splashed from getting him wet and Sammel had said that he was just like a black, taking everything. But Sammel hadn't seen that the water had sprayed away from Faryl, and Faryl knew he couldn't say anything.

Was he really a black, like Sammel had said? Even if Sammel hadn't seen and hadn't really meant it?

Faryl thought about what his grandfather had said. Then he looked at one of the small red embers that had broken off the log and rolled onto the hearthstones.

Could he just . . . sort of . . . calm the little ember, the way he'd calmed and moved the spray Sammel had made?

He looked again and scrunched up his forehead. Ever so slowly, the ember faded.

Did it just fade by itself? How would he know? He concentrated on a little spot on the side of the big log that was red-hot. It turned gray . . . but just for a bit. He tried to smooth out things around the spot, but the fire kept coming back.

So he tried a great big smoothing—all at once.

The side of the log exploded, and embers showered everywhere. One landed on his shirt, and he jumped up quick-like and shook himself. The ember dropped on the hearthstones, but then he saw wisps of smoke coming from his blanket, and he had to pick it up and shake it out over the hearthstones. He had to keep shaking it to make sure all the embers were gone.

He was shivering all over when his grandfather strode back into the room, a worried look on his face. "Are you all right?"

"Yes, ser."

"What happened, boy?"

"The side of the log . . . it crackled . . . and . . . there were sparks going everywhere. One hit my shirt, and some got on my blanket." Faryl looked around. He didn't see any wisps of smoke, and there was only one new brown spot on his blanket.

"You didn't throw anything into the fire, did you?"

"No, ser." Faryl wasn't lying, not exactly. He hadn't put anything into the fire. He'd just tried to calm a big spot on the log.

"Maybe there was a chunk of ice under the bark. That can happen. The fire heats it to steam, and it explodes. Maybe you need to move back a bit from the hearth."

"Yes, ser." Faryl dragged his pallet back and checked his blanket before lying down again. His shivering stopped after a while, and he tried smoothing and calming one little ember. It did turn gray, and he realized that he was very tired.

He'd hoped that his father would be back soon, but he couldn't keep his eyes open.

When he woke in the morning, his father was already up, because Faryl could hear the sound of the grindstone from the shop at the back of the house. He dressed quickly, although the cottage was not chill, just uncomfortably cool, since the fire in the hearth had long since died away. A bowl of porridge sat on the kitchen table. A portion of a loaf of bread was beside it. The porridge was cold, but there was nothing new about that. The bread was stale. Faryl finished both, then washed the bowls, using the water in the kitchen bucket sparingly.

Dreading what chores his father might have for him, he made his way to the workshop, where his father set aside the heavy chisel and let the grindstone slow to a halt.

"You need to go spend the day with your mother at your aunt's. She could use your help."

"Why can't I stay here?"

"I won't be home today, and your grandfather Eirl has his own work to do."

"He doesn't work. He writes things people want him to write."

"That's work. He's a scrivener."

Faryl said nothing.

"Don't set your jaw like that, Faryl. What if it froze in place? No one would want to look at you, not even your friend Sammel."

"He's not my friend. He said I was a black."

"There's nothing wrong with that."

"Yes, there is. Whites can do things. Blacks just keep things the way they are."

"Whites do things, all right, and most of them aren't good. And if you don't have whites around you don't need blacks, and that's just fine. There's nothing wrong with that. Settled is just fine." His father shook his head. "That's why we're better off without either blacks or whites. One's as much trouble as the other. Especially when they do more than they should."

"Settled . . . what good is that?" countered Faryl.

"Someday, you'll understand. Now . . . off to your aunt's unless you want to walk to Vizyn and carry slates all day."

"Yes, ser." Faryl tried to sound pleasant.

Even so, his father looked hard at him.

"I'm sorry, ser . . . it's just . . ."

His father shook his head sadly. "Off with you."

Faryl did wear his jacket, patched as it was, because there was a stiff breeze. As he trudged along the narrow road away from town toward the small stead where his aunt lived, he thought about what his father had said. Why was settled good? Or was it because unsettled was bad?

Faryl decided he would have to think about that.

Before that long, he turned onto the lane that led to his aunt's place. A hundred yards ahead, he could see the bare limbs of the pearapple trees.

The stead house was small, but large enough for Aunt Nalana. It really was just a cot, but everyone called it a stead house. It had the good slate roof Faryl's father had put on, but the worn planks of the walls looked like they'd been there forever. His aunt had never consorted. Faryl didn't know why. No one ever said. The little stead had belonged to old man Zhothar, and it had been his death gift to Aunt Nalana. No one had told Faryl why that was so, either.

When he opened the door to the front room, his mother hurried out of the back bedroom. There were only three rooms—the front room, the bedroom, and the kitchen.

"Good! You're here. Take the bucket from the kitchen and fill it from the spring."

"Yes, ma'am." Faryl didn't think of protesting. Not when he saw his mother's face.

He hurried to the kitchen and took the bucket off the side table. Usually, it hung on a peg on the wall. Then he walked out of the cot and down the path that led along the north side of the house and then east and up a low rise to the spring. It was a pleasant spring, ringed in rock. The rocks were carefully tended so there wasn't a hint of dirt or moss or the green slimy stuff.

He dipped the bucket, careful not to touch anything but water, then lifted it clear, and walked back to the house. His arms ached by the time he set the bucket on the side table. When his mother didn't come to the kitchen, he tiptoed across the front room to the bedroom.

His mother was sitting on a stool beside the bed. It was a big bed, bigger than the one his parents shared. Faryl had asked why once, but his mother had just said, "Someday you'll understand."

That had been a long time ago, at least two seasons, and he still didn't understand. He did understand that he couldn't ask again.

Abruptly, his mother turned. She did not speak.

Faryl eased closer. "What's wrong with Aunt Nalana?" He kept his voice low.

"She has a flux or worse . . . and a fever. She's burning up, and she can't keep the brinn tea down, and the poultices don't work. She needs a healer, but there aren't any here. There's not even one in Vizyn, not since Chatasula left."

"Why did she leave?"

"She said the timber mills created too much chaos."

Faryl sensed that there was something his mother wasn't telling him. He didn't say anything, though. She got upset when he did that.

"If I could only settle the chaos in her."

"She's really sick, isn't she?"

His mother nodded.

Faryl could feel that she wanted to cry. She wouldn't. She never did. He'd felt her feel like that before, but she never cried.

"You watch her for a moment. I need to get more damp cloths. You put the bucket on the table, didn't you?"

"Yes, ma'am."

"I'll be right back."

Faryl knew that. He also knew that his mother didn't need the damp cloths. Not right yet, when she'd just placed some on Aunt Nalana's forehead.

He moved closer to the bed, able to hear the low moaning sighs. He could feel the heat radiating from his aunt. It was everywhere. He looked more closely. He could see a knot of reddish whiteness, but it wasn't seeing, not exactly, because the knot was somehow inside her.

Sammel's sister Ameral had burned up and died. That was what Sammel had said. Faryl didn't want that to happen to his aunt. She'd been the one who'd told him stories when his mother had been sick. She'd made him feel special.

Grandda had said that order put out fires. It calmed things. And he'd smoothed away the water Sammel had splashed. He'd even smoothed the heat of the coals in the fire. Could he smooth away the knot and cool it? But he'd have to be very careful. Very careful.

He scrunched up his forehead, really hard, and thought about smoothing away the reddish-white knot inside Aunt Nalana. At first, it was like the spot on the log in the fireplace. The red kept coming back, but Faryl kept smoothing . . . and smoothing. Pretty soon, what came back was pinkish. He kept smoothing and stretching the ends of the knot, so that it would come loose and come apart, the way it happened when his mother spun threads out from the carded wool.

Then he felt dizzy, and he had to sit on the floor.

"Faryl! Faryl!"

He could hear his mother calling his name, but for a moment, he couldn't move. He was lying on the wooden floor. He felt so tired, but he finally sat up.

"Don't scare me like that!"

Faryl wanted to tell her not to yell at him, but he could feel how scared she was. He just said, "I felt dizzy."

"Did you eat breakfast?"

He nodded.

"You haven't been drinking enough water, then. Go into the kitchen and dip out some water into the tin cup. Drink all of it before you come back."

"Yes, ma'am." Faryl stood. His legs were shaky, but he didn't say anything. He just walked to the kitchen and did what she'd told him to do. The water helped. So did the crust of bread he saw on the corner of the table. It wasn't much, but his legs felt better after he ate it.

Then he walked back to the bedroom.

He could hear his aunt talking.

"Maelenda . . . the pain's gone . . . it's gone . . ."

"You're not as hot."

Faryl nodded, but only to himself.

His mother was still looking at Aunt Nalana. "What happened?"

"I don't know. It felt . . . like someone smoothed away the pain."

"You're still warm."

"It's fading. I can feel that."

As his mother talked to her sister, Faryl smiled. His father was right. Settled was good. He could see that when order settled things smoothly, and he took his time, and didn't do it all at once . . . no one thought it was order . . . just like Sammel hadn't even seen that the water he'd splashed had missed Faryl.

Could order smooth stones and chisels?

Perhaps tomorrow, or the next day, he'd figure that out as well.

There are games for pleasure, and then there are other games.

A GAME OF CAPTURE

The lower limb of the white sun had barely touched the gray-green waters of the Gulf of Candar on that late harvest day when the two black engineers settled onto opposite sides of the Capture board in the rear corner of Houlart's.

Aloryk set down his mug of dark lager, pulled a handful of coppers from his wallet and juggled them in his hand, then closed his fist and laid it on the wood bordering the inlaid lattices of the board, lattices with depressions for the polished black-and-white stones. "Odd or even?"

"Even," replied Paitrek, brushing back his thinning black hair as he eased the chair in which he sat closer to the table, the top of which was effectively the Capture board. He took a swallow of his golden ale, then set down his mug.

Aloryk turned his hand and unclenched his fist. Four coppers lay in his palm. "Even it is."

"Black." Paitrek picked up one of the black stones from its well-crafted box and placed it on the corner depression of a four-lattice.

Aloryk countered by placing a white stone on the corner of a three-lattice near the center of the board.

"You always do that," offered a third voice from seeming emptiness.

Aloryk looked up to see Faynal appear, smiling at him. "It works. And I hate it when you sneak up like that."

"Sometimes, it works. Sometimes, it doesn't. You need to be more unpredictable. Chaos is. And I need to practice conceal-ments. It's harder to avoid detection with people who know you."

"That makes it hard on your friends."

"You're ignoring my point about the center opening," said Faynal. "It's still chaotic."

"Tell that to the High Wizard of Fairhaven." Aloryk noted that Paitrek had added another black stone, in a way that could either create another lattice or complete a four. He debated for an instant before adding a white next to his first, then added, "You fuzzy air mage." He grinned.

"Spoken like an engineer." Faynal shook his head, and made his way toward the front door, doubtless hurrying home to his consort.

Aloryk took another swallow from his mug. He was thirsty. As he set it down, he realized that a blond man seated alone at a table for two against the wall had turned to listen to the last few words of his exchange with Faynal. His jacket was the kind worn by Nordlan merchant officers, not that Aloryk had seen many, but merchanters were welcome ashore in Nordla, unlike the officers and crews of warships, and Houlart's was close enough to the piers that some did eat there. On the other hand, warships weren't even allowed in the harbor except by approval of the Council. Belatedly, he added a white stone to a four-lattice bordering one edge of the board.

Paitrek positioned a black stone away from his others, then lifted his mug and gestured to the board.

"Who's the stranger?" Aloryk murmured as he looked up from the board after playing his next stone, convinced that the merchant officer was covertly studying them. He couldn't tell from the sleeve markings whether he was a junior officer or more senior.

Paitrek looked up and frowned. "Never saw him before. He's junior. Third mate of some sort. Concentrate on the game. I'll have you blocked if you don't. Then you won't be able to complete any lattices on that side." He reached for his mug.

Aloryk shifted his attention back to the board for the next several moves, until he realized the Nordlan had moved to observe the game. Sometimes, other engineers came by and commented, but this was the first time Aloryk had seen an outsider do so.

"What is the game?" The officer spoke Temple without an accent, but perhaps a trace too precisely.

"Capture," answered Paitrek.

"I have never seen its like before. What is the goal?"

"The black player has to build a connected set of lattices, comprising at least fifteen stones, that cannot be surrounded. The white's goal is to keep the lattices from being connected while creating a single line from one side of the board to the opposite side. The white player can go either the width or the length of the board."

"Then it is a strategy game."

"Of sorts," said Paitrek dryly.

The Nordlan studied the board for a short time, frowning, before saying, "Are you two engineers or mages?"

"Why do you ask?" Paitrek looked vaguely annoyed as he placed another black stone.

"I have not been to Nylan before. All I have heard is that mages wear black and engineers wear black, but there are no markings to tell one from the other."

"That's because, if you can't tell, it shouldn't matter," replied Aloryk, returning his attention to the board.

"That is like saying one Nordlan is the same as another Nordlan." The merchant officer sounded amused.

"I suppose so," replied Paitrek disinterestedly.

"Capture is all about balance," offered Aloryk.

"So is engineering. Is that why you play it?"

Aloryk suddenly realized what bothered him about the Nordlan. Nordlans spoke more like Hamorians, and there weren't any Temple speakers anywhere in Nordla, not that Aloryk had heard. So where had a Nordlan merchant officer learned to speak such good Temple? Also, an outland engineer wouldn't usually equate balance with engineering, since they didn't use mage-forged black iron.

Without looking up from the board, he studied the Nordlan with his limited order senses, not that his abilities were anywhere close to those of Faynal. On the surface, the Nordlan seemed to be much like any other outlander, and even many on Recluce—a swirl of order around him, dotted with hints of chaos . . . except that Aloryk could sense nothing below that surface, nothing at all.

"You an engineer?" Aloryk asked as he placed a white stone on the opposite side of the Capture board from where he'd placed the last one, except the position was "lower." He ignored Paitrek's quizzical glance.

"I am not. I am a junior navigator."

Junior navigator? Just what merchant vessel could afford that kind of extra officer? "On what ship?" Aloryk forced his eyes back to the board and Paitrek's next move.

"The *Pride of Brysta*."

"Must be more profitable than most merchanters to carry two navigators." Aloryk didn't look at the Nordlan who likely wasn't anything of the sort, but concentrated on the board for several moments before adding another white stone at an angle to the one he had previously played. "Of course, I'm just a junior engineer." Those words were the opening to another game.

"You work on building the black ships?" The Nordlan's tone was idle, as if he had asked about the weather.

"That's no secret. Any engineer who wears blacks does, in some way or another." After Paitrek placed his next stone, Aloryk could see the possible multiple linkages that Paitrek was setting up, and he placed a white stone to block the easiest linkage.

"There are no other engineers in Nylan?" The not-Nordlan sounded honestly surprised.

"Shipwrights, but not engineers," replied Aloryk. "Their yards are on the south side of the harbor."

Paitrek placed a black stone, and Aloryk placed his white next to the one he had just positioned.

"But . . . they do not use engineers?"

"All low-powered steam engines operate the same way. So do all sails." Aloryk shrugged. "Generally speaking, anyone looking for an engineer around here either doesn't understand, or is the sort of person that the black mages will take an interest in."

"Are black engineers not working ordermages?"

"Oh, we can tell when there are others around who can handle chaos or order, sometimes even when they're so good that they can shield what lies beneath the surface. But we work with engineers' tools on very hard metal." Aloryk placed another white stone, linking the three in the middle. "We leave containing chaos—except in games like Capture—to the true order-masters."

"But your black iron confines chaos, does it not?"

"Let's just say that it does what it's supposed to." Aloryk looked to Paitrek, who had just placed another black stone.

"Doesn't Maitre Thurmin come in before he heads out to brief the patrollers?" Aloryk knew Thurmin often did, so that even if the not-Nordlan could sense his order-chaos flows, he wasn't lying and the fact that it was a question as well should keep his personal chaos level low.

"Sometimes, he does. Sometimes not. He doesn't like to follow a routine. That's what I've heard."

Aloryk added to his center line, blocking Paitrek from linking a three- and a four-lattice, then looked up at the merchant officer who was far more than that. "You know, don't you, that we exile our own children if they're chaos-wielders, or even if they're natural ordermages who can't gain complete control of their abilities."

"I have heard that. I do find that hard to believe, that Recluce would waste such abilities."

"We don't waste them," said Aloryk, watching as Paitrek placed another black stone. "We just let other lands benefit. Just a couple of years ago, maybe fifteen or twenty, we sent a natural ordermage to Hamor. He ended up saving the Emperor or some such. And then there was my cousin's great-uncle. He liked gaming too much, and he ended up borrowing from a Suthyan trader. He used his access to the engineering halls to copy black ship plans so that he could give them to the Suthyan to pay off what he owed. He was found dead in the halls with the copies of the plans, frozen solid. Suthyan traders were prohibited from landing anywhere on Recluce for more than ten years. Destroyed the factor's business, I heard." Those two examples Aloryk knew well. He'd heard of the first for years, and he'd gotten more than a little tired of hearing about the trials experienced by Dynacia's widowed aunt Almyra.

"Frozen solid? I do not understand."

"Put him in a state of perfect order. Removed all the chaos from his body." Aloryk added a white stone to the one on the left side of the board. "The maitres have such perfect control that even we can't sense where they are."

"Nope," added Paitrek, "tends to keep one a bit honest." He looked to Aloryk. "Your play."

"You really think you can get all three of those lattices together?" Aloryk was just talking. He'd been concentrating more on the not-Nordlan than on the game, and there was only a slim chance he could even salvage a draw.

"You'll have to see."

"I find that hard to believe, that they are so skilled," the not-Nordlan finally said.

While Aloryk had never been able to master a full concealment, he could, for a short time, shield himself from all chaos—as could most successful engineers, those who survived. He did so, while playing another white stone, and saying, "We're just engineers, nothing to compare to the great mages. They can do so much more. Of course, they probably wouldn't bother someone returning to his ship. They could certainly tell if he were telling the truth." He looked to Paitrek. "Your turn."

Paitrek immediately placed a white stone. "That's a double-lattice."

Aloryk placed a white stone to block Paitrek from immediately linking the double to a three-stone lattice, knowing he was only delaying the inevitable.

Paitrek countered by completing a three-lattice positioned either to link to the other side of the existing double or to complete a double on the far side.

Aloryk blocked that, but Paitrek completed the double.

In turn, Aloryk extended his center, but he could see that he was going to lose. He glanced up, but the Nordlan had left. Only a faint lingering sense of chaos remained, a sense that Aloryk hadn't detected before.

He managed a faint smile, then lifted his mug and took a

deeper swallow, before returning his full concentration to the game.

Five moves later, Paitrek linked his two groups of lattices. "You see. I won."

Aloryk smiled. "I think we all won." But his words were barely loud enough for Paitrek to hear.

"Another game?"

"I think not. I've enough games for tonight."

Paitrek grinned. "You played that other game pretty well."

"I thought so. We'll have to stop and tell the guards. He might be smart enough to go back to his ship. If not . . ." *He'll experience perfect order.*

The two engineers replaced the stones in their respective boxes, then stood and walked toward the door.

While I've usually written stories or novels featuring main characters with order or chaos abilities, most people in the world of Recluce don't have those talents, and they deserve their stories as well. This is one of those.

THE ASSISTANT ENVOY'S PROBLEM

Erdyl, the temporary acting Envoy of Austra, officially the Assistant Envoy, and, as a matter of family, the youngest son of Lord Askyl of Norbruel, stood beside the desk in the study of the envoy's residence and looked out into the chill and gray late fall morning, watching as the coach pulled up the drive. He waited until Sestalt, wearing his comparatively new black-trimmed green uniform, stepped into the study.

"What did you find out?"

"Like they said, ser, it was the *Seahound*."

"Any messages?"

"No, ser. She's inbound to Valmurl from Lydiar."

Then there wouldn't be any dispatches for us, not on a vessel headed back to Austra. "Thank you."

"Any time, ser."

"Oh . . . have you and Undercaptain Demyst had any fortune in finding another suitable guard for the residence?"

"Ah . . . best you talk to the undercaptain, ser."

"Could you tell him I'd like to see him?"

"Right away, ser."

In moments, Demyst entered the study, in the dark gray uniform jacket and trousers he preferred to the black and green. "Ser?"

"Sestalt said you might be able to tell me . . ."

"About guards, ser? That'd be a bit of a problem . . ."

"Why? Lord West hasn't made a proclamation forbidding people to work for envoys, has he?" At least, Erdyl had no knowledge of such a proclamation. He was also certain that the ruler of the West Quadrant was looking for a way to inconvenience Erdyl and Austra . . . and even make the residence a target for brigands, all because his predecessor, Lord Kharl, had hired some local men as guards, enough to shelter Enelya and Jeka from Lord West's late brothers, unlamented as their passage was by anyone, including Lord West. The fact that Lord Kharl had consorted Jeka and that she had departed with him seemed to make no difference.

"No, ser."

Erdyl waited for Demyst to explain.

"He's let it be known that any man who takes a position from now on with any envoy will be conscripted into the Lord's Guard . . . or pressed into merchanter service."

"From now on?"

"The word is that the high justicer told him that he'd be breaking his own laws if he tried to conscript men already working for envoys, even if he issued a proclamation or edict."

Erdyl frowned. "So he can claim it's within his rights, and that makes it appear as though it applies to all envoys, but since we're the only ones who are short-staffed, this new 'guidance' or whatever he wants to call it won't greatly inconvenience most other envoys."

"Not for a time, ser."

"A rather long time."

"Begging your pardon, ser," continued the undercaptain,

"but aren't envoys allowed the privilege of hiring and sheltering any who remain on the premises?"

"That's not the problem." And it wasn't. Lord West wasn't about to send armsmen to drag people out of any envoy's residence, but that didn't mean he couldn't drag them off if they ever left the residence or its grounds . . . or do things to their families if they went against his wishes. Enelya had no desire to leave the residence immediately, and Erdyl doubted that Lord West even knew who she was, but most men who would be suitable guards had some ties to friends and relatives in Brysta, and even if they didn't, their usefulness would be limited to the residence grounds. "I'm not a powerful black mage like Lord Kharl who could enforce his will beyond the residence and do as he wished."

Demyst raised his bushy eyebrows.

"You're right." Erdyl sighed. "He went through a lot, and he couldn't do everything, but the fact is . . . he's not here, and I am."

"Yes, ser," replied Undercaptain Demyst. "You're a man bred and trained to be an envoy. You're you. You need to do things your way. Not his."

Absolutely accurate advice . . . and not terribly helpful. "I could start by talking with some of the other envoys." *Or assistants, where the envoys aren't available, for one reason or another.* "There will likely be some at Envoy Kyanelt's reception tomorrow."

"Yes, ser," agreed Demyst.

The undercaptain's tone was so unemotional that Erdyl understood the unvoiced suggestion that somewhat earlier action might be advisable, although Erdyl had no doubt that some envoys would definitely be "unavailable" to him since he was only an acting envoy . . . except at the reception where they could not avoid him.

"I could see a few today," Erdyl mused aloud.

"What about Envoy Luryessa? She was helpful . . . before."

"Even she at least pretends to comply with Lord West's wishes, and she's partly a mage. She also has a mage assistant named Jemelya. But I can't talk to Luryessa anyway."

The undercaptain raised his eyebrows, but did not speak.

"She hasn't returned to Brysta yet."

"What about the mage?"

"I suppose it can't hurt," Erdyl replied, not willing to admit that the thought of dealing with a woman mage from Sarronnyn definitely unsettled him. Lord Kharl had been a mage, but the man's honesty and goodness radiated from him like light from a mirror. On the one occasion when Erdyl had seen Jemelya, she'd revealed nothing.

"Good," declared the undercaptain. "Should I tell Mantar to make ready the carriage?"

"In half a glass."

Once Demyst departed, Erdyl turned, catching a glimpse of himself in one of the two ornamental mirrors flanking the hearth in the study. *Hardly prepossessing, you are.* He knew he didn't cut the figure Kharl had. The mage had been big and broad-shouldered, and Erdyl was shorter, slender, and had fine rust-red hair to boot.

Less than a full glass later, Erdyl stepped from the carriage outside the residence of the envoy from Gallos, nodded to Mantar, and then walked along the paved way to the wide covered porch and to the front door. There he dropped the polished brass knocker, once, which struck the plate beneath with a resounding impact. He waited. No one came to the door. He was about to lift the knocker again when the door opened.

"The envoy is not in Brysta at present," replied the white-haired retainer who opened the door partway.

How did he know that is who I sought? Erdyl brushed aside his own question and asked, "I'd like to speak with whoever is handling the envoy's duties."

"Who might I say seeks him?"

"Envoy Erdyl of Austra."

"I will see if Secretary Ustark is here." The door closed.

Several long moments later, a stocky, graying man, attired in gray and black, opened the door. "Come in, come in; Arias is sometimes too protective of me. You're the one who succeeded Envoy Kharl, is that right?"

"I'm officially the acting Envoy of Austra."

Ustark smiled. "Then we are in similar positions."

"You are also acting envoy?"

"In practice, if not in name. Being appointed envoy is largely ceremonial . . . or serves a purpose for the Prefect. At the moment, there is no envoy. Doubtless one will be appointed . . . at some time."

"The Prefect is not concerned about not having an envoy, particularly in matters of trade?" asked Erdyl.

"We do not trade that much with Nordla, especially Brysta." Ustark offered a sardonic smile. "Or with anyone across oceans, since our traders do not have easy access to ports. That limits the need for and duties of an envoy. Unlike Austra, whose merchanters are said to be everywhere."

"Not everywhere, although Austra trades much, even with Brysta . . ." Erdyl paused. "I came to inquire about your thoughts on something. I received word that Lord West has issued an edict that effectively prohibits any men from Brysta . . . or the West Quadrant . . . from working for outland envoys."

"Ah, yes, I have heard about that."

"What do you think?"

Ustark shrugged. "It is not good, but it affects us little. I do what I do. I gather information for the Prefect and send it regularly. One can find out much when one is well away from, shall we say, the intricacies of the ministries surrounding the Prefect."

"I've not discovered that, at least not yet," replied Erdyl. "Unlike you, I do have to deal with matters of trade, even if there are fewer . . . intricacies in Valmurl these days."

"Since your predecessor removed most of them, perhaps?"

"Lord Ghrant is not fond of unnecessary intricacies."

"Ah . . . but sometimes those intricacies can prove useful . . . particularly those that are overlooked by others."

"Such as?"

"Revealing such, my friend, might limit my ability to use them in the future. I trust you understand that an envoy or someone such as I, or you, acting as envoy, must hoard stratagems and use of intricacies . . . for at times we have little else."

Erdyl nodded. "I understand." And, unfortunately, he did. "Is there anyone else you might suggest who might prove helpful?"

"I could suggest many, but whether they would prove useful . . ." Ustark shrugged once more.

When Erdyl finished with Ustark and walked out to the waiting coach, it was only slightly past first glass. Erdyl sighed and looked to the coachman. "The Sarronnese Residence, Mantar."

"Yes, ser."

After a drive of perhaps a kay, Mantar eased the coach through a set of stone pillars and up a drive, halting in a stone circle just south of a modest entry portico.

Erdyl stepped out of the coach, squared his shoulders, and then walked up the white marble steps toward the muscular woman in a blue-and-cream uniform—with the double short-swords, if at her waist, rather than in the shoulder battle harness she likely would have worn in a less ceremonial position.

"Envoy Erdyl . . . Envoy Luryessa is not here."

"I'm aware of that. I'm here to see the Magia Jemelya."

The Sarronnese guard, as tall as Erdyl himself, and likely better at arms, at least from what he had heard, opened the door and announced. "Envoy Erdyl of Austra."

Erdyl stepped into the high-ceiled and marble-walled entry hall as the door closed behind him . . . and found himself alone. After several moments, a slender woman in a pale blue shirt, a cream vest, and darker blue trousers appeared. Erdyl recognized Ziela, a serving girl or receiving maid. She could act as either, and probably did, he reflected.

"Envoy Luryessa is not here, ser." Ziela did not look directly at Erdyl.

"I know. I wish to talk to the Magia Jemelya."

"Please wait a moment. I will see if she is in the residence."

Erdyl waited even longer before Jemelya appeared. Like Luryessa, she wore flowing pale green trousers and shirt, with a dark green vest. Unlike the silver-haired envoy, Jemelya had dark brown hair. Her eyes swept over Erdyl as they had the first time they had met and in a way he found disconcerting, as if she were weighing and measuring him as he stood there, like a butcher or cook might a piece of meat, although he had to admit that he'd seen neither happen.

"You are the Envoy of Austra now, it is said?"

"Acting Envoy," Erdyl admitted. "Only until a permanent envoy is named."

"How might I help you, Envoy Erdyl?"

"You might. Is there somewhere we could talk for a few moments?"

"The library is free." Without another word, Jemelya turned.

Erdyl followed her down the corridor, with its off-white walls and crown molding and chair rail of Sarronnese blue— and no other ornamentation whatsoever—and into the oak-paneled library, one that made Lord Ghrant's in Valmurl look modest.

With the door still open, Jemelya stopped and faced Erdyl. "What did you wish to talk about?" A pleasant smile followed her words, and her eyes met his.

Erdyl realized that her eyes were golden green, intense, and focused. He had hoped that she might suggest sitting and talking, but that was clearly not her intent. "Osten, Lord of the West Quadrant, and his veiled threats to his own people about serving outland powers."

"Such as Austra, perhaps?"

"Perhaps." Erdyl let an ironic smile surface. "But then those words and threats could apply to all of us outlanders."

"They could."

Erdyl realized that the magia was not about to offer any easy openings. He smiled in a moderately warm way. "You know that I am new to the west quadrant of Nordla and to Brysta, and I was curious to know whether this veiled prohibition is a reiteration of an old policy or something that Lord West is attempting to establish as a new custom, as it were."

"Now . . . it really wasn't that hard to come out and say it, was it?" Jemelya offered a smile that was mostly humorous; at least Erdyl thought it was.

"I suspect you know exactly the effort and difficulty, magia, just as you and your envoy—and Lord Kharl—all know more about some things than I ever will." Erdyl kept his words light and warm. "Is it an old or a new position?"

"It is a new position because Osten is a new Lord West. His father did not care who we hired. He was not pleased if we sheltered those who opposed him, but so long as they left Brysta by ship soon after we sheltered them, nothing was said. He felt that their departure was best."

"It was best for those who left, I'm sure . . . or better than remaining, at least." Erdyl decided to wrench the conversation back to the central reason for his visit. "How do you propose to deal with his threat to conscript any man who works for an envoy?"

"We don't face that problem. None of the local men would

even consider working for Sarronnyn . . . or Southwind. We both follow the Legend, remember?"

Erdyl should have recalled that. "I suppose Southwind doesn't have a problem, either, then?"

"No . . . I would think not. There are some advantages to following the Legend."

"The Hamorians bring their own armsmen and staff, and aren't likely to hire locals. . . ." Something about what Jemelya said brought up another thought, but it was gone before he could capture it. "The others . . . even Lord West would not dare to impose such conditions on the Recluce envoy. How can he expect those conditions not to apply to them?"

"You are forgetting one thing," she pointed out. "Recluce doesn't need guards. They send a black mage and an assistant. That suffices for them, and the Council of Recluce does not meddle in the affairs of other lands."

"Except when they do . . . and no one wishes that."

"Precisely."

"So . . . until I can get the envoy from Recluce interested . . . very interested, Lord West will retain his proclamation."

"Unless you can come up with a solution that fits your needs without violating his announced position."

Erdyl frowned. *And how likely is that?* He had no idea of even where to begin. He turned slightly as a bell chimed somewhere, and his arm struck the edge of a bookcase that was closer than he realized. He couldn't help wincing.

"Are you all right?" Jemelya studied Erdyl more closely. "Your arm was injured, wasn't it?"

"Yes. In the fighting against Captain Egen." Erdyl still had twinges of pain, especially when he wrote for any length of time—or when he bumped something—and not all the strength had returned . . . and might not for all he knew.

"Might I touch you?"

"Of course." Erdyl flushed, embarrassed at how quickly the words had come out. "My arm, I mean."

"I understood what you meant." The magia's fingers barely touched the back of his hand.

Almost immediately, Erdyl felt a warm tingling that seemed to flow up his arm and then vanish when her fingers left his bare skin.

"That may help. You should be careful for another season. It still has not healed completely."

"Thank you."

"You are welcome. I'm sorry that I could not offer more useful advice in dealing with your difficulty."

Erdyl was still trying to reclaim the vagrant thought he was certain he had had in the library when he re-entered the coach, and Mantar began the drive to the official residence of the Hydlenese envoy. Unfortunately, when they arrived, and Erdyl walked to the gates, he found them chained, with the residence beyond shuttered and dark.

"Another way to deal with Osten, I suppose, just not one open to you," he murmured as he returned to the coach.

"Ser?" asked Mantar

"I was just thinking aloud. Do you know where the Suthyan envoy's residence might be?"

"Yes, ser. It'd be two blocks south on the corner."

"Then we should go there."

The gates to the long drive leading to the Suthyan residence were open, and Erdyl could see that the windows were unshuttered. Once Mantar halted the coach, Erdyl got out and walked up the stone steps to the entry portico, but he did not even have time to knock before a man in brown-and-yellow livery opened the door.

"Might I be of assistance, ser?"

"I'm Erdyl of Austra, to speak with the envoy."

"I'm most sorry, ser, but the envoy is hunting in the eastern hills."

"And his assistant?" Erdyl asked.

"He is with the envoy."

"When will they return?"

"I could not say, ser," replied the slender older man.

That answer had more than one meaning, but it was pointless to press. Erdyl nodded. "Thank you."

"Is there any message, ser?"

"No, thank you."

"Good day, ser."

Erdyl returned to his coach and ordered Mantar to return to their own residence. As the coach jogged and bounced over the uneven streets, Erdyl considered the results of his efforts. *Close to nonexistent.* He could only hope that he would have more success at the Lydian reception the following evening, although he had some doubts, given the reaction of those he had already contacted—and given the absence of some of the envoys.

On sixday evening at sixth glass, Erdyl stepped from his coach outside the residence of the envoy from Lydiar—Kyanelt—and walked across the paved entry terrace to the door, where he was ushered inside and then to a large salon just off the entry hall.

"Erdyl of Norbruel, acting Envoy of Austra," announced an angular functionary.

Erdyl was all too conscious of the fact that almost no one looked in his direction as he stepped into the salon.

After taking a glass of a hearty red wine from a tray presented by a server, white being unseemly for a mere acting envoy, Erdyl surveyed the large salon, finally picking out a man not much older than himself, attired in gray and black. He made his way across the room easily enough, since no one seemed inclined to talk to him.

As he neared the other, the man smiled warmly and said, "You must be Erdyl, the acting Austran envoy. Dhorian—the assistant to Fhideas, the Envoy from Recluce."

"I am. I take it the honorable Fhideas is elsewhere?"

"He had other commitments. I do my best to fill in for him."

Erdyl gestured vaguely toward Dhorian. "Does the black represent Recluce . . . or your own abilities as a mage?" He sipped the wine, not outstanding, but somewhat better than merely decent, if with a hint too much tannin.

"In my case, more of Recluce than of magery, although I would be remiss not to note that I have some slight abilities with order."

For an instant, Erdyl wondered why Dhorian mentioned the "slight" order abilities, before realizing that, if Dhorian had such abilities, not mentioning them would be uncomfortable, because it would be slightly chaotic. *But . . . if he doesn't . . . lying doesn't hurt . . .* And that meant that Erdyl had no way of knowing whether Dhorian did in fact have such abilities. "And I, as you can tell, have not the slightest of such abilities."

"Sometimes, that can be an advantage, especially for an envoy."

"Because one is not constrained to limit oneself to the facts or truth of a matter?"

"Facts and truth are far from the same, but . . . yes . . . your point has much merit."

"Unless one has certain compunctions about taking too great a liberty with such facts."

"It's best, I've found, merely to present facts that are accurate and allow others to draw their own conclusions."

Selective use of accurate facts . . . but not all the facts. "That is indeed an interesting way of approaching matters. Along those lines, has the recent edict from Lord West come to your attention—the one that makes any man who chooses to work for an outland envoy subject to being conscripted into the Lord's Guard . . . or pressed into merchanter service?"

"I am aware of his statement. It is not properly an edict or proclamation, but a statement of intention . . . which is not exactly the same thing."

"In practice, it is."

"Ah . . . but practice and law—"

"Are not the same thing," Erdyl concluded. "That I understand, but as a strictly practical matter, it makes no difference to me . . . or to Austra."

Dhorian nodded. "You are right to be concerned, young Erdyl. It definitely does put you, and perhaps the envoy from Sligo, in a difficult position, and perhaps Gosperk as well."

"Then you might consider looking into the matter." Erdyl took another sip of the wine and offered an expression of pleasant attentiveness.

"Envoy Fhideas already has, but it is a question of the Balance. Ever since the untoward . . . incident at Fairhaven, the Council must consider all aspects of the Balance."

Hearing the destruction of Fairhaven—even though it had occurred many, many years earlier—described as an "incident" unsettled Erdyl for a moment. "Is it not somewhat unbalanced that an edict from Lord West has, as you put it, an untoward impact on just three envoys out of a number?"

"Perhaps it might seem that way, but one must balance these events over time. As you certainly know, your predecessor used a great deal of order and, in the process, killed rather significant numbers of Nordlan troopers and a number of Hamorians, not to mention several of the heirs to the previous Lord of the West Quadrant. People would rather not deal with anything that recalls such recent 'unpleasantness,' particularly when it reminds them of their inability to do anything about it. As for the matter to which you allude, I have my doubts that the Council would be much interested in creating more upheaval here in Brysta by seeming to back Austra on such a comparatively insignificant statement, not even an edict, made by Lord West, especially given the possibility that a less drastic solution or more creative resolution might be worked out." Dhorian smiled.

Erdyl returned the smile. "I had thought that might be the position of Recluce, but it doesn't hurt to ask. What might be the basis for such a less drastic or more creative solution?"

"One that complies with the letter of Lord West's word but that provides the protection you feel you, your residence, and your retainers require."

Rather more difficult than it sounds when you don't know exactly what he said and when asking directly might well make the matter worse. "I do thank you for your advice."

"My pleasure. If you will excuse me . . ."

"Of course."

Erdyl only stood there for a moment before making his way across the salon to where a black-haired man in a maroon jacket stood talking to another man whom Erdyl did not recognize. When the unknown man turned to leave, Erdyl eased forward.

"Envoy Erdyl . . . welcome to the residence."

Erdyl smiled pleasantly at Kyanelt, the envoy from Lydiar. "Thank you. This is a splendid reception . . . and I do like your hearty red wine."

"As we both know, it is a good vintage, but not great. One must make economies where one can. Few will remark on having an excellent vintage, but all will recall a terrible one."

"That is similar to decisions by rulers," Erdyl replied dryly.

Kyanelt laughed. "Too true. All too true."

"But then," Erdyl continued, "there is always the question

of taste, of opinion. What is a good wine for one man contains too much bouquet, or too little, for another, too much of the almond, and not enough of the pearapple. Like the words of a ruler, perhaps Lord West . . ."

"Rulers will do what they will, as they can, particularly Lord West, unlike the wine, which is what it is, although those who sip may taste it differently. The man who does not like a wine needs not drink it. Likewise the man who feels a ruler's intentions are harmful can either depart the land, akin to not drinking, or add something to his life or profession to avoid or mitigate those intentions . . . but it does little good for him to enlist the support of others who, if you will, do not taste the wine as he does, for the wine is acceptable to them."

Clearly, Kyanelt knew why you approached him. "That is good advice, both about wines and rulers."

"I try to be helpful, young Erdyl."

"I do appreciate that." Erdyl inclined his head. "And I do like the hearty red."

"I'm glad." With a parting smile Kyanelt slipped away.

Again, Erdyl surveyed the salon. There was no mistaking Whetoryk, the Hamorian envoy, not in his crimson tunic and black trousers, with boots so polished they gleamed, his golden-brown hair shorter than the fashion but longer than that of Hamorian troopers.

What continued to both amuse and appall Erdyl was that Whetoryk had returned to Brysta immediately after the attempted overthrow of Osten by his brothers, an overthrow covertly supported by Hamorian golds and mages—and thwarted by Lord Kharl. *And no one says anything.* Understandable as it was, given the importance of trade between Hamor and Nordla, Erdyl felt a certain sense of unreality, as though everyone totally ignored what had happened. *Because they have to?* He smiled wryly, realizing that he was just like them, with nothing to gain and everything to lose by mentioning the past "unpleasantness."

After considering that there was little point in even mentioning Lord West's intended actions to Whetoryk, and possibly great disadvantage in doing so, especially given that Lord Kharl had thwarted the Hamorian attempt to effectively control the West Quadrant, Erdyl smiled politely at Whetoryk before turning and taking several steps toward Largaan, a short, dapper man in a dark green jacket and deep gray trousers who was effectively Osten's chief factor, although he was officially called the Lord's Secretary.

"Secretary Largaan . . ."

"Ah . . . oh, Erdyl the *acting* Austran envoy . . . I hadn't thought to see you here."

"Envoy Kyanelt was kind enough to invite me, but then, given how many Austran ships port in Lydiar . . ." Erdyl left his sentence unfinished and smiled. "How are you this evening?"

"Cold. I'll be glad when winter's over."

"It's barely late fall. Just be thankful that Lord West hasn't made you envoy to Valmurl. There's already snow and ice there."

"Then I'll have to make sure Lord West finds me indispensable here in Brysta." Largaan glanced around the salon, as if he sought any excuse to escape Erdyl.

"I overheard a rumor the other day," Erdyl said quietly, but firmly.

"One cannot trust rumors. Not in the slightest."

"I see. Then, I suppose you could assure me that if I hire a few guards and retainers for the Austran residence, they would have absolutely no fear of being conscripted into Lord West's Guard or pressed into merchanter service."

"I can only speak on matters of trade, Envoy Erdyl." Largaan appeared distinctly uncomfortable, again glancing past Erdyl.

"I see. And who might address that matter?"

"I really cannot say. Perhaps Lord West himself. Other than that . . ." Largaan smiled thinly. "Excuse me. I do need to speak to young Dhorian."

"Of course." Erdyl inclined his head and then watched as Largaan sedately fled. *No one will admit it . . . but they won't deny it . . . and you can't hire men who could lose what little they have under those circumstances, not in good conscience.*

As he studied the salon again, Erdyl realized that he had not seen anyone from Sarronnyn or from Southwind. *Because Kyanelt invited no women . . . or because they chose not to attend?* He shook his head. Even as an assistant, Jemelya was certainly the equal of, if not superior to, many of those in attendance at the reception.

Abruptly, he nodded, if only to himself. Considering what he had observed . . . and what others had said . . . *there just might be another way.*

As a server approached, Erdyl handed him the scarcely touched goblet of the hearty red and took the single goblet of white from amid the other goblets of hearty red on the tray. Then he walked back toward Whetoryk.

"Envoy Whetoryk . . . Erdyl of Norbruel, acting Envoy of Austra. I haven't had the pleasure of meeting you personally . . . although Lord Kharl was most impressed with your sense of presence . . ."

"Ah, yes . . . Erdyl, is it? Your Lord Kharl was the one with presence. Quite a presence, I might add. You wouldn't happen to know where he might be posted now . . . or where he might be headed?"

"I believe, for the moment, he is enjoying the quiet of his

own estates. Like me, he does serve at the pleasure of Lord Ghrant, and I could not say where he might next appear or be posted." Erdyl had no doubts that Lord Ghrant would not hesitate to "request" Kharl's services as necessary.

Whetoryk nodded. "Lord Ghrant is fortunate to have such an ally."

"All of us in Austra are fortunate, but I understand that your emperor is also fortunate to have your services."

"I do my poor best."

"As do I," replied Erdyl, understanding that the remainder of the evening would be filled with pleasantries and veiled statements.

On sevenday, Erdyl waited until early afternoon before having Mantar drive him to the Sarronnese residence once again. This time, once he stepped into the entry hall, Jemelya was the one to greet him, not Ziela.

"You have some news?"

"No," he admitted, suddenly uncertain as to whether he should proceed.

"Then . . . on a sevenday . . . ?" Her eyebrows lifted.

Erdyl found himself looking into those golden-green eyes. He swallowed. "I'm here to make a proposal of sorts."

"Not a personal one, I trust."

Her words were so gently and humorously spoken that Erdyl found himself smiling. "Not at all." *Though I wish I knew you well enough that I could.*

"Come in and tell me about it." Jemelya stepped back and gestured, then closed the residence door and again led the way to the library. This time she nodded to the small circular table where she took a seat.

Erdyl took the chair across from her.

As the snowflakes drifted slowly out of the graying sky, Erdyl glanced through the study window at the guard wearing the green-and-black uniform of an Austran marine—a well-muscled woman also bearing the double shortswords with which she had been trained by Luryessa's senior guards . . . and then by Demyst. With a smile, he walked to the table desk and lifted the dispatch that had arrived on the *Seahound* several glasses earlier. His eyes skipped over the salutation to the important words . . . or rather the ones he had thought were important at first.

> Given your successful and creative resolution of the difficulties posed in obtaining trained and capable guards for the residence in Brysta, His Lordship, Ghrant of Dykaru, Lord of Austra, and Scion of the North, having been well satisfied in your conduct, and mindful of your heritage, is pleased to confer upon you the position of Envoy of Austra to Osten, Lord of the West Quadrant of Nordla, from this time forth, and confers on you the rank of unlanded Lord for that time that you serve and thereafter at the pleasure of His Lordship . . . You will find enclosed the sealed appointment to be tendered to Lord West . . .

Lord? Even a lower Lord? Erdyl looked to the second sealed missive, the one addressed to Lord West, containing his "new" credentials and appointment, before he continued re-reading the remainder of the dispatch.

> . . . has also have received word that Osten, Lord of the West Quadrant of Nordla, may have reached an agreement with the Duke of Lydiar to offer porting facilities at Brysta to certain vessels flying the ensign of Lydiar, vessels which have been preying on Austran merchanters. More information on this possibility would be greatly appreciated.

In addition, the envoy from Hydlen to Austra has disappeared, and his residence is chained and locked . . .
Jeranyi pirate vessels now sail openly out of Worrak as they
did centuries in the past . . . request that you discover what
you can . . .

The listing of "requests" went on for a full page.

Erdyl shook his head and set the dispatch on the desk. *You
only thought you had a problem before.* Then he grinned ruefully.

You should tell Luryessa . . . and Jemelya.

Definitely Jemelya. He'd enjoy working with her . . . at the
very least.

When I wrote the first Recluce books, more than a few readers equated "black" with good, but as this story illustrates, even in the city of Nylan, that equation is a bit too simplistic . . . especially when applied to trade and factors.

THE PRICE OF PERFECT ORDER

I

Lanciano looked across the table of the public room at me. "You still owe us two hundred golds, Trader Moraris." Like all Hamorians, he had an olive-shaded skin as smooth as lard. Unlike many, he was as burly as an Austran northlander. His hand dropped below the edge of the table, suggesting the blade at his hip.

I shrugged. "I don't have it. You know I don't. What do you want me to do?"

"You cannot escape your obligations."

"I certainly can't meet them if you use that blade on me. I think you want the golds more than you want an insignificant trader from Nylan dead."

"If there is no hope of obtaining the golds, we must uphold our reputation for not allowing ourselves to be swindled."

"Yes . . . there is that small point," I replied, trying to think of a way out. It didn't help that Skaenyr had caught me switching dice the night before. How was I to know that his snot-nosed nephew was a student mage? I'd made almost thirty golds, and I'd been fortunate to escape in one piece. But then, Skaenyr was happy to take the golds. Ten had been mine—almost all that I had left after paying off the debts on the factorage, as well as Elnora's share, all because Elnora's family had insisted that her dowry was forfeit . . . and her uncle was just high enough in the Brotherhood that I hadn't had much choice, even if she'd refused to share my bed for the last year.

And then, I'd just been getting started in winning the next twenty in the high stakes game and would have won more if it hadn't been for that little snot. On top of it all, Lanciano had ported this morning—a good two eightdays before he'd been expected—to collect on the note I'd taken to buy out Elnora's share of the factorage. "You could have the factorage."

"An empty gesture, that." His accent was atrocious, but since I didn't speak Hamorian, barbaric tongue that it was, we dealt with each other in the language of Recluce, the old Temple tongue. "Your Brotherhood will not allow outsiders to hold property in Nylan or anywhere in Recluce . . . and you cannot sell it, except to another trader, and they have no need of what little you have."

Absently, I wondered how he'd known. I'd have to do something about that as well . . . but not at the moment. "As I said, you'd prefer the golds."

Lanciano lifted a long double-edged dagger. "You have a most handsome countenance, master factor. It would be a shame if anything happened to it."

"That won't get you your golds."

"Alas, it will not, but it might remind you not to send worthless letters of credit."

"How was I to know that Sensael was about to fail?" Of course, I had known. That was why I'd forged the letter from Sensael when I'd heard of his difficulties, dated earlier, of course, before he'd jumped off the end of the black wall, with nothing left of value.

"Spare me your excuses . . ."

It was just the way things were turning out. I should have gotten a good letter of credit from Whiltar. That would have covered the two hundred golds, at least until Lanciano had left port on the way to wherever he was bound, even if it would have cost another twenty-five golds in interest—except that Whiltar was the Nordlan representative of the Hagan ships, and, after the loss of the *Northern Quarter* to Hydlenese pirates, he'd gotten word not to extend any more credit to shipping factors until the Lydians or the Brotherhood did something about the pirates. And no one else would lend me enough to cover the note. Not even with the factorage and warehouse as collateral.

"By fourday morning," Lanciano said. "Two hundred golds. No paper. Golds. You know where to find me." He looked down at the bare dagger, then stood and sheathed it. "Good evening, Trader Moraris."

I stood as well and inclined my head. "Good evening, Trader Lanciano."

I watched as he walked out, but I did not breathe easily until I had left the Trader's Hearth and covered the five blocks to my factorage and barred the rear door. Then I climbed the steps to my chambers to consider my dwindling options. By the time I fell asleep in the darkness, because I didn't want to use the lamp oil I had too little of, I still hadn't come up with a plan for acquiring the massive sum of two hundred golds.

Threeday didn't begin any better than twoday had ended. Faonyt had barely opened the factorage doors when Ruzios walked in, a broad smile on his weathered face.

"Moraris! I've got some of that prime black wool you were asking about two eightdays ago."

"How much?" There was no way I could pay for all of it at that moment, but . . . if I could get it and resell it . . .

"Three bales, cleaned and carded. Five golds a bale."

"I can take one." That would leave me with nothing, but I could sell that for twice as much to Alforyk. Lanciano would have paid more, but since I owed him . . . he'd have just taken the wool, and I'd be out my last five golds.

He shook his head. "I'm not doing it piecemeal. Three or none."

"I can give you five golds now . . . the other ten at the end of the eightday."

"Moraris . . . I'd be liking you right well . . . but not that well, especially with what I've been hearing."

"You can't trust all the rumors." I smiled openly and warmly. "Haven't I always been a man of my word?"

"You have . . . but there've been times when it took some time to keep that word, and I need the golds now. Otherwise, I wouldn't be offering the wool at such a price. Has to be good metal on the barrel. Here and now."

"Can you come back in a glass? I'd like to see what I can do."

"If I haven't sold it in a glass, I'll be back." With that, Ruzios was gone.

He probably wouldn't be back, but trying to raise the ten golds might be possible. So I left Faonyt at the counter and made my way two blocks toward the harbor and a certain large factorage with an adjoining warehouse.

The modest black signboard beside the well-oiled and brass-bound door simply read ELTARYL TRADING. I didn't go in there, but walked around to the side door, also well-oiled and brassbound, that opened into a small anteroom. It was vacant, as usual, but the door leading from the anteroom to the adjoining study was ajar.

"Ryltar?" I asked pleasantly.

"Come in."

I did. Ryltar had two open ledgers before him. In my view, at twenty he wasn't old enough to be trusted even as a clerk, for all that his wispy brown hair was already thinning. Still, with his father's illness, one that showed little sign of abating, despite all the efforts of the black healers, Ryltar was, in effect, running the family's far-flung trading business.

"Moraris . . . how are you doing?" The younger trader smiled pleasantly enough, but I could see the smile didn't extend to his eyes. He didn't offer me a chair, either.

So I took one. "Well enough."

"Word is that you're a bit . . . strained."

"Not that much, even if I did have to buy out Elnora's share of the factorage."

"Everyone knows, I think. You could have let her keep it," he pointed out.

"Are you interested in buying it?" I asked idly.

"Why?"

"Why not? That would leave one less trading factorage to compete with you."

"You can't compete with us. You don't have the contacts. Or the golds. So what's the point?"

"If you won't buy, then how about lending me twenty golds?"

"To allow you to struggle on? Or so you can lose them with loaded dice?"

I couldn't quite keep the surprise from my face.

"I have my ways, Moraris."

"You don't know everything, Ryltar."

"I'm well aware of that." He smiled sadly. "I do know that it was a mistake for you to meet Elnora's price to gain complete ownership of the factorage."

"Perhaps." But was I supposed to give up everything, just

because Elnora's cousin Clyesa had climbed into my bed when Elnora had taken one of her frequent rest trips to her family's estate outside Enstronn? And who would have thought that Clyesa would slit her wrists in her bath after saying that I'd forced her, when all I'd done was offer her some ice wine? I'd told her it was stronger than most vintages.

"You could have walked away and let Elnora run it and watched them struggle," Ryltar went on. "But that would have proved that you aren't the trader you think you are."

What Ryltar's attitude proved was that Ryltar's uncle, the one who was the councilor, had listened to Elnora's family. I managed a cold smile. "I believe I offered you two propositions."

"I believe I turned both down, Moraris. I'd suggest Sugartyn, except he never lends more than a gold. Good day."

I was seething when I left. Suggesting Sugartyn—the moneylender for ship's marines—was a gratuitous insult.

After I left Ryltar, I made my way to see three others who had lent me funds in the past. They were more polite, but the result was the same. Everyone in Nylan seemed to know that I'd been set up by Elnora and her family . . . and no one cared.

II

Fourday morning came, and I still hadn't found a way to raise two hundred golds. I had less than three golds left in my wallet because Faonyt had insisted on his pay, and I had indulged myself with decent wine after long and futile efforts on three-day. So I made my way to Hamor House—a handsome structure two blocks to the northeast of the harbor that provided rooms and studies for those from Hamor who might have some business in Nylan.

Lanciano received me in a small and spare study—after

making me wait a good half glass. He looked across the table desk at me almost pityingly. "You do not have the golds."

"Where would I get them?" I countered. "You've told everyone in Nylan not to extend funds to me."

"What makes you think that?"

"I have my ways," I replied. I didn't, but I'd liked the phrase when Ryltar had used it, and I didn't see any other explanation, since the factorage was worth far more than ten golds, possibly even a hundred golds more than the two hundred I owed Lanciano.

"What are we to do with you?"

"Give me more time," I suggested.

He just shook his head, slowly and sadly. The sad expression was an act, of course. After several moments of silence, he spoke. "Do you have no plan, no scheme to repay your debt?"

"I could do so over time."

"You have had time."

Since he was going to object to anything I offered, I said nothing.

"What might be of sufficient value to discharge your debt?"

Again, I said nothing.

"You do have contacts among the black engineers," mused Lanciano. "Is that not so?"

"I know a few." The only one I really knew was Lhean, a cousin of mine, and we hadn't spoken much recently.

"There are not many items of value that are worth two hundred golds," said Lanciano. "Especially those useful to a trader."

"Sea-green emeralds," I suggested, almost idly, because I needed to say something.

"And you have fifteen of the size necessary for your debt?"

Fifteen sea-green emeralds of the size he meant would bring closer to three hundred golds, but all I had was one likely half that size, and it had been my mother's. Besides, if I had that many emeralds, I wouldn't have needed to borrow from Lanciano in the first place.

"Black wool?" I suggested.

"Yes . . . that is always good, but who has thirty bales of prime black wool?"

Much as I had to admit it, no one did. I doubted that more than fifty bales of prime black wool appeared in Nylan in an entire spring.

"Some say that the secret to the engines of the black ships is perfect order." Lanciano shrugged. "Others claim that it is the design itself. It has been kept secret for more than three centuries."

"Surely, someone must know the design of the engines," I suggested warily.

"Who?" asked Lanciano. "Do you know anyone outside the Brotherhood who does?"

"I've never thought about the black ships much." And I hadn't, except to worry about them when I'd had "special" shipments coming in at night.

"Imagine what a merchanter could do with such an engine. It is said that they do not even have paddlewheels."

"I wouldn't know." I was getting uncomfortable with the direction of the conversation. Most uncomfortable. All of it was Elnora's fault. She'd wanted this, and she'd wanted that, and didn't she deserve this as the wife of a factor—or that? And when she didn't get whatever it was, she'd say that our quarters needed more order, that whatever it was would supply perfect order. And if I didn't come up with it, well, our quarters got rather chill . . . and certainly disorderly . . . or she departed to "rest" at her father's estate.

In the end, I'd owed more golds than anyone knew, but I'd managed to start paying them off, just by resisting whatever

Elnora had wanted to get her perfect order and using the silvers and golds that saved in being able to trade. I'd almost managed to clear all the debt—and that had meant that I saw little of Elnora. That had been fine with me . . . until the incident with Clyesa.

Then her uncle must have put out the word, because no one in Nylan would advance me sufficient funds to buy out Elnora— that had been why I'd gone to the Hamorians. Needless to say, I wasn't exactly fond of the Brotherhood . . . or the ways in which they enforced their visions of perfect order.

"The designs of such an engine . . . who knows what they might be worth?" continued Lanciano.

"A great deal more than two hundred golds," I said dryly. "More like a man's life and then some."

"If he were caught," returned the Hamorian. "If no one knew . . . and other ships appeared in a few years, who could say?"

"And if he were not caught . . . ?"

"Who could say . . . but there is little point in talking about something that has not happened." He paused, then said, "I leave for Hamor next twoday. If you do not pay what you owe by oneday evening, in some fashion, you will have no worries at all, ever again." He stood. "I believe that is all."

There wasn't much I could say. So I didn't. I just left.

III

I knew the Brotherhood had a library in the building adjacent to the engineering halls, and anyone could read what was there. They just couldn't leave with any of the volumes. I doubted that the library contained what Lanciano wanted, but I harbored a slight hope that there might be something of value there, such as rough plans, perhaps, of the first black ship, *The Black Hammer*. If so . . . there were certain possibilities.

You couldn't just walk into the library. You had to be a citizen of Nylan, and you had to sign a log. I did all that and then looked at the young red-haired engineer apprentice who sat behind the table that held the logbook, situated by the door to the library.

"Do you have any books on trading?" I asked.

The apprentice frowned. "Most of what we have is on engineering and materials. There's a shelf on factoring, ser. The one on the second carrel from the corner . . ." He pointed.

"Thank you." I nodded politely and walked to where he had pointed, and began to look through the books. Only when he returned to perusing what looked like a design of some sort did I ease over into other shelves. I finally located a volume that might have been written by Dorrin. At least, the paper was aged enough that it could have been. When I opened the book, I discovered that someone else had written it, a Jhaksurt of Feyne. He had dedicated it to Dorrin, though, for teaching him all that was in the volume. Unhappily for me, it dealt with the hull design of vessels. I had a suspicion that, while what was in the slim volume might be of great value, it would not be worth two hundred golds to Lanciano.

I went through every book on those shelves—and quite a few others as well—but there was nothing on engines, nothing at all.

After re-shelving the last book I perused, I returned to that table by the door and the young engineer. "Thank you. I'd hoped to find something on coinage weights."

"This is what we have, ser."

"Well . . . thank you." I wasn't about to ask where anything else was. That would have been calling even more attention to myself. I could hope that a factor looking for factoring books wouldn't be too out of place.

IV

Most of the Brotherhood engineers wandered into Houlart's on one night or another, but seldom on the enddays. Fourday and fiveday evenings were the best nights. So I bathed and put on one of my best factor's blues and made my way there. More than a few of the black engineers were women. I was counting on that.

I eased into the public room of the inn and made my way toward the end where some of the engineers were gathered, asking one of the servers for a dark beer. Once I had that in hand, I looked around. I ignored the pair of engineers hunched over a Capture board in the corner. Neither man looked like the type who'd say much.

To one side, a man and a woman were talking.

She was striking, and her eyes flashed as she spoke. ". . . you prize that staff more than any other possession."

"But not more than you," replied the man, also an engineer. "I mean . . ."

"I know what you meant. Words aren't your strength, Warin. That's why you're a good engineer."

They were too wrapped up in each other, and I eased away, toward two women, both young enough to be barely more than apprentices.

". . . don't know that I want to be an engineer forever," said the one, her eyes flicking past me as if I didn't exist.

"Why not? Is it the insistence on accuracy?" asked the other, a tall broad-shouldered woman with green eyes. She didn't notice me, either.

"It's not that, Altara. Perfect order, that's what everyone wants, as if . . ." She shook her head, and her short light brown hair scarcely moved. "We all know—"

The other engineer held up a hand, as if the brown-haired one were about to say something she shouldn't. "Not here."

"There are times I think I'd just rather be a smith somewhere away from Nylan."

"Is that you . . . or is it Horas?"

"We're just friends."

"He'd like more."

"I'm sure he would, but I'm not ready. I don't even know if he's the one."

"He thinks you are. He'd have returned to his family's lands and those trees he loves so much long ago if it weren't for you."

"I know. He is a dear . . . but he can be . . . impractical."

"Spoken like a true engineer." Suddenly, the big blonde shook her head. "I need to go."

That was my chance, and as the blonde left, I joined the wiry brunette. "You're a black engineer, aren't you?" I asked.

"You couldn't tell?" Her voice was cool and ironic.

"I had to say something. I couldn't just say that I'm Moraris, and I'm a trader."

"You just did."

"That was my fallback," I admitted, trying to sound off-balance and sheepish.

"Do you need one?"

"I obviously do," I said with an embarrassed and apologetic grin. "If not more."

She considered. "I'm Cirlin. I wouldn't have expected a factor here."

"Why not? Houlart's is supposed to have good drink and solid fare . . . and the prices are reasonable. Factors do consider that," I added dryly.

She didn't laugh, but she did smile. That was good.

"I've never quite understood how the engineering brotherhood was organized," I said, "or why it's a brotherhood when so many of the engineers are women."

"It was a brotherhood because Dorrin was a man, and so were most of those who followed him in building ships. Women came later. So did better designs."

"Because of the women?" I suggested.

"They certainly didn't hurt."

"You think that women are better at refining things."

"I think more women are interested in refining things. Men want to move on to the next new thing."

"So once Creslin broke away from Westwind, Megaera refined him?"

Cirlin shrugged. "Maybe."

"Then who refined the black ships and their engines after Dorrin? Another woman? Is that what you and your friend do?"

"Not yet . . ." She smiled again.

"What is the secret of those engines?" I asked conversationally. "Perfect order?"

"In a way." Cirlin smiled. "Why are you so interested?"

"Why wouldn't a factor be interested? The black ships are faster than any vessels on the sea. Just think how much faster trading ships could travel with engines like those."

"You couldn't afford to buy an engine like that," she said. "That is, if the Brotherhood agreed to make one for sale."

But the Hamorians could. That, I did know. "Do you ever think that will happen?"

"Not unless you factors take control of everything, and that wouldn't be good."

"Why not? If the factors of Recluce had faster ships . . ."

"There would be more chaos everywhere in the world."

"You don't really believe that, do you?"

"Some things aren't a matter of belief."

"Like engineering designs?"

"If they work . . ." She shook her head. "It's been an interesting discussion, but I have to meet someone." She set her
empty glass on the wooden bar, smiled, then turned and
slipped away.

I glanced around that part of the inn. I was alone, except for
the two engineers in the corner—still playing Capture.

V

By fiveday, there was no helping it. I'd have to see Lhean. He
lived in the engineers' house, the one for men, because of certain
events in his past that he doubtless regretted, but then, women
have often caused men great regret. I was waiting there for him
when he returned after work.

His mouth opened when he stepped through the door.
"Moraris . . . what are you doing here?"

"I need your help."

"I've heard about that. I don't have five golds, let alone three
hundred."

"I'm not asking for golds. I want access to some old engineering plans." I'd already decided that even Lhean wasn't about to
help me get anything recent, but, if in a few years, the Brotherhood discovered Hamorian ships based on old designs, who
would know . . . or care?

He looked at me as if I were mad. Perhaps I was, but what
choice did I have? "Not anything recent," I explained. "Older
drawings of engines."

He shook his head. "I can't do that."

"Just one set of plans for an older engine."

"You don't understand . . ."

What I understood was that, if I didn't get those plans, or something like them, I'd likely be maimed and disfigured by twoday evening . . . assuming I was still alive. That . . . or I'd be penniless and skulking through the hills . . . or the like, if not worse. None of that exactly appealed to me, for obvious reasons. So I took a different tack. "Who got you out of that mess with the girl in Sigil?"

"That was a long time ago," he protested.

"Your family still doesn't know, and they certainly don't know about those enddays you spent with Marryk."

"You promised . . ."

"I did, but I'm in deep. You said you owed me, and you do. And I need a favor."

"How old a design?" he asked warily. "And of what?"

"Old enough that the plans won't be missed any time soon. I need plans of the engines of one of the older black ships, after *The Black Hammer* and well before the Mighty Ten." That was necessary because even I knew that the engines of the lost Mighty Ten could no longer be built, even with perfect order.

Lhean gulped. "I can't do that."

"I'm afraid you'll have to . . . or . . ."

"Moraris . . . please . . ."

"I'm afraid this is a matter of life and death, Lhean."

"One of your trading messes?"

"You might say so."

He took a deep breath. Then he closed his eyes, as if concentrating . . . or trying to come up with an alternative.

I waited.

Finally, he said, "Wait here."

"Why? What are you going to do?"

"Go and get you a set of plans. What else?"

"I'll come with you."

He shook his head. "The marines won't let anyone into the

main engineering hall who isn't an engineer or an apprentice, especially this late in the day. I'll have to be very careful anyway. Just wait here. I'll either be able to get what you want in a glass or so . . . or not at all."

"It had better not be not at all. And don't cross me. I'll make sure everyone knows everything if you do."

He looked at me. "I know that." Then he added, "I'll do the best I can for you. That's all I can promise."

I didn't like leaving it up to him that way, but I didn't see what else I could do, not after what Elnora and her vindictive family had done . . . and, besides, I couldn't even sell the factorage to outlanders who'd be willing to pay for it. If what I did went against the Brotherhood, in a way, they'd brought it on themselves.

So I watched as he left, then paced around his small quarters, sat down, stood up, paced some more, and finally sat down again on a worn armchair that faced the door.

As I sat there, glancing at the closed door, I wondered. Should I have left and come back later? What if Lhean weaseled out and told one of the senior engineers? I shook my head. I was almost out of time and options, and I'd just have to trust him, much as I worried about it.

More than a glass passed before he eased back through his door. I did breathe a sigh of relief, although slowly enough that I doubt he heard it.

"Here are your plans. I put them in this half-staff case." He held up a leather case.

"Not that I don't trust you, but I'd like to take a look."

"I thought you might." He untied the leather thongs and handed the case to me.

I eased out the rolled sheets and unrolled them on the modest table where Lhean doubtless ate. The first sheet actually had a title—"Turbine Design." From the age of the paper and from what I could tell, the plans looked like what Lanciano wanted.

"You've done well," I said as I carefully re-rolled the sheets and replaced them in the leather case.

"You won't tell anyone, will you? His narrow face looked almost furtive. "I mean, how you got them?"

"That's the last thing I'd tell anyone." I certainly meant that, for many reasons. Who knew what else I might need? "Thank you."

He looked at me sadly. "Moraris . . . please be more careful in the future. I've done what I can for you. I don't think I could do it again."

I raised my eyebrows.

"The plans will be missed, sooner or later, and then they'll be harder to get to."

That made sense, but still . . .

"You'd better go, before anyone else sees you. That wouldn't be good for either of us."

I had to admit that he was right about that. Still . . . I watched every corner . . . and I took a most indirect way to Hamor House.

Even so, I kept looking over my shoulder, but I saw no one following me.

When I got there, Lanciano wasn't there. Or, if he happened to be, he made me wait for more than a glass, and it was dark by the time he ushered me into the same small room where we'd met before.

"You come to beg for more time, trader?"

"No. I have what you want." I lifted the case.

"Oh?" His dark eyes indicated complete skepticism. "You show me."

So I set the leather case on the end of the table desk, untied the leather thongs, and took out the rolled plans, smoothing them out and stepping back. I felt as though a chill descended upon the room as I did so, but that had to be my imagination.

Lanciano bent over and looked at the first sheet. His eyes widened. Then he studied the second sheet and all the others. Finally, he straightened and shook his head, almost as if he did not believe what he saw.

I didn't smile. Not yet.

"I am impressed, Trader Moraris. These will indeed pay off your note."

"And a bit more."

"Do not be greedy, Moraris."

"That might be for the best," said a third voice.

Lanciano started, his eyes widening, and I half-turned.

Just inside the door stood two figures clad completely in black. From the cut of their garb, it was clear they were black mages. I didn't recognize either, but that might have been because their faces were somehow obscured.

Lanciano's hand went to the hilt of the blade at his waist.

"I wouldn't, if I were you," said the taller figure in black.

"Who are you?" I asked.

"Does it matter?" asked the shorter figure. From the lighter voice, it was clear she was a woman, and somehow that irritated me. Always . . . always it was the women who spoiled things.

"The plans?" asked Lanciano. "They are false?"

"No . . . those are plans for a steam turbine. In fact, they're copies of the plans of Dorrin's third turbine. I doubt they'd do you much good." The taller black took a step toward Lanciano.

The shorter one seemed to be watching me.

For the first time I'd ever seen, the Hamorian actually looked angry. He glared at me. "You told them."

"No, he didn't, but it would have been better if he had. Much better."

"Why aren't the plans any good?" I found myself asking.

"They're absolutely accurate, but it takes close to perfect order to make the components. Otherwise, the turbine will fail. Sometimes, the failures have been spectacular, I'm told." The taller black mage went on. "You aren't the first to attempt to get the plans. You won't be the last."

"You've both been looking for perfect order," said the unnamed woman whose voice I did not recognize. "It would be a shame if you didn't find it."

"Perfect order," sneered Lanciano. "It does not exist."

"Oh . . . it does. Perfect order is where nothing changes. Black iron comes close, so close that we claim it embodies perfect order, but it's not quite. In people, perfect order exists when the body holds no chaos at all."

I tried not to swallow as I realized what the mage meant.

"Words," scoffed Lanciano.

"I'm afraid not, honored trader," said the taller black mage, sadly.

Suddenly, a far greater chill filled the room . . . or the space around the Hamorian. He didn't even have time to look surprised. He just toppled forward.

The shorter black mage stepped forward and picked up the plans and deftly rolled them up, replacing them in the leather case.

"What are you going to do with me?" I asked. "Give me your perfect order?"

"That would be too easy," replied the taller one. "Besides, we promised we wouldn't."

That was what Lhean had meant by saying he'd do "his best" for me! He'd put the demon-cursed Brotherhood above his own cousin. Hadn't family and all I'd done for him meant anything at all?

"We could put you on a merchanter to Hamor," added the woman, "but you wouldn't live long enough to regret your stupidity. Southwind, I think, will be good for that. The head councilor thought so."

"That's where they follow the Legend." I tried not to swallow.

"It's another form of order, just not perfect order," said the shorter black mage, "refined by women, by the way. And we have a ship headed that way, leaving tonight. You'll even get to know how good those engines are." There was a hint of a nasty smile behind those words.

"You won't be able to see for a while," added the man. "Not until you're on board. This way, the honored Hamorian trader will be found alone. His heart stopped. You will have vanished. Everyone will suspect you did it . . . somehow. And you won't be able to say a thing."

Or ever return to Nylan. Or be a trader or a factor anywhere.

I knew I shouldn't have talked so much to the woman engineer. Women . . . no matter what you do, they'll get a man in trouble every time.

Over the years, a number of readers of the Recluce Saga have asked about Cassius, and how he came to Recluce. Well . . . here's the answer . . .

BLACK ORDERMAGE

I

There was the fire, welling up everywhere on the flight deck—and an explosion and a flash of brilliant white. Everything seemed to hang in the balance. Then, blackness flowed around me, and after that so did currents of black-and-white light. The black felt calming. It was reassuring. The white *burned.*

Both vanished, and I dropped maybe two feet onto something hard. It only took a moment to catch my balance. I was used to pitching decks. But . . . there wasn't any heat, and there weren't any flames. A moment before, I'd been acting as nozzle-man on the flight deck, and now my hands were empty. Less than three yards away from me a little guy in red-and-yellow rags took what looked to be a curved sabre and slashed a bigger guy in blue and black across the back of his calf. Even before the big guy went down, a silver-haired woman in black slashed the smaller man's throat and then took out another attacker with a neat thrust.

Another crewman in blue went down, and a pole—no, a

staff—rolled across the deck toward my feet. I grabbed the staff. It wasn't that much different from the pugil stick I'd used when I'd been an instructor in SEE except it wasn't padded at the ends. They were ironbound.

The odors/feelings of blood and death shook me like I'd been slammed into a steel bulkhead. I looked out. I was still somewhere on an ocean, but the water looked grayer than the Pacific, and the air was colder. The sky was different—a really different greenish blue. I'd never seen anything like it, not even before a tornado and not in bright sunlight. I glanced down. The deck was wood. I could smell something burning. Coal? Then I could see that the ship had funny stacks, sort of belled like the old stove in Papaw's house in Hebron. But the people were wearing stuff I'd never seen, and there was another ship, lower, and sleeker, with raked sails, grappled to the railing of the higher-decked vessel where I stood on the aft quarter. Someone yelled, and I jumped. Then more of the men in the ragged and dirty red and yellow were climbing over the rail. Two of them looked at me the way Mamaw might have looked at a plump chicken.

One of the raiders came charging toward me with his sword—a wide-bladed scimitar of some kind. I spread my feet and brought up the staff from below. No one ever thinks that way. He didn't, either—not until the iron-tipped end cracked into his arm just below the elbow and his blade went flying. The woman in black ran him through with one thrust.

By then I was facing a big guy, wider than me, anyway, with a long-handled ax that looked like it could cut right through my staff. I feinted toward his head. When he ducked and dodged, I brought the staff back into the knee that held most of his weight. It cracked. Most men would have toppled. He just staggered. It was enough for me to thwack him topside. He went down then—hard.

More of the raiders were swarming up the side of the ship. Seemed to me that it was better to get them when they had at least one hand occupied, and I ran to the railing, using the staff as a lance on the first one who started to scramble onto the deck. He went flailing and bounced off the hull and into the water.

I managed to take out three more, one way or another, but that wasn't much help, because there were five of them.

Something slammed into my shoulder. I yelled. A metal bolt stuck out. But another one of the honkies in red and yellow was swinging his scimitars at me. Even with one arm barely working, I used the other one and my body weight to swing the staff across. It connected with his temple, and he went down like one of Papaw's flour sacks tipped off the wagon.

Then something else hit me.

II

When I tried to wake up, I could hear a woman was speaking to me. I tried to listen. I thought I should understand what she was saying, but the words didn't make much sense . . . and then they faded away. So did I.

When I woke again, someone was jabbing hot red needles through my shoulder, and someone else was beating on my skull with a shovel. I was in a narrow bed, lying on something like a rough sheet, and a woolen blanket covered my legs. The bed was spare and wooden. The walls of the small room were dark stone, and the windows did have glass. The only light came from a brass lamp hung on the wall, like the kerosene lamp Mamaw had kept when she'd moved from Hebron after Papaw's death to be closer to Ma.

A gray-haired woman in a green shirt, except it was more

like the tunics in bad historical movies, held a mug of something to my lips. I swallowed. It was piss-poor beer, not so bad as Narragansett, but almost that bad. I drank it all anyway.

Behind her was the silver-haired woman in black. She said more of the words I didn't understand, while the older woman fed me some broth that made the beer taste good. Before long my eyes closed.

That was the way things were for days and probably longer, except I didn't see the silver-haired woman again, only the older woman, and I kept wondering where I was and what happened. Had I somehow lost my mind?

III

The first time I could finally stay alert—and remember what had happened—I was sitting on the side of a pallet bed in a locked room with barred windows. The two small windows had glass, but it was filthy and outside the bars. My head still ached with a dull throbbing, and the continuous sharp needles in my shoulder had been replaced by occasional stabs from an invisible knife. The sleeve of my working denim shirt had been cut away, and the shoulder was so heavily bound that I could barely move my lower arm. How had I gotten from fighting a flight-deck fire to a shipboard fight on an antique steamship with staffs and swords? Had I deserted and gone out of my mind? Or just gone out of my mind?

The ironbound door opened. A guard in dirty and faded red set a platter and a mug on the floor, then quickly closed the door. The food was different, but not any better than Navy fare. Just several slices of cold lamb—mutton, really—a wedge of cheese close to rancid, a chunk of stale bread, a bruised golden-red fruit, and a mug of the bitter beer. I was hungry enough that I ate it all.

Later, two guards escorted a woman into my cell. She wore faded black. Her hands were chained together, and the chains were heavy dark iron. Her skin was tanned, like she'd spent a lot of time in the sun, and she was white. I'd have said she was around thirty, but her hair was silver, even her eyebrows and the fine hair on the exposed part of her forearms. The silver looked natural—and brilliant. But there were bruises on her face and arms, and probably elsewhere. She was the one who had fought so fiercely on the deck of the ship. I couldn't help admiring her bearing and her spirit, even though we were both captives.

With her was a man dressed entirely in shimmering white. I had a hard time looking at him for long. He spoke to the woman. His words were not gentle.

She said something to me.

I shook my head.

She kept talking. Her words meant nothing, whatever language she was using. I knew Black English and American English and what I learned in three years of lousy high school French. As she kept speaking and gesturing to the man in white, and he answered, in a tone of irritation, I had a pretty good idea they weren't speaking French, not even close.

Even though he was smiling politely, anger boiled inside him. Or something did. I could almost see it. Finally, after another exchange, he raised his hand and pointed to the wall. A tiny fireball flew and smashed against the stone. There was an acrid smell, like burning paint.

He said something else, in the tone of a threat, and he and the guards left.

She pointed to herself. "Kytrona." Then she pointed to me and raised her eyebrows. Her eyes were a muddy green.

"Cassius Barca Samuels."

That got me a frown.

"Cassius," I said.

That was how my lessons began.

In between the time spent with Kytrona in that locked room learning Low Temple, I had a lot of time to think about how I'd ended up in a different world. Or was I paralyzed, lying somewhere like Tripler, just imagining what had seemed so real? Either way, I hadn't thought things would turn out like that. I thought I'd been smart when I'd enlisted in the Navy. As the recruiter had said—clean sheets and no foxholes and no patrols with Charlie shooting at you. He'd said VC. I learned about Charlie later, on *The Sullivans*, before I got transferred to the *Forrestal* and discovered the brown-shoe Navy.

Pilots came in all shapes and attitudes, but most, especially Navy pilots, came in one flavor. That was vanilla. But, back then, black petty officers were almost as rare as black officers, sometimes rarer. My ma had just been glad I hadn't volunteered for the Marines. She didn't even mind that I'd struck for quartermaster . . . and made it all the way to second class. Chief Mangrum had told me I was crazy, that with my test scores and brains I'd already have been first class and eligible for chief if I'd gone ET. I didn't want to be a tech, especially an electronic tech. The way technology was going in the Navy, the ETs really didn't do that much tech stuff. They just figured out which black box didn't work and replaced it, and some civilian in California was the one who actually repaired the box—unless they junked it.

Chief Mangrum said that I was just copping out, that I was taking the easy way, that I just didn't want to work hard. I hated being told that. I just didn't want to be a black-boxer, but it still bothered me.

Anyway, that was how I ended up on the flight deck of the

Forrestal that January morning. We were doing the final ORI in the Hawaiian Islands before heading to SEASIA. Some of the crew called it "Nam." That didn't seem right to me, stuck in my mind like "boy" and "nigger." For all that, I couldn't say why I always said "Vietnam" rather than "Nam."

I didn't see exactly what happened, except that it looked like a rocket somehow fired itself across the deck where it exploded into one of the F-8s—at least I'd thought it was an F-8, but with flames flaring everywhere, and with that part of the flight deck an instant inferno, I wasn't sure. I was headed for the nearest hose.

There were three of us there, and I took the nozzle. The biggest danger was wing-mounted ordnance on attack birds being cooked off, and stopping that meant putting water on any bird with weapons on its wing racks. Couldn't help thinking about what had happened on the *Forrestal*. We *had* to keep things from getting out of hand.

I'd turned the nozzle on an A-6 that was already so hot that the first blast from the nozzle turned to steam. Then there was another explosion and . . . *something* shoved me into the darkness.

IV

Over the days that followed, I kept wondering about the fire on the flight deck, and what had happened . . . and Kytrona persevered, and I did began to learn Low Temple. I also learned that she was from a place called Recluce, and that the ship I'd landed on had also been from there, bound for someplace called Ruzor when pirates had attacked her. The head of the pirates was Gaylmassen, and he held us both as captives. Because I wore blue, he was convinced that I belonged to Recluce. His keep

was called something like Paraguna, and it was in Worrak. I
didn't know where any of the places were, but I'd won the grade
school geography bee once, and I knew they couldn't have been
on Earth.

I also knew there was no way I could be on another world . . .
but with every day of cold meat and cheese and beer, and an
occasional fruit that I'd never seen or tasted, I was getting the
idea that I was either a total head case or imprisoned on another
world. The other world idea was more acceptable, but barely so,
because I didn't know any way that people could throw firebolts when the technology they seemed to have was on the level
of steam engines and swords. Also, I'd never *tasted* or smelled
anything in a dream, and I certainly was doing both. And the
burned spot on the stone was definitely there.

One thing that wasn't obvious at first was that I was bigger
than most of the guards, and not just a little, but almost a foot.
At times, it almost made me laugh, because at six four I'd been
too short to play center and too slow to be a guard, and I'd gotten my ass waxed in the pickup games—until Da and Ma had
put a stop to them.

Kytrona kept talking about order. It had taken her most of
an afternoon to get that idea across—along with the fact that
the firebolt was chaos. She lined up little pieces of wood; she
folded rags into patterns. She drew repeating designs in the dust.
When I finally understood, then she kept repeating the word
for "order" and then pointing to her black tunic, and to my skin.

That bothered me, because it meant that, once again, I was
being seen as something because of the color of my skin. I suppose it helped a little that a silver-haired woman was also seen
the same way, but it was clear that I was on the other side from
my captors—just because of the color of my skin. They'd attacked
me on the merchanter for the same reason. From what little I'd

seen, I was sure I didn't want to be on the pirate side, but their view of me was another form of discrimination based on my skin color.

I learned more words from Kytrona, but I was still having trouble with the idea that she and I were somehow linked to "order" and the raiders were linked to "chaos." They seemed anything but chaotic.

Just before she was escorted off at the end of one day, she looked at me. I could sense her anger and frustration with me. "Look at the guards. Look at them closely when they come for me. Then look at you and me." She pointed to a small and recent scar on her forearm. "You have one, too."

I looked. I did have one, and it also was recent, but I had no idea how I'd gotten it, and what she had meant by pointing it out.

I couldn't do much about the scar, but I did study the guards when they came for her. There was a white mist or shadow around them, and when they brought Kytrona the next day for my endless language lessons, they still had the white mist. There was also a faint black darkness that shadowed her, but there were patches of reddish white at points on her body, and she winced when she sat on the stool. I felt twinges in the same places. How could that be, and how could people have colored shadows? Especially when there wasn't any direct sunlight in the cell?

Then I stopped. Ma had talked about people showing their colors, and how she could sometimes see them. I'd thought those were just words, but I hadn't wanted to argue with her. No one argued with Ma.

After a moment, I realized that the reddish white meant bruises where Kytrona had been hurt. She'd never said anything, either. I got off the bed and pointed. "You . . . sit . . . there."

She didn't protest, and I took the stool.

"The guards . . . a whiteness . . . You . . . are . . . black shade . . ."

"White is the color of chaos. Black is the color of order. Recluce is the home of order."

When she'd first talked about order, I'd thought she was saying that the good guys wore black and black hats, and the bad ones wore white. That wasn't like anyplace I knew. Charlie wore blue or black, or so the Marines on the *Forrestal* had said. But it was certainly possible. Now . . . now . . . I was seeing people in those terms. Was I really in this other world? Or just hallucinating in sick bay somewhere?

"You can see order and chaos. You are a mage."

"I am not a mage." I had to protest.

"You are. You can sense what others feel, can you not?"

"Times . . ." I didn't know the words.

"At times . . . or . . . some times," Kytrona supplied.

"At times," I said.

She kept her voice low. "Before long, Gaylmassen will summon you. Do not let him know how well you speak. Because of your size, no one will believe you are a mage."

More frigging bias. If you're big, you can't be anything but dumb. I pushed away the anger. "What about you?"

"I can sense what to do with a blade, nothing more. That is why I was a ship's champion. That is also why Guillum linked us. He thinks it will help you learn to speak. Before long he will sense that you are a mage. That will not be good."

"Linked?"

She lifted her hands and rattled the chains. "These are chains. You and I are chained together. The chains will grow stronger if we both live. If we live long enough, what kills one of us will kill the other."

There weren't any chains linking us. She wore the chains.

"I see . . . no chains."

She pulled back her sleeve and pointed to the scar on her forearm. "Look."

Was there a faint black line running from there? Where?

My eyes—except I was feeling as much as seeing—followed the line . . . to my good arm and the scar there.

"You see?"

I saw, in spite of myself.

"You must learn more about how to handle order."

How was I supposed to handle something like a shadow? I could buy the business of sensing feelings. Mamaw had been able to do that, but what could I do with a shadow . . . even if I learned how?

V

The very next day, the guards put me in chains and escorted me to see Gaylmassen. I expected to be dragged into a throne room like the ones in the movies. That didn't happen. I was marched into a wood-paneled office or library. There were shelves of books on one wall, and a thick plush carpet laid over the stone floor. The windows were small, and the library was dark.

Gaylmassen stood beside a desk. The workmanship was good, but every flat surface was covered with carvings, like a Chinese cabinet I once saw. That desk was the ugliest piece of furniture I'd ever seen. Gaylmassen only came to my shoulder, but he wore a sword at his waist, and it wasn't decorated. His hair was brown and short. He wore a yellow silk shirt with a vest and funny trousers.

"You admire the desk. You have some taste."

I didn't think saying anything would be wise. I just bowed a bit. I hated bowing to anyone, but there were four guards, and my hands were chained behind my back.

I didn't bow deeply enough, and one of the guards clouted me on my good shoulder with something—the flat of his sabre, I thought. Two others forced me down to my knees. Even through the thick carpet, the stone was hard on my knees.

Gaylmassen smiled and spoke. "A truly black man—that I had never thought to see. You were an expensive captive. My men tell me that you and the black bitch almost saved the merchanter by yourselves. Once you can speak well enough to be understood . . . then there will be a special place for you both in my personal guard. You would like that far better than the alternative. I could sell you as a matched pair to certain Hamorian traders." He smiled again.

I'd seen that expression before. More than once, but the one I remembered best had been on the face of Sheriff Shanklin back in Hebron, when he'd told Papaw that Papaw just had to be a good "boy" and leave things to those who knew better. I trusted Gaylmassen less than Papaw had trusted Sheriff Shanklin, but I followed Papaw's example. I just inclined my head more deeply than before and said, "Yes, sir."

"Ser, or Lord," he corrected me.

"Yes, ser." I'd had to bow twice, been forced to my knees, and had to say "ser" twice, and someone would pay for all that.

"Do you know who I am?" He spoke slowly and carefully, as if I were an idiot child.

Remembering Kytrona's advice, I replied haltingly, "You . . . Lord Gaylmassen."

"Who are you?"

"Cassius . . . ser." I almost didn't add the title, but there wasn't much point in getting clouted again.

"Cassius . . . terrible name for a guard. We'll have to think of something better. He needs to learn to speak better." He nodded to the guards. "Take him away."

VI

When Kytrona was shoved into my cell the next day, her lip was swollen, and her face was bruised. Her wrists were bloody under the manacles. From the reddish-white aura patches radiating from parts of her body, I could tell she'd been abused far more than was obvious.

I'd followed her advice, and I was afraid she'd paid for it.

I didn't know how to tell her I was sorry. So I knelt and kissed her hand.

Her jaw tightened. I could sense that was because she refused to show any emotion.

"You are kind, but you must learn to be a mage . . . or you and I will be without thought, or dead. Or worse than dead."

I think that was what she said. I could understand more than I could say. She was right, but how would I ever learn something like that when I had no idea what a mage was?

"Tell me . . . about order . . . what mages do . . . ," I managed.

"All things are part order and part chaos . . . ," she began.

My understanding wasn't much better than my handling of Low Temple. What was clear was that magic—or magery—worked. The chaos types like Guillum could throw firebolts. I'd seen that. The order types could strengthen things and make them work better.

I listened and tried to learn both words and about magery, and I worried when the guards dragged Kytrona off late in the day. Even if I could figure out how to do what Kytrona said I could do, how would that help? I was still behind stone walls and iron bars. The stone had certainly stopped Guillum's firebolt, and he was an accomplished mage.

Somewhere in the middle of the night, I sat up on the hard pallet. Strengthening and ordering things implied the ability to shift stuff. Could I strengthen things in the middle of the door in a way that weakened the wood where the hinges and the iron straps were attached? No matter how tough the iron was, if the wood got soft the way it was when termites got it, it would tear away from the hinges and locks.

That was a great idea. I didn't have any idea how to do it, though.

I lay awake for a long time, without any ideas.

I didn't sleep well, and I woke early—still without ideas.

In the gray light before dawn, I looked at the ragged sleeve of my shirt. Parts of it were so worn that it was practically falling apart. Too bad I couldn't strengthen it, with whatever this order was that tied things together. A thought occurred to me. In my world, molecules and atoms were held together by unseen forces, valences and stuff. Did order work the same way?

I ripped off a corner of the sleeve. That wasn't easy, not one-handed, because I couldn't lift my left hand high enough to reach the torn part. The old lady had changed the dressings on my shoulder several times, and the wound had scabbed over. It itched, but it didn't hurt too much.

Then I held the cloth in my good hand, and tried to look at it in the same way that I'd looked at Kytrona and the guards. I stared and looked and squinted. Nothing. I kept at it, trying to think of tiny pieces of cloth, sort of like atoms. Then I thought of them like needles. I tried with my eyes open, and my eyes closed. After a while, I tried picturing them as linked puzzle pieces.

At that point, I felt so light-headed I had to put my head down. When I lifted it, sparkles flashed across my eyes. But I thought I saw shades of white mist where I'd just torn the cloth, and blackness more in the center. I tried to move the black away from the middle and strengthen the sides of the scrap of cloth. The sides seemed to get darker, and the middle had a whitish shadow—that was what I sensed. But was I just seeing what I wanted to see?

I didn't say anything to Kytrona about what I was doing after she was thrust into the cell that morning. I just tucked the scrap of cloth inside my shirt. I was relieved not to see any new bruises. I did ask her to tell me anything she had heard about order and mages.

"There are many different kinds of ordermages . . . the first was Creslin . . ."

As she spoke, she had to explain even more words, but somehow it had become easier for me to remember them. Although I seemed to understand each sentence, trying to make sense of the world she was describing was something else.

Near the end of the afternoon, she murmured, "We do not have much time, Cassius. A few more days at most. Then Guillum will use his chaos powers to destroy your ability to think for yourself."

"What about you?"

"They will do the same to me, because the link between us might allow you to regain your memories and thoughts. I am only useful as a tool to teach you—and because they wish to humiliate me . . . and Recluce." Her words were matter-of-fact, and she was telling the truth.

After she left, I took out the scrap of cloth and tugged on both sides. It practically fell into two pieces.

I just looked at it.

That night I tried to work on the door, using the same approach.

I got so faint that I passed out on the stone floor and woke in the darkness. It didn't seem as dark as it had before, but I didn't see any more lamps or a moon shining through the bars of the window.

I barely managed to get back to the pallet bed before I dropped off again.

I didn't sleep long, because a silvery light flooded the cell, and Chief Mangrum appeared. His face was blistered and black on one side, and I could see his jawbone where the flesh had fallen away there. His working khakis were half-burned off, and the odor of smoke and burning fuel filled the cell. *Where were you? Did you cop out again? Look for the easy way out?*

I didn't have an answer.

His eyes burned as he looked at me. *Cop-out, that's all you'll ever be.*

He had to be an illusion, but the words burned into me.

Mangrum's image *twisted* into something else—a silver-haired woman garbed in silver. She stood beside the base of a massive tree that impossibly rose out of the cell and into the shadows of a forest mightier than any rain forest.

Order and chaos are twisted within you, for you come from order through chaos. You must face your fears and choose.

I didn't want anyone insisting I choose something when I didn't know what I was choosing.

You know enough to choose.

"Choose what?"

That is what you must decide.

Her image vanished, and that of Mangrum re-appeared. Flames surrounded him, and the heat and the odor of burning jet fuel was everywhere. *You left us. Deserter!* His khakis were in flames, and the heat and odor of fire rose until the cell was like an oven. Or even hotter. A flaming glob of oil flew past me and hit the wall by the window, where it continued to burn. *Deserter! Cop-out!*

"I had no choice."

You could have been an ET . . . you should have been on that deck . . .

I should have been, but that had not been my choice or my doing.

Mangrum's finger jabbed toward me, and I held up my good hand instinctively.

Hsstt! His finger burned my palm, and I stepped back.

Coward! Deserter!

I forced myself to step forward. His hands grasped my wrists, and for an instant, pain and fire ringed both wrists.

Then he vanished, only to be replaced by Sheriff Shanklin, as much taller than I was as he had been when I'd been a child. *Boy . . . you aren't going to be making trouble, now, are you? You wouldn't be wanting trouble for your family, would you?* His smirking smile was overpowering, and he held the ivory-handled revolver he'd always claimed had been given to him by General Patton.

Before I could move, the revolver barrel had clipped my forehead.

You're not worth a bullet, boy. No, you're not. The smirk was even more open.

What was the right answer, the right choice? I stepped forward. "Force doesn't change what's right, Sheriff. Threats don't make something right."

This time, my hand was moving before the revolver barrel was, and I caught it. I didn't stop it. Instead, the barrel kept swinging and threw me into the wall beside the window. I hit hard enough that I didn't feel anything for a moment. I did think that dreams didn't hurt the way I'd been hurt. Not any dream I'd ever had.

It is not a dream. The woman in silver appeared, still standing beside the tree. *This world is as real as yours. You have faced some of your fears. Now, you must find the will and the way for both*

of you to escape. Or you will die here as certainly as the man in the
fire died in the world from which you came.

With that, she vanished.

Most of my back ached. The pain had returned to my
wounded shoulder. My wrists were blistered, and so was the spot
in the center of my palm. The cell reeked of fire, smoke, and
burning fuel oil.

VII

I had to sleep on my side, and only on one side. I didn't sleep
well, and I was up early, as soon as the first light seeped through
the barred windows. Then, I just sat on the edge of the bed,
trying not to think about how many places on my body hurt.

Right after the guards half-pushed, half-flung Kytrona into
the cell, she stiffened and looked around. Then she wrinkled
her nose. "It smells like a fire in here. A strange fire."

"Burning fuel oil."

She looked at me questioningly. "Your face is red, and your
hair is singed. There are gashes on your forehead."

I shrugged. "Long night." How could I possibly explain?

"All nights are long." Her eyes were almost accusatory. "The
guards—"

"No. Not the guards." I pointed to the wall where the glob
of burning fuel oil had seared the stone. She walked over and
looked at it. Then she looked at me once more. I could feel her
worry and puzzlement. "It was fire, but you are not of chaos."

"Last night . . . there was . . . a man who was . . . above
me . . . he was . . . on fire . . . and then a woman in silver . . .
with silver hair . . ."

"An angel of the Ancients—she came to you . . . here?"

"She said . . . I had to choose," I admitted.

"She came here?" Kytrona asked again. "You had to face the fire of chaos?"

That was one way of putting it. "There was fire."

She nodded slowly, then sat on the stool and began to talk. "They say that all the great mages must face a trial, and they must confront their greatest fears. They are never the same after that, although they do not look any different, except in their eyes." She paused. "I have never looked into your eyes." She said that almost like a confession before she turned to me.

Abruptly, she looked away.

"I'm . . . sorry," I said. I just hoped it was the right word.

"You have no need to apologize."

"You looked away."

She gave me the faintest smile, then shook her head. "It is not you. It is me." But she would not say more.

At that moment, I could sense the faint black tie or link between us. It was stronger, or at least clearer. Was that because I could sense it better, or because we were more linked?

"You need more words," Kytrona said, but she pointed to the door.

After that, we worked on words, and I kept trying to re-order the oak.

That night, I knew I had to do something more, and I struggled with the wood of the heavy oak door, trying to move the strength of the door away from the hinges and lock and into the center.

I kept at it until I almost passed out, and I didn't wake until it was full light.

When I got up, I examined the inside of the heavy door. Had I really accomplished anything? I thought I could detect a whiteness around the iron straps and hinges. I pressed my fingers there. The wood did give some, but not enough to tear away from the iron. I couldn't help but smile for a brief moment.

Before that long, Kytrona was shoved into my cell. She had not been abused more, but she looked exhausted.

"Are you . . . good?"

"I'm fine." She offered a tired smile. "We need to work on more words." Her eyes flicked toward the door.

I realized that I could sense two figures outside the cell. I held up two fingers and nodded toward the door.

Her mouth opened. Then she shut it. For perhaps the first time, I saw hope in her eyes. She swallowed, then began to speak. "This is a door." She pointed to the iron. "These are made of iron . . ."

Not until the listeners left did I say anything but repeat her words.

"I . . . make the door strong here . . . less strong here . . ." When she didn't seem to understand what I was saying, I took her hand and pressed her fingers against the rock-hard center of the door, and then guided them to the softer wood around the iron. I didn't want to let go of her hand, but I did.

"It needs more work," she said, stepping away from me and the door.

I nodded. "But . . ." How could I explain that if I made it weak enough and if the guard stood right outside we could push it over on him? "We push it . . ." I acted out what we could do.

She tilted her head to one side, as if thinking, then nodded. "That would work."

I kept working on the door while she talked, and I repeated words. That went on for another two days. When the guards pushed Kytrona into the cell three mornings later, I actually held the door to support it. I'd done my best to leave the area around the lock and outside hasp stronger.

While she talked, and I tried to repeat her words, I concentrated on moving the black order from around the lock. I had to stop several times, because I got light-headed, and it was into the afternoon when I began to sense that the door was sagging on both its lock plate and hinges.

"Now . . ." I pointed to the door.

"We need to get the guard here," she said. "Can you tell when he's close to the door?"

I nodded.

"Let me know when he's near."

How long that took, I didn't know, but it seemed like forever before I could sense the guard and said, "He's close."

Abruptly, Kytrona began to moan, loudly, even while she stood on the lock side of the door. I stood by the hinges, waiting as the guard moved toward the door.

When he was as close as he could get, peeping through the small hole in the center of the door, I said, "Now."

We pushed, and the heavy door ripped away from the hinges and lock. The guard scrambled back. I thought the door would bring him down, but the wood around the bottom hinge hung on and swung away from him. That didn't stop Kytrona.

The guard stared. He was frozen for a moment, and in that moment, she leaped on him, kneed him in the groin, and then slammed the iron cuffs upward into his chin so hard that his head snapped back, and he went down on the stone with a dull thud. Before I could scramble around the section of the door that hung on the lower hinge, she'd taken his belt knife and slit his throat.

With what I knew she'd been through, I didn't blame her.

She rose, and slipped the knife into the empty sheath at her belt. Then she unfastened the guard's scabbard and fastened it to her belt—with the sabre in it.

"Now what?" I asked.

"We wait."

"Wait?"

"The head guard will come." She raised her chained hands. "He has keys."

Outside of a U.S. Navy bolt-cutter that didn't exist in Worrak, or a blacksmith, I didn't see any other way of getting the chains off her.

"This way." Kytrona led the way to the bottom of the stone steps, holding the sabre in her right hand, her left hand all too close to it because of the chains. There, we waited, each of us concealed on opposite sides of the stone arch.

We waited until the light began to fail before we heard boots on the stone. The only problem was that the head guard didn't come down the stairs alone. He came down first, but behind and above him several steps was another man. The second man radiated white—Guillum.

I didn't know what to say, and anything I said to Kytrona would alert the white mage.

The head guard had just reached the bottom of the steps and stepped through the archway when Guillum yelled, "Look out!"

The head guard turned, and Kytrona's sabre went into his side. He staggered toward me.

Whhssst! A firebolt whizzed past my face, then another . . . and another, as the mage ran down the steps and toward the arch.

I grabbed the wounded guard. When I sensed that Guillum was about to throw another of the firebolts, I shoved the guard at the mage and flattened myself behind the back side of the archway.

The sound of the firebolt and the scream of the guard as the fire struck him merged. The sound was appalling and—thankfully—brief.

Somehow, Kytrona had followed the guard's body and used the sabre on the mage. Whiteness and fire flared around the blade, and I could smell burned hair.

Two bodies lay on the stone. One was blackened. The other was not a young man, but a wizened old man. He didn't look at all the way he had moments before.

I just looked.

"Chaos ages one." Kytrona pulled a key ring off the dead guard's belt and fumbled with the key.

One key stood out. I pointed, then helped her unlock the cuffs. Her wrists were scabbed and bloody. I couldn't help but squeeze her forearm gently, wishing I could heal all she had been through.

"You are . . ." She shook her head.

"What next?"

"This way. We find a way to escape from the keep and get to the harbor. We steal a fishing boat and head west. If we are fortunate, someone picks us up. If not, we sail to Ruzor. Or we do not."

The first two possibilities were probably okay. The third wasn't, and it was the most likely, but staying in Gaylmassen's pile of stone would be even worse. "What about the screams?"

"There are always screams from down here." She started up the stairs. The sabre was back in the scabbard.

Gaylmassen's keep wasn't really a castle, but more like a fortified house. It would have been dramatic to say that we had to fight our way out. We didn't. We sneaked out through the kitchen bailey. Along the way, several attendants scattered away from us. Gaylmassen was nowhere near, but that was fine with me. I didn't need to confront him in order to prove I wasn't taking the easy way out. There is a difference between necessary courage and stupid bravado. Papaw had known that, and now I understood.

In the darkness, it was even easier to steal a boat, but I had to row us clear of the harbor, and that took much of the night. Once we were outside the breakwater, there was a breeze, and

Kytrona knew enough to set the single sail. I didn't even try to explain that I knew nothing about sailing.

VIII

The next morning we were almost a mile offshore, and Worrak lay out of sight to the east of us. The sun beat down like a furnace all that day, and we managed to use a scrap of sail as an awning of sorts, probably the same way the boat owner had.

Kytrona finally looked to me. "I did not think we would ever escape. Thank you."

I could feel gratitude and something more. I hoped it was more, but I could not act on such a feeling, not until she and I were free, and she could choose without conditions.

Her mouth dropped open. "You are honorable, like an angel."

"No," I said. "We wouldn't have escaped without you."

She frowned, as if she didn't believe me.

"If you had not explained about order, I would not have learned enough . . ."

"I wouldn't be alive if it weren't for you," she went on. "I still don't know much about you or where you come from. Tell me. We have time, now."

"From Earth . . ."

"From the ground?"

"Another . . . place . . . we were fighting a fire in the *Forrestal* . . . one of the attack birds dropped a rocket, and it armed . . ." For a lot of the words, I had to use English, but she listened. I didn't know how much she understood.

"What is this *Forrestal*?"

I tried to explain a bird-farm.

"You come from where the Ancient angels came?"

I was definitely no ancient, ancient or modern, or whenever or wherever Recluce might be. "No."

"But the *Book of Ryba* speaks of iron ships that flew between the stars."

Between the stars? That was even scarier. *When* was I?

"You have to be like an angel. You still grope for words, but you speak without an accent, and everyone not born in Recluce has an accent."

I tried to get across that I was no angel and that CVA-59 had not flown between stars. I could feel that Kytrona was still impressed by the "iron birds"—that was the best I could do with what I knew of Low Temple.

Two days passed, and we talked and sailed some distance west of Worrak, which was the only direction we could go, because that was the direction the wind blew us. While we had taken some water bottles, they were long empty, and Kytrona was trying to steer us back inshore, now that we were well away from Worrak. We'd seen several ships in the distance, but none close enough to hail.

"We can't get picked up if we're too close to shore, but we need water," Kytrona said.

My lips were cracked, but not so badly as hers. I just nodded.

"It's too bad you can't call a storm the way the weather mages can." She smiled. It was more like a grimace.

I had to wonder if such mages existed. If I could weaken a heavy solid-oak door, then I supposed they could call a storm, but I had no idea how, and neither did Kytrona.

Then she pointed. A ship was headed eastward in our general direction. She swung the sail, and we turned seaward. For a time, nothing seemed to happen. Then, all of a sudden, the ship was bearing down on us. She was a wooden-hulled steamer, but the engines were clearly shut down. Her three masts were filled with sails.

Kytrona stood. I sat.

"She's bearing the Ryall. It's a Recluce merchanter!"

For some reason, I had very mixed feelings about the approaching ship.

Before that long, a seaman threw us a line, but the ship barely slowed. Kytrona tied the line to an iron ring attached to the stem post. Then the crew reeled us in until we were alongside. They even lowered a ladder. Kytrona climbed up first. That was a good idea, since I wouldn't be able to explain much of anything.

Once we were on deck, a slender but tall man wearing the same black clothes as Kytrona moved toward us. He smiled broadly. "Kytrona! We feared everyone on the *Black Holding* was lost." Then he stepped forward and threw his arms around her.

I tried not to wince. She hadn't promised me anything, and I was a stranger from nowhere, so far as she was concerned.

"Alaren . . ." Kytrona stepped back, out of his arms, and gestured to me. "This is Cassius. He's an outland black mage, and he's the one who saved me from Gaylmassen. He showed up on board the *Black Holding.*"

I bowed politely. "It is good to meet you."

"It's good to meet the man who saved Kytrona." Alaren eyed me with open curiosity, although he had to look up some, then glanced to Kytrona, questioningly.

"The Ancient of angels has tried him and found him worthy. He will be a great mage." She smiled warmly—at me. "Even if She had not tested him, he would still be my intended."

Alaren stepped back.

I swallowed. I had never asked her, although I had dreamed.

"How could I not love a man who saved my life three times, and only asked for my respect?"

That was true enough, but how had she known?

Later, after we had cleaned up and had fresh clothes, we stood by the railing.

She took my hands. "I promised myself to you the day you knelt and kissed my hand. I could see the love and the concern. Then, before long, I could feel it." She looked down. "I had to work so hard not to let you know. Not until we were free."

That I understood.

My fingers touched the edge of her jaw, and she lifted her head. I looked into her eyes, realizing that they were not muddy green, but golden green.

Sometimes, even those things that are lost, forgotten, or passed on almost unremarked have their own stories.

BURNING DUTY

You want to know why I made you sit in that chair, Fedryrk, when I was doubtful about the truth of your words? Well . . . now that you've got children of your own, I'll tell you, and I'll even let you have the chair if you're so inclined. You must know by now, seeing how often you had to sit there, that it's not just a chair. Any time I thought you weren't telling the truth, or all of it, I sat you down in it until you got to be looking mighty uncomfortable. You remember that, I'd wager. How did I get the chair? That's a story in itself. It all happened before you were born, not long after your ma and I were married.

Stefanyk stood at his post just outside the bailey door of the Prefect's palace. His post was one of the least desirable for the Prefect's guards. It was so undesirable that it was almost always assigned to the most junior guard in that duty shift. He was the most junior. The only consolation was that he was assigned to the mid-afternoon to evening shift and the area around the north-facing door was in shadow most of the time.

He didn't worry too much when the alarm bell began clanging from the front of the palace, although he did check his gear and survey the empty bailey to see if a thief had come over the side wall. There were no thieves . . . or anyone else, not for a quarter of a glass after the bell stopped. Then the outer gate opened, and a squad of regular troopers marched into the bailey, arraying themselves as if they expected an attack of some sort. But who would attack the palace in the middle of Fenard?

He shook his head. He'd heard that some of the regulars were having trouble with the Autarch of Kyphros, but they all said the Kyphrans never crossed the borders. Besides, the border was more than a hundred kays away.

Then the palace door opened, and an officer peered out. After a moment, his eyes landed on Stefanyk. "Guard! You!"

"Yes, ser?"

"I need you inside."

"But . . . I can't abandon my post, not without authorization or my relief, ser."

"The outer door is more than safe enough with a squad of troopers there. Now! Move! This way."

There wasn't much else Stefanyk could do except obey. "Yes, ser!" He hurried toward the door.

"The second door on the right—the open one. Go in there and wait. Don't touch anything. I'll be right behind you."

"Yes, ser." Stefanyk walked quickly toward the open door, but if he was being ordered in as a shield, he wanted to be prepared. So he drew the shorter blade used for guard duty before he stepped into the chamber.

He almost stopped just inside the door, but managed several more steps into what had to be a study. The walls were paneled in golden wood, and a huge desk and a matching chair stood in one corner, and a round table in the other, surrounded by four chairs . . . except he saw a fifth lying on its back on the heavy woolen gold-and-blue carpet. Lying beside the overturned chair, one on each side, were two men, elite guards in their black tunics, trimmed in brilliant blue. One of them didn't seem to be breathing. There was no one else in the study.

Stefanyk just stared.

"Soldier! Put your hand on that black chair there."

Stefanyk looked back at the captain, confused because he was a guard, not a trooper.

"Just put your hand on it! The one on the floor."

Stefanyk could sense the anger and exasperation in the officer's voice. He reached down and brushed the top of the chair.

"On it!"

Stefanyk grabbed the top of the back of the chair with his free hand.

"Pick it up!"

The bewildered guard did so.

"Carry it out to the rear courtyard out to the burn yard. Put it in the burn pit. Leave it there and come back and carry the other four out."

Stefanyk wasn't about to question that order, not with the way the captain had looked at him. He set the chair upright, replaced his blade, then picked up the chair once more and made his way out of the study, carrying the chair back along the service hallway leading to the bailey door. He did see more of the elite guards stationed along the wider hallway toward the center of the palace.

As he walked toward the open courtyard door, he wondered why the captain was so insistent on burning the chairs. The one he carried felt cool to the touch, and yet somehow warm. But . . . if the captain wanted the chairs in the burn pit, what else could Stefanyk do?

He kept walking, out through the door and then at an angle across the wide and long north courtyard to the gate on the far end that led into the service courtyard. He had to put down the chair to unlatch the gate and open it. He felt like holding his nose when he stepped into the service courtyard that held the burn pit because of the stench from the adjoining rendering yard. A lower stone wall, a little over two yards high, separated the burn yard from the rendering yard, where all the waste offal and animal parts were carelessly and quickly dumped into a score of huge barrels, usually by the kitchen help. In the middle of the service yard was the fire pit, a circle a good five yards across, the edge being a wall of sooty and cracked bricks a yard high.

When he reached the pit, Stefanyk thought about throwing the chair into the pit, but, as his eyes took in the elegant lines and smooth finish of the dark wood—dark oak, he thought, or maybe even lorken—he decided against doing that.

"Not until you've carried out all five," he said to himself.

Instead, he set the chair beside the low wall of the fire pit and walked back across the yard to the door and made his way back to the Prefect's study, where the captain still stood, watching. The two bodies had been removed.

Stefanyk picked up the second chair, carried it out of the palace and to the service courtyard, where he set it beside the first.

Then he looked at the two chairs, identical and beautiful. He looked around the burn yard. There was half a squad in the bailey, guarding both the palace door and the bailey . . . and the entry to the burn yard, but he was alone with the chairs in the burn yard itself. He glanced around once more, then sat in one of the chairs. Somehow, sitting in it made him feel calmer. Finally, he rose and looked around. The burn yard was still empty.

He *knew* he had to have at least one of the chairs. But how would he ever manage getting it out of the burn yard . . . and over the walls . . . or out through the rear refuse gates, past the outer guards?

His eyes strayed to the rendering yard, and he hurried through the ungated opening, quickly glancing around. He quickly checked the line of barrels careful not to brush against them with his uniform. That required some contortions, but he was rewarded. There was an empty rendering barrel. In fact, there was a line of empties.

Stefanyk smiled. Then walked back to the burn pit and carried one of the chairs into the rendering yard, easing it into an empty barrel and then rolling the empty across to the line of barrels that were full, then squeezing it between two others. It took him several moments to find an end and wedge it in place, at least well enough that the barrel looked full.

Only then did he return to the Prefect's study for the other chairs. When he returned for the fifth chair, the captain followed him out to the burn yard.

As Stefanyk set the fourth chair beside the other three, the captain demanded, "Where's the other chair? I only see four."

"I already put it in the burn pit," replied Stefanyk.

"Let's see." The captain marched up to the pit and studied the ashes and the few coals remaining from what had been burned earlier.

The guard's guts tightened, but he remained calm. He was counting on the fact that the captain wouldn't think of the rendering yard and that, if he did, he wouldn't look in every barrel.

"I don't see anything that looks like it burned."

"It was there," insisted Stefanyk, trying to keep his voice firm and strong. "It was. Maybe it burned already."

The captain walked to the entrance to the rendering yard and peered into it, then walked back to the burn pit, then looked at the ashes and embers in the middle of the burn pit.

Finally, he shrugged. "The chairs are out of the palace. Put the others in the pit."

Stefanyk slowly lifted the first chair into the pit.

"Put it in deep enough so that the embers will catch the wood on fire."

It took all of Stefanyk's willpower to do that, not just for the first chair, but for each of the four. Then he and the captain waited for them to catch fire. It took quite a while, but the captain did not comment.

When all four chairs were finally blazing, the officer turned to Stefanyk. "You can return to your post, guard."

"Yes, ser." Stefanyk marched back to the bailey door and resumed his post.

Shortly, the captain returned and, without looking at Stefanyk, re-entered the palace.

More than half a glass later, another officer appeared, and ordered the squad of troopers out of the north courtyard. Even at the end of his duty, no one told Stefanyk what had happened inside the palace.

While Stefanyk had hoped to reclaim the chair before the renderer arrived to pick up the barrels, something else happened at the palace—far worse, he judged, since all the elite guards surrounded the place the next day, and the word was that several officers had just dropped dead, and that there was a black mage on the loose. With elite guards and troopers everywhere, Stefanyk could do nothing, especially since he'd been moved to duty guarding the side gates, except wait each morning at the end of the alley that ran past the palace—wearing a ragged shirt and old trousers—hoping to see the renderer before his afternoon guard shift began.

Three mornings later, Stefanyk saw the rendering wagon, with the gray-haired Raestel on the seat, turn into the alley, creaking toward the palace and the rear gates of the rendering yard. He stepped out of the early morning shadows.

"I'll help you, old man," offered Stefanyk, as the rendering wagon creaked toward the rear gates of the rendering yard.

"You're the young guard, aren't you? Mairie's boy?" Raestel tried to straighten up and look more intently at Stefanyk. "What are you trying to get out of the palace?"

"A chair that the Prefect wanted to burn. My wife and I . . . we could use it."

"How would helping me do that?"

"I hid it in a rendering barrel."

The old man laughed. "Any man who'd hide a broken chair, even a sound one, in a rendering barrel deserves it! Meet me at my place when you get off duty."

"Thank you." Stefanyk could only hope that the chair was still there.

He was still worrying after his duty shift as he hurried through the dimly lit streets of Fenard out toward the section that held the refuse gatherers, the rag-pickers, and the rendering yards.

He needn't have worried. The chair, if dripping some grease and a redolence of rendering yard, was waiting for him on the sagging side porch of the structure that served as the renderer's dwelling.

"I can see why you wanted it." Raestel's bloodshot eyes surveyed the lines of the somewhat greasy-looking chair. "Good work. You know why the Prefect wanted it burned?"

"No one ever said. They made me carry it. No one wanted to touch it."

The renderer shook his head. "Must be cursed. You sure you want it?"

Stefanyk nodded. "It's not cursed. Not for me."

"Could be the curse was just for the Prefect. Heard tell of

things like that. Strange happenings around the palace this eightday."

"No one tells guards anything, not the outside guards. A curse on the Prefect won't mean anything to us. I thought Baryna would like a fine chair like this. She deserves it."

"Deserves the man who risks so much to get it for her. Better cover it with rags when you take it."

Even walking home in the darkness, carrying the chair, Stefanyk didn't feel worried, but once he was back in the two rooms he and Baryna shared in Maman Surtyn's, it took two full glasses and most of the rags he had to remove the stench and the last of the grease.

"I won't sit in that," Baryna declared.

Stefanyk took a small square of white cloth and ran it over the entire chair, then showed it to his wife. "See?"

"You sit in it."

He did, for a time, and it was as though many of his worries vanished. Finally, he rose and turned to her. "You sit in it. You'll see."

Gingerly, she lowered herself into the chair. A puzzled expression crossed her face. "There's a comfort in it. You didn't just get it from Raestel. Where did it come from?"

"You can't tell anyone."

"You didn't steal it?"

"Not exactly. The owner didn't like it. He wanted it burned." Stefanyk smiled. He could have seated himself in the chair and said the same thing, word for word.

That's how it happened. Oh . . . it was useful a few other times as well, like when your sister—she couldn't have been a year old— when she got a terrible flux and like on died. Your ma thought I was crazy, but I wrapped her in blankets and turned the chair into a crib of sorts, and tilted it so I could sit on a stool and rock her. Anyway, after that night she got better, grew up strong and tall like the rest of you. Don't know as that would work now, but it did then. Anyway . . . any time you want to take the chair, it's yours for the asking. Fine piece of furniture even now. Doesn't look like it's older than you are, more like almost fresh-crafted . . .

Sometimes, readers want to know what happened to a character . . . looking for some sort of resolution . . . but I have my doubts if that resolution turns out exactly as they expected, just as is often the case in life.

WORTH

I

Late on twoday afternoon, Martenya watched as the blonde woman in the worn fringed leathers rode up the main street of Llysen, a single long blade at her left hip, and a knife not quite so long at the right. Her hair was cut short, not quite raggedly, and it was so fine that even the slight breeze of early fall ruffled it. Even from twenty yards, the patroller could see the weary wariness of the rider. So she waited until the stranger dismounted and tied her mount to the short railing in front of the chandlery before stepping out of the afternoon shadows toward the broad-shouldered and long-legged woman, a woman almost as tall as Martenya herself.

The stranger stopped and surveyed the patroller.

Martenya let her, then asked, "Where are you bound from?"

"Sarronnyn. Kyphros before that." The stranger's brown-flecked green eyes hardened.

"And before Kyphros?"

"Why are you asking me all that?" demanded the blonde.

"Because I'm a patroller of the Marshal, and it's my job."

"Is this Southwind . . . or Recluce?" Bitterness tinged the words as the stranger's eyes quickly took in the patroller's blue sleeveless tunic and the white long-sleeved undertunic before lingering on the twin blades at Martenya's wide belt.

"It's Southwind, and the Marshal doesn't care who you are and where you come from. She only cares whether you obey the laws and contribute something to the land." Martenya paused, then added, "Unless you're just passing through, and then you only need to obey the laws."

"Sounds as bad as Recluce." The stranger's lips curled into an expression somewhere between a sneer and disgust.

"We don't much care whether you're white or black, so long as you keep it to yourself," replied the patroller.

"Part of your laws?"

"You might say that." Martenya made the effort to smile politely. "You look like you've been a blade for hire."

"I have. When they'd pay me what I'm worth."

Martenya waited again before speaking. "There's not much call for blades here."

"You're wearing them."

"All patrollers do. That's why there's not much call for them by anyone else . . . anywhere in Southwind."

"So no one goes against the Marshal."

"So no one does anything hurtful or against the laws . . . and no one forces anyone else to. If you have a problem with that," replied Martenya evenly, "Southwind might not be the best place for you."

"I won't be bothering anyone," said the broad-shouldered woman. "Where would be a good place to stay that's clean and cheap?"

"The hostels begin one block down. Women's is one block down on the right, men's three on the left, and the family hostel is two on the left. Copper a night. Special arrangements if you have no coin."

"Slop and clean chores?"

"Unless you've got other talents besides spreading your legs or using a blade," replied Martenya with a lazy smile.

"Who determines that?"

"The hostel mistress. Who else? The mistress of the women's hostel is Eliendra. Words don't impress her."

"Thank you," replied the stranger.

"What name do you go by?"

"Wrynn."

"When did you leave Recluce?" That was a guess on Martenya's part, if not much of one, given the blades and Wrynn's attitude.

A momentary look of surprise was followed by the clipped words, "A few years ago. Maybe longer. I haven't kept track."

"And the women of Candar have disappointed you."

"Why do you say that?"

"Because of where you've been and where you've left."

"I think I'll be heading to the hostel." Wrynn turned, looked at the chandlery, then walked back toward her mount.

Martenya watched silently, wondering just how long the stranger would remain in Southwind.

II

The sun was still above the horizon when Martenya walked through the door of the small cottage on the side lane that ran parallel to the main avenue, if a good hundred yards higher on the sloping ground to the north of the main part of the town. Still . . . she knew it wouldn't be that long before twilight cloaked the hills to the north of Llysen.

She couldn't help thinking about the stranger as she removed her patroller's belt.

"Why are you so out of sorts?" The slender brunette wearing a splattered apron stood in the door from the kitchen, looking up to her taller partner.

"Out of sorts?"

"You didn't say a word when you came in."

"I'm sorry. I had to deal with another one of those Recluce types. Thank the Legend that there aren't that many of them."

"Dangergelders?" asked Paemina. "Isn't that what they call them?"

"I don't much care what they call them. This one makes a hill cat defending her young seem sweet . . . except that she's the kind of cat who'd likely eat her young."

"I can see that she made a good impression on you. Does she have any talents?"

"She's a blade and likely better than most. Recluce-trained, and she hates men. That's the way it feels."

"It's too bad she didn't go to Kyphros. Or Sarronnyn."

"She did. She didn't like either place. They didn't pay her what she was worth, I gather. Or what she thought she was worth."

Paemina shook her head. "I don't see that if she's any good. Not with the Autarch. Or the Tyrant."

Martenya had the feeling that the exile was good with a blade . . . but she didn't know. "Even the Autarch wants arms-trained women to work their way up. She and the Marshal aren't much different in that."

"That's because they believe in what works." Paemina paused. "I fixed lemon scones to go with the leftover mutton and lace potatoes . . . and some greens. And Minaeya is napping right now. I don't think that will last."

Martenya smiled, at the thought of both their daughter waking in the middle of dinner and the lemon scones.

III

Martenya didn't see the stranger from Recluce on threeday, or fourday, and she half-wondered if Wrynn had headed out, although she questioned where else the Recluce exile could go that she found any more to her liking, since the stranger had apparently passed through most of the lands of Candar and found none to her liking. Only Delapra and possibly Jerans remained. Delapra was essentially under Hamor's heavy thumb, and the Hamorians didn't care much for free-spirited women. The Jeranyi still remained horse-nomads at heart, and Martenya had doubts that Wrynn wanted to spend most of her life in the saddle, any kind of saddle.

Martenya had fiveday off and sixday as well. On sevenday she had the early shift, and it was some two glasses past dawn when she walked toward the women's hostel. To her surprise, she saw the Recluce dangergelder on a ladder, replacing one of the second-story shutters. She waited until Wrynn finished and climbed down the ladder.

The exile with a face more weathered than her years glared at the patroller.

"I thought you were a blade, not a carpenter," said Martenya mildly.

"I've more than a few skills. The old shutter was rotten. So I crafted a new one. Eliendra got the wood. I did the rest. I don't do slop and cleanup."

Martenya looked up at the shutter. To her untrained eyes, the new one, stained to match the old one, looked more finished than the older shutter. "What else can you do?"

"Most anything that needs to be done."

"Do you prefer being a blade?"

"There's no doubt of my worth there. It's hard to argue that

I'm not worth my coins when I've disarmed, wounded, or . . . disabled someone."

Martenya had the feeling that Wrynn had almost said something else, but before she could reply, the other went on.

"Besides, when you're hired to protect someone or some place, that's worth it. Isn't that one reason you're a patroller?"

Martenya couldn't argue that. Not directly. "It's especially gratifying when you can protect people without drawing iron."

"That's not always possible. Then what do you do?"

"Act as quickly as practical with the least blood possible."

"Then you're not so different as you think." Wrynn turned and eased the heavy ladder away from the hostel wall, lowered it, and, after shifting her grip, walked away from Martenya, carrying the ladder as if it weighed no more than a light stick.

"Not so different as you think?" murmured Martenya to herself. How could she not be different from the angry and hostile exile?

Even so, those words worried at her for the rest of her shift, and she couldn't put them aside. She was still thinking about them when she walked through the cottage door at close to fifth glass.

"You're a bit later than usual," called Paemina, from where she stood by the kitchen table. "What happened?"

"Nothing special." Martenya unbuckled the patroller's equipment belt with the twin blades and hung it on the special wall rack that Paemina had crafted for her, then walked into the kitchen. "Except that I ran into that dangergelder again."

"She's still here?"

"She's doing work for Eliendra. Carpentry."

"Maybe she'll find a place and stay."

"Maybe."

"You don't think so?"

"I don't know, but there's something about her that goes against my grain." Martenya shook her head.

Paemina studied her partner for a moment, then glanced from Martenya to the cradle in the nook, carefully covered with wide-weave linen to allow air to circulate but to keep the mosquitoes and other insects from Minaeya, just barely two months old.

"How is her rash?" asked Martenya.

"The brinn anointment seems to be working."

"I can't help but worry." At Paemina's slight frown, Martenya quickly added, "I know I haven't said much . . . but I do worry. She's still so tiny."

Paemina nodded. "She is. But she's healthy."

"Were you that small?"

"My mother said I was."

Neither mentioned whether Adonal had been that small as a child, necessary as he had been if they were to have a child. Martenya still wasn't certain whether she felt relieved or sad that Paemina had been the one fortunate enough to conceive . . . or whether she ever wanted to try again, understanding as Adonal had been.

Abruptly, Martenya saw, as if for the first time, the dark circles under her partner's eyes. "Dear . . . you need to sit down. I can finish fixing dinner. You'll have to feed her later."

"I can . . ." Paemina stopped. "You're right. Thank you."

"Just put the stool where you can watch her." Martenya moved to the table and picked up the knife.

IV

Another eightday passed before Martenya saw Wrynn again . . . once more outside the women's hostel. The dangergelder was carrying out a large oblong of wood, a good yard and a half wide and half a yard high, and Martenya belatedly realized that the space over the main entry to the hostel that usually held the signboard was vacant, and the heavy wooden ladder was positioned against the wall next to the entry.

As Wrynn set down the new signboard, leaning it against the old brick of the lower wall, Martenya studied it. The graceful letters were not just painted, but carved into the wood and then painted in black, standing out against the golden oak. The gleaming finish of the signboard indicated that it had also been varnished to seal the wood and the letters.

Martenya had to admit that the new signboard was a great improvement over the old one. "I like your signboard. It's well-done."

"I don't do anything that's not workmanlike or better." Before Martenya could reply, Wrynn added, "Don't tell me that I'd fit in well in Southwind. Eliendra's told me that a score of times already."

"Then I won't."

"Good." Wrynn picked up the heavy signboard with one hand, hammer in the other, and climbed up the ladder.

Martenya wasn't sure how she managed it, but the exile produced a wooden bracket from somewhere and tapped it carefully until the signboard was in place.

After that, Wrynn painstakingly fastened the signboard permanently in place, not by nailing it directly, but by using five more shaped wooden brackets, similar if not identical to the first, all of which she carefully nailed into position with the heavy hammer, leaving the signboard itself unmarked. Then she descended the ladder, nodded to Martenya, and carried the ladder and hammer around the side of the hostel.

As Martenya turned and began to walk back up the street away from the women's hostel, she couldn't help but think about the exile and her unwillingness to accept praise or, apparently, to be satisfied with anything anywhere. At the same time, Martenya wondered if she was being fair to Wrynn, since she had no real idea about what the other woman had experienced, either in Recluce or elsewhere in Candar.

V

The following threeday morning, Martenya was about to set out for the patrol station when a patrol runner, a girl in the uniform white and blue, appeared at the door of their cottage. Martenya recognized the runner, but could not immediately recall her name.

"Patroller Martenya?"

"Yes?"

"Patrol Captain Tyana requests that you not report until the fourth glass of the afternoon."

"Did she tell you to give me a reason?"

"No, ser. She said she would explain when you came in."

"Tell the captain that I'll be there."

The young runner nodded, then turned and trotted down the narrow hill lane.

Martenya walked back into the cottage and looked at her partner. "Don't bother with supper. The captain moved me to the evening shift. I don't know why." She paused. "I'm sorry. I don't know what I did."

"It might not be you," replied Paemina softly.

"I hope not." Even so, Martenya wondered.

She was still pondering what she might have done wrong when she walked into the patrol station a little before fourth glass. She didn't have to wonder long because Captain Tyana crossed the receiving room and looked up at Martenya.

"There's a Hamorian trader and his guards staying at the Black Pony. That's why I changed your shift."

"For a trader?"

"For a *Hamorian* trader with ten armed guards. For a Hamorian who has been scornful of the Marshal. Loudly and in public."

"Are they already in the public room there?"

Tyana nodded. "Nothing's happened yet. Keep your round close to the inn. I'll have Stacia cover the blocks to the north. When it gets dark, I'll send Keirin to back you up."

Martenya nodded, wondering what else the captain knew that had her so concerned.

"Just a feeling," added Tyana, in response to the unvoiced question likely indicated by Martenya's expression.

"I'll start there and spend a few moments talking to the servers."

"Sometimes that helps," replied the captain.

Martenya understood that Tyana felt the Hamorian trader's presence wasn't one of those times. "I'll check frequently."

Tyana nodded.

Less than a quarter glass later, Martenya walked toward the front entrance of the Black Pony. No one was near the alarm bell by the door, but she entered the inn cautiously, moving quietly through the doors and toward the public room.

She stopped at the archway and surveyed the chamber, taking in the aged oak tables, chairs, and backless benches—and their occupants. Outside of two white-haired men and three women, the normally crowded public room was empty.

Dehlya, the heavy-set proprietor, coming from the back hall, stepped up beside the patroller. "Hamorian bastards. Scared off most of the regulars and then left."

"Did they lift iron?" asked Martenya. "Or clubs?"

"No. They might as well have, though." She shook her head. "They said they'd be back."

"Do you think they will be?"

"Who knows? They might be. Or they might have said that to keep everyone else away."

Either was possible, Martenya thought. Just to see if the trader and his guards might return soon, she talked to Dehlya for perhaps a fifth of a glass before leaving the inn.

She saw no sign of the Hamorians on the main street as she walked south, but she also looked behind her frequently. The fact that the sidewalks were far quieter and markedly less crowded than usual in the late afternoon suggested that the Hamorians had been there not long before.

Martenya continued to walk another three blocks before she turned and began to retrace her steps back toward the Black Pony, not her usual round, but she doubted there would be problems from the shops and dwellings on the side blocks and she was close enough to them that she could hear an alarm bell if any were rung.

She was less than a block from the inn when she heard the frantic ringing of an alarm accompanied by a high-pitched yelling.

"Help! The patrol!"

Martenya increased her swift walk to a lope along the main street toward the Black Pony. When she reached the front of the inn, she saw a young server, barely more than a girl, who stood by the bell just outside the main entrance to the inn, holding a ripped blouse at the shoulder with one hand, the other on the stout post supporting the alarm bell and bronze mounting frame.

"The Hamorians," she gasped. "They . . . they . . ." She shuddered.

"Did they hurt you?"

"They would have . . . Hurry! They're after Dehlya."

Martenya moved swiftly through the half-open door and through the entry hall to the square arch leading into the public room. From the archway, she could see the stout proprietor using a stool to fend off a bearded man with a long blade, while three other guards on the other side of the public room laughed raucously. Drawing both her blades, she moved from the entry toward the Hamorian attacking Dehlya.

Martenya sensed another figure entering the public room behind her and hoped it was Keirin or Stacia, but she had no time to look because one of the watching Hamorians yelled something and the bearded guard whirled and thrust the long blade toward the patroller.

Martenya parried the blade effortlessly, catching sight, out of the corner of her eye, of the Hamorian guards closing in on a single figure. She pushed away that image and concentrated on the tall and muscular guard with the long blade who once more lunged toward her.

At the last moment, she stepped to the side, twisting away from the long blade, then used the shortsword in her left hand, not to thrust or slash, but to bring the unsharpened section just below the hilt down on the back of the Hamorian's wrist. The dull snap indicated that something had broken, and the big blade spun away. The Hamorian reached for the long dagger at his hip, then decided against it as Martenya's left blade hovered under his chin.

"On the floor, facedown . . . or you're dead," she snapped.

Slowly, the wounded man dropped to the floor.

"Hands and arms out!"

Only when the guard was prone did Martenya look farther away than the area around her.

The single figure on the other side of the public room now

faced but a single Hamorian, and, with a movement so fast that Martenya didn't believe it, separated the man from his blade, then turned to look at the stunned trader, his back against the wall. One man lay on the floor, and another cradled an injured right arm.

"Now . . . what was that you were saying about women?"

Martenya didn't know whether to smile or curse as she recognized both the voice and the face. She did neither, but kicked the blade she'd removed from the man who'd attacked her under the nearest table and walked over to the trader.

"Patroller . . . is this how—"

"Enough!" snapped Martenya. "You have one glass to leave Llysen. I saw enough. Your man attacked the proprietor, who didn't even have a weapon."

"He said all women were sluts," called Dehlya from several yards away. "He ripped poor Selica's blouse open."

"You did all that," said Martenya. "Your man drew steel after attacking a mere girl. He and you and your guards were looking for a fight. They got it. Now, get out."

"But . . ."

"You were told that drawing blades except in self-defense was forbidden."

"Our honor was insulted." The trader drew himself up. "They said we were cowards."

"Cowards with blades!" interjected Dehlya.

"If the first way you seek to prove your honor is with cold iron," declared Martenya, "then you had no honor to begin with. You have one glass."

"And then what if we don't?"

"You will leave, one way or another," Martenya said quietly. "As ashes on the wind, or under your own power."

"That is not honorable."

"Do not talk of honor. You are a trader. Your only honor is to golds. Golds and silvers deserve no honor. One glass."

Martenya turned abruptly and slashed.

A blade clunked on the wooden floor, and the guard who had tried to sneak up on her looked stupidly at the slash across the back of his hand, deep enough to have hit and broken bones, and the blood welling up across his flesh.

"The next one who tries anything is dead."

"If they're that fortunate."

The low words came from Wrynn.

The trader swallowed.

"One glass," Martenya repeated. "Any blade that's on the floor stays there."

The Hamorian merchant started to open his mouth, but shut it as he looked from Wrynn to Martenya.

Once the public room was largely clear, Martenya walked outside into the entry hall to where Wrynn now stood. "I appreciate the help. You'd make a good patroller."

"No. I nearly killed two of them. I would have if you hadn't been here. I don't have your self-control in dealing with greedy, stupid men."

"This doesn't happen often."

"I can see why," replied the dangergelder. "But you were too easy on them."

"No, I wasn't. They'll spend the rest of their lives, if they live that long, knowing that *mere* women defeated them . . . and could have killed them. The trader will know that as well." She paused. "Do you want to come with me and make sure that they leave in a glass?"

"Why not?"

The two women followed the trader and his guards out of the inn and into the darkness in which the Rational Stars blazed across the southern sky.

VI

After her report to Captain Tyana at the end of her shift on threeday night, Martenya wasn't totally surprised on fourday morning, when she reported for duty, to see Captain Tyana standing in a corner of the receiving room of the patrol station, talking to Wrynn. She eased closer, trying to overhear the conversation without being completely obvious.

". . . aren't you interested?" Tyana looked directly at the Recluce exile.

"You're all too calculating."

"Everyone with a brain calculates," replied the captain. "If they want to survive and succeed."

Wrynn shrugged. "That may be. I had a friend who told me that . . ."

"And?" pressed Tyana.

"She's likely now a captain for the Autarch. She'll still be answering to men with half her skills and abilities—"

"In Kyphros? I doubt it. If she is, it won't be for long. Besides, this is Southwind."

"That Hamorian guard ripped that girl's blouse off her and would have raped her right there on the floor if the innkeeper hadn't intervened. The innkeeper could have been killed if your patroller had been a few moments later."

"And you wouldn't have done anything?"

"Oh . . . I would have killed the bastard right there. But then I'd likely have had to run. Or risked justice here. That's the part I don't like. He should have been killed on the spot."

"He didn't rape the girl," Tyana pointed out. "He got a broken wrist, and we've sent word that Kanazar is unwelcome in Southwind and may never trade here again . . . on pain of death."

"Kanazar?"

"The trader. He lives for golds. We also sent his description with the dispatches."

"And you call that justice?" Wrynn shook her head. "It's little more than a slap on the wrist."

"If we had killed the guard, we'd still have to have prohibited Kanazar from returning. Otherwise, he'd be back in Southwind with more guards, and we'd end up killing even more people . . . and we'd likely have at least one girl actually raped. And if we make a habit of killing guards and other Hamorians who've been stopped from serious violence, then before long, Hamor would likely turn its warships on Southport. We'd prefer not to give them that kind of excuse."

"You may be right," conceded Wrynn. "So was Krys—my friend. I don't have to like it, and I can't be a part of something I don't like." After a pause, she added, "I appreciate your thinking of me, but I think I'd best be leaving."

"You won't find anyplace better," observed Tyana,

"I won't know that unless I see for myself." Wrynn gave a stiff nod, then turned and walked past Martenya, not even giving the patroller a glance.

Neither Tyana nor Martenya spoke until the Recluce exile had left the station.

"She'll be back," said the captain.

Martenya shook her head. "I don't think so. She's the type that will keep looking for what isn't there because she doesn't want to change what she believes. If her friend couldn't persuade her, I don't think we will."

"Too bad. It's a waste of talent." After a moment, the captain said, "You handled that well last night."

"It would have been worse without her."

"No. It would have been worse without you. You would have managed. Your shift today should be a lot easier."

Martenya hoped so as she signed the log, and then headed out on her first round of the day.

VII

A glass and a half later, on her second round, Martenya walked toward the women's hostel. She wasn't surprised to see the Recluce exile strapping her gear behind the saddle of her mount, but she didn't say anything until she neared Wrynn.

"I see you're leaving. Where are you bound?"

"I thought I'd go on to Southport. It's a city. If I don't like it there, I'll get a ship to somewhere else."

"Back to see your friend?"

Wrynn shook her head. "She's like you."

Martenya didn't say what she thought. She just nodded, then said, "Best of fortune."

Wrynn untied her mount and then vaulted into the saddle. She looked down at Martenya. "The same to you, patroller." Then she flicked the reins and guided her horse onto the main street, heading south.

The last aspect of Wrynn's gear that Martenya noted was the worn wooden handle of what looked to be a spare dagger strapped across the brown pack behind her saddle.

Martenya turned to see Eliendra standing by the hostel entry, under the signboard Wrynn had crafted, also looking at the departing rider.

"She can cook well enough to have her own café. She puts most carpenters to shame. She even did some masonry repairs. She could be anything," said Eliendra, "but she never will be. I don't understand some people."

"No," replied Martenya. "She's the one who doesn't understand people. Most folks are nice enough, but they expect others to do what they do without having to grovel or get out a whip to get them to do it. Wrynn wants everyone to be fair and honest, and to appreciate what she does before she does it, while she does it, and after she does it. That's asking too much of anyone."

"Sometimes . . . we're all like that," replied Eliendra with a faint smile. "And sometimes we don't appreciate others enough."

As the patroller thought about her own words, and those of Eliendra—and the fact that Wrynn had ridden away from her friend—Martenya vowed to tell Paemina just how much she appreciated everything her partner did . . . and to do so often.

After a last look to the south, she turned and resumed her round.

There are always endings . . . and this one also answers a question posed by several readers.

FAME

The boy paused at the low stone wall around the bronze statue that stood in the middle of the small square. He looked at the statue again, taking in the figure there, a man with some sort of tool in his hand, a wood plane perhaps. The statue was not particularly tall, just the height of a man, he thought, and the figure wore a crafter's or tradesman's leathers. There was a bronze plate at the base of the statue, he knew, but it was on the other side. He'd seen it often enough, but had never bothered to read it.

He took the last bite out of the apple he held and started to throw it at the statue.

"Don't be doing that, boy!" snapped a voice.

He turned to see a young woman wearing the uniform of the Autarch's Finest, looking at him.

"Take it with you, or put it in a rubbish barrel."

He just looked at her, but only for an instant as she started to ride toward him. He walked toward the rubbish barrel set against the north wall around the statue. He didn't hurry, but he didn't quite saunter. He dropped the apple into the barrel, then turned.

The uniformed rider had reined up several yards away, her eyes on him.

"It's just an old statue," he said sullenly.

"That may be, young fellow, but we'll not be having you or anyone else turning it into a rubbish heap. If everyone did that, all Kyphrien would stink, and the Autarch wouldn't be liking that."

"Who was he, anyway?" The youth pointed to the statue, although he really didn't much care.

"One of the old heroes. He saved Kyphros. That was in the great war that changed the world and cleft Recluce in two. That's what the plaque says. It gives his name, but I don't recall it. It was a long time ago. They say he lived around here, but no one knows where."

"Oh." The boy glanced at the statue. "Doesn't look like a hero." He shook his head and walked quickly across the street, feeling the rider's eyes on his back and hurrying to avoid a tradesman's wagon.

Three blocks later, he walked through the front gates of his home and then through the side entrance closest to the kitchen.

"You're almost late for dinner," said his mother, from where she sat in the small sitting room adjoining the dining room. "What took you so long?"

"I stopped for a moment in the square. There was one of the Finest there."

"What was she doing there?" His mother paused. "You didn't do something wrong?"

He decided against mentioning the apple. "No. I wondered about the statue. She didn't know much, though. Just that it was about an old hero. She couldn't remember his name."

"Well . . . go wash up, and make it quick."

He hurried to the back washroom, not even minding the cold water, not too much, anyway, as he washed his hands and face. Then he walked swiftly back to the dining room, where he waited by the door.

"How clean are your hands?" asked his father, coming to a halt in the archway. "Let's see."

The boy extended his hands.

"The other side."

The boy turned his hands over to show the backs.

"Good. No grease or grime to get on the table or chairs. That's if you eat carefully."

"Can we sit down?"

"We're waiting for your mother."

"What about Elysa?"

"She's at your aunt's this evening. She'll be back later."

Several moments later, his mother appeared, and the two followed her into the dining room, his father sitting at the head of the table and his mother at one side. He started to sit.

"How many times have I told you not to lever yourself into your chair by putting your hands on the table?" asked his father sharply.

"Yes, ser." Before his father could say more, the boy quickly asked, "Where did we get the dining set from, Father?"

"I've told you that before."

"I don't remember. It must have been a while ago."

His father sighed. "From your mother's great-aunt, and she got it from her aunt Antonia years before."

"It is a beautiful set," said his mother, looking to her husband, "even after all these years. The cabinetmaker who made it was a master craftsman, one of the best in all Candar. Some say he was the best in the world, in his time. Some even say he did more than that . . . that he saved the Autarch . . ."

"That's just a story," said the boy's father.

"It can't be just that. Otherwise, there wouldn't be the statue in the square." She turned to the boy. "That's the one you asked about. He saved Kyphros and maybe all Candar in the time of the great war."

"I didn't ask . . ."

"Don't be impertinent," said the father, setting down his goblet. "All you need to know about heroes is that they come and go, and no one remembers. In the end, he was just a cabinetmaker, nothing more, statue or no statue."

"You have to admit the dining set is still beautiful, dear, and almost without scratches after all the years."

"Too bad it started where it did," said the boy's father.

"Enough of that, dear. We don't have to talk about Antonia. That was a long time ago. What's important is that it's beautiful and we have it and can enjoy it now."

"Who was he?" asked the boy. "The man who made it?"

"I don't recall his name," answered his mother. "What's more important is that he made beautiful pieces for the Autarch—the great-grandmother of the present Autarch. Most of them are still in her palace. We're fortunate to have some of his work. Everything he did is so well-crafted and ordered that it will last forever."

"Or long enough," said the boy's father in a lower voice.

"That's why you need to take care at the table," added his mother.

"And he made this table . . . and the chair I'm sitting in?"

"That he did. Now . . . settle down and mind your manners . . . and keep your hands in your lap when you're not eating."